# The Court Of Unforgiving Gods

Abby Moore

Copyright © 2025

ABBY MOORE

THE COURT OF

UNFORGIVING GODS

All rights reserved.

No part of this publication may be reproduced, distributed, or transmitted in any form or by any means, including photocopying, recording, or other electronic or mechanical methods, without the prior written permission of the author, except in the case of brief quotations embodied in critical reviews and certain other non-commercial uses permitted by copyright law.

ABBY MOORE

Printed Worldwide

First Printing 2025

First Edition 2025

10 9 8 7 6 5 4 3 2 1

This is a work of fiction. Names, characters, places, and incidents either are the product of the author's imagination or are used fictitiously. Any resemblance to actual persons, living or dead, events, or locales is entirely coincidental.

Interior Book Design by Walt's Book Design

www.waltsbookdesign.com

This work contains material that may be distressing or
triggering for some readers, including:

Sexual content
Violent situations
Death
Reader discretion is advised.

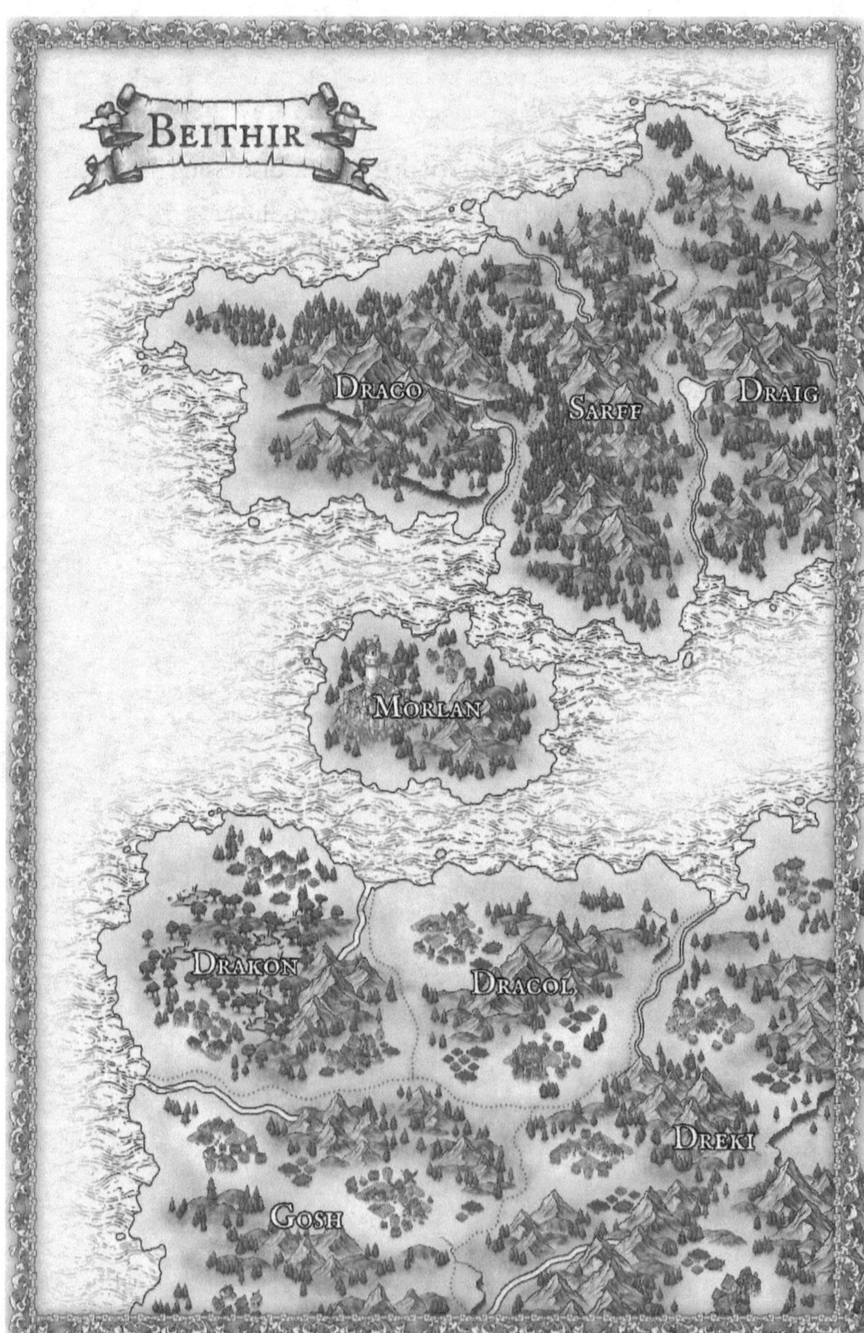

BEITHIR
DRACO
SARFF
DRAIG
MORLAN
DRAKON
DRACOL
DREKI
GOSH

Contents

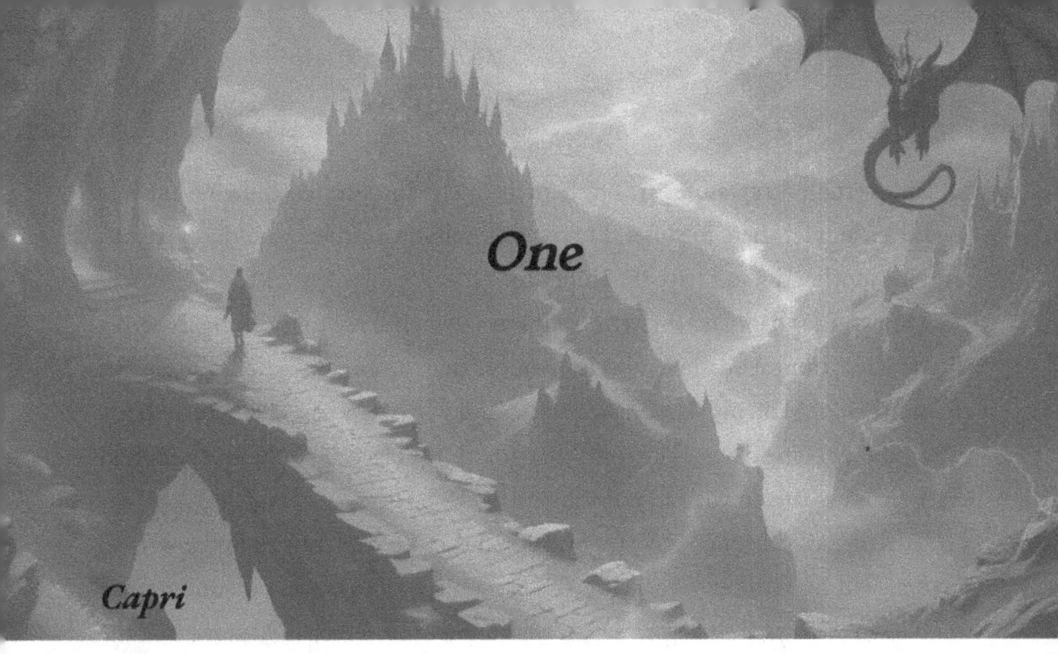

One

When I open my eyes, the blinding light hurts so badly I hiss out in pain. "What the hell was that?" I whisper to nobody in particular. I look around and see that, aside from a small monkey sitting in the tree line watching me, I am completely and utterly alone. "They got you too, buddy?" I ask, even though that thing doesn't understand me.

My hands slip into the softest white sand I have ever seen. When my gaze hits the tree line, a lush forest hums directly into my mind. I know that what I am looking for is somewhere in there. The pull of its power calls to me so strongly that I find myself standing before I can even think about anything else.

I brush the sand from my tan pants and swallow any fear I might harbor. The latest trials from my father and brothers is apparently happening right now. My boots sink into the mushy sand, making it hard to walk.

The mission I have been tossed into is a game, really. A sick and twisted type, but one the Gods play far too often. I am to steal an ancient artifact right from the most sacred place in our world. The old Gods made certain that anybody who dared to try and steal from them would be harmed much worse than the Fates could ever do.

"I guess I better get this going then, huh?" I ask the monkey who is snacking on his lunch, even though he won't answer me. I scratch my head, trying to get the grains of sand off my scalp.

I march my way through the dense trees, unsure where to go but also knowing in the same heartbeat *exactly* where to go. I push thick branches out of my way, making certain no creatures are on them first. The absolute last thing I want is to be bitten and left here to suffer. I know full well my brothers wouldn't save me, and my mother doesn't have the ability to.

This island is dark and mysterious in ways that chill me to the bone. Not in a literal sense, but the shadows are clearly more than just shadows. They reach out to me, their hold on my skin causing static, and when darkness falls here, nobody is to be alive come dawn. The souls that guard this place are unlucky enough to have struck a bargain with an unforgiving God.

"Alright, so, rule one—no cave hunting. I don't have access to my powers so no way will I be tricked into that." When I am trying to work something out, I tend to talk to myself. It helps when I feel alone as well, which is 90 percent of the time. I only have older brothers, and they aren't exactly the loving type.

My eldest brother, Atlas, is the most ruthless God there is. He sees other life-forms as a means to an end. He rules over one of the harshest worlds there is; I am not jealous of him whatsoever. Maximus, the next in line, is a bit kinder. That doesn't win him any points with our father though. He rules over a few territorial areas Atlas has staked claim over. Max doesn't like trouble, and ruling comes with all sorts of trouble. Lachlan has rule over every body of water, and his servants never sleep. The poor souls think they have it good because Lach is the funniest sibling. They don't understand the concept of sleep or relaxation. He lives with our father in the palace but isn't ever home for more than a few hours. His skin is the darkest out of us all. He spends his time swimming in oceans no others have ever been in.

"Ouch," I hiss out as a six-inch thorn presses into my leg, piercing the skin so deeply that a thick, warm trail of blood seeps down into my boot. My healing power buzzes warmly in my body. It wants to come to life; it wants to heal the wound. The potion I drank causes my powers to lay dormant; it feels as if I have a severed limb. I wouldn't wish having one's power taken on anybody, even my worst enemy.

Though I'm the youngest of my siblings, I somehow became the most power-ful. That's why I'm being evaluated so harshly by my father. I listen to the hum that only intensifies with every step towards a deep, dark, and musty cave. "This is just grand," I mutter, cursing my family for forcing me to do this.

I step into the mouth of the cave and yank my knife free from my waistband. I chant the words I learned from the old Gods' scrolls and wait. Symbols start to glow a yellowish color all over the cave walls, and almost vibrate with their humming so loud I want to cover my ears.

I cut my palm just enough to draw blood and spill it all over the stone that rests right in the middle of this dark prison. The sound of rock moving hits my ears before arrows shoot into my shoulder. My body jerks backward slightly from the impact, but I recover quickly.

"Rude," I blurt out, even though I know nobody will ever know the words that spill from my mouth in here. I yank the arrows out, knowing my brothers are going to have a full-on laugh fest over this. They enjoy my pain, and I almost wonder if they would love to watch my downfall too.

I take a tentative step inside the dark chambers of the murky cave and stumble around, wishing I had my light magic to be able to see around here. I give my eyes time to adjust to the dim light and move farther into the cave. Mist hits my face as I slowly inch forward. I pat the dampness away so that I can see more clearly.

"Of course it's a fucking body," I say as I look over the bones that lay on the stone bed. "I guess I'm glad they are just bones." It feels beyond disrespectful to take somebody's bones away from their resting space, but I need them. I go to grab them, but as soon as I touch one, they turn to dust in my hand. The grayish dust slips between my fingers, and I moan out. "You've got to be kidding me!" I yell and start scooping up the dust of whoever this is into my bag. "Maybe I'll get to scatter you in the ocean." I gather the rest of the particles into the burlap sack that I brought and quickly start my journey off of this devilish island.

My steps are quick and sure, but not panicked. My body knows exactly where the beach is, and that is my mission. Make it to the beach safely. Simple enough, right? It should be.

The shadows are getting bolder, though; they reach out, and when their palms meet my skin, it burns white-hot. Dots cloud my vision as dusk begins to set in. My feet stomp the ground as I quicken my already hurried pace, now turning panicked. The light dims around me faster than I would like, and if this isle wasn't petrifying, I would sit and watch the sunset.

I don't dare run even still; I wouldn't want to fall and lose the bone dust. Even though every time one of the shadows touches me, my skin boils. The beach is within reach; my heartbeat hammers in my chest.

"Goodbye, Mr. Monkey. I hope you always have bananas to eat and that you find a family!" I highly doubt that monkey will ever find a family, but I do hope he enjoys his life here at least. I look around the beach, searching for the exact spot I came in at. Spells are always precise; I must be right at the exact same spot that I entered in order to leave here.

The oranges and yellows in the sky turn to gray, and I rush to find the clue I left for myself. When I spot it, I make my run. I sprint as fast as I can, without any power helping me. The feeling of the wind whipping my hair makes me giggle.

Sometimes I pretend to be normal...like I am just having fun on a gorgeous beach. I crave an average life; envy is a potent threat in my life. But I am not an average girl, nor will I ever be.

I see the world where normal girls live; even the struggles they face make me jealous. My father is evil, he is ruthless, and my brothers play games like none other. The Gods know to stay clear of the God King; that's who my father is to them. He is their king and always will be. They bow to him, even though they should all work together.

I'm gaining on the spot, I need to be right as I see the moon chasing the sun away. It's a race. "Almost there, Capri. Come on." I push myself harder and faster than ever. My arms are pumping, and I just hope and pray to the Fates that I don't fall and spill the bone dust. "Let's go!" I chastise myself. My legs move like lightning, and right as this demonic island turns pitch-black and the shadows pounce on me, I touch my cloth.

Two

Capri

The door to the throne room opens, and I'm greeted by a full room of guests. The Gods and their playthings for the night are all laughing. More than likely, they are making fun of a lesser being. I look around and come up short in finding whoever it is they have decided their victim for the evening is.

The palace is so bright and large, even I haven't been in every room here. I did most of my growing up somewhere else. My mother wanted me to live a normal life; she never wanted this for me. But when I started showing how powerful I was, there was no denying what kind of weapon I could be for my father. Because that is what I am, a weapon. My worst nightmare is being used instead of cared for, loved even. My mother loves me, sure. But when your father is the king of Gods, it does very little to love somebody. Once he has you in his grasp he will do anything to get what he wants.

The conversations hush as I pass by. "Look at what she's wearing." A being whispers in disgust.

People who are eating suddenly drop their forks, as if I were pure filth that they find utterly repulsive. Some of them start drinking their wine in gulps. I meet my father's gaze as he sits upon his golden throne. The entire room is as big as some villages I've been to. The theme is bright and light, in contrast to the abhorrent behavior my father shows daily. The brightest blues mix into the whites and gold of the warm room. The throne itself is a sandy color; my family adores the oceans. I couldn't care any less about them in all honesty.

"Capri?" he questions, even though I know he feels the pull of the bones by the way his body stiffens. He knows I have what he wants; he just wants to test me further.

"Yes, Father?" I volley back, not looking towards any of my brothers. I don't care what they have to say or how they want to address me. Right now is not about them. I beat their challenge again, and I know more will come.

"You got it?" he asks me, as if I would even come back here if I hadn't passed my mission. I arch an eyebrow, unsure why he wants me to announce I stole some dried-up bones, but I'll play along...for now.

"Of course. Would you like to see?" I ask, unsure what this latest test truly is about. I giggle, the sack dangling from my neck.

The tests have recently been about me depriving myself of lovers—even though I have successfully done that my entire life—or commanding the sea for an entire afternoon. That one was dreadfully boring. Moving the waves in and out of coves, just to prove to Lach that I, too can command the waters as well as he can. If not slightly *better* than him. I wouldn't dare challenge him though because beating him would place a large target on my back.

Maximus tests my mental shields; he tries to get me to do things for him or others, and he makes me see things I don't want to see. A few of his games gave me nightmares that chased me for weeks. I think he knew they would and that's why he did it. Max seems to have a hidden agenda; I just can't see it.

Atlas is the most brutal of them all when it comes to his trials. He forces me to harm myself, then won't allow me to heal myself. I have so many scars on my body because he doesn't want me to heal them. He claims every good ruler will have battle scars, and the scars will help me in the long run. Soon, I will be made into a ruthless killer like them, but for now I enjoy talking to monkeys and having fun in ways they will never understand. I try to keep a positive outlook on my life, because if I dwell too long on the bad it will suck me up and drink me dry.

"Wonderful. Go sit," Father responds, tilting his head towards a vacant seat. I can still feel the pull of the ash hanging from my neck as I turn on my heels, wanting to be anywhere but here. Craving freedom and knowing I will never have it. "Wait." His voice could control any living being, and yet, I haven't told him it has no pull on me.

I don't want hours of torture testing it out. They already don't want me in their family, any excuse to terminate me, and they will take it. I know that's what these trials have been about. Finding ways to expose me, get rid of me or just plain and simple hurting me.

I slowly shuffle backwards, and my silver eyes meet his onyx ones. "Father?" I ask gently, because he doesn't respond well to beings questioning him. Even my brothers and I, father has killed for less, punished for much less.

I know everybody is listening in, unsure what's going to happen. A couple shuffle backwards, clearly preparing for anything he might throw my way. Chairs scrape against the marble floors, anticipating the worst to come.

My father is known for his temper; he has no grace, no compassion, and absolutely no mercy. "I want the bones." He demands with no kindness in his tone. My mouth dries up more than the sand on that very beach.

"Okay." I step forward onto the dais, a couple of steps at a time. "Here you go then." I toss the scratchy bag onto his lap. It lands right between his legs, and some of the dust falls through the fabric.

The sack still calls to me, thrumming into my very marrow. I know my powers are back because they vibrate inside my body, begging to be released.

"What is this?" he snarls at me. If there were conversations being held, there aren't anymore.

"Those are the bones you asked for. They sort of melted into ash when I touched them." I explain in a voice I don't recognize. My commanding tone is far more confident than I feel. Any weakness shown right now would be blood in the water, and there are beasts already circling me. No need to draw in more.

My father stands, but I do not back up. I don't give in to the tactic he is trying to force upon me. I don't show my fear, because deep down I know I can beat him, and I will one day.

"Did they now?" He walks around me, toying with my honey-blonde, wavy locks. I blink several times before turning my head to look up at him as he circles me as if I were his prey.

I am tall, yet he is another head taller than me. "They did," I confirm solidly. He shares a glance with Atlas and gives my brother a slight nod. Clearly, they have had conversations without me. My brother gives our father a curt nod, returning our father's gesture.

"Alright, everybody," father says, commanding the room. "Please raise your glasses to my bastard daughter, Capri." He says with malice in his tone. Every single glass is raised, and a servant brings me and my father one as well. The golden liquid shimmers in the transparent glass.

"What are they raising their glasses for?" I look around, unsure why he has them all gathered in the first place. Unease eats away at what little bits of food I had in my belly when Father's eyes linger on me, carving me up on a silver platter. "Because, Daughter, you have just granted us a new world." He doesn't smile, but amusement fills his eyes.

His words don't make sense to me; we have ownership over every world there is to own. Gods don't allow any other beings to rule, so all the realms are ours. We are the Fate's favorites; they gave us the power to control everything and every being while they sit back in their own faraway realm.

"To Capri, and of course, to me, for fucking that whore of a woman who was so scared shitless she brought you to me. If she hadn't, we wouldn't be here now, would we?" Father asks even though he doesn't expect a response. Every being in the room lifts their glass, but I don't. I have my own ways I rebel against the male who sired me. Sperm doesn't make me love him, not that I have ever loved anything before, other than mother and Val.

"To Capri. And the God King," they chant eerily. I swig my drink in one gulp. The fizzy bubbles burn going down my throat.

"What does this mean?" I ask him, knowing better but asking anyway.

"It means you've passed every test. You will now prepare for your final trial. If you pass this next one, then you will officially become a member of the royal family." Hatred burns so deeply in my blood, I am sure it might boil so hot, it'll seep from my pores. I do not want to be in their family; I want freedom. I want to live a life that is safe and far from my brothers. I want my mother not to have to walk around watching over her shoulder.

The night continues in a blur. My father hits me on the back a few times. He seems to think that's praise; little does he know about encouragement, let alone telling his own daughter she has done well. He leaves me to chat with others, more important to him. I am nothing but a nuisance to him, a means to an end. I just hope it's a swift end when it comes.

"Congrats, Sis." Max comes up from behind me, his long brown hair swept into a tight bun at the base of his skull. His bright-green eyes shimmer with mischief. The potent scent of alcohol burns my nostrils.

"Have you had enough to drink yet?" I ask, trying to tease him, but his face melts of all amusement.

"You shouldn't question me. I will be a king one day; you will bow at my feet," he declares, as if he hasn't already told me all of this before. I try but fail to not roll my eyes. "You will marry whom I say you can, and you will be lucky to live after coming back here." He says harshly. We both know he is not the one calling the shots, nor will he ever be.

His threats got boring and unoriginal after the first day here. I nod my head in agreement before checking my nails. Pretending to be bored and done with this conversation. Max hasn't caught on to me yet, and the games I play with him. Males like him want to feel important and will spill any information just to be the one who spreads it.

"Yes, I am aware. But where exactly will I be coming home from, dear brother?" My voice remains calm even though I do not feel calm on the inside.

I don't show them any weakness, ever. It is exhausting to live in a constant state of fight or flight. Atlas comes up behind Max and presses his fingers down hard into our brother's shoulders. "Are you scaring the help again?" he taunts, his deep-brown eyes locked onto mine. My jaw clenches shut, so hard my teeth might shatter. I try not to think too hard about their teasing or nicknames. Even if they wanted to like me, their mother would never allow us to get close.

"No, I was telling her that she answers to us." Maximus sneers to his back, where Atlas still stands tall. Atlas doesn't respond just yet, he watches me. Studies me, he does this often enough, I can tell when he has decided to do it. "We control her and her worthless mother's lives for the foreseeable future." Max continues on his rant to our brother, the true next heir to the throne of the Gods.

I look between them, half wondering if they are going to whip their dicks out and measure. If I didn't think Atlas would kill my mother for the insult, then I would ask them.

"Actually, you said I answer to *you*. That *you* rule over me and that *you* will pick who I marry…" I want to keep on, but the look Max gives me is enough to stop me dead in my tracks.

Atlas is the first to violence, but the others have unusual ways of torturing poor souls. I have had to sit back and watch on many occasions when they have tortured other lesser beings for fun. "You don't do that, I do." Atlas's voice holds no warmth. "I will be the king father chooses. You will all answer to me," Atlas says, rage wafting from him. I roll my eyes yet again. Something that I do often around them.

"If this pissing contest is through…I would like to get some dinner and take my mother something to eat." I move towards the door, but Atlas grips my ruined shirt. His fingers tangle in the ripped fabric.

"Wait," he hisses, his lips grazing my earlobe as he leans down and into my space; the moisture presses into my skin, as if he licked his lips before speaking right into my ear.

"For what?" I ask him, meeting his glare. It's not uncommon for them to want to keep me after trials. They are always curious about how I get through them so fast, or how I survive them in general. I would love to see them attempt the trials they have put me through.

My father, King Ragnar, cheated on his wife with my mother. It's something Gods often do, but not so often do they impregnate the other females. I am a mistake, well-hidden for years.

"Do you know what your next mission is?" His voice tells me that I am not going to like it.

"I do not. I have asked and not one of them will give me an answer." My eyes dart to Maximus who is glaring daggers at me. His eyes may be pretty, his face perfectly symmetrical, but under all of that handsome Godlike skin lays a dark demon in waiting.

Maximus is waiting to show how truly evil he can be. I wouldn't be shocked if he kills our other brothers to sit on the throne. He may desire fun and games now, but that will grow old to him soon enough.

"Well, lucky me then. I get to tell you." He chuckles against my ear but I don't find it funny. His laugh is humorless and cold, just as he is.

"Then tell me; I am starving." I snap. My mouth waters watching all of the food pass by. Trays of lavish meats and other foods that some lesser being spent way too much time on pass by me. My eyes track the food for far too long. Atlas drags my attention back to him by gripping my chin and tilting my head to face him.

"You are going to Beithir."

My eyes narrow to slits. "No I am not," I declare rapidly.

Atlas laughs as if this is all some big joke, which, in his eyes, it might all be. My life is a joke to them, I am as expendable as the meat on their plates.

"You are. It is the only realm we don't have in our grasp." His throat bobs as he watches me carefully.

There is a good reason for that, too. Gods do not return from Beithir. "I wonder why," I say sarcastically. I wasn't raised to know everything about the Gods; I didn't even know I was one until my powers bloomed in my young body. I do know one thing, though—Beithir is deadly to Gods.

"The reasons don't matter; this is your last test. Father thinks you'll survive it. I give it a week." Atlas smirks before shooting Max a knowing grin. Max smiles right back, telling me he knows something I don't.

"I give her an hour." Max chuckles, his eyes lighting up with pure hatred for me.

"I will not go there," I say firmly. "It takes days just to star travel there. I don't trust you all with my mother for that long," I hiss out, turning away.

Strong hands grip my arm and yank me backwards against a strong chest. "Just because I despise your mother for spreading her thighs, doesn't mean I hate you. You are, after all, my little sister," Atlas says, deathly calm. Little being the term he uses for me is funny. I am not much shorter than he is, and my muscles aren't that much smaller either.

My lips purse before I respond. "You are not my brother, and I will not leave my mother." I declare harshly. This is the one thing I will deny them. I will not go on a suicide mission for their amusement, leaving my mother to their games.

So far, if I do what they ask of me, they house and feed my mother and me. She lives in a chamber that I can visit daily. We have dinner together and I inform her of my progression in my power.

"You will. Father has made his mind up. It is due time we claim the land that world has to offer. Hell, maybe he will allow you and your whore mother to move there. I know *my* mother would vote for that." His firm grip loosens, and he pushes me away sharply. "Anyways, you will grant us this one last test, then you'll be one of us. I promise."

I don't want to be one of them, but I do want the safety it offers my mother. "What will I have to do?" I whisper and face my brother fully. I mentally prepare myself for the pain I am going to go through.

The devilish grin he gives me lets me know I will not like what comes from this trial. Dread chews at every last bit of resistance I have when he starts spewing the words I wish I had never listened to.

Three

I will have to travel to Beithir in seven days' time. The world in and of itself isn't big, per se; it's divided, split into two continents. On Beithir though, are beings who rival the Gods. They may even hold a flame to the Fates.

The Realm of Beithir is lush, and filled with beings of all sorts. At least that's what the scrolls say. The soil alone is worth more pounds than in any other Kingdom. The fruit is unlike the fruit here; it tastes better due to their green dragons growing it with whatever power the Fates gifted them. The animals...well, everything is better there. The texts don't say why, just that Beithir is better in every way. Father has wanted this world since I have known him, but the last time a God went to that world was my great-grandfather. He never came home from that journey. He was a powerful God King, he commanded lands. His earth ability was unmatched, his cruelty much the same.

Beithir is a death sentence for Gods. Other beings are somewhat welcome there, but Gods? Fates no. We are like rotten fruit to be thrown out, they think so little of us. Granted, the Gods also treat most beings as if they are less than a rotten corpse, to be thrown out when their use expires.

On one continent, the dragons live by the land; they don't even shift into their human forms much anymore. On the other continent, it's the complete opposite. They live in their human forms and even have villages and small cities. I haven't been, obviously, but in the ten days since I was told I would be going there, my mother and I have stayed awake doing all the research we could.

The continents are divided into territories, the northern continent into three large sections and the southern into four slightly smaller ones. From what I have gathered, the southern regions are somewhat more kind to outsiders, while the North will not be welcoming to me. That is where my grandfather went wrong. According to the records, he went in wanting to lead them; he acted like the God King. That was his first mistake. Dragons are unwelcoming because they believe that their rules are law. They do not want to be ruled, they crave freedom. They were also created to keep us Gods in check. I will not make the same mistake, I will have a different approach, a kinder one.

"How long will you be there again?" My mother's light-blue eyes shine with tears that she hasn't been able to hold back since finding out the news. Sometimes while we're researching she's just in hysterics over it all. I go to her and kneel, grabbing onto her cold hands and squeezing tightly.

"I am likable, Mama. I am not like my father and brothers are." She swallows while watching my lips move, as if holding every word I say close to her heart. "I believe that with enough research and social skills, they will accept me and my terms. I don't plan on making the same mistakes he did." I say, and she nods her head with me.

That is a fool's dream; I know it. Their two sides are at war, and have been for over a hundred years. I don't know why they are at war, but I do know the loss has been great.

"I know you are, darling. I raised you good. That doesn't make me worry any less about you." She hasn't ever said it, but sometimes I wonder if she regrets me, or at least bringing me to father. My father beat her almost to death when he found out she had kept me from him, or even birthed me in general. That piece I don't know, nor do I believe I will ever know.

"You are the best mother to have had. I will be okay because you taught me how to be kind and care for everybody. I have learned all I need to know about my powers; I know spells now, even. If necessary, I can be ruthless, but we talked about that, didn't we?" I speak to her in the kindest tone I have.

I must be gentle with her. He has ruined the once strong female she was. She is a shell of herself now, somebody I don't recognize anymore. Yet, somebody that

I wish deeply to know again. I will always look out for her, even if it puts me in danger.

She nods her head in agreement, something she does when she dazes out. "I don't think I'm going to stay here while you...while you are away." She chokes out, clearly not wanting to voice my going away.

I squeeze her hand harder now, hoping it's reassuring. But my gentle smile doesn't reach my eyes.

"You shouldn't stay here." I agree with her. Her staying here is the worst idea imaginable. I wouldn't let her even if she wanted to. "I don't know how long I will be gone, but Valor will look after you in my absence. You remember him, right?" My voice is softer than normal, something I have learned to do with just her.

"Yes, I know the boy who's been pining after my daughter since she was in cloths." Her voice sounds offended, but I know she isn't. My mother forgives far too easily to be living in a realm ruled by the God King.

"He has not been pining after me," I inform her very clearly. "And he was in his own cloths then, too, you know?"

Valor is my best friend. He is who I tell everything to, he is my shoulder to cry on when I need it, which isn't often. But since being brought into the palace as the bastard princess, we haven't gotten to see each other much. I try not to take that personally.

The one upside about being sent to Beithir is having more freedom than normal. They mostly gave it to me because they all think I'm going to die and never return. My father pretends to want me to succeed, but my brothers don't do the same. Atlas even told me last night, *"Since you're almost certainly going to die, you should get laid just once."*

Then he slipped a card into my pants pocket, and when I asked about it, the servants told me it was a business in the city that hired sex workers. I was so embarrassed I couldn't look at Atlas during breakfast. He even had the balls to ask me if I used the card; I didn't respond. There is no need to feed into his sick games any more than I have to.

My father's wife, Mara, doesn't seem to like me eating with them, but Father insists that I join his family. He claims one day I will be officially be apart of their royal family, accepted. He acts as if that is my mission in life. I don't have the guts to tell him. I want nothing to do with them.

Lach always seems to find things to tease me about. Even at the most inappropriate times. I shake my head, trying to forget the horrible things my brothers have put me through, and give my mother the attention she needs.

"I'll help you move some stuff back home if you wish?" I offer, noticing my mother's eyes wandering around her chambers. She doesn't have much, but still enough for several trips if she did it all alone.

"Oh, I don't think that's necessary. I only need to pack up my favorite clothes and a few books. Maybe a couple other things, but nothing I need help with. You need to focus on how exactly you're going to change a world that's set in its ways." She sounds almost hopeful, as if knowing that might be what I need right now. Hope, kindness, and bravery, because even though I am a God, I am scared to leave her.

I sigh, knowing she is right in every way. I just won't voice that to her. Instead, I try to help ease her heavy heart. "If anybody can change a world, it will be me, Ma." She hums her own agreement.

My mother is wise beyond her years. Gods can and do live hundreds, if not thousands, of years. Not every God has every power like me and my father, though. Some, like Lach, only possess power over water elements, while Atlas has power over every element—air, water, fire, and earth. Max with his mental powers, could control any of them if he desired. I don't see Max doing that, though.

Atlas would simply kill him if Max weren't powerful enough to finish Atlas off. Max's mental powers are stronger than most, not mine though. I just haven't shown them that.

Some Gods have smaller power that they use for everyday jobs to help control the realms. All Gods have a job that involves a realm—watching over them, helping them, however Father sees fit. He is incredibly cruel to the human realms, though.

One in particular has lost his favor. In that realm, the Fates had given the humans power to level the playing field after the fae had started to attack them. Father then started having his lower Gods snuff out the power, causing panic and unrest in their kingdom. Little bits here and there but enough to make the Fae start to stir.

I have a plan for them once I am in charge or powerful enough to help them. I must wait to help them until I have true power though. Nothing too drastic has happened yet, so I still have time to help the humans.

My mother is not a God at all though, she is just a fae. She's from our world but is a pure-blooded, normal fae. There are some ordinary fae living among us. Typically, Father moves them to another realm though. My mother was just too gorgeous, and her personality makes her a hundred times better. I know she won his heart; if she hadn't, he would have killed her when he found out about me.

Fae life expectancy just depends on the type of fae they are. My mother can live up to about two hundred, but some in other realms with more power could live for almost as long as some Gods.

Fae have magic too, but they call it from the ground, and our ground isn't magical. It doesn't need to be since Gods don't call upon anything for their powers; the Fates have just granted us with them. It is who we are when we are born. Nothing gives or takes it away from us, things can enhance it though. Magic, potions or even relics can give Gods power they don't have already.

"I want to spend my time with you, whatever you want to do. I can do my planning on the days it takes to travel there. You know star travel isn't always instant. I will be flying throughout the stars for days on end. I'll be bored out of my mind, so give me stuff to think about and things to miss." I need to give her a mission too; I need to give her a purpose or else she'll lose sight of herself again.

The trial before last was overnight, and I figured it would be okay. I needed to call the ocean to split, so that an island underneath could rise up. It took a ton of power and took me a while to get it all right. When I got back from the test, though, my mother was worse than before I had left her. She wouldn't say what happened, just that she missed me and wanted me to stay with her.

"I love you, honey. Let's help you get back to me as soon as you can." She places her palm on my cheek, and I lean into her gentle touch. I smile a genuine smile, because that's all I want...to come home to my mother. Well, and for Father to accept me so that my brothers will. And that they will stop threatening to kill my mother.

I want to learn how to harness my powers, control them, keep my mother safe, and live happily and free. That's not too much to ask for, is it?

I thoroughly believe it is not. I do not wish to rule over any realm, only to keep my mother and Valor safe. I want to help keep lesser beings safe and sound. The thought of what's been done to lesser fae and beings alike makes me ill.

I swallow the bile that threatens to overspill from my sealed lips, the nerves attacking my very body. I won't allow the anxiety to take me this time though. I have too many beings needing me to help them for me to fail.

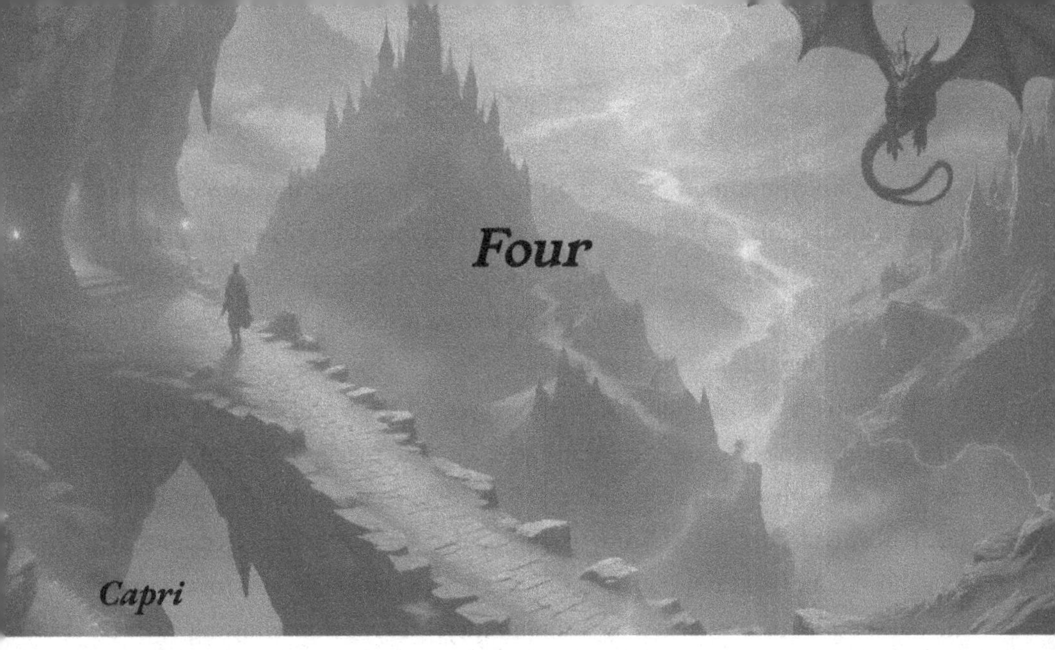

Four

Capri

I look out into the deep blue waters of our Kingdom, taking in every smell and sight. "Are you becoming an emotional nut case?" Valor asks before tossing his net into the water. I roll my eyes at him, even though he can't see it.

"No, I am trying to be sentimental. Can't you tell?" I volley right back, teasing him as he does me. He looks over his shoulder at me, a playful glint in his eyes.

He scrunches his brows teasingly. "Not really, no. It looks like you have to shit." I laugh while tossing one of his bait fish right at his face. It hits the target since his hands are wrapped up in the net. "Hey! Those cost me twenty chips." I reach into the deep pockets of my pants and toss him thirty chips. They clink into the boat, and he almost drops the net trying to catch them.

"Here, I didn't realize you had become such a cheap ass since I moved." I glower at him, my tone teasing enough. Valor always teases me; it's for fun though, not unlike what I just said to him. In complete contrast to the way my brothers "tease."

"Have you figured out how you're going to survive yet?" He pulls the net in, nothing in it. Yet again. He sighs heavily before fully meeting my gaze.

"No, but I am doing research on the beings who live there. There are many I think I could easily make friends with." I explain while he gathers the old net up and readies it to be thrown.

He tosses the net far and wide. I know it's the wrong spot—I can hear the fish under the waves—but I don't ever correct him.

"You think you can go to the most hostile realm in our universe and make friends, just like that?" He narrows his eyes at me, forgetting his net altogether.

Well, when he says it like that...no, I don't. I am not arrogant enough to think everybody just loves me, but I do know how to sway some beings. I have a certain charm about me that lures beings in.

"You know as well as I do, Val, that beings tend to start liking me a little bit more after getting to know me. I think after a month they will agree to allow me to live there with you and my mother," I say more confidently than I truly feel. He raises his already arched brow, his fishing net completely forgotten now and dangling in one hand as he faces me fully. "They will let Father visit for whatever he wants out of their world. Why wouldn't they?" I say before allowing Valor to speak. I watch as he thinks about what I have just said, and contemplates his next words carefully.

Valor's rich brown skin shines in the harsh sunlight; his hair is cropped close to his scalp, but the curls are still there. I have wondered what it would be like to run my hands through his hair. I have never taken that step with him, though.

He frowns before nodding simply and turning around to the open sea. Both his hands grip the net, and his muscles ripple from usage. He drags the net in from the water, our small boat rocking with the waves. I once would get seasick being out here, but I don't any longer.

Although, I don't like unknown water. Things lurk in deep water, like Lach, for instance. He commands all the water beings, and I know from his stories that they aren't very kind. Merfolk are evil creatures by nature, and I don't wish to ever come across one.

"I don't know, Capri...maybe because they are led by two rival dragon clans and are perfectly happy in their world of brutal war? They have been doing okay without a God telling them how they must live for decades." Val says in a neutral tone.

Valor doesn't like the Gods. He is a water fae, so he has small water abilities. That might be why he chose fishing as his way of paying back the Gods and Fates. Before we found out what I was, he was more than open to talk with me about his hatred of the Gods. Since my awakening, he has not said much about his loathing of my kind. I don't suspect he ever will.

Valor doesn't like the power we hold over every other being; he believes each species should rule their own people. I don't disagree, but Gods are the top of any food chain, dragons right under us. You can't change what the Fates did.

"Well, maybe they would like to have a queen too? What if their King doesn't do his job, and that's why they have been at war for so long?" I use my sugary-sweet voice, knowing he is getting tired of not catching anything and wanting to lighten the mood. "How is your mum?" I ask him instead of allowing him to answer my question.

His hazel eyes meet mine for a moment before he hands me the net hesitantly. I give him a bittersweet smile and toss the old, slimy, ripped net into the deep-blue waters. My hands glow a dull white from the small use of magic thrumming through my veins.

"She's doing okay. I know she's excited to have your mom come live with us for a while. Has she started to pack yet?" Val asks as he watches me call for the fish. I feel the vibration on the nets and start pulling it up. It takes little strength to pull it, but I make a show of it, for him.

"She says she only needs a few things and doesn't want to waste time on anything other than research of Beithir. We need more time, but it just keeps slipping." I know I have bags under my eyes from lack of sleep. My mother's bags match my own. I pull the net over the side of the boat, and the fish flop everywhere. I avert my eyes from them. I know it needs to be done but I hate putting them through pain. So, I end it quickly for them. A mercy I feel must be done, a swift death for their sacrifice.

Valor's eyes widen when he takes in the net, full of fish. The sizes all vary, but this will be enough fish to last him until I come back. "I still don't know how you do that." He curses under his breath before rushing over to help me, even though I don't need the help.

"Thank you." I smile at my friend. His eyes soften when he looks at me, his harsh appearance turning mushy.

"You know that I'll take care of her. She will be okay here with me. I'll make certain of it, Capri." He licks his thick lips.

I bite my lip before dropping the net; some of the smaller fish fall into the deep waters but I don't think he minds or even notices. I rush to give him a hug, and he embraces me as I tighten my grip on him. My fingers clench around the back of his tattered shirt as I grip my longest friend in a death hold, as if I might never see him again.

"I know you will," I whisper into his ear. Our hug lasts longer than it once might have. I will gladly take any stolen moments with my friend that I can get. There was once a time I wouldn't hug him like this, but throughout the years, our relationship has blurred some lines.

"So, how do your brothers feel about you going to Beithir?" Valor asks while I push the boat inland with so many fish that Val will surely be the richest fisherman yet. The back of our boat drags from the weight of all the fish. I gulp at the thought of my brothers, but I know Val won't leave it alone until I answer him.

"I'm unsure how they feel." I shrug, observing his curious gaze on my body. "They don't tell me much other than the threats they try to play off as jokes." He seems to think about that for a while before deciding what to say. That's one thing I admire most about him: he thinks before he speaks.

"I think being away from them might be nice." His gaze lands on mine, no shame in where he was just looking.

"If I live, you mean?" I watch as his throat bobs while he ponders my question.

The waters are clear here; the nearer we get to shore, you can see all the way to the bottom. Lachlan has small cities down there. He created a way for fae and lesser Gods to travel down in air bubbles. The pockets all connect in some sort of system. He hasn't invited me down there to explore, but from up here his cities look amazing. Our boat travels over a large pocket, maybe somebody's home. Only the wealthiest live down there though. The ocean is his treasured oasis, father never goes there, therefore; it is all Lachlans.

"You'll live," Val interrupts my train of thought. I look up from the mostly clear water and glare at his back.

"What makes you say that?" I question.

We pull up to the dock, and he reaches out to grab my hand. "Because everybody who meets you loves you," I smirk slightly at him, since I had already said that. He rolls his eyes at me before yanking me onto the dock. "There is something about you that one can't *not* love." He sounds irritated by that, or maybe just admitting I might have been right about beings being drawn to me. I smile and give him a huge hug when my feet hit the dock.

"You love me, huh?" I taunt and he messes with my already tangled hair.

"Okay, maybe I like you and want you to come home so I can make a living. Fates, I can't even believe you don't have a career in fishing. They just come to you." He shakes his head while running his fingers through his hair. They do. I know I have a strong water power, but apparently, I have a way to attract animals as well. They all travel to me. I don't even call to them, they just appear. Which makes it worse when I have to kill them.

I would say it seems like I may have every power Father has, but the only other God to be that strong was my great-great-grandfather...who was one of the first Gods created. I wouldn't dare say I was as strong as he was.

"Wow, Valor. You, sir, have caught more than any other bastard out today. Maybe your lovely lady brings the fish in with her good looks," a male on the dock says, not even sparing a glance at me.

It isn't uncommon for males to disregard females here unless they want something from them. Val clears his throat, obviously feeling the tension rolling off me.

"How much will you give me for this lot?" Valor's jaw is clenched so tightly it looks painful. The male doesn't seem to notice our discomfort.

"Uh...some of them are smaller fish, some are baiters. Maybe two hundred chips?" the male says almost as a question.

That is grossly underpaying Val, but to ask for more would be career suicide for Valor.

"Fine. Two fifty and we have a deal." Val says through gritted teeth, because we both know this batch is worth far more than two hundred.

The male spits something into the water and off the dock before licking his top yellow teeth. "Two twenty and I'll take them."

My fists clench tightly, but I control my anger. "Deal," Val says, nodding his head towards the fish. "You unload them then." Val concedes. The male plops a large bag of chips into Val's waiting hand.

"It was a pleasure as always, Valor. Thank you, boy." The male spits the last word as if it were venom. I wince at the term he uses for Val. The ultimate sign of disrespect in fae terms. I drag Valor away and off the dock before he gets into a fight.

"You need to find somebody else to sell to Val. We'll have to go back out tomorrow, and maybe the day after. You can't afford to live off two hundred and twenty while I'm gone." I say in a soothing tone, while I try not to offend him more than that male already did.

I offered to give him chips while I was away, and he told me that it was his job to take care of my mother. I often help him gather fish or earn other income, so I don't see why he won't accept my chips.

"I think Sammy-boy on the west side might pay better. You have too much to do to help me again. Will I even be seeing you before you leave?" Val asks his tone suddenly somber.

The thought of leaving sends my heart into full panic mode. "Yes, you will. I won't leave without saying 'see you soon,'" I promise him, giving him a half-smile, knowing he doesn't buy this whole aloof vibe I'm trying to sell him. Valor can tell I am panicked, but he won't directly comment on that though.

"You know, you're the strongest God we've seen in hundreds of years. That's why they are sending you away. They fear how powerful you are, or at least how powerful they believe you to be." He says as he looks out in the distance, averting my gaze on purpose.

His words shock me, mostly because he doesn't always speak of the Gods in a positive way. Well, he never has before. He also doesn't address my being a God very often.

"No, they are sending me there as another test. You know this, they won't fear me Val. They like playing with me, it's only a game to them." I mumble sadly.

He spins around and startles me. Our chests are so close I think he may kiss me. His cold breath mingles with mine, but instead of leaning in, he takes a step backwards. I don't let the cracks in my heart spread though. "They made you get a Fate's bones, Capri. The bones you brought back? Yes, those were from a seriously powerful Fate. There is a reason for that, if you think this is all just a game, you are wrong." His tone has a tint of warning to it.

I scrunch my brows. "How would you know that?"

His chest lifts faster now. "I was listening in on a conversation I shouldn't have been. That particular Fate was one of the first created, meaning it was powerful. There were five to begin with, and so far, your father has the bones of two. You should never have been able to even get into that cave. It should have crushed you, and it didn't, Capri. That means you are seriously powerful." He says, finally meeting my gaze.

My mind is whirling. I'm only half God; there is no logical way I'm more powerful than my brothers. Atlas is the third most powerful God ever known; I can't be more powerful than him...can I?

I grin. "Is this gossip from your club?" I try to joke but he is not in a joking mood. His eyes coldly narrow on me.

Valor is in a secret club where they drink alcohol and talk about their shitty lives.

"Maybe, but that doesn't mean it isn't true. My source is still valid." He replies.

I have recently felt like my power is still growing, but my brothers have told me I have reached my max. I don't show them everything I can do, for obvious reasons. So they have no idea, I have not reached my max. Each and everyday I grow in strength and ability.

Valor doesn't even know about my growing abilities. I just hope that after this, I can live a normal, happy life. If I succeed, Father wants me to rule Beithir's lands in his name. I think Atlas would take the throne for me if I asked; he craves more. All Gods do but him in particular, just like our father, will never get enough. I fear neither will ever be full. They will starve for power until it eats them alive.

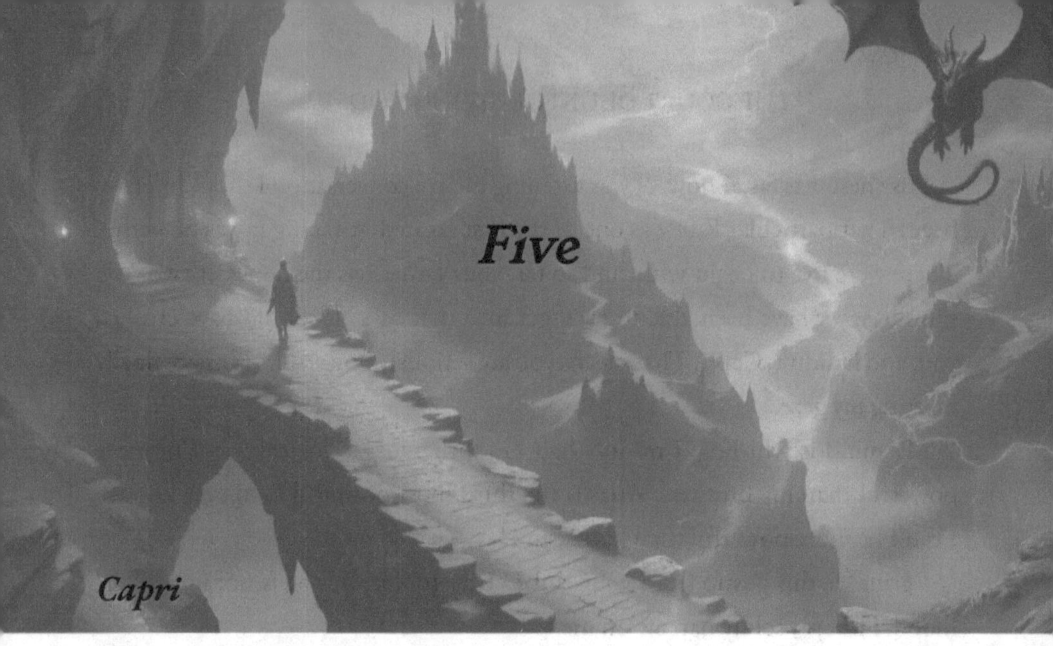

Five

I sit at the breakfast table with Father, Atlas, and Max. Lachlan is in one of his moods and has stuffed himself deep down in a pocket and won't come out. I suspect he's still angry over Father agreeing to give me total control over Beithir once I have convinced the lords and king to let me rule over them or together. His only wish is to visit once. I feel like that's totally reasonable. While I'm gone, my brothers aren't allowed to harm my mother or Valor—that was written in blood. My mother will follow me to Beithir when all has settled, as Father promised.

"I don't see how you think she could possibly even rule a kingdom all on her own," Max says to Father while taking a bite of food. Father sips on his blood-red wine, leveling my brother a stare.

"We have taught her well these last few years, do you not agree?" Father asks Max in an icy, detached tone.

I can tell he doesn't like the challenge Max is giving him, but he allows it. Max is hard not to like. He's funny in ways that shouldn't be funny but still are.

"I've trained for seventy years. You don't see me with an entire world at my beck and call," Max says, surprisingly stern.

Mara opens the large white doors and struts into the dining room wearing a very low-cut dress and heels higher than my fork.

"Do you want to go in her place then?" My father asks while he greets his wife with a kiss on the cheek.

Max huffs out a sigh. "Of course fucking not. I just don't get it." Max murmurs.

Atlas slams down his spoon, causing several things to spill. The servants rush to clean up the mess. "Do you want more, Maximus?" Atlas's voice is sharp as knives. Max drops his silverware as well, readying for the fight. "Well?" Atlas pushes.

Everybody knows Max is the carefree one—he doesn't care about anything or anybody. Max just shakes his head when he sees how angry Atlas truly is.

"Exactly, Maximus. You don't want the responsibility. She isn't going to *get* the kingdom of the dragons, and this conversation will be void when she fails. Show my stomach some respect and eat your damn food before I am too upset to eat." Atlas sprays spit as he yells.

Atlas doesn't do anything in halves; he is all or nothing. That includes his temper. I clear my throat and earn the attention of everybody sitting at the table.

"Mara?" I tread lightly. After all my years here, I still haven't earned her respect. I don't think I ever will.

She glances at me as if I were a mere speck on the floor that needs cleaning. Disgust is written all over her features.

She gives me a fake smile before responding. "Yes?" Her voice has a hint of reptile to it.

She reminds me of a basilisk, the way she moves and speaks. She waits for her prey, then, when they least expect it, she strikes. Her brown curly locks and green eyes are easy to look at, which might cause some to think King Ragnar picked her for her looks, but they would be terribly wrong. Mara's power and thirst for more rivals Father's; that's exactly why they are together. Even if they aren't mates.

The Fates wouldn't be that cruel to pair them together for all of eternity. The original five created Mates because they wanted beings to have a soul mate, another to share their life with. Each species has its own form of a mate. And after the original five Fates were created, they too began mating. The Fates are able to either birth a new fate, or create one. If one is created, they aren't as powerful, but they are still more powerful than most Gods.

"I was curious if you might be willing to lend me a few gowns to take with me to Beithir? I'm assuming what I have already isn't appropriate. I just thought you may—"

She holds up her dainty hand, and the motion causes me to halt. "You think I would give you...*my* gowns?" Her brows furrow and her lips tilt downward in a frown.

"No, not *give* them to me. I just need to borrow them. I don't have anything to—"

"I wouldn't give you anything of mine." She interrupts me again. "Your mother already took something I will never get back. Now look where we are," she scoffs in disgust. I am used to her thinking I'm a problem.

On many occasions, she has tried to have me killed or relocated. She has sent beings after my mother, and even once after Valor.

"Again...I don't want to keep them, I just figured, instead of spending Father's chips, I could borrow some gowns." I thought she would appreciate that, but I was wrong.

"If you believe you'll be returning here, you are dumber than your whore of a mother." She says in revulsion. If I thought she was disgusted earlier, that was nothing compared to now.

My entire body seizes up, until I gather control. My hands slam on the table, causing several dishes to clank. I stand up so fast my chair hits the floor. The loud *thump* causes everybody to halt whatever they were doing or saying. All eyes are on me, but I couldn't care any less.

My face burns while white hot flames lick my fingertips. With just a thought, I capture all the air inside her lungs; I grip it with my mind. Her face turns red, and Atlas realizes what I'm doing half a second before I release her.

"What the fuck?" he yells, rushing to his mother. I look to my father, thinking I might see rage there, but what I see is pride. He doesn't say anything about me trying to choke his wife, he just continues eating.

"Why did you do that?" Atlas asks while healing his mother's throat. She doesn't need it, but he is a momma's boy after all.

"I've told her not to call my mother a whore. She was warned." My voice is ice-cold. "Father?" I ask, very nicely, my sudden change in tone shocks even me. He looks up at me from his wine glass and raises a brow.

"Huh?" His voice sounds indifferent, but I feel amusement coming from him, pride even, not love, though. Gods don't love anybody other than their mates.

A mate is your fated partner. There haven't been many in recent years. The Fates have been quiet for a while, which isn't a promising sign that they are happy with us.

A mate is your other half, the true love of your life. It's said that once you bond with your mate, nothing can tear you apart. The problem is that mates don't live without the other, so if one dies... They both will die.

That's why some Gods refuse a mate. If they believe they have found their mate, they will actively try to kill them before they bond, or they will avoid them until the pull becomes nonexistent. I've been told that avoiding your mate is almost impossible though, because the urge to be with them is so strong you would sooner cut out your own tongue than be without them. I don't know how a mate bonds with the others, but in my case, it doesn't matter. A bastard like me will never have one. I will never have an equal.

"I'm going to spend thousands of chips at the beauty shop today," I tell my father. "I need things for my journey to Beithir." He waves his hand as if it doesn't affect him one bit.

I reach for a sweet pastry and take a large bite before setting it down on the table. "Thank you for breakfast. And Mara?" My eyes glide to her, where she is rubbing her throat, even though I know it is healed.

Her green eyes are slits as she looks at me. "What?" Her voice is venom spewing from her. I know I shouldn't stoke the fire, but it's fun.

"Please refrain from speaking about my mother like that again. This is your last warning." I turn to walk away, but Atlas grabs my arm near the doors.

"You really think you can speak to my mother like that? Haven't you learned anything living here?" He tilts his head towards me, something he does often in a show of dominance. His problem is just that though; his dominance is a show. Mine isn't, mine is real, and one day I will show them who the true God ruler is.

I lick my lips, still tasting the sugar from the pastry. "I have learned plenty from you all. I will demand the respect I am owed. My mother is owed some damn respect too, for letting that hairy old bastard between her legs." I don't know where the words come from, but they just start falling from my mouth. I think for a split second that he might try to hit me, but he just keeps listening. "I will be returning here for my mother. I won't leave her to you predators." I yank out of his grasp. "I promise you that," I swear, because in no realm would I leave my mother here forever.

When I pull from his reach, the anger within him shimmers to calmness. "You know, as much as I hate you, I must admit you are growing on me. Way more than Max." His eyes widen slightly. "But if you ever fucking harm her again, you'll regret it for a hundred years." He lowers his voice to a deadly level. Ice spreads on the door where I'm holding it open. "You may live to be two thousand, but your mother won't. I suggest that if you want her days—" He chuckles, but it isn't funny. "Excuse me...her *years* to be peaceful, you'll do what you're told and act like a good little princess. And when it's time for you to rule over Beithir, you will give it to me."

One by one I pluck my fingers out of the ice coating them. "And why would I do that?"

He takes a step into my chest; his fingers come up to my face, but I don't back away as they brush lightly against my cheek. "Because I have decided you'll succeed. You somehow always get out of everything unscathed. That won't happen with me though. They call me ruthless for a reason. I will tear everybody you love down until you have nothing to live for. You will give me Beithir. Am I clear?" His voice is so low I almost wonder why he is whispering to me.

"Fine, if you agree to allow Mother and Valor to come live with me there in freedom and not under your rule. I will do what I have to, to gain control over the Dragon Kingdom for us. I'm just glad you finally admit you think I'll get it." I shrug lightly.

He smirks at me; the look is almost handsome on his devilish face. "You are a cockroach. You'll survive everything thrown at you. I would like to aid you, though. You know to make the journey more enjoyable for you."

I gulp. "What kind of aid?" I don't trust him with anything, let alone helping me in this.

"I'll get the gowns you will need. I'll also send a few scrolls you might want to study. You have two days left, little sister. You'd better make them count." He warns.

Atlas actually thinks I can do this. It shouldn't matter to me what he thinks—he's arrogant and rude—but my stupid heart fills with pride from the exchange this morning. My father and brother both think I am worth something. I squeal just thinking about it, happiness warming my insides. I've been sitting under an apple tree for over an hour with my mom and Valor. Atlas did as he said he would and sent several scrolls with information on Beithir.

I didn't even know we had these here in the palace. When I went looking for information, I was given the cold shoulder. What Mother and I had been studying were things I had to steal.

Atlas, intended or not, has given me what I need to know for my trip...I just need to find it within the texts here.

Capri

It's the morning before I leave, and so far, all Mom, Valor, and I have figured out is that there are seven lords and a king on Beithir, between the two continents. Their ages are unknown, their looks—other than the one called Calix—are unknown. Calix does seem to be the most approachable, based on our research.

Calix is the Lord of Draca. The inhabitants of Draca live in villages and are accepting of most beings, especially fae. Calix, according to the texts, is extremely handsome but also mated. He is a blue dragon, which means he has water abilities. He is also said to be understanding and mostly reasonable. Blue dragons are some of the only truly kind dragons out there. Their breed is known for saving other beings.

"Okay, how many breeds are there?" Valor asks while sipping on his cofee We haven't slept since Atlas granted us the texts.

"Eight," I say immediately, because I have studied this text more than I have anything else. I have studied more than I have slept, eaten or even spoken to anyone. Mother insisted we focus, so that is what we have done.

"Which dragon breed is most likely to kill you?" he asks in rapid fire.

"Black, but sometimes pink or red will give you trouble."

He lifts a brow, and my mother makes herself scarce. "They will all give *you* trouble," he says gruffly. I huff, waiting for my next round of questions. "Which dragons do you need to watch your shields around?"

I think for a moment. "Black, of course. Red, because of their mind control, and purple because of their magic to change my emotions?" My tone is more curious than anything.

Val rolls his eyes. "Is that a question?"

I lick my lips, feeling every bit of exhaustion hitting my body. Yet I know I can't stop now. I am just getting started. "No. That's my answer," I say sternly.

He nods his head. "Okay. Where do you want to land?"

I have thought about this many times, and I know I want to avoid the northern continent—Draco, Sarff, and Draig.

After several moments, I finally answer. "I want to aim for either Dreki or Dracol." My voice doesn't waver.

"Good. I wouldn't pick any different myself. Remember, do not openly tell them you are a God. They will kill you on the spot." Val warns, even though he doesn't have to. I know dragon kind would be glad to see each and every God dead and gone.

Valor doesn't want me to leave, but with his help I could change all our lives. I can save us, start anew somewhere else.

"I know, I know. My kind is *bad*, dragons *good*." I coo, blinking my lashes slowly.

"I'm being serious." His face is firm and written with worry.

My own expression softens slightly. "Hey, I'm going to be alright. Thanks to you, I know all I could possibly know. Now, let's have some fun and go get some dresses and make me more...friendly-looking." I motion to myself and the disarray of my tattered clothes.

His face scrunches in confusion. The entire time I have ever known my best friend, I have never tried to look anything unlike myself.

"You mean...*attractive*?" He asks in complete shock, and maybe a hint of jealousy.

I tug him towards the door while smiling teasingly at him. "Well...yeah. No male is going to take me seriously when I look like I've lived most of my life in poverty."

We walk out of my mother's chambers and into the cold, damp hallways leading out of the palace. "Bye, Mom!" I call out.

I plan on getting her something special from the market, too. I want to give her something to think about while I'm gone. She rushes to me before I can make it halfway down the hallway.

"I would like to eat dinner together tonight. Would that be okay?" Her voice is soft and unsure of herself. I grab her arm and pull her into a tight hug. I cradle her to my body, my fingers tangle in her hair.

"Of course." I kiss the top of her head. "I love you." I tell her before Val and I make our way to one of my least favorite places.

While we walk through the market, Valor points out gifts for my mom. I got an extra hundred chips out of the palace just for her. I want to get her something special.

"You would for sure turn heads in this." Valor's voice is teasing as he pulls out a red gown, more see-through lace than fabric. I chuckle; even thinking of myself wearing something so revealing is funny to me. I don't dress like that ever.

"Yeah, especially if I wear the shoes that go with it." I point to the six-inch red sparkly shoes.

"Could you walk in those?" he asks, but I truly don't know. I have never worn anything that high before.

"Let's see." I grab the death-trap shoes and put them on my feet. They fit me perfectly. I wiggle my toes in surprise and stand up fully. I stumble slightly from the instability of the heels.

"Here." Val hands me his arm. I grab onto him and attempt to walk. My nails dig into the arm he has offered me.

I make it a couple of steps before trying to walk on my own. I know I look like a baby fawn trying to waddle around. I laugh at myself before leaning against a table nearby.

A cruel, low voice speaks from right behind me. "Nobody will ever believe you actually wear this type of shit." I whirl around and almost fall, but before I do, Lachlan grabs my arm. His laugh is dark and full of malice.

"I think I can manage on my own, thank you." I scoff while pulling my arm out of his grasp. I lean into the table again and take the shoes off my feet.

I place them on the ground beside the vendor's table. She makes herself scarce when she sees my brother get into my face. "Maybe if you walked around in them naked. Other than that, you will fail." He narrows his eyes, and his lips turn down in disgust. "Well, let's be honest…Atlas is sending you there to die, or whore yourself out, I haven't figured out which yet. Mother doesn't like you being here."

I turn to walk away from him, to get out of his grasp. I don't want to fight, not today and not with him.

"Goodbye, Lach," I say over my shoulder, glancing at him once more. His sky-blue eyes seem to be saying something, but I don't read into them before I grab onto Val and slip into the crowd.

Before we get too far away, I hear Lachlan yell, "I sure do hope you come back though, *little sister*! It would be a shame if something were to happen to you and I would be left with your mother and friend to play with…" Lach says in a menacing tone.

My vision goes red; I'm suddenly in front of him and all I see is my fist swinging for his face. I hit nothing as I look to see Lachlan laughing from ten feet away.

"I really do hope you can fight better than that. I hear dragons are pretty rough around the edges. They train their babies to fight from birth." I had heard that too. I know dragons are tough, but so am I.

"I would hope, for your sake, I do succeed. Father and Atlas want Beithir, so if I don't secure it, they'll probably send you since you're the *spare*," I taunt him, and that was a mistake. Lachlan's firm grip is suddenly wrapped around my throat in the blink of an eye.

He tightens his fingers around my neck, and I suck in as much air as I can. No one dares step in to help me; Gods don't fight others' battles. Let alone a fight between the prince and princess. Val curses, not knowing what to do.

"What the fuck did you just call me?" He spits in my face. I wipe it off with the hand that is not gripping his wrist.

"I said you are the *spare*. Unwelcome unless you bring value. Which you do not," I hiss through my teeth. His grip tightens on my throat before he suddenly lets go. My mind control latches onto him tightly, I hold nothing back as I grip him in my clutches.

His shields were down and that is a mistake he wouldn't have made had he known how strong my mental abilities are. Slowly, my power retreats from his mind. It's a dark place that I do not wish to stay in for longer than I must.

"What the fuck?" He looks at his hands, unsure of what just happened. He stumbles backwards a few steps, while still studying his hands in disbelief. When his eyes meet mine, pure unbridled rage lights his eyes red.

"That's what happens when you mess with somebody more powerful than even you." I prowl towards him, and he doesn't back away. Idiot. Our chests are right up against each other's.

"You are going to get what's coming to you." He curses before storming off into the crystal-clear waters on the edge of the market. The waves that welcome him seem to hiss at me in hatred.

"Are you okay?" Val rushes to me, my healing power taking away any trace of the blue bruises I'm sure my throat has already.

"Yes, I just hope you and Mom are going to be okay while I'm away." I say distantly.

Val smirks, and I don't know if I like it or not. "I have a plan to keep us safe. Don't you worry about us. You just focus on getting us a new homeland...one that doesn't smell of Gods' ass." I shove him and laugh.

We continue to shop and look around; I grab several gowns from vendors I personally know need the business. I buy some books and commission a painting from an artist, sharing a memory of Mother and me as inspiration. He's to deliver it a week after I leave. "I think I've got everything I might need," I say as we walk out of the busy market.

Most beings around here shop during nighttime. Gods tend to be nocturnal, and fae could go either way. The other beings tend to go according to their business.

"Yeah, I think you have enough stuff to live there for a year," Valor teases me. I smirk at him, unsure what to do with our last few hours of being together. I want to spend the rest of my time with my mother, planning when and how she will get to Beithir when it is safe.

"Princess?" A guard I recognize from the palace approaches us. I sense Valor tense beside me. I have never known if Val and I will ever become more than friends. I find myself wanting more time to figure that out, but having none. I don't know how he feels about it, but maybe once we settle into Beithir, we could figure it out.

"Yes? You can call me Capri. Nobody calls me princess," I inform him.

The guard doesn't seem to react to that at all. "The king wishes to have a word." He announces firmly. I look around, not knowing what time it is.

"This late? He usually is with Mara now." I don't know what his game is, but I don't want to find out. I don't have a lot of time to spend wasting. I want to see my mother and give her the gifts I bought her.

"He requests you now. I'll take you there." The guard grabs onto my arm and my blood rushes. I yank my arm out of his grasp.

I shake my head feverishly. "No. I will see Father in the morning." My tone is no longer kind, but commanding.

The guard doesn't seem to like my answer, but before he can respond, Valor grabs my arm and calms my every nerve. Just as he always has since we were children.

"Capri, it's okay. I'm sure it'll only be a short meeting. I'll take your stuff back to your mom and start moving the boxes out. I'll see you tonight." His hazel eyes shine bright with promise. I nod my head, not wanting the guard to see me hesitate because of Val. I know they will give him a hard enough time while I'm gone. I don't need to add onto his burden any more than I already have. My jaw clenches tightly, while my fists tighten into tiny balls. I don't like being told what to do, and when to be somewhere. My hope is that soon enough, I will answer to no one but myself.

I release my hands and shake them out. Giving into the calmness, I know Valor is trying to push into me.

"I'll see you soon." I give him the bags we got today; there are so many. I look towards the guard, a question in my gaze. I raise my eyebrow when he doesn't answer me. "Help him with the stuff I need to pack." My voice leaves little room for argument.

"Yes, Your Majesty," the broad guard says hurriedly. I pull Valor into a tight, warm hug.

He pats my back. "Hey, we'll see each other again. Don't worry." His voice soothes me to the core. I nod into his neck.

"I know, I just miss you already," I reply in a hushed tone. When I pull away, I take a moment to just look at him. His deep-brown skin shines from our long day in the sun. The market offers no shade for anybody. The folk who work here, work hard for their chips.

Valor's gaze begins its slow trip to my own molten-silver eyes. "I can't miss you yet, you haven't even left. But I am sure I will miss you more than you know." His voice is taunting and sarcastic. Exactly why I love my best friend. I smile my brightest smile and disappear into the air, landing right where my father's aura calls to me.

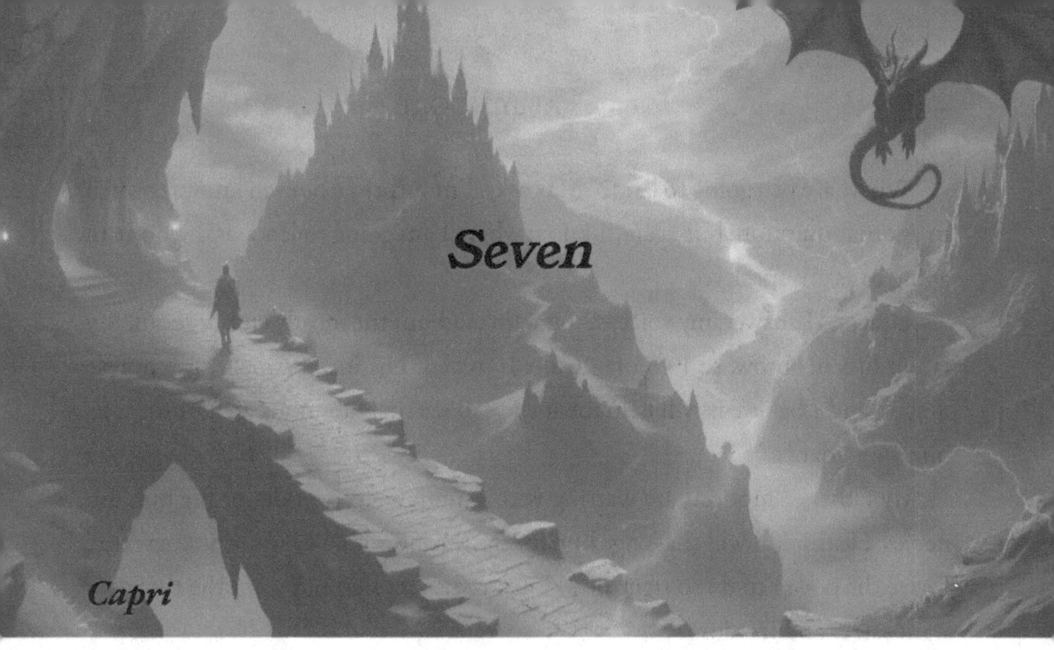

Seven

Capri

"You are getting better at that," my father says before taking a bite from his meal. Atlas and Maximus are sitting right next to him. Atlas looks as if he has just come from a shower, his dark-brown hair still damp, his clothes rumpled. I lift my brow but don't say anything to him. Max smirks at me like he knows something I don't.

"Did you want to see me?" I ignore his compliment. Father looks at Atlas before his black eyes trail to me.

"You have made many improvements in your powers. I am pleased. I wouldn't be sending you on the mission if I didn't think you could win us this kingdom." He places his fork down on the table and clears his throat.

It occurs to me in this moment that he may not even know the name of the realm, and the thought almost makes me laugh. That's the nature of the Gods though—they are power hungry. They always want more, even if they don't know what they want. They will claim it all the same. That's why they cheat on their loved ones, that's why they fight to the death, because they will never have enough.

"Which dragon is the king?" Atlas asks in a calm voice, leaning his elbows against the wooden table.

"Granger Rhodes. He is a black dragon, his powers include shadow-wielding, mind control, and fire. He can see some futures and into the minds of lesser fae. He is the biggest dragon they have ever known." My voice doesn't waver, I don't stutter. I know this.

"Where are you going to land?" Max asks. I'm surprised he even knows enough to ask that question, but again, I know where I am going to land, and who I am going to ask to speak to.

"Dracol." I answer, my voice echoing throughout the mostly empty room. My father lifts his brow, so I go on. "Calix is mated. His mate, Amelie, is a purple dragon and I believe it will help me if she can see my intentions are not for war, but for guidance."

My father's emotions are warring within him; he feels pride for me but also nerves. He thinks I will challenge him for the throne one day. If only he knew that I have the power to do so right now. I just refuse to; I do not want the throne. I want safety and freedom.

"Good. I believe you are right. Although, I wouldn't dress like he is mated. You need to gain attention first and foremost," Atlas says, and I shake my head in confusion. Flirting with a mated dragon is a death sentence for any being, let alone a God.

"You seem to know enough to do as well as any of us could. My forefathers have wanted Beithir for hundreds of years, Capri. If you do this correctly, you will gain my favor." My father stands with his glass in his hand. His other hand is in his pocket though, which I find weird. My father never shows signs of weakness; he never acts as if he might hide anything. "Do you have any questions for me, Daughter?" His steps towards me are strong and sure. Atlas and Max stay seated at the table, on either side of Father's seat. Max eats while watching whatever this is, unfold. Atlas on the other hand, glares at our father before meeting my gaze. Sorrow flashes across his face so fast, I almost feel like I might have dreamt it.

"I want to make sure my mother is taken care of. Meaning *not harmed*. I want her to live a good and free life. I need that assurance before I leave." I can't ask for anything else; he will take it as me being greedy.

My father stands right in front of me. He places his glass down with the amber liquid in it sloshing around. "If I tell you that your mother will be taken care of, alive and well, free even...then you will do everything and anything to secure my world for me?" His onyx eyes are filled with a need I have never felt before in myself. A hunger I have never craved. But I can feel it blooming inside of me all the same. Spreading like a virus throughout my body, killing any kindness I have learned throughout the years of being raised fae.

I take a step back, unsure why he is standing so close to me. "Yes, I will."

He eats up the distance. My head cranes to look right into his dark eyes. "Promise me. Say it, dear daughter. Tell me you will do anything and everything to get that world for me." I gulp, not liking all of their attention on me.

"I promise I will do anything and everything to gain control of Beithir." I croak. My voice is much smaller than I would ever like it to be when speaking to him.

My eyes dart to where Atlas sits, and I try to read him, but it's all foggy. Atlas smirks and my father reaches out to shake my hand. I take his hand and shake it, but as I do, a zap of electricity shoots through my body. "Ouch." I wave my hand, trying to take the sting away...before dread punches me right in the gut.

My father says a few words that I don't understand and then blows a black dust into my face. "Good luck, darling. I will be in contact whenever you get your bearings." My father says coolly.

My eyes dart around, utterly confused, and then it's all black.

My body is floating, there is no pain or fear, just simply bliss. The bright stars whisper things to me; they seem to like me. They keep me company in the abyss. I like them, I try to run my fingers through them as I pass by, but I am never close enough.

The utter darkness calls to me, too though; it wants me to join it. It feels so cold, but the stars are warm and drown me with their love. My body feels as if it weighs nothing and I have absolutely no problems in the world. Whatever my worries are will go away with a simple thought. Therein lies the problem though...my troubles are just beginning.

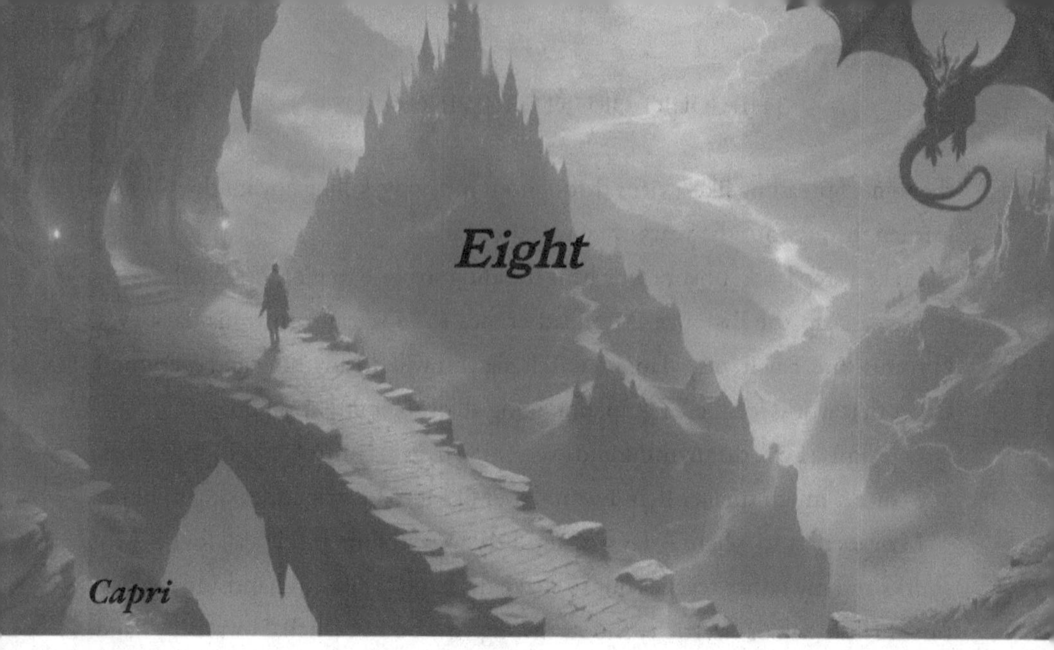

Eight

Hard ground meets my body, after days of floating in the stars. I groan and suddenly I am surrounded by males, all of whom are holding weapons. I moan as I push up onto my elbows.

"Stay down." A man with bright-blond hair hisses at me. His brown eyes eat me up, taking stock of my body without hesitation, roaming hungrily over every inch.

"Hey!" I roar as I realize I am totally and completely naked. He shakes his head and a few of the males laugh at me.

"Hay? Are you hungry, girl?" He looks confused as his eyes crinkle.

"No, I am not hungry for hay. I was saying *hey*! Like, don't look at my body while I'm naked." I look around, hoping to find some clothes, but I see none of my things. *Thanks, Father, for sending all the gowns I bought.*

"You are the one who showed up here naked." His voice seems soothing even though I know a monster probably lies dormant inside him. The group of males don't seem to take a breath; all of them are watching me with predatory eyes.

The man with bright-blond hair and chocolate eyes walks right up to me. I feel uncomfortable, so I attempt to cover my lady bits the best I can while standing up in front of a group of strange males.

"Do you not enjoy being in your true form?" he questions, his eyes yet again scanning my body from head to toe hungrily. "You are nervous...why?" His voice is calm enough that I answer him.

"Because I am naked in front of men I do not know, in a place I haven't been before." Not one of them laughs at me. I find I'm grateful for that. The male circling me nods his head, as if he understands me to a degree.

He tilts his head to the side slightly. "I see. You are hurt; what happened?" He steps closer to me, and if I weren't already covering my nipples, he would be touching them. Nudity may be normal around dragons, but it isn't for me.

"I fell from the sky," I answer right away. My heart hammers in my chest because the one being who can kill even a God is a dragon. And I am surrounded by dragons whose hellfire would melt my bones entirely into soup for them to slurp up, as a snack.

He and a few others do laugh at that. "Yeah, we saw that." His eyes dart between my eyes so quickly it's hard to track. "Your body was flailing from the sky like a doll. What are you?" His question spikes my awareness.

"I-I'm—" I can't finish my sentence before his tongue darts out and licks a place on my forehead where I know I'm bleeding. I yank backwards and fall onto my ass. Now they all burst out laughing at my expense. The laughter vibrates throughout the clearing.

"What are you, a vampire?!" I volley right back at him, even though I know he is no vampire. I have never met a vampire. They are known as parasites where I'm from, but here...I'm not so sure. The male in front of me looks pretty enough to be one. I've heard they draw their prey in. They want their prey to think they are attractive.

If I thought their laughter was a lot before, I was wrong. They all burst out laughing even harder now, some of them even dropping their weapons, seeming to think I'm no threat to them at all. Good, that means I am making progress already.

I look around, not feeling any threat to myself either. Although I wish I had clothes, I don't dare conjure anything yet. I don't want to reveal what I am, or what I can do.

"Me?" White teeth gleam at me. Through the male's laughter, I catch bits of his words. Some, I'm not even sure, are in the same language. "You have no idea who I am?" He chuckles darkly, his men still laughing so hard some of them are crying as they wipe at their tears. The man in front of me walks right up to me again, seeming to not care that I want distance.

"I am Caspian, king over the purple dragon clans and Lord of Draig. Who are you?" The laughter halts abruptly, and his smile vanishes faster than it came.

"My name is Capri." I take a step forward, unlike what my instincts tell me to do. This is a lord of Beithir, so he respects power.

"And who *are* you?" His lips purse at the question he demands an answer to.

"I am Capri," I joke, but he must not find it funny. They do not laugh any longer, and some of them bend back down to grab their weapons.

"You said that. Why are you here?" he questions, his eyes turning to dragon slits. My heart hammers and I think back on what purple dragons can do.

Purple dragons are the smartest, and they have emotional powers.

Great. He can feel when I'm nervous. School your emotions, Capri. It's fine. You're fine. He can't tell what you are, thank the Fates.

"I don't know," I say honestly. "I am just as confused as you are. I was with my father and then I was here. I don't know how I got here." I shrug and glance at my nails, acting as if I am bored. In reality, I am shitting my pants. Well, not really, since I am still butt-ass naked.

Caspian must believe me to an extent because he simply nods and chews on his lower lip. "What am I supposed to do with a female who has no memory of what she is nor why she is here?" Good question. I scratch my neck, trying to bide my time before I shrug simply. Not voicing, I have no idea where to go from here.

"You could give her to King Granger," one of his men shouts. I hear murmured agreements.

"Oh! I know, I know!" a man with white hair yells. "We keep her as a pet. I bet she can cook and clean." He bounces on his feet.

Caspian thinks about this for a moment, tapping his chin for show. "We eat all our food raw, Lou. I don't need her to clean; we live in the woods," Caspian says softly.

I forgot that they don't live in civilization. "You could show me where you live? Feed me, maybe...give me some clothes?" I speak up, finally finding my voice and running with it. "I wouldn't mind a bath, but I assume you don't have any of those laying around," I say, nervously rambling. His brown eyes scan over my body again, and I almost shiver. How many times does he have to study me?

"I could eat you." He whispers, drawing my attention back to his face. His grin turns manic, and I know I am in trouble. He is not the welcoming kind, I realize. "Do you want to know the main difference between vampires and dragons?" he asks, drawing out the last word, and I have exactly half a second to think of a plan.

"One of them sucks on necks for blood and the other is understanding and compassionate?" I ask, knowing I am wrong.

The males all laugh as if me being scared is funny. "No, but close." He nods simply. He steps against me again and I step back into a body that grabs onto my wrists. I gasp in surprise and look behind me, while trying to pull free. "A vampire enjoys an easy meal. Dragons, on the other hand, enjoy the *hunt*. The chase is what pumps our blood..." Several seconds pass by and then he leans forward. I'm unsure what to do in the face of this danger. I know I should just teleport to where I was supposed to land from the beginning, but I don't. I can't because I don't have a map to show me how to get somewhere I have never been.

"Run," he whispers...and I do, right as his male lets me go and shoves me harshly away from him.

My footsteps pound on the ground as my arms pump as hard and fast as possible.

This world is weird; the feel of its energy is different. Now that I can focus on something other than the males in front of me, I feel it. I wonder if the fae like it here because even the ground seems to hum with unused powers.

"Run, little girl, because you cannot hide from me and my family," the lord yells from somewhere behind me. My heart races for an unknown reason. I could easily outrun any of these males. The chase seems to drive my heart to beat faster than it ever has before. I enjoy the feeling. I don't call on any of my unnatural speed or agility. I just *run*. I run through the dense trees, zig-zagging throughout the maze of forest I am in.

A giggle escapes my throat and then another as I hop over a large tree trunk. I don't know what Caspian wants with me. Maybe he really would try to eat me. I finally make it out of the thick woods, and I come up to a river and don't slow down, as I launch myself into the dark cold waters. I didn't have a chance to do research on anything living in these waters, although, I could always attempt to speak to them.

"You'll die sooner in those waters, girl. Come back and I'll strike you a deal," the male says from the riverbank. I don't stop or slow down, I swim above the slowly moving water. I turn over on my back, my breasts now exposed again.

The group of males are all standing on the small rocky beach that lines the river. That should scare me...the fact that they won't even get in.

"Come back before it's too late. You're pretty enough... I think I could sell you to the Lord of Sarff. He likes them pretty and feisty." Caspian calls out.

I bite down my remark as something slimy drags down my calf. I yelp out in surprise, just as sharp fingers grip my leg. "Hurry up or they'll drag you down." They? Suddenly, I'm being ripped under the water.

I grow my gills as soon as I get pulled below the surface of the dark waters. The chill of slimy fingers causes me to regret not just teleporting before. I look around before pulling light into my fingertips. "Oh my Fates," I gasp out when I come face-to-face with a mermaid, a type I have never seen before. Her eyes are completely black, her slinky black hair is almost all gone, her skin is so pale it looks blue, and her teeth are yellow and sharp. Her eyes widen slightly, as if she's surprised that I spoke to her.

"You," she hisses, and I cringe. I know from Lachlan that mermaids value chips, jewelry, and secrets. They are vapid creatures who show no kindness or love to any beings.

"Me." I smile brightly at her, while the water moves us down the river.

"You speak to me as if you command the waters." She swims around me, her tail a dull shade of gray, swishing around. We move down the river together; I'm surprised she is even here. Merfolk don't like closed waters, so this river must flow into something larger. I know this planet has bodies of water surrounding the two large land bodies and one smaller one.

"I can." I place an air pocket around my head for good measure. She swims around me faster now, eyeing me up and down.

"Do you shift? Are you Fae?" Her voice is silky smooth.

My mouth waters, a lie coming to my tongue. I don't say it, though. "No, I am not," I answer honestly. She stops in front of me, the water still moving us slowly.

She reaches her hand out to touch my face, as if she can't resist. I look away before she can; I don't want her to know the air pocket won't allow her to touch my face just yet. She follows my line of sight, momentarily distracted.

Every time her scales bump into my legs, I want to wipe away the grime she leaves. Out of my peripheral vision, I see something else swim around us. I don't say anything, though.

She looks back at me after surveying the water and coming up empty for predators. "So, you are not Fae, you are not of *my* kind, but you have magic like a fae. What are you then, girl?" She asks me as if she is trying to put a puzzle together and can't.

What is with beings from this realm calling me *girl*? I gulp as she tries to touch me again, but the air pocket I've created doesn't allow her to. She hisses out in anger. "I can't touch you. Why not?" She tries again to press her long, sharp fingers into the air pocket and fails to get through. Her pitch black eyes widen even more than they already were.

I smile shyly. "Why do you want to?" I ask her, but that seems to anger her even more than she already was.

"You question me?" She screeches, baring her sharp teeth to me. I use the water in my fingertips to push her away from me farther, but she doesn't seem to notice as I slowly do it. "You are in *my* river," she says harshly.

So, she does live in the river, then. Strange. She swims up next to me, unable to touch me like she wants, due to the airflow around me pushing her hands away from my entire body now. "You speak my tongue, but yet, you won't allow me to know what you are." She tilts her head one way, causing what little bits of hair she does have to flow to one side. Her black eyes seem to swirl with hatred right before something grabs onto her foot and yanks her down into the depths of the dark, icy river. She screams while being plunged into the deep, dark unknown. I take this as my chance to get away, even as she tries to reach out for me to save her. I shake my head, knowing there is nothing I can do now.

I swim up as fast as I can, thinking for sure I have gone far enough down the river that the dragon clan will not find me. I release my breath when I find that I am, in fact, correct.

I look around to make certain no eyes are on me, scanning the dense trees, and coming up clear. I teleport myself straight onto the rocky beach, uneasy on my feet as the sharp rocks and pebbles bite into my flesh. Then I finally bring forward clothes from the in-between. A pair of black, skintight pants appears on my body as well as a tight band around my breasts and a sage-green shirt. The boots on my feet feel amazing after standing on the rocky beach.

I take a few steps forward before hearing a dragon roar from up above my head. I scan the skyline and see multiple dragons flying overhead. I jog over to the tree line, unsure if any of them have already seen me. When none of them descend, I know I'm safe.

"So much for purple being intelligent, huh?" I reward myself with praise because I survived coming face-to-face with a dragon clan. I think back on the map I had back home and try to figure out if I can teleport anywhere else. Clearly, Caspian isn't willing to negotiate with me, so I need to move on. I don't have extra time to spend here. I know it'll take days to come to an agreement with the dragon king. I have no time to spare on beings unwilling to help me.

I don't dare make a fire; I can warm up myself with the fire that comes easier to my fingers here. My power seems to thrum in my body, the land welcoming me. I giggle to myself at how powerful I feel here. I pull my honey hair back into a blue ribbon and start walking towards what I hope is some sort of village. If I can look at a map and see where I need to teleport, then I can get to any of the more civilized villages down south and get them to make the king see my ways.

After hours of walking, I've seen about ten different colored dragons flying in the sky. Each of them seems to be searching for something, but as fast as I am walking, they still can't be searching for me.

This world may be more powerful than where I am from, but it is darker. The sky isn't crystal clear; it has clouds everywhere. It seems to be foggy and rainy most of the time, which makes me tired, but I know I can't fall asleep out here without at least making a camp.

I don't want to sleep here, but I know I won't be finding help tonight, and the sky is so dark I can barely see, even with my night vision. There are trees everywhere here, big ones mostly. This land seems unscathed; there are no signs of the dragon clans living here.

My enhanced eyesight has never mattered much to me—I haven't been to a place that truly has no light before—but looking up in this sky, I swear I can see each and every star. It almost seems as if they are blinking back at me. They seem to be talking to me still, whispering to me as if we are connected now from my star travel.

I finally come to a clearing, and I feel safe enough from the dragons that I start to look for a tree to fall asleep in. I promise myself I'll only sleep for just a few hours, but as I lay down on the soft bed of leaves twenty feet up, I find I am much more tired than I had thought I was.

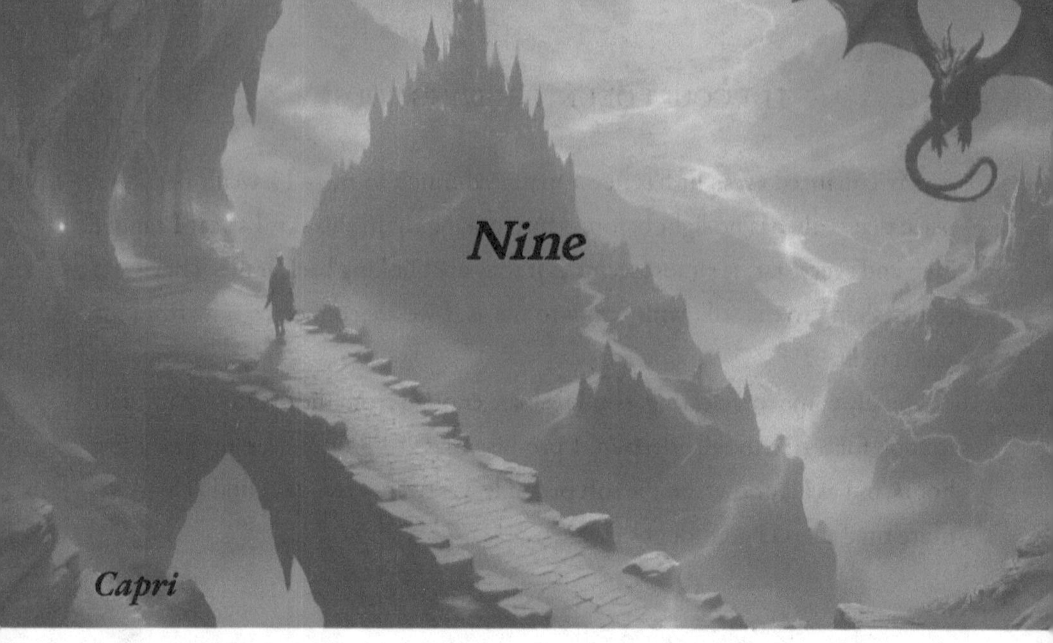

Nine

A sharp kick hits my ribs, and I stand before I am good and ready to be awake. The sun pierces my eyes are harsh I have to squint to even see blurry images.

The once dark clearing, now in the broad daylight, seems to not be as safe as I thought it would be. Caspian is leaning against a tree trunk the size of some of the shops back home.

"Good, you're awake." He says in a chipper tone. His blond hair shines in the sunlight.

I groan and clutch my side, some of my hair falls into my face and I blow it out of the way. My eyes begin to clear of any and all sleep that might have been left over. "Yeah, that's typically what happens when you kick people," I retort. His brows lift, and his lips tilt upwards.

"So, is that what you are then?" He stalks towards me, his strides eating up the distance in a few short seconds.

"Huh?" I play dumb.

"You. You're saying you're human then?" he asks, seeming to search for the answer to a puzzle I won't solve for him. His men stiffen with his tone, which doesn't bode well for me.

"I could be," I say, making my voice smaller than normal. I shrug, still playing dumb, and blink slowly several times.

"You *could* be? You don't remember...yet you showed up naked, then survived the deadliest river in our part of the kingdom, and now somehow you are fully clothed. In *fine* clothing, I might add." I chance a glance at his clothes, noticing they are fine too.

His chocolate eyes dance with amusement. "Checking me out, are ya?" He taunts me. I shake my head. He is handsome, but I did not come here to flirt. Despite what Atlas said, I needed to do.

"No," I grumble, as I back away several yards. He allows it for now. My eyes go to the ground, not wanting to meet his gaze.

"No what, exactly?" The lord in him is rearing its head, commanding him to get answers from me. Ones that I will not be giving out for free. His boots make a thudding sound as he makes his way to stand in front of me, even after I just made space between us.

Every step I take backwards, he takes an even longer one towards me. Until I am completely and totally against a thick tree. My back digs into the raw tree bark. I don't dare move when his hand comes up to my face.

His fingers grip onto my chin tight enough that it would cause pain to a human. So, I play the part. I wince, putting on a mask of pain. "No, I am not checking you out," I declare.

Some of his men laugh, but with one glance from their Lord they shut up. My heart races in my chest. Surely he is going to try to kill me now. Dragons are not like Gods, they do not enjoy playing long-term games.

My cover here will be blown soon, and I will not know where to teleport to, but I know I'll have to go somewhere and fast.

Caspian licks his lips and leans in, his hands on either side of my head. I am completely backed up against the tree, his face so close to me that our breath mixes together. "How did you survive the river? Better yet, how did you survive the night?" he whispers.

I push my back off the tree, putting away any of the distance we had. Our lips are a centimeter apart, the closest I have ever been to a male's lips.. "I swam and then I walked," I deadpan. I don't care what he does to me. My brothers have beat me to a bloody pulp before; the missions they have sent me on prepared me for this moment. Caspian can throw his worst at me, and I will take it and thank him if I must.

"You swam? What about the monsters?" He doesn't back away and I notice his males all have their hands on their weapons.

"I did swim. And that bitch drowned." I say through clenched teeth.

He finally pushes from the tree and away from me. I find myself leaning into the space he just vacated. Heat fills my face as I realize he notices and smirks. "Alright then, Miss Mysterious Girl. I have wanted favor with the other lords of the North for some time now. You will help me with that." I am about to ask how exactly I am going to help him, but then one of his men shifts into a purple dragon the size of a large wolf. The clothes he had been wearing are now in shreds on the ground. "My brothers will be so excited to meet the mysterious girl who just...appeared. Just as a mysterious man appeared *all* those years ago. Don't you all agree?" He drags each and every word out in a knowing way. My heart drops at the mention of my great-grandfather.

"I—" I start, but before I can finish whatever I was going to say, Caspian's clothes are shredded to pieces. "Oh, okay, you're naked now," I say as calmly as I can as I take in his body while it morphs from human flesh to scales.

Caspian turns into a deep-purple dragon whose scales glimmer with sparkles that should be pretty, but with his teeth being the size of my hand, I can't seem to think of him as pretty right now. He takes off into the sky, but not before grabbing my body with his claws. I yell out in fear. I can fly if he drops me, but being in between the claws of a dragon is the last place a God wants to find herself. He clearly knows what I am; my only hope is that he doesn't want to kill me before we have a chance to chat.

My body hangs between two large talons. Caspian speeds through the sky, his clan following behind. None of them fly beside him, or even within ten feet; his wingspan is a little over his own height. The membrane of his wings is transparent, the light purple of it shines almost. I can see every vein and artery he has, each line of dark purple. I take this time to watch how they interact. I need to learn everything I can about this clan. I need to learn their ways. So far, I think they think too highly of their leader. I don't like him.

"Hey, big guy, I want down," I yell, but he doesn't slow or even look to me. I glance down and out, trying to see if I can learn anything about where we are. I see the river he claims I shouldn't have survived, but it seemed easy enough. I see a large body of water and notice how the coast seems to curve around. I also see a large landmass in the distance. A castle almost the size of Father's can be seen from here. "Who lives there?" I hollar, even though I know none of them will answer me. I can also *guess* who lives there...on an island, all alone, in between the two continents.

There isn't much known about the King of Dragons. He remains in the middle of the war between the North and South though. He is completely neutral and only steps in when one side goes too far. His father, the king before him, had sided with the North and was going to end this war between them by exterminating the South. Before he could kill the inhabitants there though, his son challenged him in a battle to the death. He didn't see a point in killing an entire race of dragons just because they live the lives they do. At least, that's what the texts say back home. The scroll also says that even though the new king doesn't want to kill unless utterly necessary, he is cruel. He stays on his island alone, but when he is called forward, he shows no mercy. He is a trained killer, and I need to remember that.

I would figure that, though...considering he killed his own father and all. I don't love my father by any means, but to outright kill him in a fight to the death would harm me more than I can admit to myself. I feel the bitter sting of him sending me here without allowing me to say goodbye to my mother. It hurts so much. I think my heart might have cracked a little when my eyes first opened here and I realized what he had done.

The drop down isn't smooth, which is surprising because he probably flies more than he walks. "Watch out, dude, I have a tiny body," I say, even though none of the dragons seem to be able to communicate aloud in their dragon form. When he lands abruptly, he almost crushes my body with his claws. He drops me down onto the ground and backs away.

He snorts out smoke and a few in his clan shy away, seeming to be nervous around him. Their dragon forms retreat until some of them shift into their human forms and leave. Some of the dragons stay in their true form though; they scratch at the ground with their claws. Causing marks on the ground as they anxiously claw the dirt.

Caspian shifts and stands in front of me, still completely and totally naked. I lay on the ground, and he holds out a hand to me. I lift my brows in question.

"What? So you can scream at me the entire ride here but now you are speechless?" He shakes his head in confusion before muttering to himself, "*Women*." He scoffs as if me being female offends him. I don't take his hand, which causes him to snort out more smoke. The warmth from it blasts my face even with him being several yards away.

"I am no mere female," I declare harshly as I stand to my feet, brushing the mud from my clothes. His eyes, still purple but turning back to brown, roam over me greedily.

"No, it would seem you are not," he states plainly. One of the males from his clan walks up to him and whispers something into Caspian's ear.

We stand in the middle of a wide field; the green grass is soft under my boots. It's wet, it seems. "It sure rains a lot here?" I ask almost to myself as my feet sink into the soft soil. Caspian's friend scurries off after Caspian answers whatever he had asked him.

"It does. Our planet is mostly made up of water. So, it rains often here. I like the rain, do you...*Goddess*?" His eyes are all-consuming and they capture mine; I can't look away. I gulp at his mention of what I am.

"You know," I breathe out and start to pace, feeling unsure of what is happening here. His clan have all wandered off, all twenty or so of them. "I didn't grow up as a God," I say, trying to relate to him but also correct him. I wasn't always this powerful. He doesn't even know how powerful I am though.

"Hmm, I grew up knowing I would become a lord. It just depended on which territory I won. My father's father was there when the God came here." I can't exactly tell how old Caspian is, but he looks young.

Dragons age differently than fae or Gods do. Dragons sit in their eggs for years before hatching in dragon form. They don't earn their human bodies until later in life. I am unsure when exactly they get to transform; the texts didn't say. It did say that the oldest known dragon was over a thousand when he died. He died in battle, not even from old age. Their aging slows when they hit two hundred, and they hit their prime around three hundred. Looking around, none of these males looks over twenty-five to me. A few of them do look worse for wear though. I guess living in the woods as a dragon will do that to you.

"That must have been exciting for him then," I deadpan, unsure where he is going with this.

"He tried to come here to claim our world. Is that why you are here, Goddess?"

I bite my lip, unsure which way to go here. "I do not want to own your world," I claim, because that is the truth. "I am also not a Goddess, I am a God. In my Kingdom, there is no difference between the two." I explain because the way he says Goddess sounds like an insult.

He gets in my space in a matter of seconds, his eyes turning into purple slits, as if his dragon cannot wait to burn me. "Then why are you here!" he screams right into my face, and I notice other males coming out from the tree line.

"I would like to live here with my mother," I answer honestly.

"And why would we want *you* here?" he spits, as if I were nothing but dirt to him.

"Because I can help you." I rush to say. The king may not want to pick a side, but if it gets me this world, *I* gladly will. This seems to calm him enough that his eyes turn back to their normal shape and color.

"Why would we want your help? Do you know what happened to the God who came here before?" My great-grandfather, but I don't say that.

I grind my teeth, unsure of what happened to my great-grandfather and even my grandfather at that. My father has never spoken about his father, so I have no details about his whereabouts. Nor do I care to learn them.

Father didn't tell me when I asked him, and I didn't pry any more than absolutely necessary. "You need my help," I rush to say with more assurance than I feel. I don't dare tell him I want to know what became of my great-grandfather; I won't give him that. I don't need to know if he was eaten alive. I do not care for my father's family enough to risk my life here.

He takes a breath, and about a hundred males come out into the clearing with us. Two males walk past the crowd that has formed around us; they are dressed in finer clothes than the others. One of them, about Atlas's height, has deep-brown skin. His short brown hair is shiny in the morning sun. His oak-colored eyes scan me over, and then he sets his gaze onto Caspian.

The other male has a kinder face than the first. His tanned skin tells me he probably spends most of his time in the sun. It's golden-brown and freckles are splashed across his face. He has long brown hair that's tied in a tight bun at the base of his skull. It reminds me so much of my brother back home, the way he wears his hair slicked back into a bun just the same.

This lord, though has black eyes, but they have swirls of white throughout them. They seem kind and welcoming. A lie, I figure, to draw in prey. Not one of these males is going to be nice to me, and I need to remember that a handsome face does not mean kindness.

"Lord Eamon." Caspian nods his head to the male with the black eyes and the bun. "Lord Rafe, good to see you again." He nods his head towards the male with the deep-brown skin. Neither of them bows or shakes Caspians hand though; they just simply nod their heads towards him. They don't say a word to me, as if I'm not standing right here.

"Lord Caspian. We gathered as soon as we heard your call," the male Caspian called Rafe says. I scan over his clothing, trying to gather any information I can. His wrinkled black shirt fits his body like a second skin, his pants in the same manner. Both seem too tight for his muscular body, but also I don't mind it.

"I am glad you came when you did. This is going to be how we win the war." Caspian says in an ominous tone. Caspian steps aside and puts his arm around my shoulders, pulling me flush against his warm, bare chest. My eyes look up into his.

"Huh?" I question, but he doesn't answer me. He just looks to the males standing in front of us.

"This is Capri. She is willing to do anything and everything we tell her to do." Caspian says coldly.

Lord Eamon looks at me finally, and I clear my throat. "Is that so?" He smirks, and Lord Rafe chuckles. "And why would she do that?" he asks, but it sounds like a threat.

"Because she and her mother want to live here with us," Caspian says back to him.

"Oh really?" Lord Eamon says with amusement pouring from his lips. I look between the three of them, wondering what is going on.

"We could just...eat her," Lord Rafe says darkly. Caspian *tsks* at him in a way that reminds me of a mother scolding her child.

"She holds more power than the one who came before her. I think she could be useful, Rafe," Caspian claims. I don't know how he would know that. I would assume he is talking about my great-grandfather though.

Eamon's black eyes swirl wildly, the white and black mixing, turning his eyes gray. I sense his emotions, and he is skeptical. "Well then...I think we have a lot to discuss. But first and foremost, welcome to Beithir. I will not eat you...yet," Eamon says, but it's Rafe who chuckles.

I will not call them lords anymore, because they do not act as lords. They act as if they were Gods as well, playing games they don't want to start with me.

"What a warm welcome you have given me," I plainly say. My voice isn't cheery, and I know I should try harder to be kind. I just don't think Atlas was right in thinking these males will be easily flirted with. Rafe smirks at me, and I know then...I am in trouble.

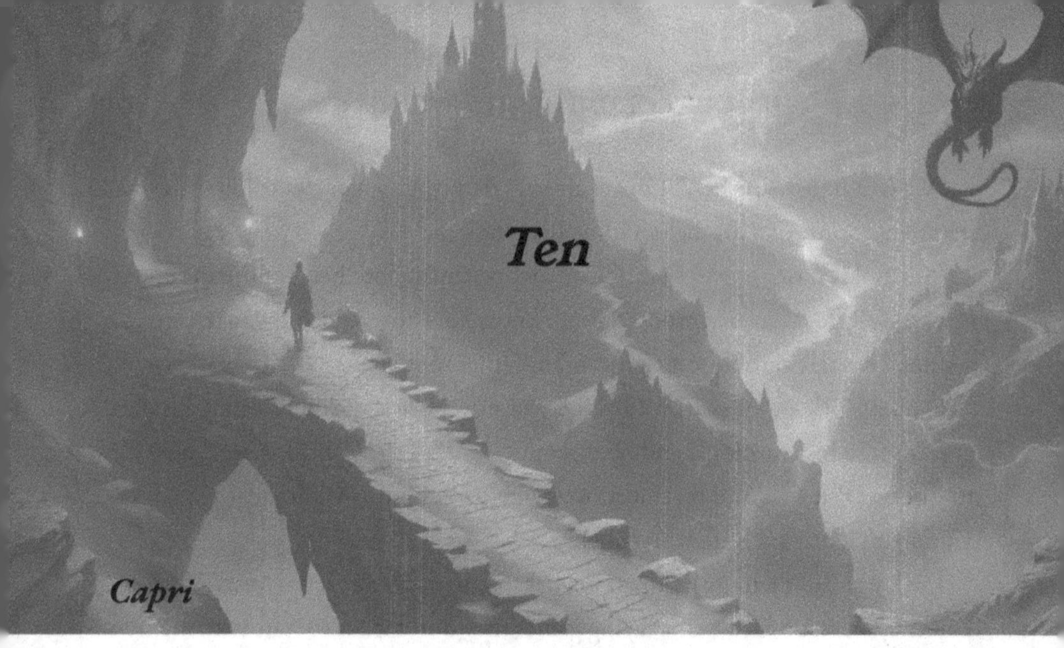

Ten

I'm standing in the middle of a male circle. There are about a hundred different males, some in their dragon forms, staring right at me. I am in the plain clothes I thought I would be alone in, completely unaware how many roaming eyes would be on me.

Rafe has a flirtatious personality, unlike Eamon, who seems less than enthusiastic about me being here the more he hears. His mood continues to sour as he listens to Caspian talk about me, and his plans for me.

"We do not need her to win the war. Call him and have her put down," the lord in question says in a hushed tone, one that everybody can hear though, and not just because we all have supernatural hearing. He wants me to hear him, it is a scare tactic I know far too well.

"She is a God, I know you can feel her power. This is exactly who we were told would come." Caspian's words pique my interest.

"Who told you I would come?" I barge into their conversation, not for the first time either.

I feel the heat of the three lords' eyes on me, but I don't back down. "Come on. I am not just some low-life fae you can ignore," I say in my most charming voice. Eamon rolls his black eyes; the white swirls seem to whisper hateful things about me.

"You are just some bloodsucking God who doesn't know her place," Eamon says harshly, while taking a large step towards me. I take a step towards him as well, and I hear hushed whispers from his males, I assume.

"My place is here. That would be why I want to live here. I can feel it in my bones." I say right back.

I really can feel a pull, a thrumming so strong that it almost hurts. The ground seems to call to me. I feel at home for the first time in my life. My mother would be safe here; I just need to take her to the South. I wouldn't bring her to this continent. No, I think these lords have no interest in me being here. They want to use me for their gain, then toss me out with their trash. I won't let them.

Rafe scoffs, as if disgusted, but it's Caspian who speaks. "Do you not know?" He asks in a curious tone.

My mind whirls with what he could be referring to, and my face must betray me because his eyes dance with my ignorance.

Eamon smirks cruelly. "Your father didn't tell you, did he?" Eamon starts walking circles around me, but my eyes don't leave Rafe's.

I feel as though he might be the only one who can see clearly. "I am unaware of what you all seem to think I need to know. If you could please tell me." I gesture towards Rafe, hoping he will continue whatever the others wouldn't say.

His males call out, "Let her be our first queen! Come on, we need a female!" One of them says and the others cheer encouragingly.

A first? I look at Rafe in discomfort. He stands stoically, not looking away from my commanding glare.

"No females live here?" I ask before thinking about it. Eamon runs his clawed paw along my neck; goose bumps raise in response. My eyes don't leave Rafe.

"No, we do not allow females to nest here with us. Do you see any?" Eamon answers for Rafe. His tone is harsh.

I scan the crowd, but I know I haven't seen any. I just figured they were somewhere else nearby. The males here seem oppressive enough to make females stay behind and care for the children or cook.

I bite down on the rude remark that I want to say and play my role. The happy God who wants nothing but peace.

"I haven't seen any yet. I just figured you handsome males wanted them safe at home." My voice doesn't stutter, but the words taste like bile coming up. I could never picture a world where males forced their females to stay home and do all the work while the males played.

Even still, I smile to the lords, whom I must suck up to for my mother. My smile is as sweet as a sugary pastry could ever be. Eamon scoffs as if I have offended him with my fake kindness. "What?" I ask, looking around to see if I can read anybody.

In order to read somebody, I have to have complete focus. I have gotten better, but not 100 percent accurate. I haven't had time to practice like I would need to be able to perfect it.

I look towards the male I know is from Rafe's clan, and dig my claws in. I notice him wince, just slightly, but still there. My goal is for them to not even feel me inside their mind. I'll get there someday, with practice.

"She doesn't even know anything about this world...yet she wants us to let her live among us?" I race past useless thoughts, attempting to find what I came here for. *"She is hot. She wouldn't make a bad plaything."* Okay, gross. Moving on to something not about me. Come on...come on. *"No one tell her about the whereabouts of our females. We don't need the extra trouble of keeping her away from our nests."* I can feel other minds brush against me in his head. "Why aren't you all speaking?" I ask the group suddenly.

Caspian smirks. "As if you didn't already hear him, God."

My face heats. "I don't know what you're talking about." I decide I do not want to be in the middle of this male circle any longer.

I teleport right behind them and take several deep breaths, trying to calm myself. *This is not going well, Capri.* I turn to face the group of male dragons, but when I do, Caspian is standing right behind me. The rest of the group is gone. My eyes dart around searching for where they all went.

"Where did they go?" I take a step backwards, suddenly feeling unsure about this.

"What is your goal here, Goddess?" His question makes me uneasy.

"Where did your clans go?" I ask instead of answering him. Eamon walks up beside Caspian, then, out of thin air, Rafe walks up beside them both. "Answer me, Goddess." His voice sounds inviting, and makes me want to answer him. I should be concerned about how easy it is for him to draw my attention elsewhere. I am not, though.

I am strong and could erase every single male here, I must remind myself of that. "Let's play a game," I say in my most taunting voice, then I start to pace. One foot in front of the other.

"What games do Gods like you play?" Rafe asks, with genuine curiosity in his voice.

My one advantage is that these males have no idea I grew up Fae. One thing fae, is that they are excellent at tricks.

"It's something I like to play back home." My voice is sweet as can be, polar opposite of who I really am. My steps are sure, and I notice Rafe bouncing on his feet. I reach out with my mind and grip his tightly. His body now hanging in my hands, his mind is mine to do with whatever I please. He will die if I put any more pressure into his fragile skull.

"Hey! What are you—" Eamon steps towards me but halts abruptly.

I hold my hand out to Eamon. "I told you. I want to play a game." I smile, but this one is anything but sweet.

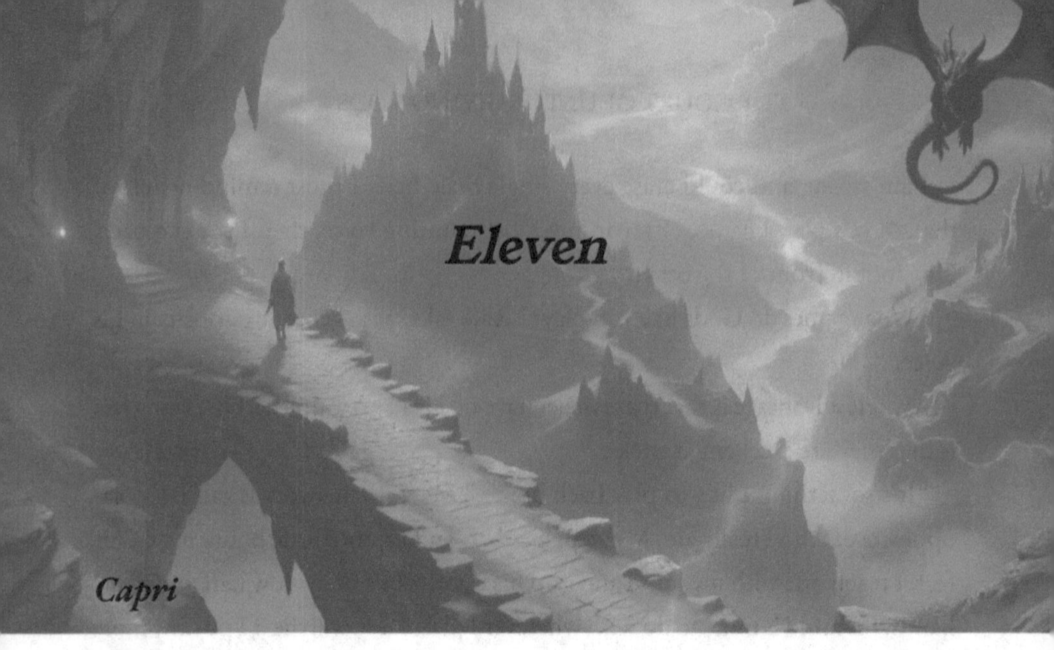

Eleven

My hands grab onto one of Eamon's men. They thought I wouldn't catch on to their games. They were wrong. Noone plays games better than a God raised by a fae.

I noticed the way the light moved around a large space. I only guessed about being able to grab onto one of the males. I was just lucky I grabbed his throat and didn't miss. Fates forbid I accidentally touch something I do not wish to.

The male I hold in my hand is light enough that I hold his limp body dangling in the air. "I will ask one more time...*nicely*. If you do not answer me, I will kill him." My tone is icy-cold but calm. I sound every bit the land-shattering God my father wished any of his children would become. I would bet chips he would have never thought it would be me.

Eamon turns bright red; he grinds his teeth but doesn't say a word as his jaw flexes. Anger is burning inside of him so hot I can feel it all around me. My eyes track the scorching path in the land around his feet.

I feel vines from the ground moving under my feet as I focus on every little thing around me, and I *tsk*. "Do not attempt to harm me or I will tighten my already firm grip and kill him. If you answer incorrectly, I will know and I will kill him. Do you know what will happen if you make any sort of movements towards me?" I ask, leveling a gaze at the lord I fear might cause me trouble.

Caspian smiles at me wildly and unruly, drawing my attention away from Eamon. "Let me guess, you will kill him? And, I'll add for good measure...everybody else?" Caspian questions playfully. My smile doesn't reach my eyes.

My feet slowly lift from the ground, and I start to hover. I've known I can fly, but I haven't ever really tested that ability. I guess now is as good a time as ever. I still hold Rafe's mind in my tight grip, and the other male's body in my hand hangs limply.

Their eyes track my movements; my fingers press so hard into his flesh that they are white. "Our females do not live here," Rafe grunts harshly, through clenched teeth as spit drips from his mouth.

The once nice male is completely gone. His mind is a tricky thing, but I hold on tight while he battles me inside of it. He is a strong male, and somebody I need to watch out for.

"Not an outright lie, but not enough information." I chastise. "Tell me, Lord, where are they?" My head tilts to the side, in a show of power and dominance. The group of males reappears, Eamon's light magic dissolving away completely.

"They nest off the shore. We want our hatchlings safe, so they do not come here. Ever. Unless there are problems. We go to them." Rafe says in exacerbation, sweat slicking to his brow as he fights me.

I don't push for their exact location. I feel the male's pulse start to slow under my tight grip. I do not wish to kill him yet, or at all if I don't have to.

"Where is your king? Tell me about him." My heart thumps in my chest, unsure what they might say.

"I will tell you, Goddess...but first, let Brock down, please." Caspian drawls. He seems to be the only calm dragon here, maybe it's all an act.

I look at the male dangling in my grip, then I drop him onto the plush ground. His body crumbling at my feet, I step around him. I take a deep, long breath before responding to Caspian. "I have already told you Dragon shifter. I am a God." I declare, feeling my temper rise.

"No, you are a Goddess. You are female, aren't you?" He argues right back, playfully yet again. I do not play with respect, though.

"I see no difference in being female or male; I will still always be more powerful than you will ever be." Silence lingers after my declaration.

Eamon's eyes turn to dragon slits, the white swirls in his black eyes going frantic as his males drag their friend away from me. Making certain they do not get too close and clearly sensing the growing danger within me.

I feel bloodthirsty, I feel powerful. As if the very ground I stand on gives me more power than I have ever had. The longer I stay in this Kingdom, the more I feel power overwhelming my senses. The more I desire to stay and fight for a life I have never allowed myself to ever dream of.

Before I can harm his mind irreparably, I detach from Rafe as well, setting him free. I don't know enough about this world or my strength here to test my limits. Especially not with a dragon lord.

The power I feel thrums through my blood. It feels as if a drum is beating inside my body, egging me on to take all it offers, and then some. I could easily live here forever, I could see myself drowning in the power if I let it overtake me.

"What is your goal?" Rafe asks, rubbing his throat as if thankful he can breathe on his own. My toes barely touch the ground before I plant myself solidly on the lush grass. When I look around, only a few dozen males stand circling me now. The rest have backed away, as if they fear me.

"I will answer this if you tell me about your king, your kingdom, the war, maybe?" I tilt my head, mimicking their own head movements.

I notice even in their human forms, they move like serpents. Their dragons lay dormant under their flesh, waiting to be needed and used just as the fates wanted for them. Some dragon shifters are even powerful enough to use their dragon abilities in human form, from what I have read.

"Our king hates Gods like you, and if he finds you here, you will be dust and bones. Just the way we like our Gods," Eamon spits at me, and fire comes to my hands without warning. My fingers dance with purple flames.

Light assaults my eyes, Eamon no doubt using his power against me. "Okay, you want to fight. Fine, let's fight," I say with more enthusiasm than I truly feel. Throwing my arms out in frustration that these beings might not be as easily persuaded as I had originally thought they would be. My charm has met its match, and it is dragons and they are fierce competitors.

Eamon rips his shirt off without hesitation, and the other lords back off. "What...don't you want to gang up?" I taunt them, readying myself. I have fought Atlas enough to know what to expect. This will hurt, but I will gain respect. That is what I truly desire here: respect is earned and valued among beings of this caliber.

Caspian shakes his head. "Not our way, God. You fight one-on-one." At least he calls me God now; that is progress.

I shake my head right back at him. Of course they have respectful ways to fight. An all-male continent would have to. "I still want answers," I grind out, watching this large male circle me. I know what he is doing...he's looking for weaknesses. I don't have any, so I search for his.

Just to taunt him, though, black smoke swirls around the base of my feet. His eyes bulge slightly. Where my boots once were are now high heels, and my plain outfit turns into a red silk glittering gown. "Are you trying to get us to breed with you now?" Rafe chuckles, and my gaze snaps to him. The fire in my eyes must shut him up. "I'm sorry to inform you, even if we wanted to stop this fight, we could not." Rafe starts to explain from outside the circle, as Eamon and I circle one another. "Once challenged, you cannot back out, unless you surrender, or you want to admit he is your better and bow to him?" Rafe tauntingly explains the last part.

My red silky dress has a large slit down my tanned legs; sweat glistening down them for good measure. I laugh manically. "I wouldn't want to breed with one of you anyways. Hatching an egg doesn't sound enjoyable." I circle Eamon faster now. His eyes are filled with pure hatred. He says nothing about my outfit change, telling me he sees nothing but an enemy in me. Atlas said males have one thing on their mind—sex. He told me once I get their attention on my body they will not be able to resist. He was wrong.

"You haven't been with the right males yet then, God," Caspian yells. "Some males in our clan are big enough to help ya out." Caspian continues his rant. Rafe laughs at his comment. I don't dare look at them, not when I have a deadly predator right in front of me. I roll my eyes, still watching every move this male makes.

"No male is as big as an egg is, therefore, nothing could prepare me for that," I say, trying to distract the male currently circling me.

I hope not, at least. I wouldn't know about the different sizes of penis's, let alone a dragon's dick. Father should have known I wasn't ready for this, maybe he knew I wasn't and this was all for nothing. I needed more time before coming here. I don't have enough experience talking to males yet.

Before our conversation can go on any further, I rush at the male in front of me. He sidesteps my kick before he pushes a hand to my chest and shoves hard. Light beams into my molten eyes. It burns so bright that I stumble a few feet backwards, rubbing on my shut eyes. "Oh, but you can use magic then, huh?" I ask, right before pushing his own power right back at him. I use the sun to my advantage, shoving the bright rays into his face, and rush him.

My low-cut dress swishes around my ankles during my run. I almost stumble in these Gods-dang shoes. Eamon moves as swiftly as the river I was just in, he is a trained warrior.

But I survived that river, and I will survive this one too. I land a punch to his jaw; this results in his clan chanting to him. Which seems to urge him on as their chants grow louder, stronger, and more encouraging.

He grabs my hair and yanks me back. Fire springs to my palms and I shove my hand right onto his face. "Bitch!" he hisses out. When the sizzle of his skin meets my ears, pride blooms deep inside my gut.

"I am no bitch; you will call me *Queen*," I say through gritted teeth. When I yank my hair out of his grip, I whirl around to see the handprint my fire left on him. I quickly call to water, and it flows smoothly throughout my veins.

"Eamon," Rafe says nervously. I can't get through his mental shields any longer, but by the way his face contorts, he is scared I will win. That maybe I will kill not only one of his fellow lords, but a brother to him.

"You can call the fight," I say, water swishing in my palms, floating throughout my fingers and hands. Eamon's face turns vile and cruel. He rushes at me, and I easily evade him. I push the two water pools that lay in my hand towards his face. I cup them around his nose and mouth. I don't allow him any breathing room. His eyes go wide, as if he doesn't understand how I could drown him while he stands on solid ground. "Blink twice for surrender," I say, my chest heaving.

Right before my eyes, his dragon form takes over. Scales replace flesh, clothes fall from his growing form. I look to Caspian to see if this is allowed, and he doesn't act as if it isn't.

This pale white dragon that stands in front of me blows steam out of his nose. I call to a sword, even though my swordplay isn't great, it is my best bet. "You know, I will kill him if he doesn't back off," I inform the lords, still not taking my eyes from the predator in front of me. Caspian and Rafe exchange a sort of concerned glance from my periphery.

"You will not kill a dragon lord, young God. Do not worry yourself," Caspian calls out. I lick my lips and lift the sword up with both hands. It's heavy and strange in my grasp. When I find the right placement for my hands on the cold metal, then I stand face-to-face with a dragon the size of a large horse.

Eamon roars in anger, spittles of fire falling from between his jagged teeth. The sunlight reflects off his large body and right into my eyes. The slit in my red silk gown gives me room to be able to move freely. I swing the sword once, twice, then catch it right as the blade stops near my dirty face.

The dragon moves like a snake towards me, his long tail swishing behind him. The tail itself is almost as long as his body is. Eamon's clothes lay on the ground at his feet in ribbons, his front right claw kicks them out of the way. As if his dragon form is disgusted by the material.

The serpentine way he glides to me makes me falter enough that his large paw shoves me on the ground. I grunt when my body hits hard on the suddenly solid ground. Everywhere else is soft except the one place I land? My gaze travels over to Rafe and he gives me a knowing smirk. "You shouldn't help," I say, right as I shock Eamon, and his dragon form roars out in pain. I keep sending lightning right into the paw that holds my body down. He releases me with a snarl; his black eyes have no white remaining in them whatsoever. His black eyes against his white scales make him look scarier than ever.

His tail swings out from behind him. I jump high enough to evade the damn thing, but it keeps coming. I rush under his body and thrust my sword into his leg; this gives me enough time to call another sword.

His dragon form roars, and I can hear the other lords shouting at him. Whatever they are trying to say comes out as a gargled mess. Black blood is spraying everywhere and it's hard to see through its warm thickness. My dress is ruined, especially when I shove another sword into his back paw, one in the front, and another in the back. He starts to stumble and thrash around.

"Yield!" I yell aggressively. I rush out from under him right before he falls to the ground. I jump on top of his large, scaly body, sword in hand. He tries to throw me off, but I dig my feet into his scales and climb up to his long neck. I press the sword into his neck and scream, "YIELD!" He tries to throw me off several more times.

Rafe yells now. "Eamon! You're beat, bud. Come on!" He tries to mask his nerves, but he fails. I press the sword deeper and it cuts into my own palm. Red blood starts to fall, but I don't let go.

Suddenly, I am on the ground, standing over a naked lord, blood seeping from both our bodies. "I fucking yield," he spits at me. When I bend down, he shudders. I never would have thought that seeing a naked male cower under me would make me happy, but I smile at the sight.

"You yielded. I am not going to hurt you." I press my palms—even the bloody one—onto his warm, bare chest. The light-blue light that shines from my hands presses into him, healing him faster than his dragon form could ever. His eyes look at me with mistrust but also respect.

"Your ugly dress is filthy," Eamon says right as Rafe and Caspian rush over to us. My blood stains his firm chest, while his blood stains my hands.

"Dinner tonight. We will eat at the palace," Rafe says in a clipped tone. I lift my brow in question. "You have earned our respect, though your fighting could use some help. We will give you some answers tonight. Not all of them, and not details, but some," Rafe informs me. Caspian helps Eamon stand. I nod softly, understanding dawning on me. These males do not want my body; they want my power. I will give it to them without fault so long as they allow my mother and me to live here.

"You have a palace but live in the woods?" I question as I follow Caspian. He looks at me with some sort of amusement. Caspian is a bright light, whereas the other lords are cautious, mistrusting even. As they should be.

"We have a palace for when we meet with the king, yes." Caspian confirms.

My heart almost leaps out of my damn chest. "Is he coming tonight?" I ask, almost too eagerly.

"No, he is not. We wouldn't very well be able to answer your questions about him if he were, now, would we?" He places his hand out, as if wanting me to grab it. I blush at the gesture- males, even in the palace back home, never gave me the time of day.

"No, I guess that would be rude, wouldn't it?" I half smirk at him, and the look he gives me back is devilish. My belly is doing flip-flops at the way his eyes seem to chew me up and spit me out within the same moment.

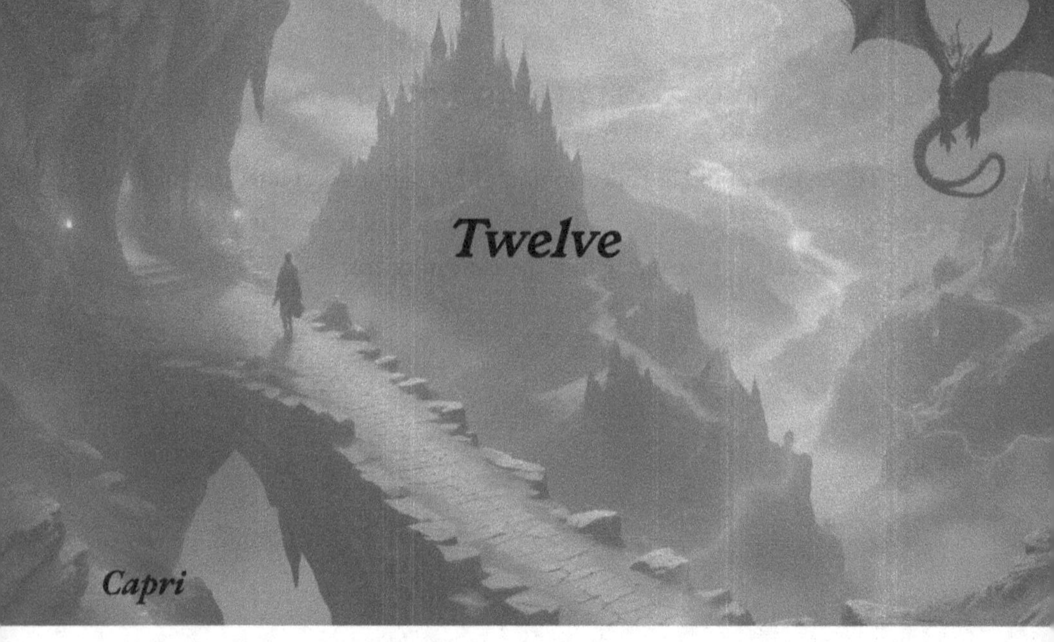

Twelve

I find myself on the back of Caspian this time instead of kidnapped by his talons. We have been flying for hours and his purple dragon form is becoming soothing to me. I watch the seas; I look into the woods and watch the creatures that roam here. I haven't seen any fae yet. Then again, maybe I have, and they are in the form of a woodland creature. I haven't spotted anywhere that would host their females or nests. I know the males are much larger than their females, so maybe they hide them.

At some point, I started to pet Caspian. I was just wanting to find something to do with my hands. He seems to not mind it very much. At first, I think it tickled him because his scales shimmered, and his body writhed beneath me.

"You sure are a good boy, aren't you?" I coo to the large deep purple dragon. His throat makes a warning sound. He has already thrown me off once, but I teleported right back to his back. I am certain he knew I could before he tossed me off. "You don't like praise, do you?" I pet talk to him. "I like it that you try to communicate back to me without words in your dragon form, it's sweet. I think you should all stay in your dragon forms." I bite down on my lip, trying to suppress the smile I know is building up. Caspian shakes his head, and I giggle. I'm having fun up here—taunting him, playing with him. I like Caspian; he is funny. He seems to understand me on a deep level, which would make sense considering the fact that purple dragons are best with complex emotions. The hours pass by quickly while I joke with Caspian.

The palace comes into view, and my thoughts race. The gray palace isn't very big, but there are already circles of dragons and fires in the field beside it. When we land, Caspian shifts right away, dropping me onto the ground without warning, his cock and balls dangling right in my face. "Oh my Fates, get away with that!" I shriek out.

The sideways smirk he gives me is the picture of a devil, and not one somebody would easily resist. "Oh, God, you are lucky to have seen my ba—"

Rafe tosses clothes right over Caspian's face, cutting off whatever in the Fates he was going to say to me. "Cas, she doesn't want to see your junk." Rafe takes my hand and guides me down the dirt path that leads to the palace of the North. Eamon doesn't speak one word to me; he doesn't even glance at me. I can't find it in myself to feel any guilt over our fight. He challenged a God. Not many walk away from a fight like that.

The dragon-made path is rough and uneven. As I look out at the land here, I can tell they cherish their kingdom. The hills make waves as the long green grass blows in the wind. Mist hits my face as I make my way to their palace. I notice some yellow flowers here and there, even a faraway field that houses hundreds of flowers. Then drastically dropping into the harsh sea below. The cliffs are high enough that impact into the water could kill a human, maybe even a werewolf.

I noticed on the flight here, Eamon's clan gave him a wide berth. Unlike Eamon's, Rafe and Caspian's clans flew with them. I still don't know how many males are among them, but I get the feeling there are way more than what's just right here.

The large wooden doors creak open, giving me a glimpse inside the palace. "So, does anyone live here?" I ask while walking past two males who hold the doors open.

"Some do," Rafe answers while Caspian pulls one of the males into a tight embrace. I continue walking side by side with Rafe. Even though we are close to each other, our arms do not touch. "Were you trained?" His question startles me, I can sense he is truly just curious with me. There is no malice in his question or tone. He doesn't know what to make of me, and honestly, I don't know what to make of myself either. "Sorry, you just don't seem like any other God we have met. None of us know how to read you." His honesty catches me off guard.

"Are you not angry with me?" I ask shyly, unsure if I really want the answer.

Rafe stills, then starts to walk again, catching up to me. "I cannot be angry with you. You are fighting for whatever you believe in, just as we are. My kind have been at war for as long as I have been here." He stops talking for a moment, as if the emotions of it all surprise him. "If I were mad every time somebody threatened my life, I would have no friends." He breathes out on a laugh.

We head up a large staircase, which winds upwards towards the second and third floors. "I wasn't always a God," I admit to him, though I don't know why.

"Oh?" His tone is higher than earlier. He leads me down a dim and dusty hallway, lit only by candles and the falling sun.

"I was raised as Fae. I only found out my father was a God in my teens." He stops in front of a door, seeming unsure what to make of this information. He licks his lips, his deep-brown eyes gleaming with questions I know he won't ask.

"Dinner will be held in the main dining area. Be prepared to be interrogated." He warns, as he turns to head back down the enclosed hallway, I stop him.

I grab onto his hand. "You can call me Capri, you know." I could sense he didn't know how to address me, none of them do. "I am not a power-seeking God. I want freedom, like you." I clench my jaw, hoping he can't see how much I need this to work. His brows furrow but he doesn't comment.

"I will send my second to come gather you in an hour...Capri." His white teeth shine against his deep-brown skin. A small dimple greets me before he turns on his heels to leave.

The room I have been locked in is small and simple. I can tell these dragons do not want to live from anything but the land. The room itself has a simple bed with one pillow, white sheets, and nothing else. A window overlooks the sea and the castle in the distance. I catch myself looking towards the castle, where I know the king of the dragons lives. I rub my thumb and forefinger together, trying to take away some of my anxiety. When I walked around the tiny room earlier, I found a small bathing chamber that housed a pot, a tub, and some oils.

"Well, alright then." My gaze doesn't leave the castle in the distance. "I wonder if I'll meet him anytime soon. I sure hope not." I need to know my enemy before I come face-to-face with him. I do wonder how Mother is doing. We've never been apart for longer than a few days, at most. I wonder if Val is taking good care of her.

I also wonder if Atlas is keeping his word and watching out for her. If Lachlan does anything to harm my mother, I will kill him. These are the thoughts that haunt me as I make my way to the bathing chamber.

I use my water and flame ability to take a steaming bath, turning my tan skin red with the heat of it. There is no soap at all, so I don't wash my hair. I do put some of the oil in it though. I let my long hair hang over the side of the tub and pool on the ground. My long locks often keep me sane. I run my fingers through them when I am missing mother, or when I am feeling overwhelmed by the mission at hand. I am not a normal God, and I know that. I know it isn't normal for Gods to question themselves, but I wasn't raised as one. I was raised by a female who taught me the opposite.

"Questioning yourself means that you are willing to learn from others, and that will make you a damn good God. It will set you apart from the others, be better than they have been, Capri." I keep telling myself that, repeating it in my head. Her words suddenly echo in my brain as I think back on them.

When I am ready to get out of the bath, I realize there is no towel or anything in here. This palace seems to be empty of everything, really. I groan and call for a towel and a gown. I grab the towel and wrap it around my body tightly. The gown waits for me on the bed. I am used to this; I don't need help getting ready.

I try my best to braid my hair away from my face, pulling the braid apart as I go, then I pull the other side into a tight half-up, half-down pony, bringing the braid into the mess. I am pleased with myself when I look at my reflection in the window.

I put charcoal on my lashes to darken them, a deep maroon powder on my eyelids, and a simple nude paste on my lips. I call to everything I have ever touched from Mara's collection. Surely she won't be missing it.

I want simple. These males seem to adore simplicity. Although, the dress I have *will* showcase my body. They seem to not mind showing off theirs, so I will do the same with mine. My mind goes back to Caspian shoving his balls and cock right in my face. "Ew," I mumble, right as a knock on the door drags me out of my thoughts.

"Hang on," I yell through the thick, pale, wooden door.

"Hurry up, girl. I am hungry." A male says through the door.

"Alright," I chant back in a singsong voice, although very annoyed that he would speak to me like that. I pull the black dress over my head. The full-length gown grazes my feet, and the slit up to my hip showcases my full leg. The dress hugs my waist in a way that makes my body look like a God's. My breasts are squeezed tightly in this gown, and the glitter all over it almost makes me choke out a laugh at myself. This is so far from who I am, I feel foreign in my own body.

I open the door and am faced with a male who is freakishly tall, his features sharp and defined. His body is on full display with the outfit he wears. "Enjoying yourself, huh?" the male asks, and I realize I have been staring at him for several seconds.

"I'm sorry, I just haven't seen many...uh...dragons as tall as you are." I am unsure of what they call themselves outside of their dragon form. I know they aren't Fae, but they aren't human either. Some of the more powerful dragon shifters have power in both forms. That is rare though, at least from my research. The male starts to walk, and I figure he just wants me to follow him. So, I do just that.

"You look fine," the male says sharply from in front of me. "Everett couldn't come get you. You will meet him downstairs momentarily." He says in a harsh tone.

"Oh, thank you, I think." It didn't sound like he really meant what he said. "Everett is Rafe's second then?" I venture curiously.

"I wasn't complimenting you. You keep incessantly fixing your dress, where it doesn't need fixing. And I do not speak to Goddesses about the ranks of my brothers." I look down and notice my hands are in fact grazing lazily on the fabric of my black shimmery dress. The glitter feels nice on my fingertips.

"Thank you for drawing my attention to that detail." I smile sweetly as we halt at the base of the steps. He whirls around to face me, eyes to...well, chest. Even though he is several steps down, he is still taller than me.

"I do not like you. I do not like your kind. You are here for power and power alone. I will not be swayed by your pretty words or the body you are so obviously trying to flaunt for attention." He speaks so dully I almost start to snore.

I gulp down my response, though and just simply nod. I keep my damn mouth shut, because that is what males expect of females.

"I don't know where the main dining area is. Would you be a doll and show me?" I coo and grab onto his stiff arm. His entire body goes rigid at the contact, and he tries to pull away, but I do not allow it. I merely pat his arm, trying to soothe him. "Oh, these darn heels are so high I struggle to walk. Would you mind?" I bat my lashes, feigning a damsel in distress.

If they want to keep their beasts hidden under prettiness, as will I. I can pretend, I have done it my entire life and will keep on doing so.

I really could walk on my own, but it's a power move. Walk in with one of them on my arm...as a toy, maybe? I bite down my laughter as he leads me to the area that will host us for the entire evening.

Thirteen

Capri

The dining area is a large room with candles everywhere; they dangle from the large beams that adorn the ceiling. The long table seats around twenty males, all different ages, shapes, and colors. They each share one thing though—they all hate that I'm here. Some of them outright hate *me*. Their putrid thoughts should startle me, but I drink them all up. My anxiety is now forgotten and replaced by pure adrenaline.

"Hello, everybody," I say to the room, then turn to the dragon next to me. "Thank you for walking me down here. That was very kind of you to offer me your arm." I smile at him, and his mouth hangs open as if in disgust about even touching me. The table is bare other than empty plates and the platters of food, which seem to mostly consist of meats, some possibly raw and bleeding out. I grimace but don't ask any questions. Instead, I take the seat that is vacant at the head of the table. I hear several gasps, but none of them say anything to me as I sit. My chair scrapes against the floor, I wince at the uncomfortable silence in the room. Caspian smiles at me before waving to the food.

"Everybody, load up. We have much to discuss." He announces to the room.

At Caspian's command, all the males fill their plates. I grab what looks edible and cooked. Some of it has fur still on it. I don't typically eat meat, but right here and now I will not question it.

"That right there is...a type of rabbit. You'll like it."

I smile at the male speaking to me. "Thank you." I bite into the meat and almost gag. I hold back my distaste as much as possible.

"Don't you like our food?" the same male asks me. I swallow the meat that tastes like it died ten months ago and rode here on the back of a donkey in the hot summer days.

My eyes crinkle in disgust, but I swallow the bile down. "I don't mind it. We don't have, uh...fresh food like this in my home." I say slowly while trying to breathe out of my nose instead of my mouth. I slam my hand over my mouth to contain the contents quickly coming back up my throat.

He nods and I hear a few snickers around the table. I know they all are feeling nervous, but also, I get the sense they are messing with me.

I heat my hand up and grab onto a leg of some type of bird. With the food being mostly cooked after I heated it up, the taste isn't bad. Although, these males act as if this is a gourmet meal.

"Do you like this?" I ask softly, noticing everybody else is conversing. I reach my hand out to shake the male's hand, after of course, wiping my hand off on the seat since apparently they do not believe in napkins. He looks at me with a question in his eyes, but he grabs my hand and shakes it.

"I do; this is a delicacy to us. We mostly eat what we find in our dragon form. We don't travel unless in form."

I ponder this for a long moment. "So, you live in dragon form, truly?" I whisper, not meaning to actually say it out loud.

His blue eyes travel over me for a long moment, then he nods his head. "Yes, we live, eat, breath, and fuck in dragon form." I almost choke on my food and several heads swing our way.

"Ev, leave her alone. We have important matters to discuss, not our sex lives, you freak." Caspian chuckles before turning to Rafe. "What kind of second are you training?" Rafe half smirks before whispering something to Caspian that causes him to laugh loudly.

The meal goes by smoothly, and several hours pass by as they all chit-chat around me. After a while the conversation slows, and I notice now might be my time.

So I start doing what we are supposed to do here, figuring this shit out. "So, I need to know things, and you all want to know things. Please, let's share." I look back when a hand touches my shoulder. A male is offering me a goblet of blood-red wine, I take it hesitantly. "Thank you." He nods, then goes to the next person at the table.

"I would love to share *you*," the male Caspian called Ev says to me with a wink and a shit-eating grin. While he is handsome, I don't feel a pull to him. His shirt looks two times too small, he has freckles all over his chiseled, tanned face, and his blue eyes sparkle with mischief. Any other weaker being would get lost in those ocean eyes. Just not me.

"Thank you for the offer." I then swing my gaze to Caspian. Just to gain their attention, I change my eye color to red. Several males right by me stand and back away several feet, fear radiating from them. "Please do keep on acting as if I am a test you are conducting. You ignore me further and see how I will react. I find it amusing but I don't have time for this, sadly." I push my seat back and the sound of it stops all the chatter.

"She is a devil God," Eamon says with a sneer, and I growl at him, showing my teeth in more ways than one.

"Oh, boy, I am no devil, but I will haunt your nightmares if you don't give me the answers I seek." I look them each right in the eyes. I just want to scare them a little bit.

Caspian is now the only one sitting at the table. Even Rafe grabbed his goblet and backed away. I put my heels on the now cleared table and lean back in my chair. My hands intertwin behind my head, before I speak to the group. "Care to share your story? Well, more importantly, your king's?" I ask slowly, drawing out the last word.

I look over the rim of my goblet, right at the only lord brave enough to sit here with me. Caspian says nothing but takes a long chug of his drink, sporting a grin. I bite down on my lip as I lower my goblet. These males are going to make me work hard for any sort of answers.

They will never respect me or trust me. So, I will have to force them to bow to me. Caspian's eyes dart to the doors for a split second before meeting my gaze again.

"You are just the type of female we needed here," Caspian says right as the doors swing open and slam into the wall. I don't even have time to think about what he is talking about before a voice chills me to the bone.

"Are you talking about *me*?" My heart stops in my chest, and suddenly my face is completely red. I no longer breathe, as my lips part slightly and my eyes widen comically.

"We were. Come in and meet our new friend," Caspian says with humor in his tone. The male who strides to me is the most handsome male I have ever seen.

"I would rather her not be here. What has she promised you? God babies and winning a war, neither side will likely win?" he huffs out. His long strides make it to the table quicker than I would think he could. All the males seem to relax in his presence, as if he would keep them safe from me. I scoff, and that earns me his full attention. Although, he already had mine.

He wears a tailored deep-navy suit that fits just right on his muscular body. I swallow hard as my eyes drag down the firm planes of the dragon king. His eyes are golden, and his hair looks completely unruly with the way the brown waves are swept to the side, but also look perfectly in place.

"Why are you here?" His eyes burn with an intensity that could kill me if I'm not careful. His nostrils flare as he sniffs the air around me, as if he can decide what I am just by smelling me. He stops right in front of me. My feet are still on the table, ankles crossed. I look far more relaxed than I truly am.

"I decided I wanted dragon babies; isn't that why most females come here?" I smile, biting into my bottom lip. My gaze is right into golden eyes that make my heart stop and beat within the same moment. He growls at me, and the room seems to still under his scrutiny. His hand lands on the back of my chair, and he leans it back enough that I yelp. My feet dangle in the air while he holds my chair in balance. My breasts almost fall out, and he trails his gaze down my body in a predatory way that tells me he isn't uninterested in me.

"We don't want your God blood tainting our children. Leave here and go home. That is my final offer." His tone holds none of the warmth that I know I see in his eyes. Every set of eyes is on us. Caspian still sits at the other end of the long table, chuckling at our interaction.

I shrug sarcastically. "I would leave, but I can't until I claim your undying love and loyalty." The slow flutter in my lashes seems to upset him. He snarls at me, and I take the chance to teleport away from the dark gray smoke wafting from his nostrils. I now stand behind him. Even in my heels I must still look up at him. That must mean he is taller than even Father. "Hello," I say, tapping on his shoulder. He whirls around before gripping my throat and tossing me over him as if I weigh nothing. I thud onto the table, luckily, nothing else remains on the empty table or else it would all shatter. Caspian holds his goblet close to his chest.

The King puts his forearm on my neck while pushing me into the table harder than necessary. The shuffle of feet and shoes across the ground is the only sound in the entire room. "Oh, you're handsy are you? I wouldn't peg you for a male who does it in a crowd. You seem too possessive," I try taunting him.

If he challenges me and I win, then he will have to bow to me, which will mean that no matter what stage the war is in, I will be their queen.

"You, girl, are barely in heat. I do not want you." He presses me harder into the table. If I weren't a God, it would hurt me. Maybe even snap my neck.

My brows lift, "You don't? I wouldn't be able to tell that from your hard-on." The rumbling growl that greets my ears should scare me, but it doesn't. I look down at where his crotch touches my upper thigh. The gown's slit has completely moved, my bare skin on display for all to see.

He pushes away from the table and looks to Eamon. The dragon shifter shakes his head at his king, as if they are speaking in each other's heads, and I am not invited to their conversation.

"Hey," I say, interrupting their conversation. Apparently it was an important part because they don't even look at me. The king looks about half a second away from killing the Lord of Draig, his eyes heating more intensely as they lock with Caspian.

I don't understand why, but when I look at Caspian, he is still half-smirking. As if he has done something that the king and Eamon don't like.

I hop off the table and straighten my gown. I stride over to the two males and insert myself into their heads. Both of their eyes look dazedly at me, and I notice the other lords closing in on us, probably thinking I am trying to kill the two males, so I force them back with air magic and dig my claws in.

"*She isn't—*" the king starts to say before he realizes I have joined them. "*What the fuck?*" His head whips towards me and then they both must notice none of their males can get to them.

"Will you two listen to me now?" I ask sweetly, as if I weren't holding back their clan's strongest males. Caspian watches with more interest than he had during dinner. "We will listen, God," Caspian says while leaning into the chair, still looking relaxed as ever.

"I am not here to take your world or whatever you think. I want to help stop the war—" The king scoffs as if I am some stupid girl. I keep on, fully knowing he thinks I am nothing but a silly female. "I want to live here with my mother and best friend. I need to. Their lives depend on it," I say with the sincerest voice I can muster.

"Is that all? Do you truly believe you can just come and rule a world you know nothing about?" the king asks, disbelief written all over his face.

My mouth hangs open, I can't believe that's what he got from all that. "I-I don't want to rule this world. I want to help lead it. I don't need to be a queen. I can't very well bring my mother here if your war will put her in danger though. Now can I?"

He shakes his dark-brown hair, some of it falling into waves of complete and utter chaos. He shoves his fingers through it, attempting to tame it. "What did your father send you here to do?" the King demands answers, so I will give them to him.

I mourn the conversation between Caspian and me. The kindness, the playfulness now snuffed completely out of the room.

"I am to take control of Beithir so that he may have access to the kingdom, just once, he would like to come here. Then I will live here to maintain the peace." Chaos erupts around me.

After more than thirty minutes, Caspian convinces the king to sit down and hear me out. The other dragon shifters left the room to the lords and their seconds, leaving me in the room with the King of Beithir and his three Lords of the North.

I should feel terrified, nervous, or even shy. I feel nothing but complete and utter power. They don't know what to do with me because I am too powerful for them to challenge and win. I smirk to myself and take a sip of the wine I was handed a moment ago. I have already downed two other glasses; it tastes so sweet. I never allowed myself to drink large amounts around Father or my brothers—I didn't want them to take advantage of a possible impaired state—but here I see it as a way to relate to the dragons.

"Speak." The king's voice sends chills down my spine. Goose bumps prickle my arms. I don't hide them though; I think showing him I'm vulnerable will help me. I haven't ever come across a male who commands with the level of certainty he does. His voice brings a calmness to me, even knowing he wants me dead and gone.

"I will. Give me a minute." I hold up a single finger to him. This seems to anger him even more than he already was.

I take another sip of my wine and wait for all of them to be seated. "You don't need to make yourself a show to earn our attention; you already have it." The king says as he sits in the seat I once had been sitting in. I take the one right next to him. Caspian glares at me, as he searches for a new place at the table.

"I just want to include everybody here on our conversation. Is waiting for others to sit down such a bad thing? That's probably why your world has been at war for so long. You don't communicate well." I sigh. The king's golden eyes burn with hatred, and I squirm under the harshness of them.

"Now, now. No need to place blame on our king, God," Caspian says, trying to get our attention off one another.

"Well, there is a war, is there not?" I question, even though I know I shouldn't.

All eyes are trained on me; I puff out my chest and simply drink the sweet wine.

"There is," Rafe dips his head slightly while agreeing with me, and I'm shocked.

"So, it would make sense that we come to an agreement, while everybody who needs to be here is sitting down with us, wouldn't it?" The king smiles softly at my response, which is in complete contrast to his hard features. His dark, thick and long lashes brush his cheek as he blinks slowly.

"We don't want to agree with you. We want our brothers to stop stealing land and power from us. We want our king to see the right side of this, and we all want *you* gone," Eamon spits out. "We *need*-" He says the word desperately, his voice cracking. "Them to stop murdering our babies, our females, and families."

I look around the table and all of them are nodding in agreement, except for Ev. Everett sits stiffly, his knuckles white while clenching his goblet.

"I will not be leaving unless I am to be bringing my mother back here to live," I state clearly, and none of them warrant me a response.

The king runs his hands over his face, seeming annoyed by this when he blows out a long breath. "We have been trying to come to an agreement between the North and South for decades. You think you can come here and fix it?" His golden eyes bore right into my soul.

I clear my throat and shift under the eyes on me. "I think we can come to an agreement. If I only knew what started the war, I might be able to help. Aren't you the king? Can't you make your lords behave?" I say my internal thoughts out loud and regret it right away.

Eamon growls, Rafe looks about two seconds away from mass murder, and Caspian chugs his wine.

"If it were that easy, I would have ended it before the death toll went over a million dragons and our numbers dwindled to what they have become." The king says gruffly.

"The war is over power and control. The South thinks their way of life is better, but that is not the way of the dragon. We do not see eye to eye on the amount of power we should use and how we use it. They live in villages and even smaller cities; the Fates did not want that kind of life for us. The war may have killed many, but we are at a standstill for now. There haven't been active battles for many years," Caspian states in between gulps of wine.

I mull over this for many minutes while everybody sits awkwardly. "Why would you care how they live, if you live so far apart?" I ask hesitantly.

"Because they want to control us and force their villages and cities on us. They attacked our nests; they killed our hatchlings. Our king has tried to force them to see reason, but they will not accept it." Caspian pauses for a moment before continuing. "Just as they cannot accept us, we cannot accept they do not live by the code of the dragon."

The king watches me with so much interest that I look down to make certain my breasts haven't popped out.

"They haven't," he says right as I look up.

"Huh?" My face scrunches in confusion. He licks his upper teeth before smiling widely at me.

The smile he gives me causes flowers to bloom *deep* in my belly. His warm smile takes me to another universe entirely. Star travel forgotten, the King of Dragons merely has to smile at me and I will bow to him. My chest fully on the ground, worshipping at his feet.

Then he speaks and the entire moment is ruined.

"Your tits are still right where you desire them to be." He says so low I almost can't hear him.

My jaw unhinges from its place at his crass words. Faces whip to us and our conversation. I school my features, gently placing a mask over my shock. "Thank you for noticing." My voice is clipped. I hadn't been that obvious, had I?

"I wouldn't be able to *not* notice. You have them on display like you wish to be ogled," he states plainly while motioning to my chest.

I shrug, as if I couldn't care any less. "Well, you all seem to enjoy being naked half the time, so I figured this is modest." I play the part I need to.

The king's eyes don't leave mine while he says, "I do not allow others to see me naked outside of a bedchamber, and between my sheets." He leans forward, resting his elbows on the wooden table. His shirt stretches with the muscles moving. My brows furrow and my body heats at the mention of his body being naked. Then I picture whoever is lucky enough to be between his sheets with him, and my mood sours.

He smiles almost, when my face turns down and into a frown, not a full smile like before, but a teasing one. As if knowing what he did to me and my insides.

"Anyways, they want our clans to live how *they* live. They will do anything to force their ways upon us, including killing our babies to force our hands. Our land has more potent power than theirs." That brings up several more questions, but I won't ask them just yet. "They want what we have, we just want them to live by dragon law. They breed with non-dragons." Rafe states this fact with a look on his face that shows how disgusted he feels about that. I must bite my lip to stop myself from asking why they aren't allowed to sleep with non-dragons.

Caspian must read my face and answers it for me. "We can have sex with non-dragons, but to have babies outside of our kind is forbidden. They do this knowing it is against the law. The Fates created dragons different from other beings for a reason. *They* accept anything on their cocks and in their pussy's." He, too, makes a face that says he agrees that non-dragons are disgusting. I push my tongue into the side of my mouth before turning my gaze to the king.

"Why don't you force each side to compromise?" I ask because I know the power this male holds is strong enough to level most battlegrounds. I can feel it. The dragon king sitting in front of me holds more power than I have ever felt.

Each time I talk to him, his eyes meet mine in the most intense way. Our eyes lock, as if caught in a siren's song. I can't look away and neither can he. His thick lips part slightly as a cool breath leaves him.

"I lost my father to this war. He tried to force each side to listen to him, to follow dragon law. I took to my isle when I won as their king; I will come to fight in this war when the time is right." I know he says this directly into my mind, but I didn't know dragonkind had that ability. *"They don't."*

I blink back at him several times, my eyes narrowing on him. *"I'm sorry about your father."* This seems to startle him enough to make him break eye contact.

"Are you two done mind-fucking each other?" Everett asks, and I almost choke on my drink. The way these dragons speak is unlike anything I have ever heard. They have no manners at all, each of them, even their king has a foul mouth.

My mind feels fuzzy; I place my fifth empty goblet down and stand up, swaying on my feet when I do. I place both hands firmly on the table in front of me. "It seems we may have much more to discuss, but I am tired." My fingernails dig into the hard wooden table as I attempt to calm myself down. I look down the table to the lords. "Thank you for this information. I would like to help you even if you don't accept me here with you since I am not a dragon. You deserve to live the way you want." I turn to leave and I take several steps away from the table before Rafe grabs my arm.

"You may sleep in here. You are not a dragon, you don't have to sleep outside with everybody." My mind whirls because I hadn't ever planned to sleep outside with them. He is right, I am no dragon, I am a *God*. Gods do not sleep with their enemies, especially out in the open.

I smile sweetly at him before patting his upper arm and walking to the palace doors. My heels clink as I take each step slowly, and not just because the room is now spinning from the drinks. "I won't be." I say as loud as I can over my shoulder.

The doors open, the brisk air hitting my warm face, and I make my way to my new home. For now, at least. I hear the males follow closely behind and then several gasps and curses as they see what I have done, but I keep walking.

To the place I will bring Mother and Val. The place I have never had before but will not give away lightly. I can feel what this land is doing to me, and I won't give it away for free. If they want me to leave forever, then they will be starting a new war with a bigger opponent.

I walk myself *home* for the first time, and not the last. I have a home, and one I can say I am proud of. The field has cleared out of any and all dragons, other than the ones gawking at my masterpiece.

Fourteen

"What have you done?" Eamon grits out.

I continue my walk towards the raging sea. "I made myself a home. You weren't very welcoming with yours, Eamon," I say from over my shoulder, as I almost skip to the shoreline.

A hot hand grabs onto me, and then I'm spinning to face the king. Not *my* king but one all the same.

"What did you do here?" he growls in my face, his golden eyes turning to slits of pure, blackened rage.

"I built a home to live in while I try to help your Kingdom." I gesture towards the castle I've created, and when I look at it, a large smile pulls at my face.

I can feel the moment the king relaxes, his grip loosening on my arm, but not yet letting go. I turn to look at him, and my breath is taken away from me in one fell swoop. He isn't looking at the castle at all, his eyes are on me, on the place where his hand still holds me. No longer are they void of happiness, they are lit up with an emotion I can't place, but a good one, I know.

I worked the entire evening to put this together; I mentally built each stone and moved them in a way that made a home as well as a fortress. I pulled the land up above the sea. I wasn't sure I would be able to do it let alone finish it. But I did it.

Then all too suddenly, his mask slips right back on. "I can see what you are trying to do here. Why did you build your...uh..." His large, tanned hand waves towards my new place of residence. His veins bulge and pulse across his muscular arm.

I smile at him before walking out of his grasp. "This will be my home. Any other meetings will be held there, with real food." I lick my lips, thinking of the food from home, my stomach growling with a need for real food. Then, as if he cannot contain himself, he grants me another smile, a full one with dimples and all. One that I think might very well be my undoing.

"You can't live there." He says, almost painfully. "We haven't decided if you can even stay here, let alone build yourself a castle. How did you even do this?" His eyes don't leave mine, even as the castle I built from scratch taunts him behind me. His tone is filled with disgust, mistrust, and...lust?

I enjoy the last one more than the first two. And I know very well I will enjoy living here with these males. I turn away, even though my heart tells me to stay with the King of Dragons.

I shrug my shoulder slightly, making my way to the icy-cold, murky water. The tide brings in dirt, seaweed, and other things from the open waters.

"I simply just thought about it and moved the stone with my mind. You should see the inside," I tease him, knowing it won't gain me his favor. I am just unable to *not t*ease him.

I hear him take a step towards me, his dragon clans standing right at the water's edge now. They all look out towards my castle in awe, when I make it to the shoreline, I turn around, I just need one more glance. Every dragon shifter is looking at my home. Granger's eyes are glued to me still, as if he refuses to look away. Even for just a moment.

"Are you inviting me to stay in your home?" He tilts his head in a way I saw some dragons do earlier. In a predatory way, his eyes narrowing and his golden eyes turning to black slits. My skin flushes bright red at his lustful tone.

"Would you accept it if I were to? I'm no dragon shifter, I'm afraid," I bait him and bat my lashes slowly. I take a step towards him, brushing my chest against him. I in no way, shape, or form, think I can truly seduce him; I'm sure the dragon king has his pick of females here, if not somebody already waiting, warming his bed, which gets me thinking.

"Do you have a mate?" I ask so airily, I wince. I shake my head, knowing I must revise my words. "I mean, don't you have to have a queen?" I hate the way my voice betrays me in these moments with the handsome dragon king. I might have to kill him someday, but I can't look away in this moment.

The way my eyes go to his heaving chest should embarrass me. They then drag up to watch his throat bob, gliding up to his chiseled jawline, then stopping on his puffy lips as his tongue darts out to wet the top and bottom of his mouth. The smirk he gives me makes my knees weak.

"Do you want to know this because you are curious about my world or because you find me attractive and want me in your home?" He takes a step closer to me, pushing me back several feet. "Maybe even...in your bed?"

I shake my head, my hand going to my temple. I need to get a hold of myself, I need to remember why I am here. And it is not to get into bed with my enemy.

"Good night, Dragon King. I will send word when I am ready to host you all." I teleport to my new castle, ready to be in a bed that's soft and inviting, something I can call my own. But before my body dissolves into thin air, I think I hear Granger say, "I haven't claimed my mate yet."

The isle I created isn't much bigger than the castle that sits atop it. I wanted to create something that other Gods haven't yet. That's the thing about Gods from where I live—they create simple-minded things, like a dress here and there. Father is powerful enough to create amazing structures, and he has before, but nothing like this. His father and grandfather worked alongside the Fates in creating realms and other amazing things. They were powerful. My father, though? He cares only about himself, and about filling his own pockets.

When the Fates helped create other realms alongside the Gods, they worked together. A God could never alone do something like I have just done. I don't think too long on that, truly, because I don't care to.

I walk up the stone pathway towards the place I am most proud of. This will be all mine and Mother's. I thought of her while sitting through the dinner, which took far too long for my comfort. I ate raw meat tonight in hopes that one day it will give my mom freedom to live in a place she can call hers.

"Mom, if you can hear me, I love you. And when you get here, we will bring so many books in that we'll have to build more rooms." I open the bronze door and take my first step inside my new castle home.

The first thing I see upon entering is two stairwells on either side of the main hallway. Under the stairs, in the middle, is a hall that leads directly to the dining area and the scullery. To the right of me is the massive library that has no books in it yet. I want to wait for Mother to place the first ones in there. To the left is a sitting room that hosts a large green velvet couch and a liquor cabinet that I have already stocked up with wines and whiskey I found in my mental search of the dragon manor. Heading up the steps, I take my shoes off only three steps in. Then, on second thought, I dissolve the clothing in general and go for the nude look. I am completely alone for the first time in my life. I want *the ladies* out.

I hum to myself while taking the stairs, with a new pep to my step. The second story is full of guest rooms for the friends I might make, but also royal guests who will come visit. I keep my feet moving, not wanting to stop because I worry once I see a bed I will fall into it and sleep. I want *my* bed, *my* blankets, and *my* comfort.

At the third-story landing, I start up the steep spiral staircase that is no longer open but enclosed by gray stone. I walk up the long flight of stairs to get to the bedroom at the top of them. My room is secluded from the rest of the manor. I finally make it to the top and let a relaxed breath escape my mouth at what I have done.

The large room has a golden four-poster bed frame, the white comforter and massive pillows are stuffed with feathers. They look so soft and inviting, I might as well sleep on a cloud. My gaze makes it to the large open window, the archway inviting. I walk over and look directly at the king's palace several hundred feet away. From this high up, it doesn't seem as far to me as it did on the ground. I chew on my lip, my thoughts racing to King Granger. My body has never reacted to a male the way it did to seeing him. Speaking to him was on another level entirely. I haven't ever felt the amount of comfort in a random male or female before. Shaking those scary thoughts from my mind, I make my way to the bath.

The large tub could easily fit several beings, as well as conceal your entire body. I wanted a deep tub so that I could submerge myself. I still need to practice my water magic; I am not perfect by any means. As Father always says, if you sit idly by and allow others to work harder than you, you will be killed for not being good enough. He would scream and yell at me that if I didn't practice every moment of every waking hour, I would kill myself and others around me from my lack of effort.

So, I did just what he said to. I practiced...in secret. My brothers never had any clue as to what I could do. I didn't allow them to see or even sense it. I knew if they smelled blood in the water, they would attack. I am strong, but not strong enough to take on three powerful Gods and come out unscathed. I worked my ass off. Now I have a castle to show for my ability.

The scalding hot water drenches my body. I lather on the honey soap and allow myself these moments. I haven't had time to process the fact that I am in another Kingdom far from my mom and best friend, the only true family I have ever had in my life. They are both away from me, and unless I make the impossible happen, they will never come here, and I may never leave.

I grant myself an hour, just one hour, of self-loathing and hatred to fill my body. I scold my body and my mind, beating myself far worse than my father ever could. Every hateful thought I have passes through my head. Anything and everything I can think of.

Then, one affirmation at a time, I talk myself off the ledge I've walked myself onto. My toes are dangling over as I teeter a very fine line, I take the steps I need to backwards and into myself.

I am *powerful*, I am *strong*, I am *not* like other Gods. I care about other beings and their lives. I could create a realm that is made for peace. I could help others, and I will. I will be better because of my upbringing and not worse. My mother raised me to care deeply about everything and so I will. Even just one life matters in the grand scheme of things.

My hour is up, and I feel better, now relaxing in the plush bed. I have a glass of wine in one hand and my thoughts are racing. The self-hatred session has given way to pure curiosity.

"So, they don't have their females here. Where could they be?" I chew on my finger while thinking about everything that was said tonight. The king doesn't have a mate yet. Interesting. He isn't married, if they even do that here. "I wonder, do the lords in the South have the same feelings about their females? They must not if they would attack the nests of others." I talk to myself while pulling the lush comforter over my chest. I chug the rest of my wine and fall asleep with my thoughts pulling questions out that I don't know if I want the answers to yet.

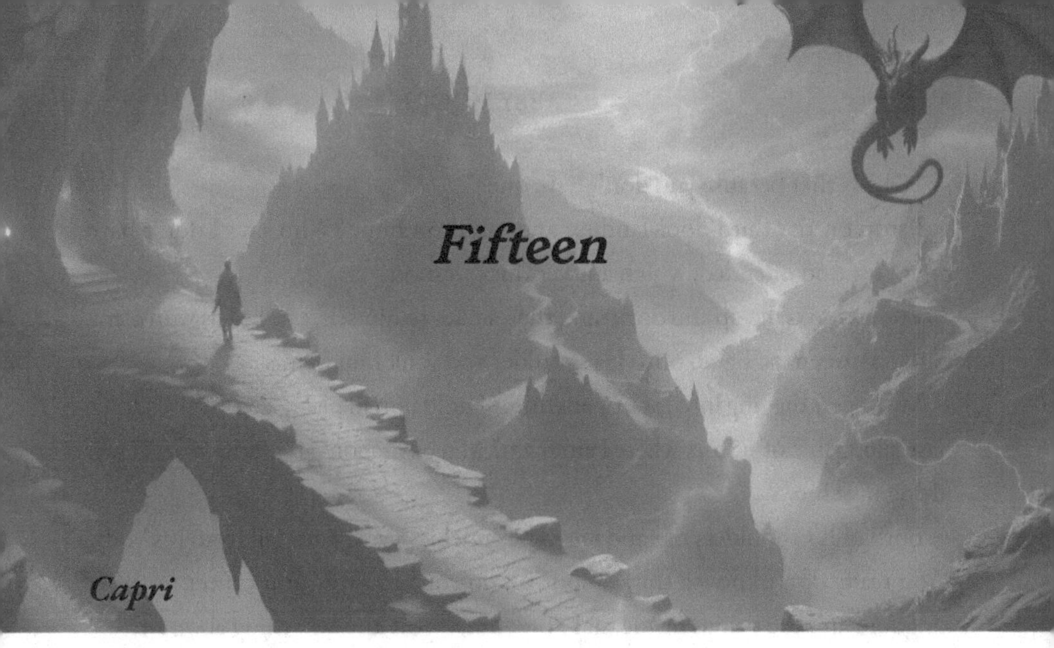

Fifteen

"What have you done?" Everett asks in awe, walking around my room in nothing but his skin and sweat. It has been three days of silence from the dragons, and I have slept for most of it. I yawn from my bed, and sit up covering myself even though I slept in a nightgown last night.

Everett has just let himself into my home, and if I hadn't already heard him outside wandering around, I might have killed him. I am desperately trying to bring the beings of this kingdom together though, so opening my home for them is the first step.

"I built myself a home. I have never had one to be proud of before, so I figured it would be good practice." I shrug and conjure up some clothes for him.

He lifts a brow, a silent question written on his face. "Are you not enjoying my nudity?" He teases, in an upbeat tone. I bite my lip out of embarrassment, then I meet his bright, ocean-blue eyes.

"I do not enjoy staring at your dick, no," I answer, keeping my eyes away from his privates. I walk to the set of stairs and make my way down, just hoping he follows me.

"Oh, you like females then?"

I clear my throat; my mind is on other things. More important things...like how I am going to cook.

"I don't think you and I should have those types of conversations. I am more interested in figuring out my food situation than my love life." I take the steps two at a time, Everett right behind me, his salty scent overwhelming my nostrils.

"Oh? Is that because you don't have one?"

I stop on the third-floor landing and whirl on him. "Who says I don't have one?" I sound offended, which answers his question.

Everett looks me up and down and then smiles to himself, as if he has won some battle between us. I grab onto his shoulder and yank him to me.

My fingers digging into his upper arm, as I hold him in place. "Who says I don't have a long line of suitors where I am from? Maybe dragons aren't my type," I say, lifting my chin.

Both of his shoulders rise and fall as he chuckles. My hands fall from his body. "You really don't know a thing about us, do you? How do you expect to rule a kingdom and the beings inside that kingdom, if you know nothing about it?"

I roll my eyes, scoffing, even though a small part of me knows he might be right. "Of course I know things about you and your clans, as well as your world."

We make it to the first floor, and I make my own way to the scullery. I think if I conjure up some fruit and maybe eggs I can figure out how to cook it into a nice breakfast. I have never had to make a meal before. Mother either cooked for me, or the fae brought out the meals in the palace back home. Everett keeps speaking but I have long since drowned him out. I need food, I don't do well without it. I might be a God, but I still need rest and food. Some Gods even go into a dream state for years, they need it to sustain their power.

I look around the sandy stone of the scullery, and Everett huffs in frustration. "Are you listening to me?"

I search frantically for something that I conjured to be edible, but I come up short. I can only call to things I have had in my possession, things I have been around and touched or felt. The stones of this castle are from a mission I had from Lachlan. He sent me hiking up a mountain back home, I had to bring back seventy different animals. It was more for kicks and giggles on his part, but it works in my favor considering I now own that mountain and have made it into my home.

"No, I am not listening. Do you not see the issue here?" I gesture around the scullery. There are open windows that look out at the lush green grass outside, right before the large drop-off into the unknown waters. I can hear the waves hitting the rocky shoreline on this side of the palace.

His brows furrow. "What? You are a virgin and have fallen helplessly in love with me and I can't be with you?" His taunting voice is a lot for this early in the morning.

My hand slams onto the countertop. "Ugh. No, that isn't true, nor would you not be with me. You find me attractive." I can read him without having to.

"Well, honey, just as your mind can read my emotions, I can *smell you*. And I know what sex smells like. You reek of it. You want it, and yet...you still have your blood. So, you have not been bedded yet." I gulp down the spit that has gathered in my mouth. Everett takes another taunting step towards me. "But yes, you are a pretty thing. If you want me to, I will take that blood from you." I wince; that sounds awful. I hold my hands up and take several steps backwards. "I do not enjoy this conversation Ev." I turn away in an attempt to hide my bright red face.

Horror hits my guts hard and hot. My eyes widen comically, as my mouth falls open. "Wait," I stop everything I am doing and whirl to him. "Can all of you smell that or..." I leave the question open-ended. The smirk Everett gives me has me pausing. I walk right up to his chest and harshly push him back onto a countertop. My hand grabs his thick throat; he doesn't back away. "What is it, dragon shifter?"

He speaks even though my hand is on his throat. "Yes." His one-worded answer doesn't help me much. I growl in his face and that just seems to make him happier. "You can threaten me all you like. I *enjoy* it. And yes, honey, we can *all* smell *you*. It's part of our dragon nature."

I yank my hand from his warm skin and grab onto the first fruit I can find. My steps are quick from the scullery and even more so from my home. I want to visit the South today; I need to hear their side of things. If I am truly going to help this kingdom, then I must hear from them all. I don't believe that civilized beings attacked the North's nests. Calix is said to be the kindest dragon lord, I need to meet him first.

"Where are we going?" Everett asks while he tries to keep up with my fast pace. I don't pause at the front door; I even leave it open for him.

"Make yourself at home, Ev. I'll be back later today or tomorrow." My feet lift from the ground as I fly to the mainland. I see the groups of males already up and about.

As soon as my feet land, Everett lands right behind me. The thud of his body shaking the ground before he shifts right back into his human form. "Hello," he chimes in a singsong voice.

"Why are you following me?" I make my way through the crowd. I need to find Caspian.

My outfit today is one for battle, but not the physical kind. I will meet with the other lords today, even if they don't want to meet me.

"I am to stay with you. King Granger wants you to remain safe." I can feel his breath on my neck.

I shake my head, attempting to get him away from me. "Why would he want that?" I scan the firepits, and walk around large dragons until I finally find Caspian.

"I'm unsure. He likes you more than Eamon does, that is for sure."

I huff a laugh. "A dead slug likes me more than Lord Eamon does. He doesn't like losing," I say loud enough that said lord can hear me.

"Oh, you are asking for trouble," Everett says, amusement pouring from his words. The Lords are gathering around a large fire, and the flames lick my face. The brisk morning seems better with the warmth. The smell of their breakfast makes my stomach growl.

"You want some food?" Rafe asks while taking a bite from something that looks better than what I came up with.

"I'm okay. I have come to inform you all that I will be travelling today. No need to wait for me. I will be gone the entire day," I say, not seeing any reason to ask permission.

Rafe slows his chewing; I almost take the food from his hands. Caspian smiles widely, and it causes my stomach to flutter enough that when Everett leans in and whispers, "See, we can all *smell* that here. I am not opposed to...helping a friend out," I move my shoulder in a circular motion to try and push him away from me. Eamon chokes on whatever he is eating, while Caspian smiles with some new amusement and hunger, not just for his food.

My face turns beet red and I whirl on Ev. My hand reaches for his throat, and I bare my teeth at him. This time I hold nothing back, my fingers grip tight enough to harm him. "I may not be a dragon, but I will eat you whole if you don't back off. I am not turned on by *him*. He looks good, yes. But I will not be sleeping with you or him or any other dragon shifters during my stay here, thank you very much." My tone is sharp and cruel. I don't understand why, but I am angry. Everett must see this and backs off, holding his hand up in surrender. But not before commenting on the fact that I laid my hands on his throat twice today already. I don't respond to him. I don't need to. "I will be going for the day, as I said earlier. Alright?"

The three lords look at me and have the good sense to seem nervous. "Considering the fact that you almost just ripped my second's head off, I don't see how I could argue with you exploring." Rafe's tone is light, but I catch the slight edge to it. Everett has moved away ten feet or so. I swallow, unsure where my outburst came from. It didn't feel like me speaking at all.

"Where are you wanting to go?" Caspian's friendly demeanor stays in place, but I get the feeling he isn't always so friendly.

"I will be travelling to the South. If I am to help around here then I will have to meet everyone." Eamon turns a purple color before dropping his food and walking off, to only then shift into his white dragon and leave. When his wings start to beat, wind blows in my face, as well as dirt and twigs, things I think he *meant* to blow at me. I run my hand over my face to get all of the debris off.

"What was that about?" I ask, unsure why I even care that he left.

"Uh...he does not like the South and doesn't like to hear about them unless it's new ways to kill them," Everett says from behind me, rubbing his neck.

"Alright. Anyways, I will be going now." I look one more time at the food and then decide against it. Surely the South, being more civilized, will have loads of food to stock up on.

"Wait, I think we should speak with Granger about this." Caspian stands and roars. The sound almost pierces my eardrums. I cover my ears just in case; it feels as if they might burst open. When it finally stops, I glare at him with an annoyed expression.

"He is not my king, and I will not be listening to him. I have a mother to get home to, and food that needs to be eaten. I have made my choice. Thank you very much." Without another word, I spin on my heels and leave.

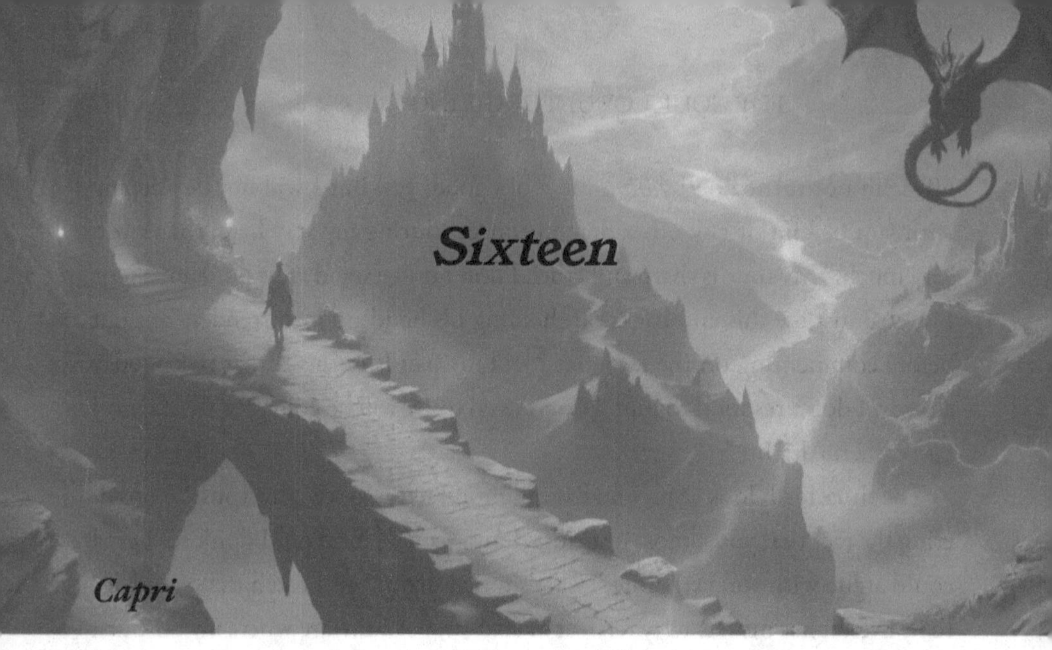

Sixteen

I sit on a tree trunk alongside the king, Lord Rafe and his second, Lord Caspian and his second, Callahan, as well as Asher, who is apparently Lord Eamon's second. They all sip on wine and eat their food as if they hadn't heard my belly growl with hunger. Maybe they don't remember that I have a mother whom I need to be with, either here or my home kingdom.

When I tried to leave earlier, Everett wouldn't let me. He kept distracting me with stories for long enough that Caspian was able to get Granger here. Now, here I am. Watching the dragon shifters chow down on another meal, laughing and just chit chatting while I am ready to leave.

"Uh-huh," I say, trying to gain their attention again. They all look up as if I am interrupting them, and I scoff. "Anyways... As I said an hour ago, before this big ole party happened, I need to get going." Granger's golden eyes scan me. The light-blue dress that clings to my body shimmers with silky layers of white lace on top. He runs a hand over his cropped beard, which somehow grew within the span of twelve hours, since I last saw him trying to enter my home. I didn't let him, and he didn't push it.

"You would like to go speak with the Lords of the South and...what, Capri?" His tone doesn't suggest he thinks I am stupid, so I answer.

"I think that maybe there is some misunderstanding, and we could come to an agreement." The laughter that fills my ears makes my blood spike to new temperatures. "Why are you all laughing?" I ask while looking around to see even the king is chuckling. It makes him look boyish and even more handsome.

I shut down those thoughts right away. I wouldn't want them to smell me thinking the king is anything but just a king, and my enemy at that. His eyes bore into mine in that intense way that makes my heart pause for just a moment. I am sure they can all feel how the king makes me pause.

"You know nothing about dragon law and yet, you wish to go and fight for us when you don't know what we are actually fighting for?" Granger asks in between bites of whatever meat he is eating. I eye the food with interest, but I won't dare ask for a bite of it. I won't beg, even though I am getting close to eating a bunny I just watched hop away from the hole it came out of.

I stand up and walk right over to the king. Asher leans backwards so that I don't brush against him. I read it in his mind...he hates me. His lord hates me, therefore, he does as well. I hit his leg, just for fun, as I walk past him. I chuckle when he hisses like I have burnt him or something. Dragons don't burn though. Now, their homes can burn...and they will if I don't eat soon.

I step between the king's thighs, right in front of everyone. I crouch down so that I am just a little lower than eye level. The closer I look into his enchanting golden eyes, I see bits of light brown and speckled black pieces. "Dragon law states that under no circumstances will nests be harmed. The problem with this is that the North and South do not see eye to eye. The North think that you should all still nest, while the South hasn't had a nest in over fifty years. They have live births instead of dragon births. Which is strange because red and pink dragons are so strong...you have to wonder why they have so many of them if they have live births instead of hatchlings," I start to ramble on, mostly because I need to get out of here. Every moment I waste fighting with them is another moment my mother is without me.

"Anyways, dragon law also states that clans do not mix the breed of dragon, which yet again, the South has no issue with doing. Fates, they even breed with sirens, fae, werewolves...all the beings I have read about. They don't seem to have high standards according to your law." Everett chuckles but I push past his sounds. "I know the North wants to live as dragons have forever. The problem is that the South keeps growing in their population and they need more room. They want to live in the North since the North doesn't have the same numbers. That's why the South keeps fighting and killing them, isn't it?" I question, but I don't dare stop, because I am on a roll. "Although, the land and soil here are better as well, so that could be another reason why they wish to reside here. Maybe their powers aren't as strong. I won't be able to tell if it's that until I get there and test my theory. You will not stop me from going, so I suggest you don't try to. I am here to—"

Granger stands up so fast that I almost fall right into the blazing orange flames. "To help, I heard you. So, you learned a few new dragon laws and you believe yourself to be our savior?" His eyes dart to Everett and the dragon shifter shrinks down into himself.

"He didn't tell me a thing." I come to Everett's defense, even though I don't need to.

Granger's eyes meet mine and for a second my breath catches and it's as though we are the only two standing here. "No, he didn't," Granger agrees, we are so close together that my chest brushes against his stomach. "You read his mind because his shields were down around you. You are a stranger to us and yet you want to fight for us?" His voice is so stern and commanding I struggle to piece together the kindness I have seen inside of him. The passion I know I just saw flicker in his eyes.

"I will fight for a better place to live, yes, where both sides get what they want. There will be comprise, but each side will live…if you will give me a chance to show you how strong I am." I almost whisper the last bit, suddenly feeling so unsure about myself.

The king doesn't say anything for a long minute, and when he does, he looks to Callahan and then Everett. "Get ready to go." He commands.

I don't dare take my eyes from his face; not just because it is the most perfect face I have ever seen, with his ten freckles dusting his nose and cheeks, or his pearly-white teeth and perfect smile. No, I can't look away from him for no reason other than I am completely caught in his net. My body won't allow me to look away from him; I can't move farther from him. I, for some reason, would rather cut my own arm from my body than look away from this male right now.

"I don't need a bodyguard, or two, for that matter. I am coming back today." The two seconds in the circle both stand and take their damn food with them.

"You will do as I say. If you would like to stay here with your mother, after all is said and done, you will listen and obey me."

I balk at the way he speaks to me, my feelings and thoughts out the window. As soon as I feel like I may make progress with him, he pushes me backwards. His shields go up, and I must back away from him. It takes everything in me, but I do just that. I sigh heavily when I notice the animal thigh in his hand. I watch as he slowly brings it to his mouth, then bites into the dark meat. I can't seem to think of anything else other than wanting to be that freaking thigh. Juices spray from the meat, and I watch as his teeth tear the pieces away. I watch as he chews and chews so slowly...and I think he is taunting me. His throat bobs once, then twice, before he finally wipes his mouth clean. Then I do what any rational being would do.

I grab the thigh in his hand and take a large bite. It's still steaming hot, so I take another one. His eyes widen slightly. None of the lords utter a word but I can feel their shock rippling through my body.

"Are you hungry, Capri?" The way he says my name sends chills down my spine until it hits the base of my belly and warms it right up.

"I was," I agree after taking another very large chunk from the meat. It tastes like smoke and everything good in life. I moan then realize I have almost eaten his entire meal. I shove the almost bare bone right into his hand and wipe my mouth on the black shirt that clings to his body. At least he had the decency to wear one; most of the males here don't believe in clothing.

I don't feel any embarrassment, I just smile sweetly and say, "I will listen to you, King Granger. But listen when I tell *you*, I may not adhere to everything you say. You are not *my* king after all."

His golden eyes look down to the spot on his shirt where my lips had been, the food now on him instead of my face. He licks his lips slowly, wetting them down before pursing them. "Good luck, Capri." He turns and Caspian jogs after his king. I look around to see gawking faces and wide-open mouths.

"Got anything to say?" I ask the group, though none of them respond. They shake their heads and leave one by one, their food untouched. I take full advantage of this.

Seventeen

Capri

"I still don't understand why I can't just teleport there and meet you all," I huff out in frustration to Everett.

Callahan nods in agreement with me. "I don't want her riding me." He sighs and I turn to him; his violet eyes are gleaming with hatred.

"I don't want to ride you either, dragon boy." I shake my head, unsure why Granger cares how I get there.

"You rode Caspian here, didn't you? I am just as good a dragon. I won't let you fall, I promise. And then afterwards, if you want to ride me some more..." Everett stops his sentence there and winks at me.

Granger fumes with anger; I am unsure why he would care what my sexual habits are but he gives Everett a glare that could kill. "I might think on that. Thanks." I turn to Caspian, "You aren't coming then?" I ask sadly. I have grown to like Caspian in these days. He is kind, funny and caring in ways I didn't think a dragon could be to a God.

His answering sad smile tells me all I need to know. "I need to check on our nests and the clans in the west. I have duties here as lord. I am happy to know you will miss me, though. I will not miss your hanger." He nods his head towards me. I don't know why I do this, but I reach out to hug him. Maybe it's because I am feeling homesick, I'm missing Val and need a friend. His firm body stiffens, then he melts into me. He gives me a side hug and then pats my back, releasing me to find the two seconds have already shifted into their dragon forms, clothes in a tattered mess on the grass.

Everett is the size of a large bear, his scales shimmer a deep forest-green with shades of light green mixed in. His paws are the size of my head and the claws on them are longer than my hand. I take a moment to marvel at how beautiful this creature in front of me is. His scales are sharper than some of the other dragons I have seen.

When I turn to find Callahan in his dragon form, he is shaped more like a serpent than the others are. I don't know if that is why the purple are the fastest, but the way he moves is slick and predatory. The purple is a dull shade of lilac; his neck is long and slender. His claws are sharp and thin, unlike Everett's, whose are thick.

Granger walks up behind me and places a hand on my shoulder. "I have business to attend to with Caspian in the western parts of Draig. I will meet you in Dracol when I can." He says gruffly.

I nod, unsure why I care when he will meet us, but I find that I might just be counting the moments until I am with him again. "You don't have to meet us; I will be fine. Unless you are worried for me, dragon shifter?" My tone is teasing, even though I really do want to know. I need to know...is he worried for me?

I walk towards Everett's green form, but before I can grab onto his scales to climb up, Granger has my arm gripped tightly. "You need to take this seriously, Capri. They look nice, they *seem* nice, but they are not as nice as one might think. They may fuck everything that walks but there is a reason for this war." The warning isn't just in his words, but the way his eyes seem to scream at me.

I resume my ascent onto Everett's back, getting as comfortable as I can on the back of a flying beast. The scales are so sharp they almost cut into my thighs.

"Would you like to tell me, or no?" I ask, because I have a feeling they have not been completely honest about this war. "I will listen to whatever you feel I need to know, I just need information if I am going to help."

The king takes a large breath in. "When we see each other again, I will play my part. As you should too."

I shake my head and adjust my hips to take some weight off my center. "I have no parts to play, King. I am myself to a fault."

He pulls something from his pocket and tosses it to me. I catch it, unsure what is in the gray bag. "Amelie enjoys pretty things, the sparklier the better. Give this to her in an offering, and I suggest you do not look her mate in the eyes." Everett takes off and I think on Granger's words for a moment.

I hadn't even thought about what them being mates might mean for our interaction. I don't know what being mates looks like in dragons. I have done some research on Fae mates, but werewolves and merfolk don't have mates; they have open relationships only, as do sirens. What if I am unable to speak to the Lord of Dracol due to his mate?

I pat Everett on the shoulder blade and he takes off higher into the sky. I shout loud enough that his body ripples with what I would assume to be laughter. I watch Callahan's reptilian, purple dragon form slither through the sky. I know then that if I had been introduced to these males as dragons I would have teleported straight home. I conjure up another piece of meat and it earns me a growl from Callahan. I look over at him and lift my brow. He flies close enough that I could jump onto his back, that is, if I trusted either of them to catch me if I were to fall. I could always teleport back, but it would be nice if they caught me.

"I guess it's just us and the open skies, huh, buddies?" I say in a voice that must upset Callahan; he does not share Caspian and Everett's carefree attitude. The fire he blows from his mouth sprays hot and bluish-purple. I think those flames would melt my bones. "Alright, you are not my buddy then." I hold up my hands in a silent offering. He is not my friend, nor will he ever be.

After a while I get bored and start telling stories of my childhood to the dragons. I also ask about theirs, knowing they can't answer right now but still hoping they will divulge when they can. When they are in dragon form, their shields are far more powerful. I can't break through them to speak. Even in their human forms if their shields are strong enough, I may not be able to get through.

After many hours of flying, my hips hurt so bad I try to adjust them. A huff from Everett has me stopping, and I realize how my writhing may have come across. I clear my throat. "My hips hurt. I wasn't trying to rub one out on you. I'm sorry if that...uh, violated you or whatever." Cal looks over at me, seemingly thoroughly unimpressed by my apology. I have started calling him that. He doesn't seem to mind the nickname. Well, he didn't burn me to a crisp when I tried it out during my story about the time we confronted my father about having a surprise daughter.

"Land," I huff out in a whisper. I see the southern continent sprawled out in front of us. We are still so high that the land seems little, though I know it's actually massive. I can already tell there isn't as much vegetation here. The grass itself looks lush, but there doesn't seem to be many trees or plants...not from up here at least. I don't know if that is because the green dragons don't live here or because the soil itself is not as prosperous.

We start our descent right as I see a large navy-blue dragon heading towards us. Its claws are out, teeth bared. This is not a welcome sign; this is battle.

The navy-blue dragon shoots water at Callahan. Cal avoids the water right as it turns to ice and plummets to the ground. My eyes widen; that dragon meant to freeze Cal and kill him. Nice first impression, dude. Two more dragons come from below and I hear a roar escape from Everett, all signs of the friendly dragon shifter gone. Three against...well, I guess two and a half. Not great odds, but I get the feeling my two dragons are far more cruel than the other three. The blue dragon starts a storm of water, while a gray dragon hits us with hail. The large chunks of ice hit my head and bounce off Everett's scales before I use air to shield us.

Callahan closes in on a pink dragon and tries to bite it, but the pink sprays him with fire that melts against Cal's scales, causing him to roar with anger. Both Callahan and Everett are trying to get to the ground. I start to stand, hoping I can help them, but one growl from Everett's mouth tells me he does not want me helping anyone. The blue dragon comes back around, ice daggers aimed right at us. I block them with an air shield right before Everett dips enough that he would have taken the brunt of the attack. The blue dragon roars with fury and turns to the gray, probably thinking that the gray's air power stopped the attack. I watch in amazement at the way these dragons move throughout the air, they glide and flip around each other.

"Just get to the ground. I will shield us enough until then," I yell over the rain and the hail, covering us enough that the hail doesn't hit anymore. Callahan is in a one-on-one battle with the pink dragon, and I throw as much air into that dragon as I can to allow Cal a way out. His serpentine neck slithers to me and he nods in thanks. The gray dragon follows, obviously upset that its powers are being taken and used against them. It doesn't understand that they are *my* powers.

A roar sounds from behind us right as the gray dragon hits my air shield with lightning, causing my shield to weaken enough that the pink dragon rams into us. I am thrown into the air; my body falling at a rapid pace.

I should stop myself from hitting the ground, I should. I haven't yet though. I was several hundred feet up, but now only a hundred to the ground. I blink back as the air collides with my face, bugs hitting me in the mouth, and I just free-fall. I smile and then laugh. I might have lost my ever-loving mind, because I enjoy this fight.

Fifty feet above the ground, Callahan catches me in his thin, sharp talons. I gasp at the impact from going so fast downward to being yanked into the sky. A mighty roar sounds from Callahan's throat and then fire hits his side; he takes the brunt of the colorful blaze. Finally, my mind begins to work right, and I throw everything I can into the pink dragon assaulting us. I see the gray and blue dragons teaming up against Everett in the distance. His green form isn't as big as the blue—he's more similar in size to the gray—and I'm afraid he might be outmatched. "We have to help him!" I yell, then realize the only way to do so is by leveling the playing field.

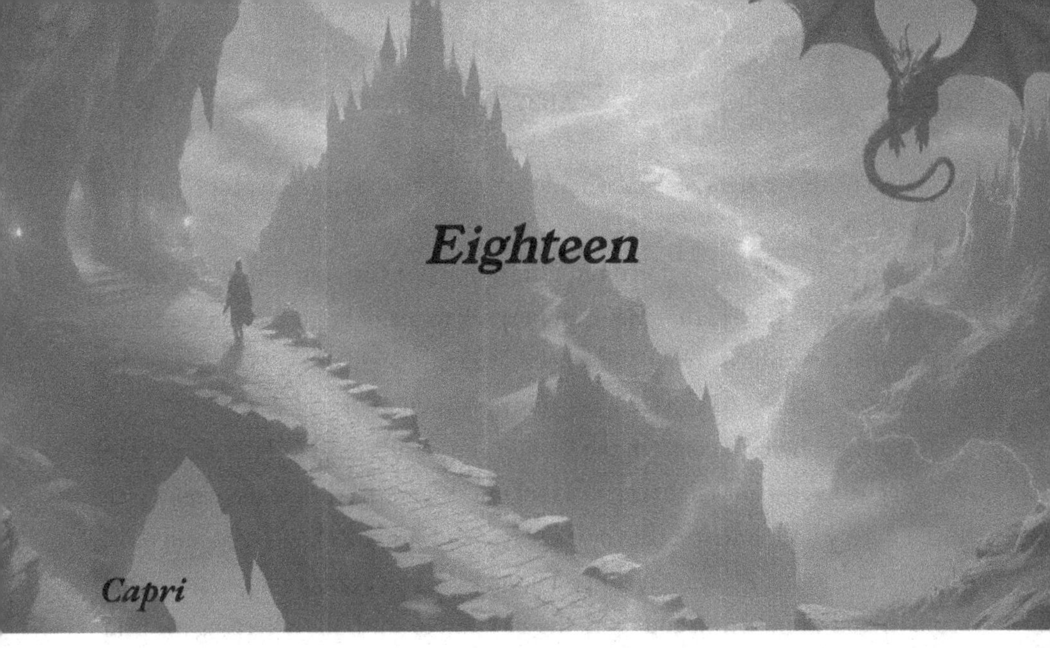

Eighteen

Capri

Callahan tosses me onto his back, even though I know this is the last thing he wants me to do. He doesn't like me, but I know I will earn his respect some way or another.

"Higher." We race the pink dragon; Callahan's speed is in our favor. I know what I need to do, but I don't like the thought of doing it. I knew coming to this planet would require bloodshed, I just didn't think it would be within the first week. "Faster," I say, exhaustion coating my words.

Our speed is picking up as we race to where Everett fights against the dragons. The two of them work together, throwing ice and lightning at him. Both of them moving as one in the sky, fighting together against Ev. He fights back, vines coming up high enough to yank down the dragons. His opponents break them immediately. "Come on," I whisper, fully aware that I may not know Everett very well, but he doesn't deserve to die just because I wanted to come here. No one deserves to die because of me. Yet, I have a feeling countless will.

"That is pathetic. You shouldn't care about the mere lives of dragons; you need strength and power. Give up that part of your fae nature and learn to be a God. Gods do not care for other beings; we are all that matters." My father's words come back to me. I had told him I wouldn't kill even if provoked. *I lied.*

I jump right onto the gray dragon as Cal speeds by. My body is suspended in the air for several beats before I hit its hard, sharp scales. My arm is cut when I thump into his firm side. The gray hadn't seen us coming; Callahan was so fast we were almost invisible. I hold on with sheer force, digging my fingers into his scales. I wouldn't be shocked if there were marks on its body after this. I will apologize as soon as this is over.

The gray dragon drops down ten feet, trying but failing to throw me off. It roars out in anger. I like that they cannot speak to me right now. I don't want to know what he or she is saying. "If you will stop this, I will not kill you. Go to the ground now...or else," I threaten, begging it to listen to me.

A lightning bolt shoots from the sky and almost hits me, but I dive out of the way. "I guess you want a fight then," I huff out, angry that the dragon would pick this. I dig my heels into its scales near the rear and conjure two daggers and place them in the holster in my tight pants. The gray dips yet again, trying to throw me from its body. I hold firm and tight; the air I pull towards me is keeping me held in place. "One last chance, buddy. I will give you one more ch—" Its tail swipes out and throws me forward. "Looks like I need to work on my freaking shields." I grunt before pulling the dagger free and slamming it into its hind leg. The gray bellows in anguish and my heart clenches at the pain it is enduring. All because it wouldn't back down and listen to me.

I slam the other dagger into its other hind leg, and both back legs gush grayish thick blood into my hands. "Ew," I say trying to wipe it off. The heads of its two friends whip in my direction, enough of a distraction that Cal and Ev take control of the situation. I make a sword engulfed in orange and yellow flames, then I run up the spine of the beast that wants to kill me. My feet pound against its flesh. I don't slow, even as I hear its heart race, clearly nervous.

It doesn't understand what I am, and honestly, I don't either. It will soon find out what death looks like. And it is a female named Capri.

I use all my strength to plunge my flaming sword into its neck. The flames are so hot the sword severs its head but gets caught on the bone. I can feel a burnout hitting my body so I try to focus. My fire is purple and blue, the strongest fire there is. I throw everything into it, and then there is silence. I hear distant screams from a female, but I have to ignore her. I cleave the sword through the rest of the bones and muscles and then *whoosh*. I float right there as I watch the dragon form fall to the ground. The pink and blue dragons freeze, eyes widened for a moment before halting their fights and rushing to the ground. I watch almost in slow motion as the gray falls from the sky, something a dragon should never do. I watch as his friends race to catch him, but they will not save their friend. They hurry to the ground, my heart pounds in my chest.

To their friend, maybe family they try to save even though there is no coming back from this. Callahan and Everett race towards me and I point at the ground, unable to find words. I don't want to speak; I don't want to face what I will when I make it to the ground. I will slip the ice-cold mask I have right into place. I just need one moment.

I count to ten, pushing my fingers into each other while I take deep and long breaths. I swallow and follow the dragons down, to where I know I have done irreputable damage.

Right as my feet hit the ground a small female is in my face, screaming at me, but I don't listen to her. My eyes go to the dead dragon and its friends' naked bodies crouched beside a female who's wailing.

"Who are you? What have you done? You killed him!" the small female screams at me; I keep my mask in place, where it needs to be.

"Who I am is nothing to you." My voice betrays nothing of how I am truly feeling. I walk straight over to the male I know is Calix. I look him in the eyes, like I am not supposed to, and introduce myself. The other dragons I have just fought still stay with the female who is crying next to the dragon. Calix looks at me furiously, and even with all the anger he is still incredibly handsome.

"I am Capri, daughter of King Ragnar, first of my name. I will rule this Kingdom. If you do not adhere to me, then you and your mate will meet the fate your friend just met. If your lords do not bow, I will make them."

His green eyes shimmer with hatred, which is a damn shame because he is hot as hell. The female who was just screaming at me is right next to him. "I tried to stop her, I'm sorry." She wraps her arms around his and eyes me with strong emotion. *Hate.* They all hate me.

It is okay, Capri. They don't have to like you to bow down to you. They are not your friends, nor will they ever be.

Callahan runs over, Everett rushes behind him. "Hey, we came in peace. We never meant for this to happen, Calix." Everett holds his palms up. The group is getting rather large. I try to keep my emotions separate from this. It's hard when the wailing female continues to cry, even when the limp dragon form is laying in a thick pool of blood, she does not move.

I motion with my hands to clean up the mess. It disappears, but her seafoam eyes lock onto mine. "What did you do!" she screams even louder, then when she was crying.

"I figured you would like to say goodbye...with him whole. Am I wrong?" I ask, and Everett grabs onto my arm yanking me back and into him.

"I'm sorry, Calix. This was not the way we wanted to come. If you hadn't sent your commanders out to fight us, maybe he wouldn't be dead." Everett actually sounds remorseful. He turns his gaze to Calix's female, "Amelie..." Everett bows his shiny locks and Callahan does the same. They both look at me.

"I will not bow to them." Disgust is apparent in my tone.

Calix growls at me. "And why would you think to bring *this* to me?" Calix's green gaze locks onto mine, disgust written on his face as well. His mate shares the same feelings.

"Capri is not from here. She doesn't understand what she has done," Callahan says firmly.

"I don't care what I did or where I am from. That dragon was going to harm my friends. I simply will not allow it," I say firmly. Calix moves to me as fast as I can see.

His hand is gripped firmly around my throat so tight I almost can't breathe. I have been in this situation many times over though, and at this moment I am glad my brothers beat me many different ways. Maybe, they did care for me. Maybe they did teach me something after all.

"Is this the foreplay you are speaking of, Everett? If so, I think I enjoy it." I smirk halfheartedly at the handsome lord in front of me. Suddenly, Amelie punches me in the face so hard I black out. Calix's mate must have not enjoyed my comment.

Nineteen

My head hurts, and I don't remember what happened. I know one minute I was standing in the field where the dead dragon lay. I know I killed him...and that thought alone causes me to sit up quickly and vomit everywhere.

The light wooden floors are unfamiliar, so I know Everett didn't bring me home. The bed I am in is hard enough to cause my back to be sore. The contents of my stomach keep coming up. I throw up everything, then when I am done vomiting the meager food I have eaten the past week, burning bile follows it. My vision is blurry, I don't know where I am. I start to panic and stand too fast, but strong hands grip my arms and for some reason I trust whoever it is.

"So, you aren't heartless," the calm voice says to me. When I meet violet eyes, I know Callahan is holding me up. "You got vomit on my shoes." My eyes widen and look down to see that we are both, in fact, covered in vomit.

"Where are we?" I ask, not recognizing my own voice.

"We are in Dracol." His tone is hushed.

"Okay." I nod in understanding.

"I appreciate you saving my life. I owe you a life debt." His tone suggest he hates that very fact.

I look around the room. "Where *exactly* are we?"

The more I look at the room, it seems as though we are in an inn. I bite my lip and swallow; my nerves are racing. I can't win a world over if they think I will just kill them, but they have to fear me. I can't lead people if they don't respect me. I wish I knew how to do this better, how to be a leader. Father wasn't a good example. Atlas wasn't either.

"I can tell you are struggling with your choice to kill the commander."

He was a commander... I don't want to know. I wish I didn't know that. I don't want to picture personal things about him. Callahan doesn't seem to notice I have zoned out until he waves a hand in front of my face. "Are you listening?" he asks in a softer tone than he has used before.

"I am. Sorry, my head hurts," I answer honestly.

"Yeah, Amelie is a red dragon. She blew your mind up not knowing you are a God. She did nothing but give you a small aneurysm. Probably why your head hurts so badly. I could have a healer come in." he says nonchalantly.

My brows raise at that, I had thought she punched me. "You have healers?" I didn't know dragons could heal.

"Well, *we* don't, but I am sure they have some fae around who would be willing to help. When Granger found out what they did to you he went ballistic."

My mind stops on that fact. "He is here?" My eyes dart around the room, as if he might be sitting in here. When I don't see him, my heart sinks a little.

Right as I say those words, I hear a commotion in the hallway. Banging, then screaming. "Where the hell is she?" I hear the voice of the king say, the one who doesn't even know me. And yet, he is hurrying through a hallway to find me. My heart feels as though it calls to him and he answers. My blood is pumping at the thought that he is just on the other side of that door.

"Majesty, you cannot see her. She is asleep," a voice tells him, then a thud sounds on the other side of my thin wooden door.

I rush to the door, and right as I get to it, he kicks the damn thing in. His chest is heaving, his hair ruffled in a way that makes me want to run my fingers through it.

"Are you okay?" His golden eyes are crinkled with worry.

"Yes. My head hurts but—"

He is in front of me in half a second. His hand reaches up to touch my face. "Your head hurts?" His hand pauses as though he is remembering I am his enemy. He hates me, our kind hate one another. Don't they?

Concern eats away at anything else in his body. It overwhelms my senses to feel. I can feel that my hurt is hurting him for some reason. "Yes. I threw up, so..." I gesture towards the vomit covering not only me but also Callahan and the floor.

"I see." He bites his lower lip, drawing it into his mouth.

Then the king takes a step backwards, away from me...his enemy. The female who is trying to take over his kingdom so that her father can control him. Bitter cold hits my heart as I realize none of these males will ever like me. They might pretend, but I can't ever let my guard down around them. I had thought this could be a home, but now I am thinking it might be my prison.

I just know I have disgusted him. I don't even have to reach out to him to know; his face turns beet red. I twist the fabric of my dirty shirt with my fingers.

"Cal, clean this fucking mess up," Granger growls, then walks towards a doorway. When I don't move, he halts and motions for me to follow, his eyebrows completely raised. "Do not make me beg you," he drawls. I shake my head, wondering who he is talking to. "Capri...please." He grits out, then he shuts his eyes, as if even saying my name pains him. When they open, he meets my gaze. His gold eyes plead with me, for something that I don't recognize. I balk backwards.

"Please...what?" I ask, unsure what he is talking about.

"Please follow me so I can clean that mess from you." I almost say no—I almost say *hell* no—but my feet move, and I don't know why. My feet move as if he has commanded me to; they move to follow the male who causes my heart to stop.

"I can draw my own bath," I say when I realize we are in a bathing chamber.

"Then draw it," he says, tilting his head towards the tub, no harshness to his tone.

"Aren't you mad at me?" I question and suddenly wish I hadn't. I don't need or want the answer. I just need right now with him.

He rolls his white shirt up to his elbow. "Put the warm water in, love." His term of endearment makes me realize he is playing some sort of game here.

"Oh, yeah. I forgot you have a role to play. What are you doing? A king doesn't do this for a nobody, let alone somebody who just killed one of your kind."

At the reminder of what I did, he growls, but I realize it's not directed at me. "He asked for it. Now get in, please." The smirk he gives me makes him look less like the dragon king and more Godlike. His tanned arms are on full display while he gestures for me to get into the bath.

"I don't bathe in front of strangers," I say, chewing on the side of my lip. He lifts his brown eyebrow and I almost laugh.

"We are hardly strangers, love. Your isle is right next to mine. I could watch you bathe if I wanted to, and fates, maybe I have already."

My mouth drops slightly, "Have you?" Then, without waiting for him to respond, I swallow any and all pride I might have had before this. I let go of any expectations I have and just trust my instincts.

I shut the door, and for some reason, I take the vomit-covered shirt off. So slowly that I think Granger might just stand up and rip it from my body. His eyes burn with so much intensity that they turn almost black. I suck in a breath when I take the band from my chest. His breathing stills when my breasts break free from their restraint. The way he looks at me almost causes me to believe he might *want* me. More than just for show. But that can't be true. I am a God made by the Fates to hate dragonkind.

I swallow thickly and then bend to take my pants off. When I reach my waistband, Granger gets on his knees in front of me. I don't dare move. His eyes look all the way up my body, and my chest heaves.

He places his hands over mine. "May I?" His eyes swirl with want, but want for me? He is the King of Dragons, the King of Beithir. I am here to take his role away from him, or at least co-rule with him. I nod my head even though I know I shouldn't. How many times will I have a dragon king on his knees begging to take my pants off?

The slow descent of my pants causes my heart to stop beating. I step out of them and then his fingers slide right under the waistband of my underpants. They aren't anything special. I had changed before I left this morning, knowing all too well that I couldn't ride a dragon in the dress I had on.

I should be embarrassed that I picked undergarments that would cover every-thing in case the pants rubbed me raw down there. Granger clears his throat and doesn't take his eyes from mine, even with my chest on full display. I nod, giving him the approval he so desperately wants, his eyes full of need. I realize it's a need to take care of me. So, I allow him. He pulls my undergarments from my ankles and I step into the warm bath.

I sit in the warm water while it laps right above my chest while Granger sits behind me outside the tub. His rolled-up sleeves are still getting wet from where he's rubbing the hand towel up my legs. He pauses at the crease that separates my thighs and I give him permission to continue. This doesn't feel like I thought a sexual drive would feel like. This male is handsome, yes. But he is more than that. I feel it in my very bones.

After scrubbing every part of my body, we sit there in silence. I hear others in the hallway; they are yelling. We don't look away from each other. I am not certain if he has even looked at my chest. Maybe he is just a gentleman and I am being weird about this.

That thought still on my mind, I finally speak. "Am I in trouble?"

Granger's hand stills in the water, he hangs his head, the brown locks falling onto his forehead. "You are not. I am king; if they want you, they will have to go through me."

I turn to face him fully, not shying away from the fact that I am completely exposed. "But...they wanted me to be in trouble?"

He places his wet hand on my face; water droplets fall into the still tub. "They wanted your death for their commander's. I informed them of what would happen if they attempted to harm you." I lean into his touch, even though my mind tells me to slow down.

I feel as if I were back outside, racing to the ground without any sort of power to slow my rapid descent. Although this time, I feel like when I crash to the ground I might like it, enjoy it even.

"And what will happen if they harm me?" I hear the want and need in my own voice.

"They will die a death worse than anything they could ever imagine." His voice is so convincing, I almost believe he would do just that. "They would be waking a beast who has long been asleep, yet eager to awake." The undertone he uses causes me to stop breathing entirely.

"Why would you do that for me?" I question even though I can hear Callahan calling out for us. I know our time is limited, yet I am a selfish being. I crave more time with the king who looks at me as if he deeply wishes we were not enemies.

"I don't know." His answer hits me like a stone wall. I am about to reply to him when Callahan calls from the other side of the door.

"They are asking for a formal dinner."

"We will be out in a minute," King Granger growls so low goose bumps rise on my arms.

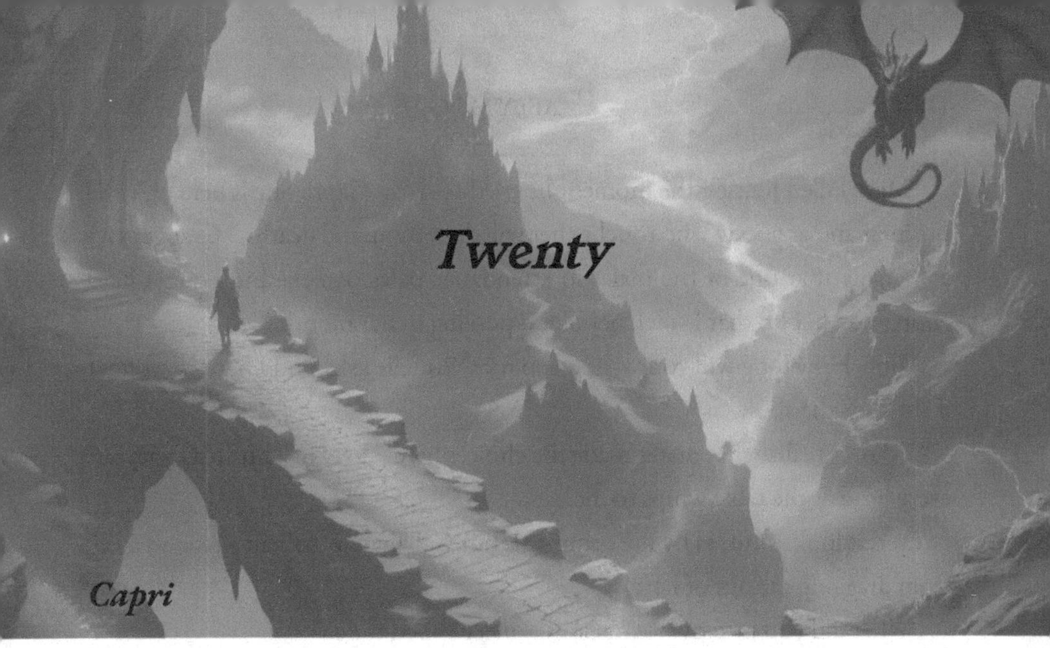

Twenty

Capri

I am sitting at a table that I am thoroughly unwelcome at. It reminds me of the first dinner I went to when Father announced that I would be living with them in the palace. Atlas tried to kill me upon site, Max cursed every Fate in the universe, and Lachlan tried to drown me. I would prefer that over this any day.

"So, you found her and thought you might bring her here, Majesty?" Calix's voice sounds like smooth liquor. He sounds like he has experience with twisting words and saying pretty things to get what he wants.

"I believe she can offer us peace in a way we have not had before, this war has gone on for far too long. Don't you agree?" Granger speaks similarly to Calix, in a way that makes me believe he could also twist words into something they are not. Granger Rhodes is a fierce King in more ways than just on a battlefield, and I almost wonder if the biggest battle he will ever face is right at a table speaking.

"I would like nothing more than peace, you know this. I want peace for my beings. We have suffered loses far greater than *you* could ever know." Granger flinches at Calix's words. "*They* must agree to my terms though, King. And to do that, they will have to change their laws. No *female* can change the other lords' minds, let alone my own."

I stew on his words. I don't know yet what is causing them truly to be separated but I get the feeling it is more than they are letting on.

"The girl needs to go. She will not help us...she *killed* Mave," Amelie hisses out, and I wince at her tone. I am glad I disposed of the jewelry Granger gave me, to gift to her.

"Mave killed himself the moment he tried to harm Capri. She is here on royal business and anybody who touches her will die a thousand deaths," Granger says so harshly that one of the males in attendance pales. Amelie bites down hard enough on her lip that I smell her blood pooling in her mouth.

"Fine. How long will your visit go on for?" Amelie asks, and I have to wonder if she runs the show.

"I didn't realize that mates made the choices here," I say in a hushed tone, but every head at the table whips to me.

Everett looks amused by my comment, but Callahan looks half a second away from dragging me out of here.

"What did you just say?" Amelie asks in a clipped tone.

I smile at her and lift my brows. "I said what I said; I didn't stutter. Maybe the issue here is that the Lord of Dracol listens to a hateful female instead of doing what is best for his world."

Amelie spews every hateful feeling my way. I am unsure if she knows I can feel everything she feels. I wouldn't doubt it if it made her happier knowing I can feel all her ire towards me. All I feel from Granger is pride.

"You dare speak to my mate that way?" Calix asks, and I decide he isn't as handsome as I had first thought.

"I do when she causes the world you live in harm. The North and South need to come to an agreement, and it would seem as though she holds you back from convincing your southern lords to speak about any type of agreement that might be made." I shrug and take a bite from the meat on my plate. I hate eating meat, if I had any other choice here I would pick something else. It seems the dragons only eat meat though, so I am out of luck.

"Well, that is your opinion of our world after...what? A day of being here?" Amelie starts to continue her tirade, but Granger stands and hits the table. Plates shake and some of the mugs fall to the floor.

"Leave." His golden eyes glow, and Amelie's mouth gapes open.

"What?" She breathes out, and Calix looks half a second away from breaking something. His fists clench so tightly his knuckles are white.

"You heard your king. *Leave*," Callahan says, seething.

"Just go. I will inform you of anything we discuss, darling." Calix looks almost soft while he speaks to his mate. I wish I didn't have the feeling that she might be the cause of this world's pain. She seems to love her mate. I need to do research on dragon breeds. I need to learn this kingdom more, and I hate that I haven't.

"So, let me get this straight. All the North is asking for is for dragon law to be upheld. They maintain their lands and they keep...everything they have." Calix breathes out, steam wafting from his nostrils.

"Correct. Although, I think if we all got together, we could come to an agreement. I realize that some of that is not fair to you in the South. We all will have to compromise on many things. I think we should be able to though, don't you?" Granger asks, and I can't help but nod along with him.

Whatever he says, I seem to agree with him. Granger Rhodes has a way about how he speaks and leads that makes me want to listen to him. Calix takes several deep breaths.

"It will take several days for me to get ahold of Draven; he is out on a hunt. I haven't heard from Killian in a few months, so I will have somebody reach out and inform him of the...*situation*. Airus will be easy enough to get ahold of. I will have him here by the day after next." I take a sip of the wine and listen to the male speak. "You all can stay here. Or, if you would feel more comfortable in the inn, I will have rooms ready for you to stay there for a while."

It is weird being in a real village after so many days in the wild. The North and South live such different lives. I can see why they would be so upset with the changes each want to make.

"We will stay at the inn. Thank you for your kindness." Granger stands and readies to leave, but before I can stand with him, I pause. Everett halts beside me, his hand on my arm, ready to drag me from here. Callahan is close enough that I can feel his nerves over what I might say or do next.

"I am truly sorry for the way we had to meet. I wish it hadn't ended the way it did. I will tell you though, if this changes your world for the better, end this war for you all, then it is worth it. Isn't it?" I ask, unsure if he will answer, but he nods at me.

"I hope it will be." Calix might have kissed my hand if his mate wouldn't kill him for it.

The four of us make our way from the palace. "Good job," Everett says from beside me, and I can't help but smile at him.

"Thank you. I hope this is the first of many good evenings. I just hope we can find peace for you all." I say this genuinely, with my entire heart.

"So that you can live here?" Everett asks, then adds on quickly, "I heard you want to rule...with your mother."

We make the journey to the inn, down the cobblestone path. Granger and Callahan are in an intense conversation. "I want to make this world better for you. For your people. I don't care if I can't live here forever. Everybody deserves to live a happy life, Everett." His smile is genuine and kind. I know why I feel so calm in his presence...he reminds me of home. He reminds me of Valor and how he radiates kindness and compassion. I miss him, I miss Mother. I hope they are doing okay.

"You would do all of this...even if you must leave after?" he questions.

I grab onto his arm. "I won't lie to you, I want to live here. I want peace here, but not only because I wish to live here with Mother." I chew on my bottom lip, unsure how much I want to share with him.

"My life hasn't been easy. Mother struggled back home, we didn't have enough chips to be able to afford food some months. I learned to live without, and I will again...for her." He watches me so intensely I wonder if he truly cares about me and my story. "I want to live free too. I want to live away from my brothers and my father. I need to...for my safety and my mom's."

The two-story inn comes into view; I pause for a moment before I continue. "That is not why I am doing this now though. I might have been forced to come here, but after meeting you all, I know I can't leave if you guys aren't safe."

My words must shock him, because he doesn't respond. He simply nods and gestures inside the inn.

I realize now that what I said came from deep inside my heart. I might have come here, been forced to come here by father to co-rule this kingdom. To grant father access to the lands, but now I realize I crave their safety. I can't leave until I know the dragons are safe from themselves.

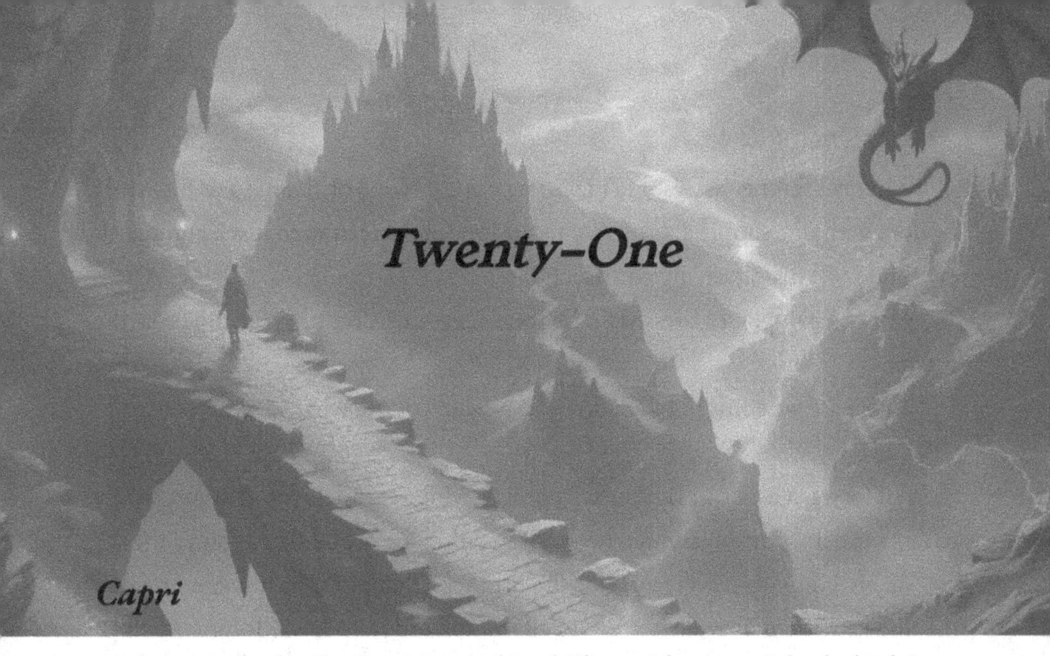

Twenty-One

I lay in the bed at the inn. My mind is whirling with energy I don't think I can expel. I practice my fire magic to try to alleviate some of this. I'm tossing a fireball up into the air, right above my face, when a knock on the door distracts me, causing me to miss the ball completely.

The small ball of flames lands right on the bed. "Oh shit." I throw some water magic at it, hoping the fire will stop, but it doesn't.

"Capri?" the king asks from the other side of the door. I am patting down the blanket where the flames are starting to grow, trying to get the flames to calm themselves. When I don't answer, Granger kicks the door across the room.

I huff out an exasperated sigh. "Are you kidding me? Again?" I ask, and suddenly the flames are snuffed out by his shadows.

"Oh, God." His eyes sparkle with interest, a soft smile reaching his lips.

I clear my throat. "I guess you really do have shadow power. What's that like?"

His golden eyes turn black. "Capri, why did you try to burn your bed down? Are you attempting to get into mine?" The way he asks makes me wonder if he might actually want that.

I pull backwards when he grabs onto my shoulders. "Um, no. I actually was trying to expel some energy, and when you knocked... You know what, never mind. No, I don't want to be in your bed," I say with as much confidence as I can muster. His smirk tells me he knows what I had been doing, he just wanted to tease me. It worked. My face is bright red. I feel flustered and out of my element. This male does that to me; I don't understand it. I have been around countless

Gods in my lifetime, handsome males, sexy even. None of them do to me, what he does with one simple glance. A smirk, a lone chuckle or even just a glint in his eyes and I feel myself caving entirely.

"We are leaving. Get dressed." His tone suggests I don't have a choice in the matter.

"Where are we going?" I look down at myself, unsure what to wear.

"The tavern."

I call forward a pair of tight black pants, a white sleeveless top that just barely covers my belly button, and red heels. Atlas would be proud that I found these.

"We are going to the tavern, not the brothel. Change." His hungry gaze eats me up like I could be his last meal. I lick my lips and stalk towards him. My hips swaying as I make my way to the dragon king.

"I like what I am wearing; does it distract you?" I don't let his comment about the brothel hurt me, although I am curious if he has been to one. I don't dare ask that though, I am not jealous. I just met this male, and although he makes my heart pause, I do not like him in the slightest.

"You distract me, yes. Especially when I picture you drinking and falling over due to your outrageous shoes."

I look down at my feet. "Now you have an issue with my feet?" We walk to the door, which is now on the floor, step over it and head downstairs.

"Not your feet, love; I would kiss those. The shoes I do have an issue with."

I take the steps down as slowly as I can. "I like the shoes, and they will stay until I need different ones. If I feel like they are making things difficult, I will change." I notice Callahan and Everett at the bottom of the stairs waiting for us. I can feel Granger's annoyance, but I don't pay him any more attention.

"You look lovely," Everett says, while Callahan looks as though he might try to sell me to the highest bidder. The cobblestone road we walk down is uneven, so I hold onto Everett's arm to steady myself.

"Thank you, as do you," I say, giving him my best smile.

Granger turns around; his growl is low but loud enough that Everett lets go of my arm. "I told you those shoes were not the correct ones." His eyes roam so slowly over my body that Callahan clears his throat.

"I will meet you all in there," Cal says as he makes his way down the road past the tavern that looks like it has seen better days.

"He isn't coming in with us?" I ask as we step into the loud and busy tavern. The king sits at a table in the dark corner, Everett right across from him. I choose to sit beside Granger, and as I take my seat the waitress comes over.

"He is meeting someone tonight. It shouldn't take long," Everett says softly while Granger gives our order. The waitress eyes Granger up and down, flirting with him. When I dig into her emotions, I can sense lust; she finds him attractive. I mean, who wouldn't? He is the King of Beithir, he is handsome to the core, his heart is pure and kind. Granger is out of every league there will ever be.

"I didn't realize you all knew beings from here," I say, taking a sip of the whiskey shot Granger had placed in front of me a few minutes ago. He had made his way to the bar after quickly finishing his, not wanting to interact with the barkeep again after she not-so-subtly tried to give him a lap dance for his service to the Crown, her words not mine. I wouldn't dare correct her by saying he isn't servicing the crown. *He is the crown.*

I saw red in those moments, and I am glad he is gone while I finish the rest of my pouting.

"Well, of course we do. The North isn't evil, Capri. We just want certain things to be upheld. Not every being here is bad." I nod in understanding, hoping he knows I just want to help.

"I guess I just haven't figured it all out yet," I admit.

"Well, that's because you've been here all of...what? A week, two maybe? It will take time, but you will get it," Everett assures me. A spark flickers in my chest, that I might be making headway with these beings.

I place my hand on his and rub my thumb across it. "Thank you."

He looks confused, but before I can read more into his expression, his eyes widen and he pulls away from my minor act of affection. "Majesty," Everett says over my shoulder. I look over my shoulder to see Granger standing right behind me. His jaw set firmly in place.

"Everything okay?" The king's voice seems raw.

"Yes, I was just telling Capri that we know beings from here. She would like to understand more about us." Everett takes the glass Granger offers him. "Thank you, Majesty. I am going to go and...well, find someone to talk to." Ev gets up so fast his chair almost falls to the ground, he catches it quickly and scoots it into the table before excusing himself rapidly.

"Thank you for bringing me out with you guys," I tell Granger, making direct eye contact.

"Well, I didn't want you burning down the only inn in the village." He sips on his drink while watching me carefully.

I slap his shoulder playfully. "Oh my, I wasn't trying to burn anything down." I guzzle down more of my drink. I have had two or three now, while he was at the bar the other bar keep brought Everett and me several rounds. The burn of the alcohol is diminishing and my mind is becoming fuzzy. This liquor is hitting me differently than the wine the other night. Granger gives me a smile that says he knows exactly how tipsy I might be.

"Did you drink back home?" He faces me fully, his knees hitting against mine. The contact is torture because I need more of it.

"No. My father and brothers do. I just chose not to. I wanted to train and not have anything in the way." He nods simply.

I don't feel the need to explain that I also didn't want my brothers seeing me weak, impaired or intoxicated and yet I am sitting at a table with a being who the fates created to kill my kind, and I feel *safe*.

I grab his drink and take a sip from the mug. His eyes burn with something I can't feel in this state. I don't like it.

"Oh?" It sounds like a question, one that I don't know the answer to. I finish his drink and a new barkeep comes with four more glasses. "You were training to come here?" He pushes a glass towards me, his warm skin brushing against mine, making me sigh. The small amount of contact our fingers had causes shocks to electrocute me in all the right areas. He takes his mug back from me as I take the glass from him.

If he heard my sigh, he doesn't make any comment about it. "I was training to become a God." My answer is immediate despite being intoxicated.

"But you were born a God, correct?" His lips purse, his eyes studying me. I take a moment to think of my response. I don't know why I feel so comfortable in telling him what I do. I couldn't feel any more comfortable if I were with my mother, and that should startle me.

"I was born with God blood, yes, but I wasn't raised with the powers of a God. I was raised by my mother. She's a fae; she is the best female there is." I give him a warm smile, my heart aching when I think of my mother. "I love her with my entire heart. She is the only reason I am here. I want her safe. She gave up everything for me. I owe her a life that she can be happy in."

Granger runs his hand over his beard. "Interesting." He chugs the rest of his drink then stands up suddenly.

The King of Beithir takes my hand in his warm one and I stand and follow him. I think I would follow him anywhere, sober or not. He guides me to the center of the tavern.

"What are you doing?" I laugh when he spins me around and then pulls me into his firm body.

"I am not doing a thing; we are going to dance together." Beings stare, vampires hiss, showing their teeth. But when they realize they just threatened their king they shrink back. I laugh freely when they do that. "I like that." His statement startles me; he whirls me around. There are no sounds other than our feet and the busy tavern.

"Like what?" I beam at him, my body pulled flush against his. I unbashfully lean completely into him.

"Your smile, your teeth, your lips...hell, even your happiness. Everything about you." I grip onto his tight black shirt. My fingers dig into the fabric, crinkling it up. He doesn't seem to mind or maybe he hasn't noticed yet. I think for just a moment he might kiss me as we swirl around the room. We dance between tables and chairs.

The only thing that matters is me and him in these moments. One of his hands is on the lower part of my back, the other gripping tightly onto my hip, possessively.

I look into the golden eyes of the king; he is a fierce predator. I am his enemy in every way possible; in every realm we are supposed to hate one another. Yet, when I look at his face I see nothing but *home.*

The male holding onto my waist has killed more beings than I could count, and yet, I can't help but to look into his eyes with passion. I look into his eyes, ready to drown in them, fully knowing I would never come up for air.

I grip onto his shirt with enough force one might think I was being yanked away from my future. I hold his gaze like I will never see his gorgeous face again if I look away. I press my toes into my shoes, leaning completely on him, my chest right against his. Every movement sends chills down my spine. I feel every place where our skin touches, in more ways than just physical. His fingers grip tightly around my waist, the skin right there showing slightly beneath the cropped top. He rubs small, tight circles on my hip bone.

My face is right by his, our lips are close enough that one small movement would cause them to touch. I lean in, smelling his crisp pine scent, hoping to just brush my lips to his. I feel a pull whispering to me. The whispers are telling me he will be my savior. They tell me he is mine. I close my eyes, my weight on his body, and he holds me upright.

Right where I thought his lips might be is now empty air. My eyes snap open, my lips still pursed and ready. He has moved his head to the side, away from my touch. Panic hits my belly right as I realize, he does not want me.

He leans into my body and whispers in my ear, "We need to talk." I pull from his grip just slightly; suddenly realizing I must look insane. He never asked to kiss me, he wanted a dance. I took this too far, and now things might get awkward.

"Okay." I nod before making my way to the table that now houses Callahan, Everett, and several new rounds of drinks.

The King follows me but doesn't say a word. He doesn't stop me as I plop right down next to Everett. When he takes his seat guilt is shining in his eyes, and confusion in mine.

Twenty-Two

Capri

"What were you doing with her?" Callahan sounds harsh, but I don't get the feeling from him he feels any sort of way about what he saw. I don't let the king answer though. I place my palms down on the table.

"I wanted to dance. I asked him." I shrug and the king looks at me, as if wondering why I would say that when he had been the one to drag me onto the floor.

"And why would you think our king would want to dance in a tavern with you?" Callahan asks, his face morphing into something of embarrassment for me. My mind spins, and I'm unsure if I should continue drinking.

Alas, I throw caution to the wind. I believe I am safe here with these males. At least for now anyways.

I throw back the drink and then look Callahan in the eyes. "I guess I just wanted to see if your king could dance like a *real* king. You never know with dragons." I shrug.

"What does that mean? Of course, he can dance. When he gets bonded, he will have to at their ceremony." Callahan hits the mark he was trying to hit, his eyes light up when he sees how bothered I am by his statement. My mouth falls open; realization strikes me blind. He might want to speak to me because he has somebody else. "And he is a *real* king. Don't forget, God, the Fates created dragons to equal you all." I ignore his jab, my mind on other things. "Our hellfire would melt you into soup." He licks his lips, Granger slams his fist down onto the table.

"Enough." Granger growls, Everett shrinks into himself.

Of course he would have a female. She is probably a gorgeous dragon shifter. I don't know why I didn't think about that fact, he is their king. He will have to bond and have babies at some point.

"Oh." I stand suddenly, my knee hitting the table, knocking over the ale Everett has in front of him.

"Damn, it got on my pants." Everett stands up, wiping his pants off with a cloth.

"I'm sorry, Ev." My words start to slur enough that I know all the liquor is hitting my system at once.

"Here, let me help you back to the inn," Granger says to me, but I yank from his hold. Hurt flashes across his face before he schools himself.

"I can make it back myself, thank you," I say solidly enough that he nods his head before taking his seat again. I think I might hear somebody hit another but I don't have the energy to think too long on it.

"I could walk ya back, Capri?" Everett asks, eyeing Granger with fear, but I won't ruin his night.

"No, thank you. I just need some sleep." I bite my lip, not trusting myself to not spew out my disgusting jealously.

The males all watch me exit the tavern; *he* doesn't stop me from leaving. My heart aches for some stupid reason. I don't know why, that is what hurts me most. I don't even know what I thought would happen between me and the king.

Once outside, my steps become slow and unsure. There is a reason I don't drink. "I hate this. I *hate* myself." I groan, feeling gross. He wouldn't want me; I threw up all over myself after killing a dragon. I got so drunk I can hardly stand up. He definitely doesn't want me. I keep telling myself every hateful thing that comes to my mind.

I am a God here to take over his rule. Why would he even keep me alive?

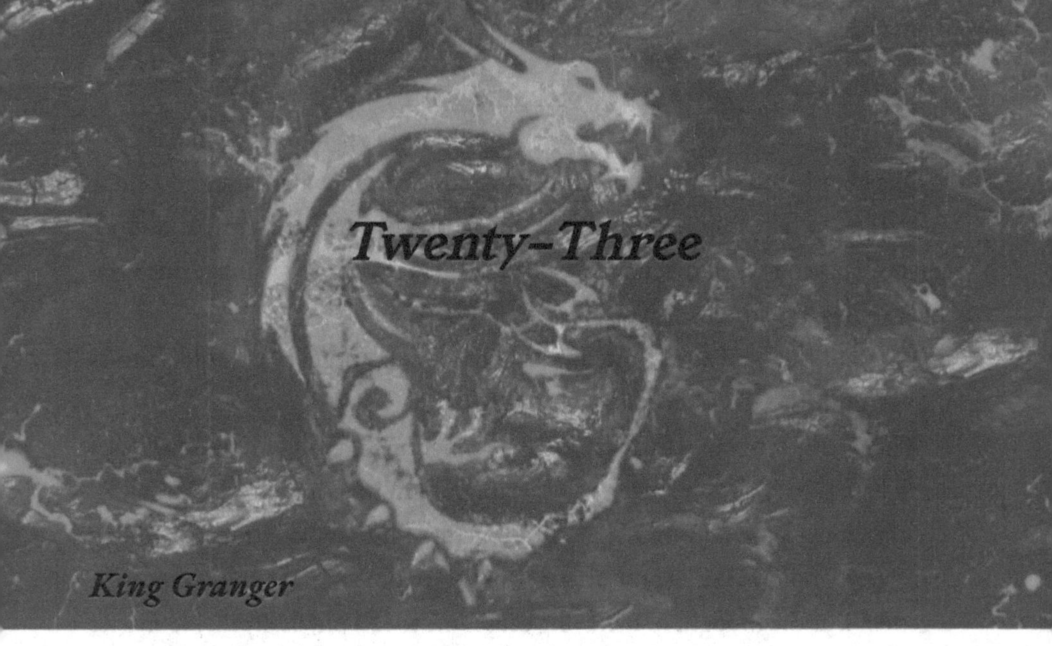

Twenty-Three

King Granger

S he *left*. She didn't want to be here with me.

"Grang?" Cal asks in his usual indifferent tone.

"Yes?" I sip from the ale Ev brought me after seeing how the God's departure affected me.

"Are you okay?" I know I am, but I feel like my heart was yanked right from my chest the moment she left this tavern. That annoys me more than anything.

Dragons are possessive to a fault, and she might as well be my tressure because the moment she walked out, as did my heart, my soul and my very being followed her out the fucking door.

"Of course," I snap, but not meaning to. Cal is one of my oldest friends. I quickly correct my tone. "I am fine. I shouldn't have drunk so much tonight. I have a long day ahead of me tomorrow, I need some sleep."

At the reminder of the day ahead of us, Cal asks, "Yeah, what am I supposed to do with the girl while you and Cas travel?" Callahan asks. I empty my glass and stand up, feeling like I need to go after her.

"You will do whatever she asks of you." I halt and spin back around. "*Unless* she requests for your pants to leave your body. If you allow *that* to happen, you will regret it."

Callahan scoffs. "As if I would ever sleep with a God." The way he speaks about her makes my blood boil for no reason. I don't want him to sleep with her, nor would I allow that to happen.

Our kind hates one thing altogether—Gods. They are arrogant and believe themselves to be better than us. Little do they know, the Fates created us both equally. I haven't taken the time to explain to them that little detail, the one I was told as a boy, the story which changed it all.

I am not the kind to ask questions before killing though, it would seem as though my little God is the exact same way.

When her great-grandfather came to our kingdom, he showed us exactly why we all hate Gods. Then he gave us an even bigger gift than his life.

I am shocked my clans haven't rallied together for the sole purpose of killing her. They would make a show about it too. Her death might bring our clans together. But the thought of her dying causes me to feel physically ill. No matter what decree I put in place, it will never be enough to keep her completely safe here.

There have already been many decrees made, just for my little God. I already informed every lord that if they have a member of their clan even attempt to harm her, their fate will be worse than what happened to her *grandfather*.

"She wouldn't sleep with you either," I scoff, sounding more offended than I should.

"Oh? Would you like to place a wager then, Granger?" Cal asks sounding more amused than he should. If he only knew how close he was to death right now, he wouldn't be teasing me like this. I clench my jaw so tight it should break my teeth.

My closest friends do not call me *King* when it's just us. Even though we are in the tavern, none of these beings are focused on us. They give me the privacy I desire. I also don't wear my crown out anymore. Other than a few lone females wanting to warm my bed, I don't gain much attention.

"I wouldn't bet anything with you about her. She isn't a prize to be won for me." I claim, even though I know I would claim her as the price of my life if I could.

I make my way to the door; unable to keep holding off the feeling that I need to be somewhere. The draw is so strong I almost can't handle it. Callahan follows right behind me before yanking me to face him.

"And why is that? You can't have her, Granger. Be real with yourself." The disgust in his tone causes my fists to clench, I almost kill him right here in this dirty tavern. I know all too well that I *cannot* have her, even though my chest pounds around her.

The moment I saw her bright silver eyes and honey-blonde hair that shines in certain lighting, I was *done* for. The way her teeth bite into her lip when she smiles makes me want to grab her lips with my own teeth. She tries to not laugh sometimes and the sound she makes while quieting herself, to not be as much of herself, makes my dick harder than my dragon scales. I groan just thinking of the dresses she uses to taunt me, hoping I will get another glance at one tomorrow, even though I know I won't. My heart still craves it more than beating, my eyes scan everywhere searching for her.

"I am being real with myself, Callahan. I am your king, and you will not question me." I walk outside and the air is brisk, foggy, and full of potential. I feel a pull calling to me, my dragon instincts on high alert.

Callahan looks me up and down. "What's wrong with you?" His face doesn't give away any worry, he wouldn't though he is my strongest friend.

"I don't know. I just feel like something is pulling my body in a way that...I don't understand." I admit through clenched teeth.

He sighs before responding, leaning against the doorframe. "It's probably your cock telling you it has been too long." His face is stone-cold serious, yet his eyes say something different.

"Yeah, I'll take care of that myself tonight. You go back and take care of yourself," I say while nodding towards the tavern. Then I turn on my heel while looking out into the large village.

Callahan, being a purple dragon, reads into every situation; he studies everything before taking action. He overthinks and analyzes absolutely everything.

"I will be okay, Cal." I assure him softer this time, knowing he needs it. "Go enjoy yourself for a night. You won't get this when we get home." He pauses for a moment then he nods his head before conceding.

The two sides have been at war for far too long; the North doesn't ever get to relax. I find that I relate more with them. I feel for them. I too want to live a dragon lifestyle. I don't like other beings being here with us, they deserve a better life than the one here. Other beings other than my little God...

"Hello, King, are you alone tonight?" A female dressed in almost nothing walks towards me.

"I am okay tonight. Thank you." I give her some chips and continue on my path.

I regret allowing Capri to walk back to the inn alone. She isn't even from this realm, not to mention that every single being hates her. Even the fae from here hate Gods; they aren't to be trusted. Fae will turn on any being if it will get them chips though. Fae are ruthless and tricky in their ways. I almost hate them as much as I do Gods. There is a hell of a realm just for them, and I would love to send every one of them there. I don't have that power though. I hear the Fae there haunt the human lands, taking them and using them in ways that make me sick. The Fates finally felt badly for the humans and gave them power to fight back, I haven't heard how that is going for them though.

One strong God and a Fate created the other realms before I had even hatched. I had been told it was from love, a Fate and a God together creating the realms and kingdom within the realms. My father had once told me the story. Now I wish I had paid more attention to it. I loved my father, and I deeply wish he hadn't died the way he did. I wish he had made different choices in his life.

The ale hit my stomach hard about ten minutes ago, but I try to hold out until I get to the inn and have my eyes on the female who plagues my mind.

"King!" A little werewolf runs up and hugs onto my leg. I stumble backwards due to the amount of alcohol in my system. I chuckle, almost forgetting about the calling dragging my body towards something. *Almost.*

"Hello, little one. How are you?" I ask while smiling down at the child latched onto me. The tiny girl yelps with joy as I pick her up. Her mother runs up, halting when she sees who is holding her child.

"I'm so sorry, King Granger. She got away from me." She tries to grab her daughter from my arms, but I pull away.

"Oh no, I don't mind. Now, let's see…" I make a show of thinking, tapping my chin several times. The tiny werewolf giggles. "You like candy, don't you?" She claps loudly and laughs while her mother looks half a second away from falling in love with me.

"I lurve candy! The hard candy is my favorite." She almost drools on me; her mother *does* drool on me.

I draw the shadows into a storefront that has candy I know she will like. "Here you go, sweetheart." My shadows hand her the blue hard candy and I place her back on the ground, patting her head as her feet plant firmly on the ground.

"King, you are too kind." Her mother pushes her chest out, as if I am even looking at her when I have Capri on my mind.

"I appreciate that." I pay no attention to her while I say goodbye to the two of them.

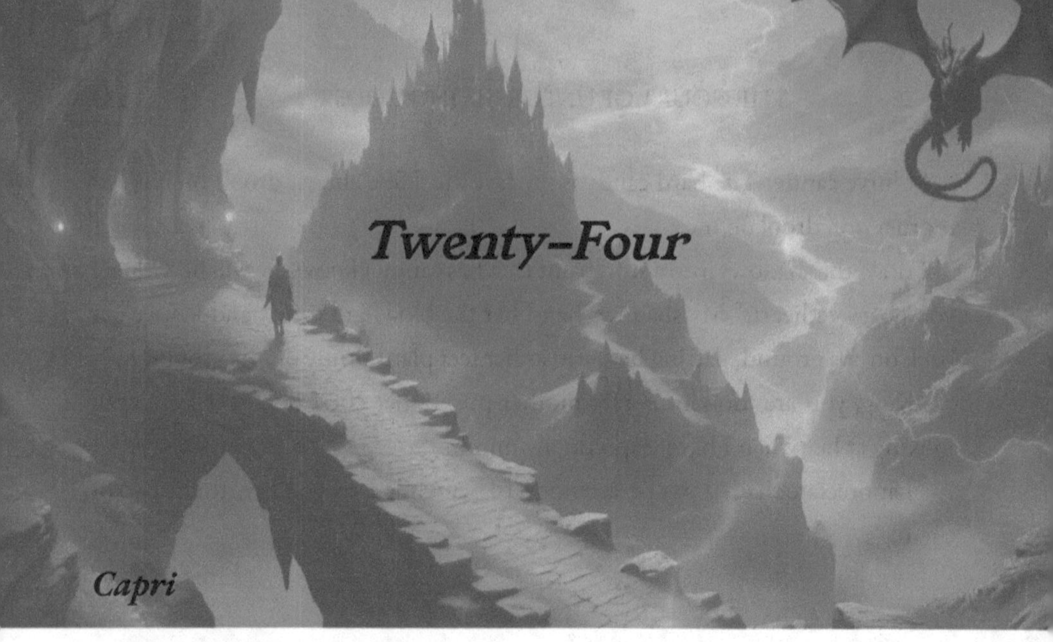

Twenty-Four

Capri

My face burns in the brisk air. My body runs hot in general, but this realm feels different. The foggy air makes everything seem wet and sticky. I rush into the inn, holding my shoes in my hand and ignoring every stare.

I took my heels off as soon as I got into the inn; I barely made it up the stairs and into my new room. Since Granger knocked another door down, the front desk vampire stopped me and made me swear it wouldn't happen again. I couldn't make any sort of promise for the king. He seems to think *after* his actions. I did toss the vampire several chips, then started the treacherous journey upstairs.

I soak in the tub while I think of the way Granger ran the towel up my legs. I think of the way his warm skin touched my body. The way it made me feel when his eyes never left mine, like I would never know another moment of being alone again. He makes me feel safe, unlike anything I have ever felt before. He hasn't said anything to make me think this, but somewhere deep inside of me I wonder if he would protect me, even against his brothers. I have no reason to think that way, but something about him calms something inside of me.

Not in a sexual way, but more. A way that scares me. A pull to him that I don't know if I want. I may not have a choice in the matter though. My heart seems to be making all of my choices when it comes to the dragon king.

I must doze off in the tub because by the time I open my eyes the water is freezing. "Oh shit," I hiss out before standing and drying my body off with my air magic. "You need to never drink again, Capri. You made a fool of yourself," I chastise myself harshly.

My father seems to hold me to a much higher standard than my brothers. They could parade themselves around with countless females and males alike, they could drink themselves to the point where they slept for days, but I am not allowed to do anything like that. I could barely enjoy life, let alone actually live it.

The palace may have given me a father, but it took away my freedom. It took away my mother. After being here, I realize how much we both need this to work. We can't continue living under Father's rule. He won't ever allow me to completely leave him; he is a God after all. He is the God King. He controls everything and one. He rules a ruthless kingdom, and will kill any being he believes threatens his reign.

My thoughts are halted by a strange feeling taking over my body. My body buzzes with this feeling to follow something unknown. A song sounds in my ears, and it completely captivates me. My entire being seems to want to find the source of this sound and please it. I open my door, completely unclothed, and follow the sound that makes my body buzz. I don't know where I am headed to, but I know I need to go. My feet move accordingly, the sound becoming louder in my ears the closer I get to it. When I make it to the lobby, several beings are there but none of them pay attention to me. It's as if I am completely invisible to them, and I am okay with that. So long as I get to the sound that makes me feel alive.

The cold air hits my nipples, and they harden immediately. I realize I shouldn't be outside naked, I know I should have waited out whatever this calling is, but I had felt like my body would burn alive if I didn't follow the pull. I walk past buildings and beings, none of whom bar my way. I don't know any of them, but if they try to stop me, they will understand the wrath of a God.

I shake my head, unsure where that thought came from. "What the hell, Capri?" I question myself out loud when I come upon an old, abandoned cabin on the outskirts of the village. The lights are dim inside, and for some reason I feel as though I need to go in. I look around and realize I am alone; there isn't anything stopping me from peeking in there. "Why not?" I shrug before walking towards my calling.

This place looks as if it should be torn down. The windows are broken, the floorboards are so worn there are pieces missing. My home back on my planet wasn't much better than this. Mother worked hard for every chip she earned.

That lifestyle wouldn't be ours any longer when I proved to father who I could be. What kind of God I could become, and have already started becoming.

"Oh goodie, you answered," a voice that sends a chill down my spine says. The tone makes me feel as though I am *in* love. I look at a shirtless male and think he is the best-looking male I have ever seen. The sound in my ears is unlike anything I have ever heard before.

"Do you hear that beautiful song?" I ask in a dazed voice. He smiles and my knees buckle before his hands are under my armpits, lifting me up. Like a savior meant to keep me forever.

"Oh, don't worry about my song. I'll make sure you feel really nice tonight. I saw the way you looked at me, sweet cheeks. I knew you wouldn't outright come to me, so I followed you." Alarm bells go off in the back of my head, I know I should run. The words he is saying to me are concerning, but I can't stop thinking about how his greasy hair would run smoothly though my fingers. I know exactly how I should please him to make him want to keep me.

"I am glad you did." I nod my head with him. I don't remember him, and it feels like a damn shame I don't. I would have danced with him instead of the dragon king who won't give me the time of day. He has a betrothed, he won't ever be mine. For some reason, that stings more than anything...the thought that Granger could never be mine.

Lost in the song and my thoughts, I don't even realize the male is touching me. "Who are you?" I ask, confused as the male's fingers glide down my arm.

"I am somebody you will not remember tomorrow. We will have a good time, and that is all you will think about. Your friends need not know." The male drags his slimy fingers over my shoulder, as he moves all over my body. "You are truly gorgeous. It is a shame that Gods are frowned upon here." His fingers slow down and I want to like it, I want to please him, but I don't know how.

"Why is that?" I ask, feeling buzzed. I hear something outside, but I don't stop to figure out what it is.

"Because I would fuck you every night." For some reason, I want that as well. I gulp, unsure what to think or say to make that happen.

"I think I would like that." I whisper and look over my shoulder at him.

The door blasts across the room so fast, the male doesn't have time to move away from me before shadows choke his throat. "What the fuck, man?" he screams at the shadows. The shadows tighten so hard that the song in my mind finally stops and everything comes to light.

"Oh my Fates." I cover my chest up, then realize all my lady bits are on display. I call to some clothes, but I am still tipsy enough that the only items that come to my body are tiny shorts and a cropped T-shirt. Of course it couldn't be anything that covered my body more. I roll my eyes and realize I have been siren-called.

"I will burn your *fucking* eyes for looking at her," the king roars as he makes his way into the shithole of a home. His boots pounding on the wooden floors as he fiercely comes to my defense.

"I will break your fucking hands from your body, you parasite." Granger is screaming so loud it causes beings to start to crowd the home. I feel uncomfortable being dressed in clothes that show off almost everything. I could call to another outfit, but my mind is whirling so much I cannot focus. *Damn it.*

"Hey, she wanted it!" the siren yells, holding his hands in surrender as he cowers away quickly. The shadows are still dancing across his throat, not as tightly as before but still there. A reminder of how brutal his king can be.

"I don't care what your twisted mind thought she wanted; she doesn't want you. If she did, she would have come to you without your fucking song, and you know it." Granger growls. I bristle with his tone, unsure why he would care if I slept with this nasty, wrinkled male.

"I didn't mean to. I wouldn't have do—" His voice cuts off when Granger snaps his neck. The crack sounds throughout the entire cabin.

"Oh my Fates," I gasp out when his body hits the floor with a *thud*.

Granger rushes over to me, using his shadows to slam the front door and cover the windows so that we have as much privacy as possible. "Are you alright?" His face is plagued with concern. His palms grip onto my hips, and my body leans into him, even knowing he can never be mine.

"I think so. I was just...I was taking a bath, and all of the sudden I felt as if I had somewhere to be. It took over my self-control. I guess I didn't have time to stop and think." I admit shyly.

The drinks tonight surely didn't help anything. I shouldn't have fallen for his siren song. My God blood and mental shields should have been enough to keep him away from me.

"He was strong, Capri. You're lucky I found you when I did." That thought alone sobers me right up.

"I am strong too; I won't have you forgetting that, Dragon King," I state almost offensively because…who does he think he is? He's acting like my savior, as if I need him to be, and I do not. I came here to take over this world even if he has a say against it. I will do what I need to for my mother.

His face contorts with an emotion I can't read, and don't recognize. "It sure looked like it when I walked in to see you completely nude, him running his fucking grimy hands all over your body." His tone is bitter and cold. I scoff in disgust at the visual now painting my mind. Granger must think I am scoffing at him because his defensives go right up and slam into me.

"I am sorry you had to see me naked. I am sure your betrothed will be understanding that you thought you were helping me, or following me just whatever you were doing. Anyways, I need some sleep. Tomorrow is a big day, right?" Tomorrow Granger is going somewhere, and I will be left here. I need to make these folk like me.

"My what?" He seems genuinely confused.

"You know what. I heard Cal in the tavern." I seem so jealous. I hate it more than anything that he can probably smell it on me.

Strong hands grip onto me, and spin me around into a firm chest. "What are you doing?" I hiss out.

"I am speaking to you. While you are in my kingdom, you will treat me as the king I am. Am I clear?" The intensity in his voice should scare me, but it doesn't. I avoid eye contact, afraid he may see how much he truly affects me. "Are we *clear*, Capri?" He grips my face, not tight enough to harm me, but enough that it forces me to look right into his eyes, just as he likes it to be.

"We are clear that you are an asshole who needs to let the hell go of me," I say through clenched teeth, grinding them shut.

I won't fall for his charms anymore. I know I need to have my guard up; I need to be the heartless God my father is trying to raise.

"An asshole, huh? I don't think I mind you calling me nicknames. Although, I believe you are smart enough to come up with something far more creative."

I punch at him, unsure where this violence is coming from. "I can call you anything I'd like to, *Granger*." He lifts his brows at me in question. I answer him by swinging at him again. He avoids my hit, so I go again. "You are engaged to somebody, and yet you danced with me tonight like you wanted me." I bring my lower lip between my teeth, trying to hide the quiver in it. I don't understand males, let alone how one could captivate my heart without doing anything to earn it.

I hit again and again before he dodges completely and grabs onto my arms. I yank out of his hold quickly, and try to gain some traction in this fight. He tries to put me in a headlock, I pull out from him, dropping to the floor and sliding under his legs. I stand up behind him, knocking his knees out.

"Ah, smart little God," he hisses, but then rolls away from my next hit, meant to be to the back of his amazing head.

"I am not some *little* God, and you will not treat me as such," I hiss out in frustration. I punch at him, and this time it lands right where I wanted it to. I don't feel any better after hitting him though.

"I have no idea who you are speaking of. I am not bonded to a soul. Callahan teased you and you took his bait." He doesn't hit me back, which makes me angrier than anything. I struggle against him, to no avail.

"Fight me," I say through my gritted teeth.

"No. I will not hit you. I might as well be hitting myself. If you are in pain, I feel pain." He declares gruffly.

I don't stop to think about his words, I just act. I throw my body into his, hoping that it will force him onto the ground and I can finally get a good hit in. Anger bubbles up in my body hot enough to burn my skin.

I push and push until finally he trips on a piece of rotten wood, and goes to the ground. My body falling with him. I move as fast as I can and hold his arms down onto the floor and sitting atop him.

I straddle the king, my knees on either side of his body. "Is this all you wanted, Little God?" His voice is taunting, yet I don't feel like he is making fun of me.

"No," I snap at him. I know there are beings trying to watch from the broken windows that the shadows barley cover, I can hear them speaking about me.

"Then tell me what you would like me to do for you." His eyes plead with me, a silent command that I cannot interpret. It isn't a question but a statement.

"I don't want you to do anything other than give me the control I need to get my mother to safety." I almost beg.

I shouldn't have said that. I don't want him to know I am vulnerable; I need him to think I am all-consuming power. I need to portray that better than I have tonight. *No more drinking, Capri, no more flirting with the hot dragon king who makes your heart pause and beat within the same moment.*

Granger stills underneath me. "I can give your mother solace here. I am unsure if this world is a much better place for her though. Although, I cannot give you the control you seek. Your father wants what he cannot have." His throat bobs as if he hates what he is saying more than I hate hearing it. I swallow, unsure if I am disappointed or if I knew deep down it wouldn't be as easy as just asking for the power and control I need.

"My father just wants to come see your world, Granger."

He shakes his head, sitting up so that I sit on his lap, our chests are completely pressed together. "Your father wants what he cannot have," he repeats. "As did his father, and his father before that. The Gods all want more than they can have, Capri." His voice sounds as if he personally knows this.

"You cannot know what my father wants," I say, hoping I sound more convincing than I feel. I want to get up from his lap, but I can't bring myself to do it.

"I do know. I have met him once or twice before. I wasn't king then, but all of that is history you clearly do not know of. Tonight is not the night we will figure it out." His eyes search mine, for something I am unsure I am able to give him.

I don't know what to think. My father hasn't been here, surely. "You are lying to me." I stand up and when I do he falls backwards. I rush to the front door, but before I can open it, a hand that is mist and smoke clamps down on the doorknob pushing it back closed.

"I am not lying to you," he says while stalking to me. "No, you do not know everything there is to know, but you will in time...if you will just trust me." I open the door, and he allows me to. My hand is still on the open door knob, but I turn to look into his kind eyes.

"Trust is earned, Granger, and you have done nothing to earn mine." He rears back like I have slapped him across the face.

"I have killed for *you*. I have warned off my people from harming you, I have set laws to keep you safe. I have earned *something*." His face contorts in pain, as if I truly have harmed him.

I look deeply into his golden eyes; they seem to swim with shades of black and brown. "That wasn't something that earned my trust, King. Those were acts of a good male. You did something kind, but I know nothing of you. We don't know each other. You did what any good and decent king would do for a guest of his kingdom." I sound defensive, even though I wish I didn't.

When I turn to go back to the inn, he follows me but gives me space, staying five paces behind.

I'm wishing I hadn't yelled at him, I am already regretting how I treated him. He is the best male I have ever met, other than Valor. I need time to think. I never think well when I am tired and hungry. I cannot possibly be feeling the emotions I am right now, so I need time to think about them before I do something stupid. Like act on them.

I feel confused, but also, I don't. My heart knows exactly what it is saying to my head. I just don't want to accept it.

When we get to the inn, I slam my door in his face when he tries to come in and talk. I don't know why I am so angry with him. But I am. I feel it deep in my bones that he is changing things inside of me. He is making me question things my father has said to me, and I don't like it.

Granger doesn't try to speak to me, but I hear him outside of my door pacing the floor. I lay in my bed, listening to his footsteps as if they were a lullaby soothing me to sleep. My father could have lied to me, but I don't see how he would think I could win over an entire world on a lie. It's with these thoughts that I fall into a deep, dreamless sleep.

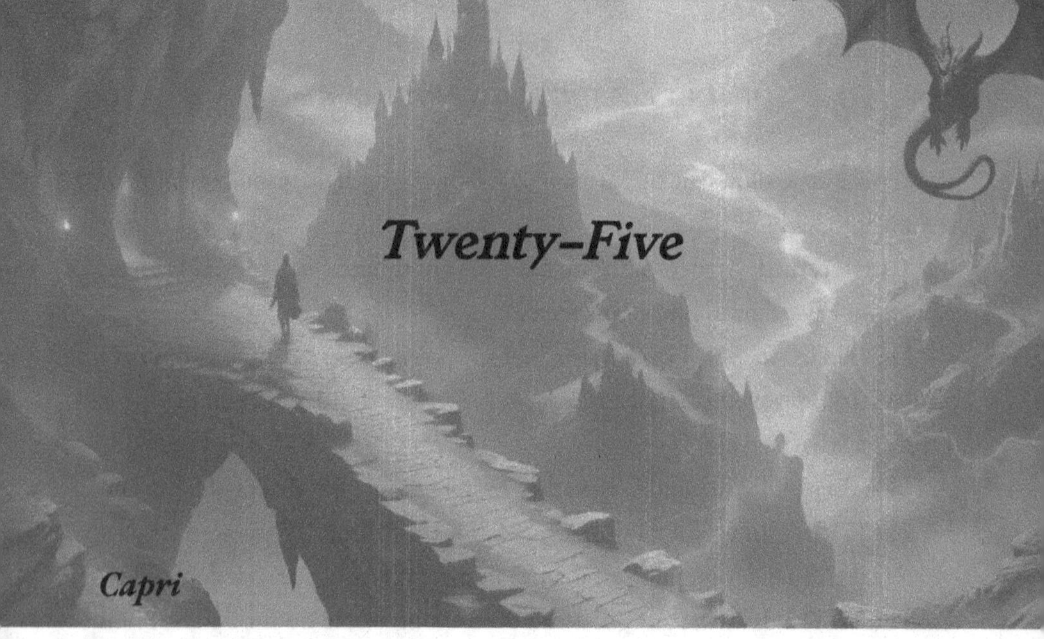

Twenty-Five

Capri

"It's been three days, Ev. I do not want to shop in the same village shops we have been...for the last *three* days. I already have every book from that store;" I point towards a pale yellow shop. "We got some flowers from there." I wave towards a gray shop which has moss growing all over it. "I can support a village with all the chips in the realms for the rest of my life, but I want to do more. I want to see more of this place." I huff out in frustration. "I need to start making bigger changes." I kick some dirt off the cobblestone, under our table, that fell from my shoe.

It was supposed to be one day without *him*. One day...and now it has been three. I worried after the first day, unsure if I should go find him. That would have been crazy though. I have no reason to seek him out. I have no reason to lie in bed wondering what he is doing, if he is safe. If he might be cross with me? I groan, thinking I might have upset him the other night by letting him stand outside my room for the *entire* night.

"You sound like a paranoid partner," Everett says without looking up from his brew.

"Partner, huh?" I ask shyly.

His eyes glance at me before going right back to his brew.

"Yes," he says while nodding his head solemnly.

"That's a very human term," I deadpan. I don't know what to make of Everett today. He seems glum, almost sad. I almost think he wishes he could have gone with the others to wherever Granger took them.

"Yeah, well there is no way you are his mate, therefore, I wouldn't use *that* term." He takes sips as he's speaking. Slurping the hot beverage, just to annoy me. I have found that Everett's favorite thing to do is annoy me.

"Why is there no way I could be his mate?" I wonder out loud, then wince when I realize I said it loud enough for him to actually hear me.

Everett puts his brew down on the table in the alchemy shop. They make more than just brews here; they make love potions, potions to make somebody have bad luck, things that will change your appearance. I haven't searched the entire shop yet, but I am amused by it all. Especially the lust potion, I could see how that would be appealing to somebody.

Everett cut that part of the morning short, of course, when I finally started having fun. He does not believe in taking potions; he claims the fates gave us all a purpose. A reason, and that is another thing the North and South do not see eye to eye on. I am learning, I think I lean more towards the North's beliefs. I can see and understand the reason for their brutal war. I just hope I can help fix things.

"Because you are a God. The Fates made our two kinds hate each other so passionately that the moment our ancestors saw one another, a war bigger than anything we have ever learned about before happened. Our one sole purpose was to keep each other in check; we cannot be equal in any way, therefore the fates would never pair our kind together." I think about that for a moment and decide it's best I don't respond to him, because I do not agree.

"Are you ready?" Everett asks after I pretend to sip on my brew that has been empty for over an hour.

"Yes. What is the plan for today?" I have been away from mother for almost three weeks now, including the star travel to get here.

"We are going to Drakon. Killian has sent an official greeting card; Caspian will meet us there."

I nod before asking, "May I have a map, please?" I am ready to be out of this village. We walk out of the alchemy shop and into the brisk, dewy air.

If they aren't outright staring at me, then they are whispering about how I killed the mate of one of their own. I hate it here; I would rather be camping in the North. I felt safer there. No wonder they are at war. The South thinks it's their way or nothing.

Before Everett can even think about my question, I snatch a scroll from the cart on the cobblestone pathway and glance at it.

"Why would you want a map?" His eyes narrow in suspicion, and then I grab onto his arm. His eyes widen in shock for just a moment. The smile I give him makes him nervous, but I don't wait to grant him an answer. I teleport us right into the very middle of Drakon...which just so happens to be the jungle. And I guess in this realm, the foggy jungle has large bodies of sticky water.

"What the fuck?" I whisper-hiss. We are in the middle of a black, mucky lake. "Oh my Fates." The water is so deep it feels chilly; the color of the water so dark that I can't even see my legs kicking. I look frantically around for Everett and see him just before he shifts into his green dragon form.

His scales glimmer in the sunlight, while black, almost slime-like water falls from his dragon form. His wings send wind so strong that it is pushing me further from him, and almost under the surface. I teleport to the edge of the lake, right after something touches my foot. I don't know what it was because I couldn't even see my hands in that water. I think I would rather not know what touched me, or who.

When Everett meets me on the shoreline, he shifts and vomits everywhere. "Ew. Are you okay?" I run to him, unsure what to do with a dragon shifter who is sick. My clothes drip the black gooey water onto his hand, and he shakes it as if the water has offended him.

He holds up a hand, asking me to wait while he expels everything in his belly. "Can I do anything for you?" My face scrunches with concern, my mouth turning down into a frown. I could try to heal him, but that could go wrong since I haven't had enough practice. My brothers didn't want to teach me what they knew, so I had to do it mostly on my own. I think that was because they feared that once I learned how to heal, I would be unstoppable.

"No. You are..." He bites down on his lip hard enough to cause blood to spray. My eyes widen, and I take several large steps back. His pupils turn to dragon slits, and steam wafts from his nostrils.

"What are you doing? Why are you hurting yourself?" I watch this male make himself bleed, his fists clamping down on the grass in front of him.

"I cannot say what I would like to say to you because I promised Granger I would be kind and the best gentledragon I can be. So, I will refrain from what I wish to call you right in this moment." He says, hanging his head down so that I cannot see his face any longer.

I take a second to process that and bend down so that my palms are on my thighs. "Oh?" I ask, unsure what else to say. I hunch over even more, just trying to level with him, but not close enough he could spring on me.

"Yeah, *oh*. But I will have you know, that body of water..." He tosses his hand towards the black water. "That is the deadliest water in this realm. The things that live there..." He shakes his head and shivers. "We are damn lucky, Capri," he says with a barely suppressed scream. I feel like I need to make this up to him somehow, but I don't know how. He may be my only friend here.

When I scan the dead-still water, I see a pair of black eyes looking right at me. Whatever being they belong to is sickly white that I shudder, long black hair goes down and into the water. Chills race up my skin, but I don't dare look away from this being. The dark eyes never leave mine, they don't even blink. I decide not to tell Everett I believe something may be hunting us. After several long moments, the eyes slowly go under the surface of the water and don't breach it again.

"Alright, so it looks like you know exactly where we are. Maybe you could show me on a map where we need to go?" I shake that haunting interaction from my mind and turn back to Ev. I think those black eyes might follow me into my sleep. I venture away from the shoreline even further; I don't want to be in those waters ever again.

"I won't let you drag me through whatever demon God thing you just did ever again. That wasn't natural, Capri. You shouldn't be able to rip through space like that." He says this so genuinely that I don't think he is being mean to me. I also don't think he realizes how unnatural it is that he shifts into a *freaking dragon*. I don't think now is the best time to bring that to his attention, though. I think he really believes that Gods are more powerful than they should be.

"Isn't that what Gods are though? Isn't that why the Fates wanted Gods to rule for them?" I ask, wondering what he will say to me.

"No. The Fates didn't want...that. Now, get on my back. Also, clean me up a little bit and I will forgive you." He declares, so I listen. I pull my water magic to the surface, taking my time to get every bit of the black lagoon from his body, along with the vomit and even things I can't discern. My powers caress his body; it's as if my own fingers were touching him. My mind wanders to Granger and how it would feel with his powers touching me.

"Are you done feeling me up then, huh? All you had to do was ask." He shrugs, one brow arched. His tone is more teasing than I would think it could be after the last ten minutes. That is one thing I love about Everett: he forgives and forgets quickly.

I have gotten so used to him being naked all the time that I don't even notice he is anymore. "You are as appealing to touch as my own brothers," I claim, and that is the truth. My heart doesn't race when I see him, I don't feel flutters like when Granger is near.

He rolls his eyes at me. "Yeah, well, I bet your brothers don't shift into a huge green dragon that can call to the world. I can make flowers for you," he says defensively. I giggle at him, knowing he is only teasing me.

"Are you trying to plead your case with me, Ev? Do you have a crush?" I bagger him. I wipe my hands on my pants, which are still soaked through.

"You know what, maybe I am. I don't know, maybe we could be good together. You with your evil abilities and me with my charm and flowers." He blinks several times slowly, tilting his head and giving me a pouty look.

I slap his shoulder. "Maybe so, but you don't get my blood pumping." I sigh before my mind wanders back to the king who does, in fact, make my blood do insane things.

Twenty-Six

Capri

My mouth drops when we come upon a sprawling estate. The castle that sits in the middle of this land is bigger than even the king's.

"What is this?" I ask, because disgust is wafting from Everett. We wait at the metal gates while the dragon shifters confirm who we are.

"A castle?" Everett says teasingly while lifting a brow. "Did you hit your head, Capri?"

I roll my eyes and place a hand on my hip, scoffing loudly enough that the guards for this estate look at me with worry in their eyes. "I know *what* it is, Everett. I mean, did the king live here or something?" The metal gates open and the guards motion for us to go on in.

"No, this is all Killian's. Stay by me, alright?" Everett's eyes drag down my body, not in a lustful way but a protective one.

I take a step away from him with that comment. "I don't need you protecting me. I am strong enough on my own." These dragons need to learn, I am not some docile female they need to take care of.

Everett grabs onto my hand, stopping me in my tracks. I yank my hand away from his grasp. "You are not *in* danger here, Capri. The opposite, actually. Just pretend with me, alright?" I don't know what that means but I won't fight him on it. He holds his hand back out to me, and I nod slightly before giving into him.

I may be powerful, but power is nothing without support. Everett wants to pretend, I will give it to him. I hold onto his hand while we make our way to the large castle.

Everett walks ahead of me, while I trail right behind him. Our hands still connected, as if holding hands would keep me safe.

Everett says this is how the lords here like it. The females all bow to the males here. He insisted when we walked up the path that I calm my aura...whatever that means. He says he can feel my anxiety from a mile away, which is bad because he isn't even purple. I just decided to trust him and do what I need to gain favor here today.

As soon as we make it inside the doors, my eyes adjust to see that the floor to the ceiling is black and white marble with gold accents everywhere. The large staircase spirals up several open floors, encased with white swirls everywhere. This entire castle is an eyesore, and it hurts me deeply to look at it. I blink several times before realizing we aren't alone anymore.

"Lord Killian will see you all now. I give you my deepest apologies. He was...busy." The young man in the black butler's suit bows his head. I realize then that he is just a boy. I can't feel any power from him. He feels nervous and overwhelmed.

"It is alright, Hankie boy. How have you been?" Everett seems to know everyone, and I don't know how. I thought they were all at war. I need to ask him later.

"I-I have been m-most good." He nods his head several times while stuttering out his words.

"Hi." I put my hand out to shake his; this seems like a good idea until he starts backing up.

"Oh, no thank you, m-my l-l-lady." The small boy stutters out. I give Everett a look and he gives me one that tells me he will explain later.

"Okay. I am Capri." I pull my arm back almost awkwardly, before hanging my arms at my side.

"I know wh-who y-y-you are." The boy turns, walking away from us. Everett motions for me to follow.

"What's happening here?" I ask as softly as I can without Hank hearing me.

Everett eyes Hank, then me. "He is different. They don't know why. One day he showed up here, didn't know who he was or where he came from. Killian, the bastard he is, took him in; he lets him play butler. Although, it annoys Killian because he doesn't want Hank thinking that's all he is worth." Everett explains softly.

Interesting, I have never met a full human before. I didn't even know they still lived...among us. I thought they had all been relocated to another realm. A realm where humans live right above the Fae. I would deeply like to visit there someday.

"How do you know all of the lords here so well? You seem so friendly with them, Ev." He pushes his tongue to the side of his mouth. He then drags his lower lip between his teeth, clearly not wanting to voice something.

He finally caves. "I am from here. I was born from a female who had been kept captive here, after having me and my siblings, she escaped. She was killed here when she tried to come back for us. I was kept here as bait for the lord then, he had underground rings where beings would bet who would survive. He didn't care much for anything other than chips and sex, so I just lived here. So long as I kept winning, he didn't mind what I did." Everett pauses for a moment. I grab onto his arm and squeeze tightly so he knows I am here with him. "That is, until Granger's father got me out and placed me where I belong. I don't hate them here like some of my other brothers do. I understand them a bit better after living here for so long."

Before I can respond, we make it to a hallway that has some very graphic paintings and drawings. "What are these?" I ask, the subject of Everett put on pause for now.

My eyes are burning with images that make me feel uncomfortable. Everett chuckles. "That is why I said you are not in any trouble here, unless it's your pants that are in trouble of leaving your body." His voice is low, almost to the point I can hardly hear him.

"I don't understand what these are." I stop in my tracks, feeling uncomfortable with the boy—Hank—seeing these. Even though that is a silly thought, considering he lives here.

"These are Killian's...um...adventures." The paintings before my eyes are difficult to look at. My face heats with embarrassment, but also something maybe *more* than embarrassment.

"These are interesting adventures," I state as plainly as I can before we come to a large door that has gold accents everywhere. "There is a lot of gold around here," I observe out loud.

"Yeah, well, he is a dragon lord after all." Before I can deem him a response, the doors are opened to a grand ballroom.

There are two long tables that house flowers unlike any I have ever seen. A throne sits on top of large steps that overlook everything happening in the room. In that throne sits a male who is handsome; he has cropped brown hair and a face that looks as though he gets anybody he wants.

Judging by the paintings in his hallway, I think he *has* gotten anybody he wanted...and maybe even some he didn't want.

"Lord Killian." Everett bends down slightly, but I do not.

Killian's eyes meet mine. He smirks at me before saying, "This is the God then?" The way his eyes trail my body makes me feel as though he might be able to see right through my clothes.

"She is. This is Capri, and I would remind you—"

Killian waves his hand, cutting off Everett. "I know, I know. I cannot harm her." Killian stands and takes the steps down two at a time. "I wouldn't dare harm this fine lady." My cheeks flush, he is extremely handsome; the closer he gets to me, the more I see he is defined in a way that Gods are. I guess huge lizards sort of have to be strong, but this male is *strong*. "I extended my invitation for you all to stay here. I didn't receive a response. What a shame." His head tilts and slithers in a predatory way.

Everett steps in between me and the lord circling me. "I think we will stay in the village nearby. Thank you for your kind offer Lord Killian." Everett says in a polished tone.

Killian stops in front of us, his tight outfit showcasing every single muscle he is clearly proud of. "Nonsense. I will inform the king that you will have rooms made up here. I will have Hank take you to them now. Dinner is in two hours, and you both smell like bog shit." His nostrils flare as he inhales with disgust written across his face.

My eyes widen in surprise; I thought I had cleaned us off well. "I cleaned us up after that fall." My tone is defensive. I smell myself, unsure if this male is just teasing me.

"I am a dragon lord, Capri...I could smell your blood if I wanted to. I know what you had for breakfast. Nothing slips past me...including your interest," the Lord of Drakon says, a smirk written across his face. He winks at me suggestively.

Maybe Atlas was right, and I can win these lords' hearts with my body. The thought of doing that, though, causes bile to burn my throat.

Everett yanks me into his body. "She is taken," he hisses at the lord. I look to him, feeling unsure of what to do in this situation.

"You don't still share then?" the lord asks, genuine curiosity in his words.

I search Everett's eyes, trying to find an answer I may not want. "I am not to be shared. I appreciate your interest in me though." I smile sweetly at the lord. This wasn't the right move for me. My smile only gets him going. His own arousal is now apparent to me—I can smell it, which means Everett can too.

"I would have to be blind to not be interested in your body." He leans into my space, even while Everett holds onto me. Killian's breath tickles my neck.

Everett releases a low growl, one he cannot actually act on unless he wants to start something neither of us wishes to finish. "If you change your mind about being shared, or even if you want to dump the second for a true Lord of Beithir, I will be hosting a get-together tonight."

Before I can even answer, Hank walks back up. Killian clears his throat, and I notice him straightening his pants.

"Your rooms are ready. I will take you to them now." I turn to follow Everett and Hank.

"Please let me know, Capri, and I will save myself for you only." Killian winks at me, and I just wave awkwardly back at him.

"So that is Lord Killian?" I ask when we make it to my room. Everett's is right next to mine.

"That is. His parties are not something you want to be involved in. I promise you, Capri, if you want to get laid a group orgy isn't it." I listen to Everett talk about Killian and his parties for a solid twenty minutes. He doesn't let me speak while he goes on and on about how disgusting the South is.

"Is there anything else you would like to talk about?" I interrupt his new rant before it gets out of hand.

Everett looks at me sideways while leaning against a small desk in the corner, his ankles crossed over one another. If I didn't already know he had just been complaining for the last half hour, I would have thought he was the picture of calmness.

"Granger and Caspian are coming tomorrow." I walk to the large windows in my room that overlook a lush garden. I lean into the window seal.

"Callahan isn't coming?" I ask while looking at the expansive flower statues.

"He has other business. Caspian is coming instead, even though he isn't happy about it." I don't dig into the other business; I know full well Everett wouldn't tell me, even if he wanted to.

"Shame," I whisper.

"What?" Everett comes to stand next to me.

"I just said it's a shame they will miss out on the party tonight." I turn around, needing to get ready since we have wasted too much time talking.

"Granger doesn't do that," Everett says softly. My heart pitter-patters in my chest.

"He doesn't party?" I ask, fully knowing what I am really asking and hoping Everett will catch on. When he doesn't, I press a little more. "You know what I am saying," I say shyly.

Everett stays by the window, leaning into the seal. He doesn't look at me when he responds. "He doesn't sleep around."

I swallow and simply nod my head. "I have to get ready. I'll meet you down there in about an hour." I walk right into the bathing chamber without waiting for him to say anything else to me.

Twenty-Seven

Capri

I stare at myself in the window; my reflection looks bleak. I give myself several moments to just *feel*. I feel sad about missing my mom and Valor. I feel angry about my father putting me here and not giving me any instructions on how to rule a world. I don't know what I am supposed to do here other than try to stop a war I know nothing about. I don't understand this war, I don't understand these beings, this kingdom. They are not outright fighting at this time in their lives. They are not what I expected. It would be easier to take over a realm if they were actively at war right now, if they were killing each other. But they aren't. I can't stop thinking about what Granger said either...about having met my father. But that can't be true, can it?

I know most Gods would be happy in my position; these beings trust me. To a degree, they think I will not outright take them over and hand them to my father on a platter. But won't I? If it comes down to my mother's life versus this planet, I will choose her. I know I will. She is all I require to remain good and sane. I need her. If I take them over with force, it will cause more war and fighting, but against me instead. How am I supposed to rule a kingdom that wants to kill me? I can't. I must get them to like me, to trust me. I need them to hand over the reins willingly. I need their king to fall, and me to rise in his stead.

A loud knock on the door causes me to jolt away from the window and my inner turmoil. "Coming," I say through the door, but before I can get to it, the thing slides open.

"Oh, I'm sorry, I thought I heard that you were coming, and I figured you might want some help with that." Killian laughs, like what he just said is the funniest thing he has ever heard, or thought of.

"Oh," I say, not sure what else to say.

He doesn't seem to notice anything but himself. "I will walk you down. I wanted to get some alone time with you." Killian's eyes roam my body so slowly I shuffle on my toes.

"Where is Everett?" I ask while walking into the hallway.

"He went ahead with Hank. I wanted to get to know you, since I hear you will be staying with us."

I look at him, which isn't hard because in my heels, I am eye level with the lord. "Hopefully. My goal is to end this war you all have started for yourselves and rule alongside the king," I answer honestly. Killian must not have known that because surprise ripples into my own emotions.

"Hmm," he hums; the sound is calculating. "And what do you know about our war?" He tilts his head the same way he did earlier. It isn't hard to remember this male is in fact a dragon, a ruthless killer, and someone I will not be trusting.

We walk slowly down the steps, Killian grasping onto my arm. I don't pull away because he isn't bad company if you get past his gross remarks. "I know very little." I play coy, wondering what he will say.

"I see." His eyes go straight to my breasts, which are somewhat on display. My light blue gown hugs my waist, forcing my breasts upwards. My hip bones are also visible in this gown. The sides of the dress are cut out in an intricate way right where my hips are, which catches Killian's attention.

He licks his lips slowly. "Enough talk about wars for now, Goddess. I would like to get to know *you*." His smirk is inviting; he ripples masculinity. His calling me Goddess annoys me though.

"What the hell?" Everett yells from the top of the stairs, causing me to jolt backwards and almost fall. Killian catches my arm, steadying me. "You just left then?" Everett asks me, and my eyes go to Killian's who is now looking anywhere but at me.

"I was told you would be down here with Hank." I pinch Killian who hisses out in pain.

"Ouch. You wound me, Goddess." Killian spares a glance at Everett. As if Ev being here is a bother to him. "I must have forgotten to tell Hank about getting you. I am truly sorry, Evey. Will you forgive me?" He asks, but I don't get the sense that Killian really cares if Everett forgives him or not. I feel some serious tension in the air, so I take matters into my own hands.

"Come on, Everett. We have food that needs to be eaten." I grab onto Everett before he can do anything stupid, like hit the lord and cause the war to become active again. I chance one more glance back at Killian. His shit-eating grin is all I needed to see to know exactly what he thought he could get away with.

"What did he say to you?" Everett whispers, barely loud enough to be heard.

"He was just talking to me, I don't know." I have never felt this amount of anger come from him, even when I landed us in the black waters of that lagoon.

"What did he say?" Everett's grip starts to hurt. My defenses rise instinctually. I zap him right in the hand and he hisses out in pain. "Why did you do that?" he says, but his eyes go to behind me.

"Is there a problem here?" Killian asks, clearly reading our mood perfectly, knowing we are fighting. I don't know about what, though.

I walk away from both the males. "Everything is fine. Now let's eat," I say over my shoulder, my tone clipped. The doors open and I gasp when I see how many beings are here. "I didn't know so many would be attending tonight." I look to Killian, and he smirks right back at me.

"I told you it was a party. They usually get a meal beforehand. You can sit by me." He leads me away from Everett, who has to sit at another table on the other side of the room.

I take my seat next to the lord. I notice several females glaring at me. "There are all kinds of beings here," I state while grabbing my goblet. I shouldn't drink, but I am nervous enough that I throw caution to the wind. Killian eyes me in a taunting way, as if asking me if I want to change my mind about his party.

"There are." He nods towards the long table. "I enjoy the company of many. I don't usually like one-on-one interactions. Although, looking at you makes me curious if I might enjoy it." He gives me a lazy smile. I blush. I know I do because my face is hot. That statement shouldn't make my cheeks heat, it should insult me, but it doesn't.

"I just meant that there aren't *only* dragons here. I am surprised." I sip lightly on my wine. It doesn't taste like anything I have ever had before. It's bitter and not sweet at all.

"I thought you were aware that our side of this war enjoys bringing in new friends. We like all different types of beings." His voice is like liquid silk. The way he sounds is fluid and light, soft and inviting. "I cannot see how that is so insulting to my brothers of the North but here we are." He motions towards a siren walking by, goosebumps riddling my legs. I decide not to look too long at the siren.

"Other than Gods, correct?" I ask, but he doesn't answer me. Killian stands up and raises his glass. Everyone stops to listen to their lord speak.

"Hello, friends. We have here a Goddess in our company tonight. She is our friend, and we will treat her as such." Every being sitting at the two tables raises their goblet. "Here is to our friend, Capri, and hopefully her help with the war." The nice moment suddenly feels ruined. I lift my goblet even still, locking eyes with Killian. I know there is more to him, but I like him so far. He seems like honest and good company, even if he is creepy. It also helps that he is sexy; his bronze skin glistens with sweat. I drink slowly from the goblet, already feeling the effects of the strong wine.

"It's good, huh?" Killian asks when he takes his seat. Plates and plates of food are brought out and laid in the middle of the tables.

"It is, what kind is it?" I ask, while swirling the liquid around.

"I am not certain. The fae are the best at brewing new drinks. You should go to a village of theirs with me sometime. It is the best party of your life. They know how to *live*." I smile at the lord. I enjoy how easygoing he is, even if he is too flirtatious with me.

He may be a sex addict, but I don't intend to sleep with him, so it doesn't bother me. "That sounds nice," I answer. Killian hides his surprise well on his face, but his emotions are shot right to me.

I giggle at his expense. "What?" I ask before reaching for some bread. I take a small bite from the bread while I wait for whatever he is going to toss my way.

"I am just surprised you would agree to go with me." I put the bread on my plate before loading up with tons more food.

"I agreed to go check out their wine...not you," I say smoothly. His eyes darken slightly.

"We will see about that, Goddess."

I raise my fork to him. "Yes, we will." I notice several females now walking around the ballroom floor, seeming like caged animals. "And I prefer to be called a God." Killian smiles widely, something about it looks rehearsed.

"You may be trouble for me, darling." His voice is as smooth as the wine I am drinking and the silk that clings to my body.

"Why is that, Lord Killian?" I ask in a taunting voice, batting my eye lashes at him. They are darkened; my skin is bronzed with the same makeup. I feel lighter after even a few sips of wine.

I need to slow down or I might do something I shouldn't. Like join his sex party. That would be one hell of a way to lose my virginity. I don't want to prove Everett right and regret joining an orgy party.

Killian leans in so close to me that our breaths are mixing. "Because I was told that under no circumstances am I allowed to touch you, but I hadn't seen you when I agreed to that." His voice is low and almost threatening.

I lean into his ear and whisper to him, "And now that you have?" My voice is sultry. I know I am playing a dangerous game with this lord, but for some reason I don't feel like I care. I feel like Atlas may have been correct in saying there is an advantage to sleeping with the enemy, especially if they are good in bed.

Killian gulps before pulling away from me. He picks up his goblet, looking down the cup at me while he drinks his wine in the most seductive way I have ever seen somebody drink. "Now that I have"—he places his goblet down, his hand going to my thigh, the opening in my dress giving him access to my warm skin—"I don't think I will ever get my fill." I gulp, not sure what to say back to the handsome lord as his fingers press into my flesh.

Twenty-Eight

Capri

I came here to learn their ways. I came to this kingdom to rule these beings. And to rule them, I will have to become what they want. I mingle throughout the room, making my way around every being. I read them all—some hate me, some of them are curious about me. I show them what I am. I show them what I can do. They all watch me, as if I am their entertainment. Maybe I am.

The ones who hate me are jealous of what I can do. The vampires want to drink my blood for my power; I almost offer just to gain favor with them. That is when I realize I have had enough to drink. I am only on my third goblet of wine and yet I feel like I am floating. I laugh at everything; my face hurts from smiling so much.

I'm talking to a dragon shifter when Everett finally breaks through to me. "You have gained quite the crowd here, Capri." I look around and notice how many have gathered to talk to me, to watch me use my magic.

"I guess I hadn't noticed," I answer him, feeling like he doesn't want to be here any longer.

"It's time for us to retire." He grabs onto my arm but I yank away.

"No, I still have others I promised to speak with." I look around and I do notice many other older beings are leaving.

"Unless you want your virginity to be taken from you tonight by strangers, you should leave with me now." Everett warns. I don't recognize the icy tone he uses. I look and find that beings have indeed begun coupling up. Some are even undressing, and I avert my eyes.

"You are right," I agree with him.

I go to say good night to Killian, but when I see him with two nude females—one straddling his lap, the other kissing his neck from behind—I get a good dose of reality. He fucks anything and everything. I don't know why that hurts, but it does. He is exciting and handsome, but he is another dragon shifter who would rather have his own kind than me. The cold realization hits that if I live here, as my father intends for me to, then I will be utterly alone in my life, other than having my mother. Valor may not leave his family behind, and I wouldn't make him.

Everett's gaze goes to where mine is and he is the one who pulls me out of this ice-cold realization. "He is never anyone's. Remember that when his sweet words come out to you. It will never be you and him only. He doesn't know how to love, Capri. The South care about themselves. There is a reason I left here."

I nod numbly, and before Killian can see me watching him with them, I leave with my chin tilted up. "I didn't want him," I state when we make it into the silent hallway outside the ballroom. "I don't know what I want, but a male who has no loyalty is something I am not interested in. He wasn't offering me that tonight though. Just so we are clear, he didn't promise me anything." I say firmly. Everett's eyes look concerned. I don't want to see it, so I teleport right into my room. My head hits the pillow on my bed, and I fall right to sleep.

I don't know what wakes me, but it is so loud I can't help but go into the hallway to check it out. "Surely the party is over," I say to myself. I roll my eyes; I do not enjoy being woken up. It is well into the night. I wander down the dim hallways which are only lit by the lanterns and candles. I don't see another being, so I continue timidly. I hover above the floor, slowly but surely moving while floating down the steps. I am curious now, so I don't stop when I hear the soft grunts and moans. My body is no longer visible to any beings. Atlas taught me that trick when I gave him information on Lachlan's whereabouts one time. I am not invisible per se, but I blend in with the background of whatever I am in front of.

I teleport into the ballroom and almost immediately want to go right back outside. I stay though, for reasons I don't fully know. This is unlike any sex party I would have ever imagined. There are females riding males, while other females ride the male's face. There are two males inside one female, and she seems to enjoy it. I tilt my head, trying to study this.

Every being here seems to be having a grand time. It almost convinces me to join until a bucket of cold water is thrown on my curiosity when my eyes land on Killian while he is ramming into a female. He watches another female ride another's cock, her breasts bouncing as she finds her pleasure and rides it out. The look on Killian's face tells me he is thoroughly enjoying his view, and his partner as he kneads his partner's breasts in one hand while the other hand plays with her entrance. His lust slams into me so hard I almost mistake it for my own. He greedily shoves himself rapidly into the female on her hands and knees in front of him. I shake my head, trying to get this out of my mind.

I teleport out of the room, unsure why I feel the way I do. Nothing was going on in that room that they didn't want to happen. A cold hand slams onto me, and I halt.

"Enjoying yourself, Princess?" I am looking into the golden eyes of the king. I don't know how, though. I look down at myself, trying to figure out if he can see me.

"I-I heard something." I look down again because I am not visible to him. I shouldn't be. "How can you see me?" I ask softly, now very uncomfortable with the loud moaning on the other side of the door.

His eyes are lit with rage and jealousy. "I control shadows. There is nothing I cannot see and nothing that can be hidden from me. The shadows tell me things, Princess." His voice is thick, almost like he is out of breath.

"When did you get here?" I want to move away from this door; I want him to erase every moan from my memory, from his.

"Just now. I rode as fast as Caspian could keep up, until he couldn't any longer, then I left him." Granger says his chest is heaving. My brows furrow with confusion.

"Why?" The king takes a step towards me; I don't back up this time.

"Because I felt you getting aroused and there is no way in any world that *that* will happen without me." His voice is full of a commanding tone, which makes my undergarments wet. My chest heaves with my breathing.

"And why would you want that? I am not a dragon, King." His eyes roam over me in a way that leaves heat in every spot they touch. I don't even notice I am in my sleep attire.

"You are exactly what I *need*, Capri." The way he says my name makes me think he might mean those words. I step into his firm body. I don't get on my tiptoes...no, I float to be eye level with him. "You are everything I have ever wanted and never allowed myself to have."

"Prove it," I taunt, daring him to make a move. The moaning is now setting a mood I do not want to ignore any longer.

Granger looks almost pained when he says, "I cannot."

I plant my bare feet back on the cold ground, the marble biting into them. "Why is that?" I ask, unsure if I want the answer, but knowing I need it.

"We need to have a conversation first."

I scoff and cross my arms over my chest. "There are many individuals who fuck without knowing the other one's favorite color, King." I purse my lips, needing release from whatever is going on in my center. I rub my thighs together, and this only makes it worse. Granger tracks the movement and groans while running his hand down his face. I decide right here that I will be the one to make my choices.

"It's not about your favorite color, although, yours is blue. Not dark blue, not royal blue, but a candy blue. Like the sky but bright and cheerful." I grind my teeth together, not knowing how he would know that.

"Then what is it about?"

He blinks several times, his thick dark lashes fanning his cheeks. His face contorts in pain as if this conversation pains him more than he is letting on.

"You know what? You don't have to tell me." I move to the door of the party, but before I can reach the handle, Granger's strong hand grabs me and pulls me flush against him.

"What do you think you are doing?" he says through clenched teeth.

"I will be fucked tonight. I gave you first choice, and you don't want me." I shrug him off my body before he pushes me against the door.

"I am your only choice, Princess," he growls in my face, his hands on either side of my head.

"Then do something about it." I am unable to ignore the feeling in my core right now, so when his body presses flush against mine and I feel his arousal against my belly, I can't help but jump and catch myself on him.

He holds me, my arms interlocked behind his neck. My legs are crossed at the ankles, locking my body onto his. "Show me how much you desire me, King, before another does," I whisper, hoping to drag him so far into this he can't stop. I want him to fall as fast as I am, to crash as hard as I know I will.

"You are going to wreck me Little Goddess, aren't you?" he asks before his eyes scan my face. Then, without letting me answer him, he whispers softly, "Take us to your room." His whispered words tickle my ear, but I do as he requests of me.

"I was kind of hoping you would do the wrecking tonight, King." I say before teleporting into my room. Granger drops me as he watches me slowly back up. I stumble backwards until my legs hit the mattress.

My eyes drag down his body, and the *V* shape of his abdomen as it goes down his pants is enough to dry my mouth. The way Granger stalks to me while I lay on my bed causes my heart to stop beating.

"Once we do this, Capri, there is no going back. Do you understand that? You will be mine and only mine. I do not share. If you even *think* of another, I will kill them on the spot." He threatens. I watch him watching me. I nod my head eagerly at the dragon before me. His eyes turn to slits, before changing back to normal. "Say it. Tell me what you want."

I lick my lips, and his predator gaze tracks my every movement. "I want you," I whisper, closing my eyes. When my eyes open once more, they are met with golden ones already taking my body in. "I want you completely. I want you to ruin me so that I will never look at another. I want to be your only," I say in a hushed voice, almost embarrassed. His fingers catch my chin, drawing my attention onto him and only him. "I need you more than I ever knew I would another." I claim, and wish I could take the weakness away.

His grip on my chin tightens, and my eyes lock onto his. He leans completely over me. "Do not be ashamed of your feelings; embrace them, Capri. You are the most beautiful female I have ever laid eyes on. You deserve everything you want. Voice it, demand it, take it for yourself. You are not like the other Gods, you are so much more." I gulp down any leftover anxiety and allow myself this one night of stolen moments with the King of Beithir. My enemy, just not tonight, because tonight he is going to worship my body.

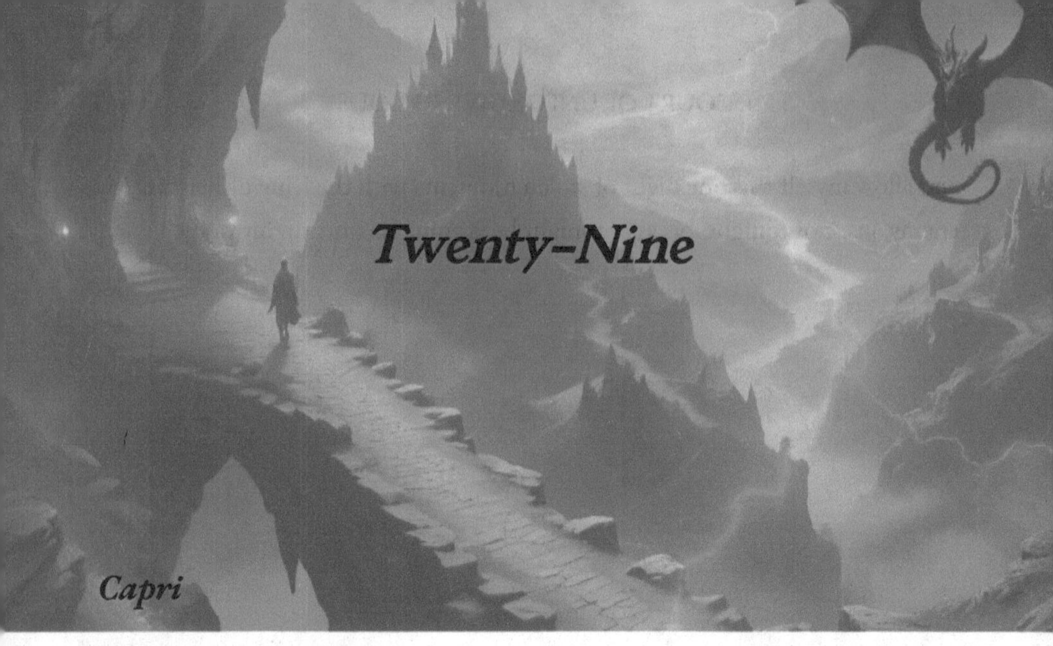

Twenty-Nine

Capri

Granger stands between my legs; I am still in my nightclothes. He asks me once and only once, "Do you want this?" His voice is gruff and low.

I rake my gaze over his perfectly sculpted chest and abdomen before answering. "I want you, all of you. I want you to ravish me entirely."

His abs flex before his fingers run over the waistband of the pants he wears. When he pulls them down, his cock springs out from under the soft material. I swallow once because seeing his cock right now, compared to the many others I saw downstairs, I realize how much bigger he is.

"You are *big*." I whisper. I don't allow myself time to feel any type of nerves. I sit up on the soft bed on my elbows. His gaze burning into mine, I gulp down every fear I might have and embrace that I want the Dragon King to ruin me.

He moves back slightly so that I can completely sit up, and take in his long, thick length. I run my fingers up and down the long shaft playfully. Granger grips the back of my head, his fingers digging into my hair so hard it would have hurt if I was tender-headed.

"Tonight is about you, Princess." He pushes me down onto the bed and I fall eagerly. Not just on the bed, no; I am falling for this male in front of me.

I bite down on my lip when he cages me under his warm, tan, firm body. Granger runs kisses from my feet up my legs to the crease of my thighs, my belly, my breasts, my neck and then finally he claims my lips in a way that I may never recover from. My heart is completely paused; I don't think I even take a breath. His tongue sweeps against mine and I moan into his mouth. I run my hands between us and grab onto his cock. Not knowing what I should be doing, but also in the same sense, knowing whatever we do will be life altering.

Granger groans out, "I said tonight is about you. Your pleasure is all I care about." He moans as I run my hand once, twice, up and down his length.

"Your pleasure is mine too," I say against his swollen lips. He lays his forehead against mine, the passion in his eyes burns right into my soul.

Granger deepens the kiss, and I place both of my palms against his chest. I feel him run his fingers so slowly to my thigh, I feel the moment he gets to my center so heavily it might crush me. The moment he runs his fingers through my slickness, I groan into his neck while pressing sweet kisses to his warm flesh.

"You are ready for me?" he asks, as though he might not know how much I crave him.

I answer immediately, unsure if I can wait any longer for him to be inside of me. "I need you inside of me like I need my next breath of air, Granger." He groans and then presses hot and wet kisses against my lips. A single finger slips inside my core, and I feel as though my entire body is hot lava. "Oh my," I pant out. His thumb plays with me while his finger does more to me than I would have ever guessed a finger could. One single finger just changed my *life*.

"More," I moan out, now understanding the noises I had heard.

"I will, but I need you to cast an air shield." When I pause my panting and raise a brow, he explains. "Any beings that hear you will die a most unfortunate death." He growls. I chuckle which causes his fingers to pause mid-thrust.

"Do not stop," I hiss out.

"Then do not laugh while I am pleasuring you." He warns. I cast an air shield so that not one being could hear us. Even if I were to scream out. Which should concern me, considering I am literally in bed with the enemy, but I am throwing caution to the wind again, and this time, I might become more intoxicated than I have ever been on their wine.

The sounds that come from my mouth are unlike any others I have ever made. When my core creates more fluid than I have ever felt, I guess it only makes sense, because this male is doing things to me with his hand, mind, heart, and soul that I have never experienced.

"I love how responsive you are, Princess. You are so wet for me." He purrs as he removes his fingers, and I mourn the loss of them. That is, until I feel his hard, thick length sitting at my entrance. "Are you ready to wreck me, Princess?" he whispers against my mouth, and my answer is instant.

"Yes. Yes." I must sound almost pleading to him. When he pushes into me, dots cloud my vision. Granger grunts in pleasure and I follow his grunt with my own soft moan.

"Are you alright?" He stops his movements, going no further. His voice is soft, unlike what you would expect from a king. When my eyes meet his, they stay locked. My lips are parted slightly as I feel a single tear slip down my face. Something inside of me shifts, a dull pull tugs me in a direction I have already been trying to follow. He wipes the tear from my face with his lips as he kisses all over my face.

"Yes. More, please," I beg, suddenly feeling like I don't have enough of him. My fingers run down his back in a way I picture a beast scratching up a tree. I feel as though he is more to me than just a king. I feel as though he is the beginning and end of me. My very existence is based on him. Those thoughts stop for a single moment when he pushes all the way inside me. I can feel my body stretching to accommodate his thick length.

"Eyes up here, *love*." My eyes snap from where we are connected to those golden eyes that now feel like *home* to me.

"Okay." I lean up to press a soft kiss to his lips. He hasn't moved since pushing all the way inside me. The movement caused by kissing him sends painful shocks of pleasure right to my core. "Move," I say against his lips, and all too suddenly he moves his hips in slow, torturous circles. The movement causes his navel to touch my bead of pleasure, sending shocks that feel like the best drugs the world has to offer.

Granger's body is a drug I feel I will never recover from.

"*You won't ever have to recover from me.*" His voice echoes in my head as though he just spoke into my very mind, even though my shields are firmly in place. That can't be true though, so I ignore that little voice telling me it is true. His eyes don't leave mine when his pace quickens and I feel as though I might crash and burn. I might explode from pleasure and pain. I may very well die from feeling this many emotions. *"Over my dead fucking body,"* he seems to growl right into my subconscious.

My body chases pleasure from Granger's, like I may not live if it doesn't happen right in this moment. I don't know what I expected, but when my body starts tingling, and his thumb ups its pace on my core, I never would have thought my body would convulse with pleasure. I never knew my body would soak his. "Oh my Fates!" I scream out. His eyes heat with passion and triumph.

"I am no Fate. I am your one and only *king*. Am I clear, Princess?" His pace doesn't stop, which causes my pleasure to feel as though it will never end. "Am I clear?" His tone is biting and harsh.

"You are," I moan out as the waves of this orgasm wash over my body. His movements become erratic, and for some reason I hear his voice so soft inside of my head.

"You are only mine, and I am yours." His voice sounds passionate and hushed as he spills himself inside of me. *"Mine."* His forehead leans against mine as he claims me in every way I claim him.

Granger doesn't move. Our chests brush against one another while we wait there, neither wanting to depart from the other. I feel as though if I were to leave him, I might not survive it.

"Don't move yet," he huffs softly against my ear. His body still caging me in. "I want to memorize every single feature on your face so that when I think back on this moment, I can remember what this felt like." My heart starts pumping so fast, I think it might give me a heart attack.

"And why would you do that?" I question.

His eyes roam over my face in wonder. The way he looks at me makes me wonder if he might be feeling how I feel. "You don't know yet?" he asks me, and I don't know what to say. Instead of answering him, I lean up to press my lips firmly against his. The warmth of his body makes me feel like I finally have a home here. Like I may belong here.

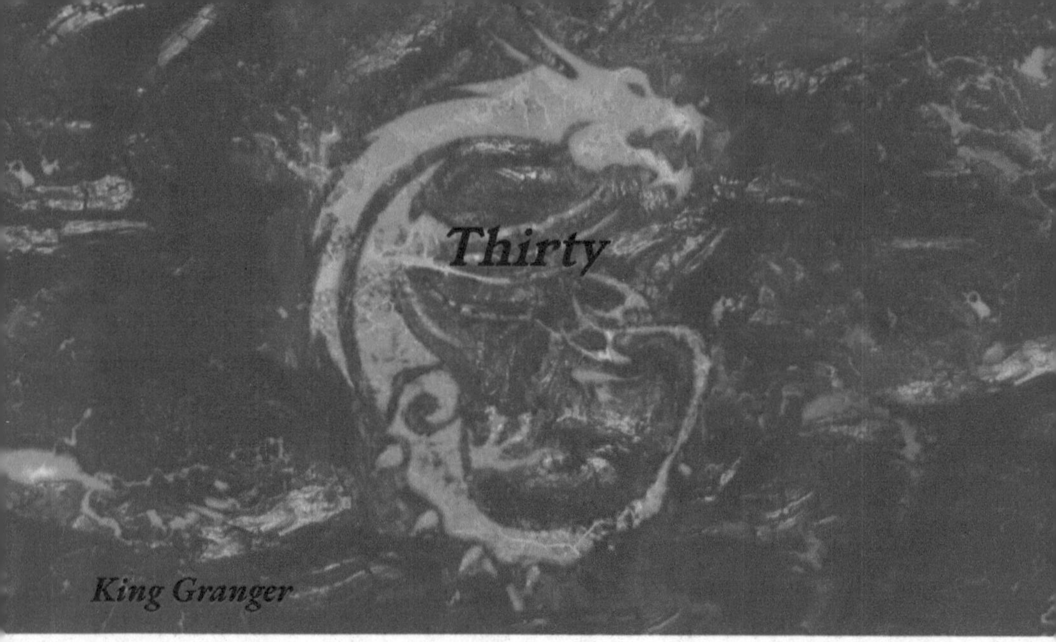

Thirty

She is my mate, and she doesn't know it yet. I don't know how she wouldn't know. Only mates can speak telepathically outside of clans, but when I did it the first time her face scrunched in that adorable way when she is confused, when I did it during our moments I figured she would know what we are. When she still looked confused that I could brush past her shields, I wasn't going to explain to her during the throes of passion that she is now bonded to me forever. She will forever be mine, as I am hers. She owns me now, every part of me is hers. I had a feeling before this, but it all solidified when I entered her and claimed the bond as mine.

Caspian had wondered when he smelled us together. We had gone to research if it was truly even possible for a God to be bonded to a dragon. We are enemies in species, and yet, here we are...mated. I know in my very bones that she is mine.

Dragons are greedy by nature; the bond will only strengthen from here. I will not tell a soul who doesn't need to know about it. I will not allow her to be harmed because of this. There are still so many who will try to take my spot as king and will take any chance they can to weaken me. The lords grow restless with the war never ending; they do not know what I do. Airus, Lord of Dreki, has been rumored to be making big moves against me. He, more than any other, is tired of living this life. He wants to end the war with bloodshed, and I simply will not allow my friends and family to die for something that will not change our world.

Capri rests next to me. When I finally had my fill of her after going for hours, she passed out. Although, my fill only lasted a few minutes at most. Now I sit here with a hard-on. I wonder if waking her up would make her happy. I get the feeling she would beat my ass if I did, so I decide on a walk instead.

I walk out of her room, wishing I wasn't this far from her. I'm in gray lounge pants that hang dangerously low on my hips, and nothing else. I feel my nerves rambling about inside of my body the further I get away from her. My entire soul demands I go back to what is mine. I get to the base of the stairs when I finally decide I am far enough, I stop and begin my trek back to my heart. When I turn to go back to my God, the front doors open wide to show an angry dragon.

"Seriously, Granger?" The sun is blossoming on the horizon, which means he more than likely stopped somewhere to rest.

"I needed to confirm something," I state plainly, not needing to explain myself to him.

"And? Did you confirm it?" he questions, and the only reason he is still standing here is because he is the closest thing to family I have left.

"I did." I nod and his eyes glaze over. Caspian's body stiffens when he figures out we were right.

"How is that possible?" He makes his way to me, not caring that he is stark naked. That is a normal thing around our kind, although I suddenly feel as if any of them saw Capri naked, it would be the last moment they ever saw anything ever again.

"I am unsure. I guess that is a question for the Fates, if you would like to question them?" I taunt him, knowing he won't call them for a meeting. We have tried before, and the calls went unanswered.

"I would not like to tempt fate." Caspian looks at me, his nostrils flaring, and I know what he smells. "You smell like her already." When dragons bond, they bond entirely; it intertwines the souls. When the Fates allow us to have a mate, they make certain there is no other. Not that I would have ever looked at another after seeing Capri Ragnar. The moment I saw her, I was beyond done for. The way she sat at a table filled with her enemies and didn't bat an eye when she saw me. Capri Ragnar is the bravest being I have ever known, and will ever know.

"Thank you," I say in answer, although I know he didn't mean for it to be a compliment.

"Granger." His voice all too harsh for my liking.

"I understand your concern, although, I cannot change fate. They decided this before time and space; you know we cannot question them. She belongs to me and I to her. That is it." I shrug my shoulders. My heart aches to be with her already. I need to hint to her what this means for us.

"Does she even know?" We walk side by side, the sounds of Killian's party still going on in full force around us. Several females stumble from the ballroom and throw glances our way. If Caspian didn't hate Killian with a passion, he might join.

"She does not. She doesn't understand our people yet, but she will with time." I will teach her everything she needs to know about the ways of our kingdom.

I had long since believed myself to be dead; I was no king to my kingdom. Not like what they deserved.

I was a worthless piece of space that honestly needed to be taken out long ago. Now? I finally feel like I have a reason to live. I never wanted to be king; I never wanted this power the fates gave to me.

"She doesn't feel the pull yet? How are you feeling?" Caspian has not found his mate, if he even has one. Fate can be cruel like that; some may not ever meet theirs. Or maybe they just don't have one.

"I feel as though my heart is breaking because I am not with her right now. I feel protectiveness like I have never felt before," I answer, in the most honest way I can, without sound.

"Even more than when the power shift became yours?" He asks, and I don't even have to think about it.

The day I became king of the dragons, every being became my ward. I protect them all to the best of my ability, which is why I cannot actually pick a side in this war.

"I would burn this world for her. I would kill for her if she even just asked. The mere mention of her from your lips makes me wish I could kill you." I clench my fist tightly, trying and failing to make my anger towards Caspian go away.

"Well, that sounds like a problem," he says. He doesn't back away from me because he knows I wouldn't hurt him unless he came in between me and my *mate*.

"It shouldn't be one. I will make certain that all will know in time, but now is *not* that time. Am I clear, Caspian?" He rolls his eyes at me before stalking towards the rooms that were made up for him. "Caspian?" I call down the hall.

"Yes, sire. We are clear." He waves me off in his normal teasing tone.

I hate it when he calls me that. He is my family, and I care for him deeply. He knows I have to play my role or else it will be stolen from me. The price will be my life, or worse. *Hers.*

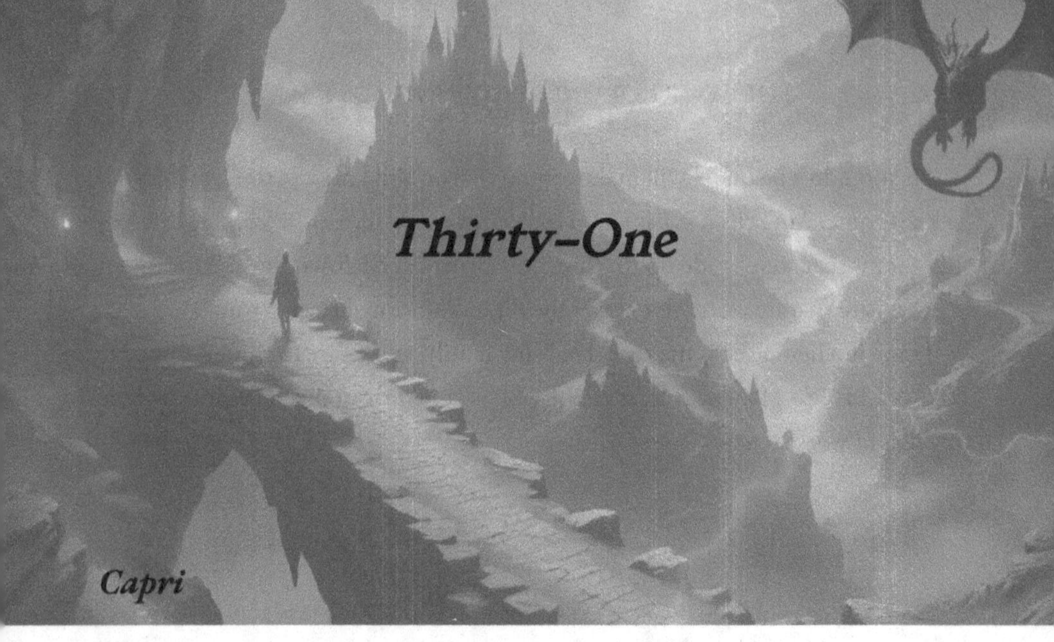

Thirty-One

Capri

My eyes open to a dimly lit room and for several moments I have no idea where I am. The bed I lay in is still warm, which means...

It all comes back into view, right in the forefront of my mind. "Oh, my Fates." I sit up, suddenly feeling uneasy, and sore in all the wrong places.

"You mean *king*, right?" The king's voice comes to me from somewhere in the room. When my eyes finally lock onto his, he looks like paradise. His tousled dark brown hair is waved in a way that suggests he has been running his fingers through it. His ankles are crossed in front of him as he sits casually in the armchair right beside my bed. His dark suit fits his body so snugly that I can't help but wonder if he had it tailored just for him.

"Enjoying the view then?" His voice is taunting in a way that tells me I have been staring for a long while.

"I was until your voice happened," I tease right back. When I go to move from the bed, I wince out in pain. Granger rises fast from his seat, crouching in front of me.

"Are you okay?" His eyes are filled with worry, and my heart aches for it. I have only ever wanted to be cared for like this, as stupid as it is for a God to want to be cared for. I have always craved this kind of... passion.

"I am okay." I say as firmly as I can, even though the gap between my thighs aches.

His fingers roam over my face in a way that tells me how much he truly cares about me; his gentle caresses turn eager. I yank on his shirt to pull him right on top of me. His warm, firm body cages mine in the bed. "You didn't get enough last night?" he asks as he tilts his head into the crook of my neck. A blush creeps up my cheeks, but I don't dare back down. I don't feel the need to with him.

"I don't think I will ever have enough of you," I answer honestly, and it surprises me. I don't understand this tether between us, but I know that if I don't grab onto it, it might go away.

"I couldn't agree more. Although, we are needed downstairs for a meeting." He pulls away slightly from me, to look me in the eyes.

I groan and turn over in the bed, hiding under the massive, feathered pillows. Granger laughs at me and pulls the pillows from my face. I close my eyes, hoping he might just lay back down in bed with me. "I can't," he says, but I scrunch my face at him, unsure what he is referring to.

"Give me a few moments. I-I don't know if I am able to walk," I admit to him, unsure if it is because I lost my virginity last night or because we went at it for five hours afterwards.

Before I have a chance to see if he has left me to crawl my way to the bathing chamber, strong hands grip onto my naked flesh and pick me up with ease. "What are you doing? I just need a moment to clean up." I know I look a mess, I know there is blood, and I do not wish for him to see any of it.

"I am aware of the female body, Capri. I will not allow you to clean up my mess." I try to look down at the bed, but Granger stops me. "You are *mine*. My heart will only beat if you are in it. My life is only worth living if you are living it with me." He presses a solid kiss to my lips, not letting me respond to his declaration. "Am I clear?" He whispers against my lips. I nod eagerly hoping he will continue to kiss me if I don't respond.

He does.

He makes quick work in the bathing chamber. The tub is already filled when he places me inside of it. The water is so warm I moan, and I don't think twice about it when he bends down to my face. "You are mine. I would like to be yours...what do you think?"

I blink several times. He is giving me a choice in this. He has claimed me, but he wants me to claim him too. I nod my head feverishly. "I want you to be mine,"

I whisper, not because I feel shy but because I don't know how we will make this work.

His lips sear into mine; the passion in this kiss alone makes my body go weak. I feel as though I am falling from the sky, and I have no powers left to keep it from happening. I embrace the falling feelings. Although scary, they comfort me in a way that I feel in my bones is okay. I feel like I am claiming the home I deserve. Our kiss continues while Granger washes my body, his hands running cinnamon-scented soap all over me. His fingers brush over sensitive places with ease. I moan into his mouth and that gets him going.

By the time my body is cleaned up, the water is cold, but I don't seem to notice. "What do we do now?" I ask him when he stands to get a towel for me. I step out of the tub, drying myself off and then realizing he wanted to do that. Before he turns around with said towel, I call back the water I had just dried from my body.

"We take it one day at a time, Princess."

A knock sounds at the door and we both look. I already know who it is, and from the look on Granger's face, he does as well. I lift the air shield from my room, that way he is not surprised when his king opens the door.

Granger yanks the door with more force than I would have. "Oh, My King, I must have gone to the wrong room. I am deeply sorry," Killian says while backing away from my door. I walk forward, no longer in my towel but in a white lace dress. It isn't a gown but more of a sundress. I enjoy the way it flows and swishes around my bare feet.

"No, you are at the correct room," I say from behind Granger. I watch Killian's nostrils flare and then he realizes.

"Interesting." Killian places his hands behind his back, and steps away from Granger.

"Did you need something?" Granger asks in a tone that tells me he doesn't really care what Killian might have needed.

"I did. Breakfast is being served. Capri is needed." Killian says with more authority than I would have thought for a lord speaking to his king.

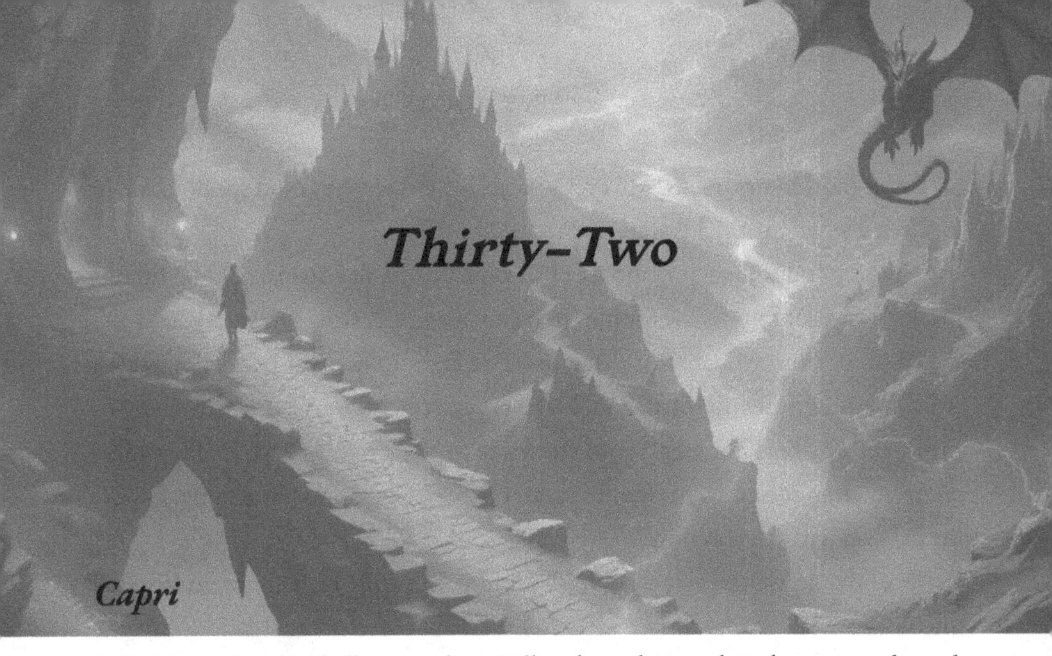

Thirty-Two

Capri

The walk to the ballroom where Killian hosts his meals is the most awkward walk of my life. I don't know what I expected, but every dragon can clearly smell something even though I bathed.

"Do I smell weird to you?" I ask Everett, because after the third time Granger growled at Killian I stepped back and told him I needed to walk slower. He wanted to walk with me; Killian pulled his attention elsewhere.

"You smell like you, plus the king and his offspring." I almost choke and that draws looks from not only the two males walking ahead of us, but also several other beings.

"I am sorry. I'm okay, I just swallowed wrong." I say before Granger does something stupid. Granger lifts his brow in question; thankfully, Killian draws his attention to more pressing matters than my ability to swallow. "You can smell...*that?*" I hiss at Everett. His all-knowing smirk is answer enough for me.

"Yes, we all can. Especially Killian's little vampire friends. You smell just like the king, and he you. You must have gone to Pound Town all night for your scents to be so intertwined. I cannot scent the difference between the two of you." Everett says, lifting his chin higher.

My brows furrow in confusion. "What does that mean?" I ask softly, not wanting every being here to hear me, although I have a feeling they already can.

"It means that if I were to shut my eyes, I would not be able to tell the difference between you two. That only happens if you have spent a long amount of time doing...*you know what*, or if you are mates, bonded. Which you aren't, so it—"

I stop dead in my tracks. My eyes widen. Is that why he could speak to me in my mind when my shields were up?

The king and Killian head into the ballroom but I wait outside, holding Everett back. "Why is it impossible for him to be my mate?" I ask in a hushed voice.

"Well, because you are not a dragon. The Fates have never bonded a dragon with anything other than a dragon. Mates are extremely rare, Capri. Most dragons never get a mate. They aren't going to waste the king on...well, you." He winces as he says it, but I know he doesn't mean offense. Their kind hates mine. I know he believes what he is saying.

"So, how do we test this theory?" I ask him, knowing he will not want to tell me.

"I guess wait to see if you still smell like him after you have been away from him for a while."

The thought of being away from the king for any amount of time makes me feel like I cannot breathe. "I don't like that plan, is there another one?"

His face turns almost sad. "I promise you, Capri, you are not mated to our king." He sounds so sure, but I am not.

We turn to walk into the ballroom when one more question strikes me. "What if...what if he could talk into my head?" I was unsure if that happened or not, but now...I know it did. "What if he could read my thoughts, even if my shields were intact?"

"What do you mean?" His eyes go wide.

"Like, he spoke into my mind. I heard his voice, answering something I had only thought of."

Everett grabs onto my shoulders then. "Are you sure?" His eyes are filled with what looks like worry.

"Yes?" I say, more of a question than anything. "I know what I heard." I sternly say this, because I know he read my thoughts.

He gulps and it's so loud I feel like it echoes. "You go on in," he says. "I'll be right behind you."

I shake my head, not wanting him to leave me with this question unanswered. I guess I could ask Granger, but even after all of what we did last night, it feels like an intimate question. "Answer me, Ev." I almost beg.

Before he turns to leave me to the ballroom vultures, he speaks again. "If he truly spoke into your mind, then yes, you are mated to the strongest dragon there has ever been. But, Capri, you are already targeted for what you are. You do not want this to be true." His tone is filled with warning.

I step into the ballroom, unable to not stare right at Granger. Many females cater to him; the sight alone makes me feral. I don't know what comes upon me, but I see red. My steps are directly to where he sits at the head of the table, but before I get to the king, I am stopped.

"Hello, darling." The term should be of endearment, but when he says it, it feels like anything but.

"Hi, Killian," I snip, wanting to walk straight past him and to where I see a female running her grubby hands through *my* Granger's lush hair. I bite down on my lip, unable to stop my growl. Killian follows my gaze and chuckles to himself.

"Ah. I see the king is getting accommodated here."

My eyes go wide for half a second before I chill myself. Literally, I use my magic to calm my body, cooling off my blood that is boiling hot right now. "He got plenty accommodated last night with me." I smile sweetly right into his eyes then float myself to his eye level. I do not like males looking down at me. I am not short, these dragons are just large.

The smallest dragon male I have seen was probably my height, and I am five feet ten inches. He was a blue dragon; he looked younger. Even the few females I have seen here have been large, their build all similar in the way that their muscles ripple from every part of their body. Granger's cock even flexed last night, the veins in that damn—

"Hello? Did I lose you?" Heat spills across my face when Killian waves his hand in my eyes.

"Yes. I mean no. You didn't, I was just thinking about something."

He doesn't miss a beat. "Yeah, I can certainly smell it all over you." His voice is playful but the way he says it makes me wonder if he is upset about me and the king.

"What? You cannot tell me you are jealous," I tease, trying to release some of the tension in his shoulders.

"No, I am not jealous. Surprised that *you* could screw our king, sure. But jealous, no. I fucked over ten females last night." He shrugs and I wince while scrunching my face. "Does that make *you* jealous, darling?"

I giggle. "No. I saw you with two females right after you told me you would wait for me. I wouldn't ever waste my time on a male who cannot keep his word." I say simply.

Killian shows the anger I was watching for, waiting for. I know their reputation isn't for nothing. "I do not answer to you," he sneers out. I turn and walk away without responding to him.

When I make my way to the king, I see several other beings have crowded around him. They all paw at him and ask him things in voices that make me want to kill them. I sit down right next to Caspian, and he side-eyes me, looking closer at me than he has before.

"How are you?" he asks me, though I don't know what answer he is looking for.

"Just grand." I pour myself a glass of brew. Caspian lifts his brow at me. Before responding, he picks up the jar of brew and pours himself one as well.

"Cheers to being in enemy territory." He tips his glass and clinks it with mine.

"Cheers to whatever you just said." I chuckle, but the happiness is not long-lasting when I hear a female compliment Granger on how sexy he has gotten since taking his leave of absence. I look down the table and our eyes lock in that intense way they do, but all too soon he is being drawn away to be fawned over yet again.

"It will be hard, you know," Caspian says in a hushed tone.

"I don't know anything that is worth keeping that isn't without some difficul-ty." I take a large bite of my eggs, then another.

"I guess that's true, but you already have it hard here." His eyes are so genuine; he's being careful with me, instead of his usual carefree attitude. "I just don't want you getting in over your head."

"What? Are you becoming a softy for me?" I taunt, but his face turns serious.

"I am being as hard as I can without hurting you, Capri." He leans into my ear, although he doesn't have to. "Being mates with a dragon king is dangerous on its own, let alone you being a God. You have a target on your back, and I am scared to see what he might do if you are threatened. We have never had a king mated before." He licks his teeth, and his throat bobs.

I place my brew down on the table; I am ready for this conversation. "So, it's true then?" I huff out.

"Yes, I can scent you in him. In his very essence, Capri. You don't just smell like him...you are both part of each other now." I shake my head, not fully understanding. Before I can ask more, Killian taps his wineglass with his knife, drawing every being to look at him.

Thirty-Three

Capri

"I would like to welcome our king, first and foremost," Killian's voice booms throughout the entire ballroom.

"To the king!" every being in the room says.

I even lift my own glass, but instead of saying "To the king," I say, "To Granger." He is more than just a title; he is a kind male, he cares about his people. Yes, he is more than just one thing.

"We welcome him with open arms...although, he has brought unwelcome guests here." Killian's eyes dart to Caspian, then darken when they land on me. He clears his throat before continuing to speak. "We will celebrate the guest he did bring, who is most welcome here. Capri, darling, stand up." He motions for me to stand, and for some reason, I do what I am told, even though I know I shouldn't. I wave around the room even though nobody waves back to me. My arms slowly lower to my side awkwardly.

"We will meet in two days to discuss a peace agreement that King Granger has asked us to consider. In honor of the event, we will throw a ball." Cheers erupt around the room so loud that nobody hears my question.

"What all comes with being mates?" I whisper to Caspian.

"Go to the fourth floor, third door on the right, top shelf, midsection."

I arch a brow, but don't ask him for more.

"The ball will welcome all seven lords; invitations were sent out this morning. There will be a dinner where we will all discuss what the possibilities of a peaceful kingdom might look like. It is all because of Capri. You sure have brought us together, darling. So, cheers to the Goddess." His eyes dance with mischief, I feel unsure about why he would call me out, but they all clink their glasses to a peaceful world. Not to me, of course. I also don't miss his insult by calling me a Goddess when I have repeatedly asked to not be referred to as a Goddess.

Breakfast goes by in a flash; I eat fruit and eggs mostly. I don't like meat very much; I don't feel like my life is worth more than others. I will eat it if I must, or if it is insulting if I do not.

"How was your meal?" Granger asks softly, kissing the skin under my ear.

"It was good. Were you even able to eat?" I ask in a petty voice, no one sits at our table they have all long since left.

"Yes, yes I was. Were you?" he asks before pulling me away from the chair and dragging me alongside him.

"It was hard to digest my food while watching all those females fawn after you," I say bitterly, unashamed of how jealous I sound.

"Oh, yeah?" His voice is filled with teasing, and I notice others watching from afar. They do not stop us from leaving the room though.

"Yeah," I say sharply when we make it into the hallway.

Granger pushes me against the wall where no others are in sight. I wrap my arms around his neck and gently press fast, firm kisses onto his lips. Mine still feel swollen and bruised from last night. I pull at his shirt, wanting it to be off.

"Not here," he growls.

"Why?" I ask in a whisper against his lips.

"Because I don't want to kill every male here who will watch you, who will smell you and your arousal. I am ruthless, sure, but there doesn't need to be so much killing when we could go to a room."

I chuckle, suddenly feeling unsure if I should ask him about being mates now or after I get some of my own information on it. I decide to wait. I would like to have all the information before starting a conversation I am not ready for yet again.

"I must go to Gosh to get Draven. He is being difficult with us, and for us to have any sort of discussion, he must be in attendance. Would you like to come with me?"

I bite my lip, unsure if I could really go that long without him, but also needing to go to that room.

"When would we need to leave?"

Granger seems to study me for a moment before saying, "We could leave tomorrow, if we need to?" I don't deserve this male, but I will gladly take him if the Fates deem it so.

"Would that be too late?" I know the ball isn't for a few days' time, and it shouldn't take that long to fly there.

"I will do anything for you. Do you have plans today, Princess?" I don't know why he calls me that, but I like it.

"I actually think I might." I am vague for a reason; Granger doesn't press me for information.

"I will have to busy myself then, which shouldn't be too hard around here."

That thought makes me think back to the types of parties Killian has, as well as the females who were basically throwing themselves at him during breakfast.

I grip onto Granger's shirt, teleporting us into my room. He doesn't even seem to notice, nor does he act like he cares. "I think you should not busy yourself with the types of activities that are popular around here."

One side of his mouth tilts up in amusement at my statement. "I wouldn't dare do that to you, Princess." He claims, and something soothes in my mind.

I believe him. I know it in my very being that he wouldn't dare look at another in a lustful way.

"Of course I wouldn't. Look at you, Love. None other can compare, you are beyond beautiful."

I balk, unable to cover my surprise at his intrusion. "So, you really can speak into my mind then?" I question him.

"I can," he deadpans but doesn't add anything further.

"Interesting. Can I do that to you then?" I know my powers allow me to hear thoughts if I focus very hard, but I haven't been able to do it to anybody of his caliber. Maybe a child or two back home, a weaker dragon sure, but never a powerful dragon king.

"You can if you try to. Would you like to try?" He grabs my hands; his warm ones wrapping around mine.

"I would, yes."

"Okay, so you know how you can feel others' emotions?" Granger's golden eyes shine into mine, as he teaches me more about myself and our bond.

"Yes, sometimes I can even push emotions into them. Like if they are sad, then I try to push all of my happy thoughts to them."

He rubs his forefinger on my thumb. "Okay so it is kind of like that. Pull the bond between us and push your thoughts down it. Like a string connecting our minds, but it's clear."

I close my eyes; his fingers ground me somehow. I think about my mother, the last moments we had together.

"She is beautiful. You look just like her."

I open my eyes, unable to not show my surprise. "You saw that?" I gasp out.

"Yes, you showed me your mom. She has your spirit." I blink back several tears, one slipping down my cheeks. Granger wipes the stray tear away. "Why are you crying? I am impressed that you were able to do that. You are so strong, Princess."

I sniffle, my sorrow from missing Mother invading me full force. "I never wanted to leave Mom. She was supposed to come with me. I didn't realize that Father would send me here this fast; I thought I had several more days of training and getting ready." I take a moment to think about the events that got me here. *"I wasn't ready to leave her. I miss her so deeply it aches in my heart. I didn't get to say bye."* I surprise myself by being able to say that much down the bond.

"You wanted to bring her with you?" His eyes bore into mine, and in this moment I feel as though we are one. Just like what Caspian had said, I feel it in my bones. He is me; I am him.

"When the time is right, yes. I wasn't done with her. We weren't done," I whisper, hating myself for being so weak.

"Hey, you are anything but weak. You came to a planet you knew nothing about and are trying to do something that has not been able to be done in hundreds of years. You are brave, Capri. I envy that about you. That also wasn't goodbye...you will bring her here." He pushes a stray hair from my face and then runs his fingers along my cheekbones. "You will be able to show her the castle you have built, the life you are going to make. I can see it. I know how good you are, and the good you are going to do here."

The fact that he is taking this time to teach me, something that even after all those years with my brothers not one of them did, means so much. They always felt threatened by me. I guess that is the difference between our kinds. Dragons can show kindness, whereas if Gods show it it's considered weakness.

With his words tasting like the sweetest sugar on the planet, I kiss him passionately. I leave not one place on his body untouched. My hands run up and down his firm length that is calling for me to release him. Granger's groan tells me he wants the same. "I need you," I say into his neck as I press kisses to his tanned skin while my fingers fumble pulling at his waistband. "I want you," I say in between kissing the outside of his lip, then nibbling on his ear.

He turns feral for me, throwing me under him. His eyes turn completely black. If I didn't know any better, I would say I am looking right into death's embrace. He yanks my pants down before licking up my entire center, his hands pressing my knees apart. "You taste just like what I envision the rest of my life tasting like." He licks his lips as if he can't get enough of my flavor.

I moan while my fingers run through his hair. He licks me savagely before toying with my entrance. He pushes two fingers inside of me while swirling his tongue around the bead of pleasure at my core. My head falls back against the soft blanket, the feeling of bliss already promising everything it shouldn't. Forever doesn't sound as bad when I think about him being right next to me.

I pull Granger up to my mouth, needing to kiss him, to feel him. When I grab onto his length and push it to my core, I moan into his mouth. He presses kisses that taste like me to my lips. When his tip presses just slightly into me, I push him back.

"What are—"

I don't let him finish his sentence before I push him onto his back and place my palms on his chest. I sit down on his length, allowing it to stretch me completely. Slowly I continue my journey down his hard length, my head lolling back as the bliss of Granger fills me completely.

"You are beautiful," he breathes out when I make it all the way to the base of him. I start to rub myself, moving up and down. He leans up to press kisses to my neck while his hands make quick work of taking my shirt and undergarments from my body. My breasts spring free, and my nipples are already peaked when he runs his tongue over the firm bud.

"Granger..." I groan out, feeling like I might explode.

"I know, baby." His thumb runs slow and soft circles on my bead of pleasure while I ride him, upping my pace. His other hand grips onto my waist hard enough that if I weren't a God it would bruise. Bliss hits me at the same moment Granger grunts out his own pleasure.

The warmth of his pleasure spills inside of me, the feeling of him finding his release causes my waves of pleasure to intensify to the point that I don't think it will ever end. I ride him for what feels like an eternity. This feeling of our bodies intertwined, alongside our mating bond taking root inside of my soul, is a drug. I won't ever recover from this, from him. Granger has imprinted on my soul. I am not the same being as before I met him. I am not the same Capri my mother knows. I just hope she wants to know the new me.

Thirty-Four

Capri

When I enter the room I instantly know I am not supposed to be in, I scan the shelves for the book I need. I find it right away. The spine is a dull forest green; some of the pages are worn and torn, but most of the words are visible.

The small library houses ten bookshelves, five shelves each. Most of the books appear to be historical in nature, and I suddenly wonder if there is anything about the war in here. Maybe I can study them before the ball in a few days. I need to know everything I can before meeting with all seven of the lords. I know Granger will back whatever I have to say. The lords have no reason to want anything to change; each side believes they want what is best and maybe in their own eyes they do.

I take the book that is titled *Dragon Bonds, Breeds, and Power* and make my way outside. I had seen a garden from my room, and I want to explore it. I pass by several beings, mostly dragon shifters, but a few are sirens or fae. The fae seem to have mundane jobs here and there. Other beings, I have noticed, tend to be more respected by the dragon shifters. I get the feeling fae are not well-liked here. They do have a tendency to play tricks and games on others.

I walk out the back door. Many beings watch me closely, as if I am going to harm them. I smile sweetly at them, attempting to appear as kind as possible. They still fear me; they hate me, and some even wish for my death. They throw feelings into my head. I don't even have to use my power to read them. I try to not allow it to sting, but it does. I don't understand why they would hate me for what I am.

They have no idea that what I want for them is a much better life than they are living. I don't want the fae to feel less than. My goal for this planet is for every being to be loved and welcome. Whatever their beliefs are, they deserve to live their own way safely. So, maybe my goal is for them to live on their own.

I kick my sandals from my feet and leave them so that I can walk barefoot on the lush green grass. I crinkle my toes up and out several times; the grass feels amazing on my feet. They must have a green dragon shifter living here for this amazing grass to grow. The plants here are some of the most gorgeous I have ever seen. I haven't seen any greens here, but I could have missed them. I have watched several pinks, purples and reds fly above.

"This looks like as good a spot as any," I say about a perfectly lush spot right under a tree that has pink flowers flowing from the branches. The flowers themselves are small in size, but they make up for it in number; the entire tree is covered in them. They float all the way down to eye level. I breathe in and the scent is so sweet I almost want to eat it.

I cross my ankles and lean against the large trunk of the pink-flowered tree and start to read. I open to a page that describes dragon breeds and their powers. Most of it is exactly what I thought I already knew. Other than one dragon breed—the black dragon, which Granger is. He doesn't only have shadow power like I had originally thought. No, he can control thoughts and emotions like the red dragon, and he can call an army of beings by just a thought. If I didn't know him better now, that would scare me. I haven't seen another black dragon yet, but I hope they are good enough to not control somebody. I don't like the idea of beings becoming puppets for others.

I shrug off the feeling that there are going to be black dragons who might use their considerable power for evil. I can't focus on things I cannot control. "Come on, Capri, focus on yourself and what you need to figure out."

I scan through text after text, page after page. The book itself isn't huge, but the words are tiny and some even smudged. "Aha! There we go." I finally find the chapters on mating bonds. I look around, hoping nobody heard me. I don't want others to find out what Granger is to me. I know he is worried about me getting harmed because of him, but I worry about what might happen if some of his lords figure out our secret.

Dragon mates are rare. Most will never have a mate, some will never meet theirs. Dragon mates are typically of the same breed. Intermingling of mates of different breeds is even more rare than having a mate.

"Well, great. That means we are basically the only ones." I huff, scanning the texts for any information that might help.

Mates can reject the bond that the Fates grant them, but this is ill-advised. If you do not accept your Fated mate, the Fates will abandon you. It is the highest of honors to be granted a bond backed by the Fates. Once mated bonds are accepted, fate will do the rest. The souls of mated pairs are interchanged; two will become one. The powers of one will become the powers of both. The very scent of the dragon pair will mingle into one. If one mate is harmed, the other will feel it, and in some cases, if the bond is strong enough, then both will become harmed.

My eyes widen slightly at that. That means if I get hurt, Granger will feel it. I don't know how I feel about that. I gulp down some of my anxiety before reading some more.

Mates cannot be far from each other for long periods of time. This will harm the bond, therefore, harm the pair. The pair will be able to communicate telepathically with each other, even if they do not possess the power to do so.

The ceremony to accept the dragon bond is a show of loyalty to the Fates. Both dragons must cut into the flesh, spilling blood onto the sacred ground. The blood will mix on its own. Both dragons need to say these words: "I will accept the bonded mate the Fates have granted me with. I will follow my every instinct to take care of my mate, to love my mate more than I love anything else. Above all, I will carry out dragon-bound duties to protect my mate over any other, including myself." Once the words are spoken, the mating bonds will be unbreakable. The only way to refuse the bond after a ceremony is to kill your mate. This may kill you.

Until the bond is secured, you will both feel a pull to accept it. This will overpower every other instinct you have. Fates do not grant mated pairs lightly. The dragons must both be very powerful for the Fates to allow you a mate. This is an honor above any other.

The very thought of ever harming Granger causes my stomach to plummet. I feel so sick about that possibility that I start to dry heave.

"Whoa, are you alright?" Granger bends down in front of me. My eyes widen for half a second before finding solace in his calming gaze.

"I-I was reading on mates, Granger," I rasp out, showing him the book.

"And this is your reaction to it?" His brows furrow and I wince.

"Yes, I mean. This is intense shit."

He chuckles and takes my hands in his own. "I know. Why do you think I hadn't mentioned it to you yet?" I start breathing calmer with each moment in Granger's company. "How did you even find this?" He takes the book and starts scanning the pages.

"I— Well, Caspian told me where it was."

He places the book down on the ground before sitting in front of me on the soft grass. "I see." He takes a long, deep breath before responding. "Did you learn what you wanted to?" He sits crisscross with his arms dangling over his knees.

I think on that for several beats. I don't really know. I feel like I have more questions now than before. "No," I answer honestly. "I don't understand how we can be mated, but I know it in my very bones that we are. I don't know how I know that...but I do."

His face softens with my admission to him. "I don't understand it either. That's where Caspian went with me when you first came to the South. We went searching for answers."

I look out at the gardens, suddenly unsure of how I feel considering he hasn't mentioned that ceremony to me. What if he rejects our bond? I didn't get to that part. I am not a dragon, so the Fates may not care if he does reject me. My pulse races with those thoughts before his thumbs presses into my palm, calming me instantly.

"I didn't mention the Copian ceremony because I didn't want to frighten you. I also didn't want to make you feel like you have to be with me, because...you don't. You have a choice." I lean my head against his shoulder. "You were just sent here by your father when I saw you and knew in my marrow that you were mine, I would've gone through the ceremony right then and there. My breath was taken from my lungs, Capri. I just wanted to give you time to figure it out. To figure *here* out. You came for a mission, not a mate. I wouldn't blame you if you needed time."

I don't know what to say to him, because I don't know what I feel. I know that I care for him deeply, I know I could love him, but can I bond myself entirely to him right now?

"You being a God, you may not feel the bond as strong as I do until you accept it...if you do." He swallows. "We can wait until all is figured out with the lords." I nod softly before turning around and lying between his legs.

My head rests in his lap while I look up into the eyes of the male who my life is bonded to. "What did you find out?" I ask in a hushed voice, because I see some females walking around.

"We found out very little. There has never been a mated pair outside of dragons before, sure, fae have mates but the fates have never granted a fae a siren mate." I close my eyes for just a moment. "The Fates did this for a reason, and we can figure the reason out later as well. None of these questions are pressing down on us. Nor do they really matter. You are mine, bond or not." My eyes open and drift onto the tree that seems to have swallowed us whole. "I will tell you, Princess, the longer we are in each other's company, the stronger the bond will get, until we either accept it or reject it. We won't be able to be apart, we won't notice the appearance of others, and the bond will strengthen any feelings we have tenfold. I have seen a few mates before, and it is a beautiful but scary thing. They will die for one another. I haven't seen any die due to the death of their mate, but I know it can happen."

I listen to his words. The way he explains love feels like it could be ours forever. I want it to be, after we figure out this war. I want my mother here to witness the ceremony; I want Valor to see it. To meet and understand Granger. Maybe even Father would come. I think back on all the many trials my brothers and father sent me on. Maybe it was all a test to see if I was ready for a mate. Maybe the Fates play with us more than I had realized.

My eyes drift shut listening to Granger talk, on and on. His voice is so soothing and comforting; the way he speaks is a calming presence that I don't think I could ever live without again. I know I would die if I could never listen to him ramble again.

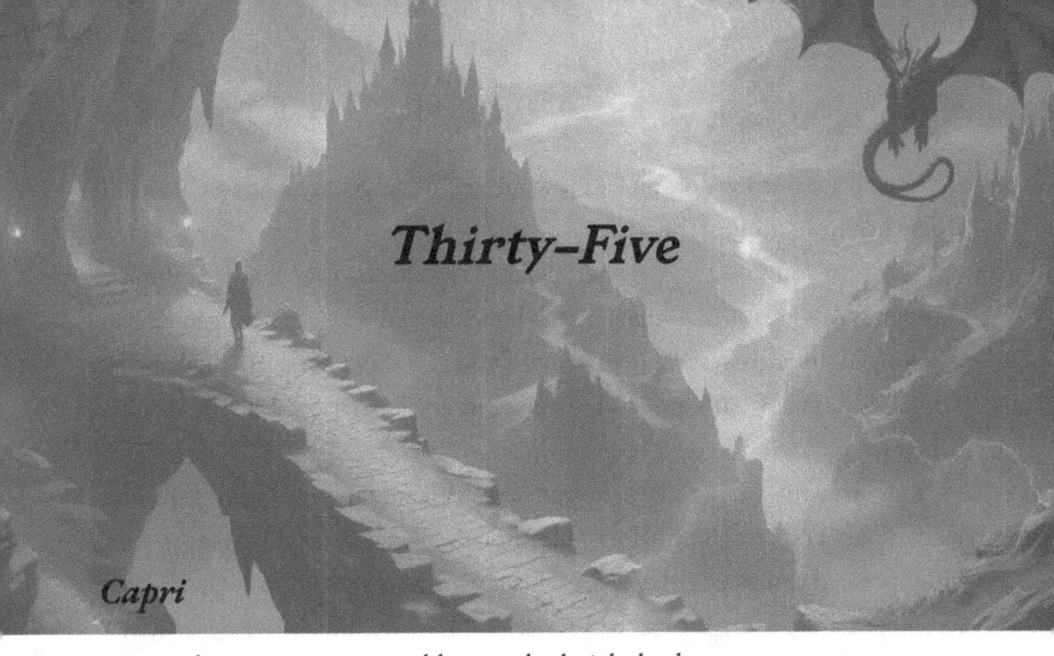

Thirty-Five

Capri

When my eyes open, golden eyes look right back at me.

"Good morning." Granger smiles down at me, his pure white teeth shine in full force.

I sit up quickly, my eyes widening in shock. "I slept the entire day away?" I ask in panic. When I stand up, I hear grunts from males nearby.

"No, of course not. You did sleep long enough that I thought you might be dead though." He jokes as he shrugs and starts walking away from me.

"Where are you going?" I ask, unsure if I should be offended that he's so casual about thinking I was dead and isn't more concerned.

As I follow behind him, his fingers grip the hem of his tight shirt. "What are you—" Before I can say any more, Granger is tossing his shirt on the ground. I bend down and grab it. "Don't worry, I'll get this for you?" I say in question, but he only smirks over his shoulder at me. We walk through the tall maze of the garden.

At the exit of the garden maze, there is a dirt circle; in the middle stands Killian and Everett. Both are shirtless, their seemingly endless muscles on full display. Killian's pale skin is completely opposite from Everett; their bodies move like liquid. They dance around on quick feet. Killian throws a fireball directed right at Everett's face. Ev dodges the ball and throws his fist right into Killian's cheek. I wince when the blow lands. Killian growls in Everett's face before Granger steps forward, revealing himself. I walk behind him.

"You all are putting on quite a show for me," Granger says with a chuckle. I stop when he heads into the circle.

"What do you say...two-on-one?" Killian says, his natural charisma shining through. He winks at me, which grants him a low growl from Granger. Killian throws his hands up in surrender. "Hey, if you two think not every single being can already smell what's going on, you are insane." My face heats up, turning bright red.

"I accept your offer, Kill." Granger makes his way over to them, slow and meticulous. The way his muscles ripple just by walking, I wouldn't want to fight him. I trained alongside Atlas and Lachlan, even Max sometimes, when he was feeling generous enough to grace us with his presence, but I have never seen a male move in the fluid way Granger does.

Everett rolls his neck several times before making his way to stand next to Killian. One more moment and Granger strikes at them both. He throws his body into the air, flipping over both males. Killian reaches up to grab onto Granger, but he is too high above him. Granger kicks out Everett's legs and gets him into a headlock first thing. Killian calls for his fire before Granger *tsks* at him.

"In this, Everett is your ally. You cannot harm him. How will you win this fight, Kill?"

Killian's face turns to one I can only describe as fury. "I would kill him; therefore, any weak links are gone from my clan," he hisses out before Granger shoves Everett to the ground. Shadows start licking the outskirts of the circle. My heart hammers in my chest as I wonder if Killian would outright kill Everett.

"You would kill your brothers?" Granger says in a taunting way. He is trying to anger him enough to get Killian to strike at him.

"I would do anything that needed to be done to win this fucking war, *King.*" The way he spits *king* is spat out as an insult. My instincts have me taking a step forward, my blood pumping in a way that calls for bloodshed. "He is also not, nor will he ever be, *my* brother. I lay no claim to him." Killian says the venomous words, trying to hit Everett where it hurts.

Everett goes to hit Killian, even though they are on the same team. Killian burns his face when Everett tries to punch him. Killian's flaming hands grab Everett's wrist in a tight hold. I can smell Everett's flesh melting from his bones.

"Stop!" I yell. Granger doesn't stop me when I walk into the circle. "Fight me," I hiss out. "You want somebody of your caliber? Your king is too kind to you. I will not tolerate you treating my friend like that." I yank Everett from Killian's grip and Granger grabs onto him before calling for healers to come. Everett tries to refuse, but in the end, his face is half melted off and he concedes. His bone is showing from behind, melted, dangling, steaming flesh.

"You think you are stronger than a dragon? I thought you were smarter than that, *girl*." His words are spat at me as if I were mere dirt on his shoe.

I shake my head, finally seeing the true Killian. He isn't the male who flirted with me. He is the male who killed a nest of hatchlings. Looking into his handsome face, I see it clearly now. I see why this war has gone on for so long. The South is ruthless; they are brutal and have no loyalty whatsoever. Not to their own kind, not to others. Their only goal is for what they want to come true.

Killian looks to Granger, who has stepped out of the circle. His smirk tells me he believes I will win this. "You will allow this?" Killian asks in disbelief.

"I do not *allow* anything; she is her own being. I will stand back and watch whatever she decides to do with you." He shrugs and I look towards Killian. "If I were you, I would start praying to the Fates." Granger warns in a playful tone.

"Are you hoping your king will rescue you?" I ask in a taunting voice.

He snarls at me. "I do not need rescue. I just want reassurance that he will not skin me when I wipe the floor with your face. As pretty as it is, I will do just that, *darling*."

Granger's anger radiates from him, causing me to be angry as well. "Whatever you think, *darling*." I volley right back at him.

We circle one another. I wait and watch his feet. Whenever he attacks, he starts with his right foot, meaning he is dominant on his right side. He calls to his fire and throws a ball of orange-and-pink flames right at my feet. I jump up high enough to go over his head. He twists around, meeting me when I land. He throws a punch, which I easily avoid. I call to my water magic and throw it right in his face, holding it there to form a bubble around his entire head.

He screams before lifting his hand and dipping it into the water surrounding his face, causing it to boil. I wince when I wonder how that must feel on his skin.

"Ouch," I say before he whirls on me, his pink dragon form showing itself. I know pink dragons have the worst temper of all the dragons.

"You bitch," he spits at me before sending fireball after fireball hurtling towards me. I suck out the oxygen from each and every one of them.

"This is a fight. Could you try a little harder? Your king is watching you, Killian," I tease him with a wide smirk on my face.

Killian's pupils turn to dragon slits as his temper gets the best of him. I look to Granger who gives me the go-ahead. I shrug before calling to his shadows; that is one thing I think the mating bond will give us now.

The ground beneath Killian turns completely black as I suck the life from his body, the evil calling of the shadows sending chills racing along my spine. I twist the shadows to my beck and call, twisting them around his form. He gasps out, trying to suck in breath, but I don't allow it. When his body collapses onto the ground, I pull Granger's shadows back. I stalk towards him as if he were a baby fawn and my prey for the evening. My steps are slow and methodical, a trail of shadow following in my wake. When the shadows completely thin out from Kill, Killian groans in the dirt. He rolls around, attempting to suck in the air I had deprived from his lungs.

"So, you want to fight again or...?" The rage on Killian's face is apparent, but it softens into a mask of cold disinterest when Granger walks up next to me. Granger holds his hand out to help Killian stand up.

"Well, it looks like it's true then, huh?" Killian snorts out, looking at me with disgust.

"What is true?" I ask in confusion.

"Yes, it is. I will announce it at the ball." Granger's eyes turn blackish-gold when responding. I look between the two males for a few moments, then decide it's better to just listen. "That is as good of a time as any, Killian, and you know it."

The lord shrugs his shoulders, circling them as if they are sore. "I guess so."

Granger walks right up to Killian, their chests both heaving and pressing against each other's. "Tell me you will not tell a soul until we can figure it out. Then, if she accepts me as her mate, I will tell the others."

Killian snorts out a laugh, but the sound isn't very amused. "*If* she accepts you? She would be—" He stops speaking as if deciding that whatever he was going to say would get him harmed. "I will give her as much time as I can," Killian says, even though he looks like it pains him to speak the words. Granger growls, his eyes not once leaving the predator in front of us.

"You know, for a lord who should want to please his king, you don't seem very appeasing to him," I chime in, almost immediately regretting it when Killian's death glare is turned to me.

"I do very much want to please my Majesty. I will keep your secret, for now, King. I suggest you do not take much more time in deciding though. You smell like the fucking God filth she is." With that last statement, Killian walks away, leaving Granger and I standing completely alone.

"Is Everett okay?" I ask shyly. Granger's glare softens to a small, sad smile when he looks me in the eyes.

"He is okay, thanks to you. I wasn't expecting you to step in for him." His words hold no jealousy, just adoration. "You did not have to do that, and yet you still did. Why?" His eyes search mine.

"He has become my second-best friend, and I had a very bad feeling that Killian would have done anything to harm him and not get into trouble for it. His feelings for you and the other Lords of the North are just plain rage and hatred. I still don't understand why," I say honestly, hoping he'll give me more information before the ball.

"I will explain it all to you if you agree to have a meal with me." His cheeky smile reaches his gorgeous eyes, and I can't help but giggle like a little girl when he picks me up into his arms and twirls me around.

"Of course I will eat with you, so long as it's something you cook yourself." His brows reach his hairline, but he agrees to cook for me...so long as I teleport us back to my home, right next to his.

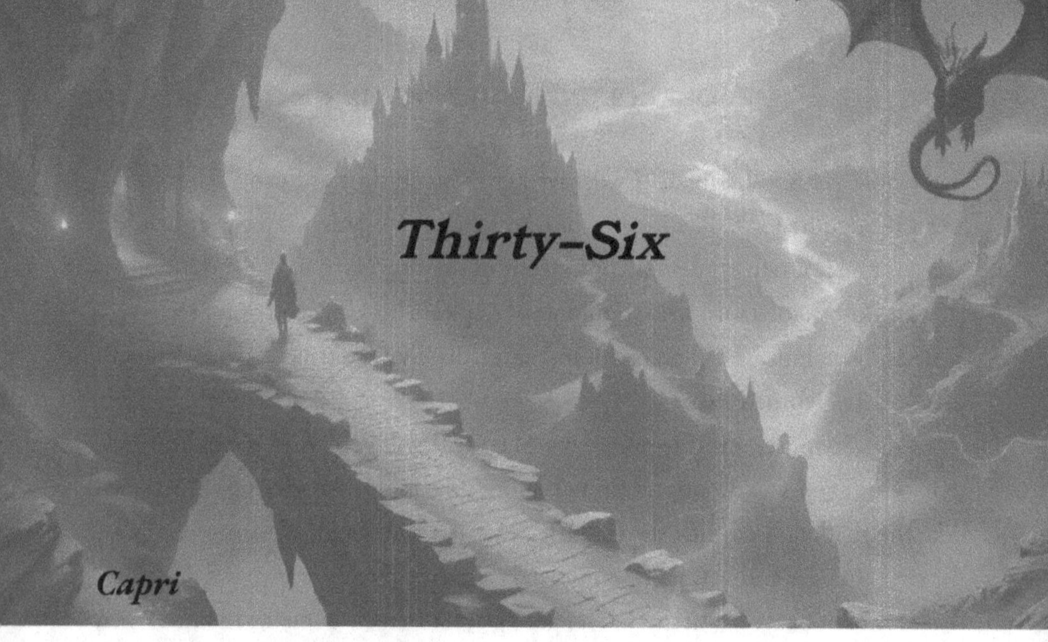

Thirty-Six

Capri

I stand in front of the dark wooden table I created for my scullery. It's laden with various meats. Granger says he hunted and killed them himself.

"Don't look at me like that." He warns softly.

I wince when I realize I have been staring at where he's chopping the carrots from my very own garden. Yes, I used magic to grow everything, but that doesn't mean I don't have a green thumb. "I just feel bad for whatever animal you killed, is all," I say while walking around the table to grab two wineglasses.

"What if I told you that the species of deer we are going to eat is endangered because of their numbers? That if we didn't hunt them, they would die anyways due to overpopulation. They overbreed, then they all get sick and killed by other predators in a far worse way." He stalks towards me, putting the knife down on the table, and leaning his hip against the wood.

"I would say I hate that they struggle, and when I rule with you, I want to help them." I lock my eyes onto his, and he does the same. His golden hue is more of a brown-gold tonight. His smile is warm and causes all sorts of butterflies to be let loose in my belly. Granger scratches the back of his neck before replying to me, his shaggy brown hair tilting over his brows.

"So, you are telling me that when you rule beside me, you will care for the animals while I am left to the dragons?"

I move to stand in front of him, grabbing the knife to chop the carrots. Strong arms wrap around me and Granger places his hand on top of mine. Both of us work together to chop the vegetables in front of me.

"I will if I am to help you rule. I will even care for the werewolves. That should help you out enough, right?" I question teasingly. Even though we both know I am not joking.

His deep, low chuckle vibrates against my back. "Princess, you could contribute nothing to my kingdom, and it would be okay so long as I have you."

I look over my shoulder and into eyes that feel like home and warmth to me more than anything. "You think I would do nothing once I win your heart?" I say in a taunting voice. We chop the vegetables and move on to putting seasonings on everything.

"Oh, Capri, you have already won the war for my heart. I am afraid that battle was a short one. The first moment I saw you, I knew something was different about you. My heart finally started beating again because of you." He kisses the place right under my earlobe, and it tickles when his short beard scratches against my delicate skin.

I swallow, unsure how to feel about his declaration. Granger reaches around me to grab the spices.

"Enough about love and other serious things. So, what do you typically eat if you don't enjoy meat?" His words hold no judgment, just curiosity more than anything.

"I eat *some* meat." I shrug, unsure when I started to feel bad for animals. I am the only God I know of who thinks of things like this. Most Gods go about life as if nothing else matters but their own world.

"What makes a difference for you?" He starts a fire over the charcoal.

The scullery is complete with a deep, white marble sink, a chopping table, a large round table for meals, and the charcoal. It's simple really, but all I wanted. The icebox is in the adjoining room. I keep it cold with my ice magic, even when I am away.

"I don't know what makes a difference. I guess if it's rude to not eat what's placed in front of me, then I will. I just prefer not to extend my life by ending another one. But I will eat it tonight."

Granger glares at me, I can tell he feels annoyed. His body is rigid, and his knuckles are white. "You should never lower yourself to please others, Princess. You're values are what make you, you."

I bite my lip, averting my eyes from his. "I must. I came here to win you all over and help save your kingdom. That will not happen if I can't win the hearts of your beings."

Granger drops the spice right into the lettuce to walk over to me. I suck in a breath when he grabs onto my face with his thumb and forefinger. "This is my world. I am responsible for the war; I alone am accepting this burden, Capri."

I grab onto his face with both of my hands. "It is no longer just you though, Granger. You are mated, and if I understand it correctly, then what happens to you, happens to me. So, we are in this together." I say wholeheartedly.

"You are accepting it? The bond?" Tears gather in his eyes, and when one slips down his stubbled cheek, I wipe it away, alongside all his other worries.

"Yes, after the ball I would like to have the ceremony with you, Granger. I doubt the Fates would steer us wrong." More tears gather in his eyes, pure bliss shoots into my body. As if he had thought I might reject him, and hearing I'm not is overwhelming to the point that he cannot contain his emotions. "I feel unlike how I have ever felt for another before. You feel like *home* to me."

Tears start to brim from my own eyes now, happiness and sadness both gathering. His callused fingers graze my face, wiping away any sadness I might have felt because I know deep down my mother might not get to watch my mating ceremony.

"After the ball, then." He declares, emotions clogging his throat, making his voice gruff.

I lean up onto my tiptoes and press the softest kiss I have ever given to the corner of his mouth. Then another to the center of his lips. My kisses are slow and calculated.

A growl rumbles in his throat when I kiss the base of the column of his neck. "If you would like to eat *food* tonight, I would halt your advances on me." The heat in my body starts pumping deep inside me.

"Well, are you on the menu?" I ask tauntingly, a full and bright smile lighting up my face.

"*You* will be, but not before you eat the meal I have prepared for you, Princess. Go set the table, please." He tilts his head out of the scullery and shoves his fingers through his thick hair.

I wave my hand dismissively, walking away from his warm, comforting body.

"Where is all the meat you had?" I ask when Granger sits down at the round, intimate table instead of the long, formal one. His choice to sit here, I didn't mind where we sat.

I placed large white flowers in the middle of the table, and when Granger sees them, he moves his place setting right next to mine, instead of across.

"I need to see your pretty face. Also, I don't think I can go the entire meal without touching you." He sets his stuff down right next to me.

I look down at my plate, then ask again. "But where is all of the food you cooked?" I stare down at a plate of rice, broccoli, and some type of nuts with a brown sauce drizzled on top. On the side is a type of noodle with a green sauce and some cheese sprinkled on top.

"I will donate the meat," he says, placing a napkin in my lap and sitting down beside me.

"But *you* eat meat," I counter because I am talking to Fated dragon.

"Yes-" He confirms, before placing a napkin in his own lap. "But not tonight." He grabs his fork and starts digging in. I don't need any encouragement to do the same. The moment the food hits my mouth, I know I want him cooking all of my meals.

"This is amazing," I say with a gasp while covering my mouth. He half smirks as he takes a bite of his rice.

"Thank you. I grew up watching everything. I studied it all; I wanted to take care of myself, even as a toddler, I wanted independence." I look at this male in a different light. Not because he can cook, but because he *wanted* to.

Granger was born royal; he had no reason to want to learn anything, other than how to be a king. Yet, he did.

He learned to cook, and it is delicious. Warmth spreads around my body in a fast pace. I am falling, and don't think it will stop anytime soon.

"So, this is where all of the scheming is going to happen?" Granger asks when we make it to the top of my tower, where my bedroom sits.

"I guess so. You better not ever break my heart, King. I have a very clear view of your castle, and I have always wanted to test how far I can throw a fireball."

Granger moves to the open archway that overlooks the water parting our two bodies of land. His hand goes to my lower back in a protective type of way.

"When did you hire so many beings here?" He asks, and it seems so random.

"I don't know. I guess after I built the castle, I thought the fae may want some work. We had traveled through a village that seemed hungry before getting to Killian's manor. I told them if they wanted a place to live, they had one here." The dim moon sets the tone for the evening. Granger turns to me, fully embracing me in his firm arms. "It is the least I could do really."

"You are too good for me," he whispers before pulling my face to meet his, peppering kisses all over me. He lifts me in his arms before walking over to the bed in the middle of the circular room. He holds me there in his arms while he is leaning against the mattress. "I do not deserve you Capri." He whispers against my lips. I shake my head, about to speak, but he stops me with a kiss. "I cannot afford you. And yet, I will fight for you, for *us*. I will earn you for the rest of my life. Each and every day, fighting to be the male you deserve." The emotion in his voice cracks slightly as he opens up in ways I would have never thought a brutal king could.

Granger lays me gently on the bed. I watch as he crawls up my body, kissing everywhere he comes in contact with as he goes. When he makes it to my waist, he stops before pulling my dress up and over my head. I lay in just my lacy undergarments, baring myself to him completely, in more ways than one.

"I will worship you and your body every day that you allow me to," he whispers against my belly, sending hot lava into my very core. His golden-brown eyes burn with pure passion and love.

"Then do it," I whisper out, hoping he will claim me in every way possible. His eyes turn bright red, and I gasp in surprise before he does just what I wanted. He claims my mouth with such passion I think I will feel the leftovers of him for the rest of my life.

His kiss is full of devotion, his tongue sweeping over mine before I draw his bottom lip between my teeth. I suck his lip into my mouth, drawing a small amount of blood. I yank his shirt over his head, tossing it to the side. When my fingers tremble over his buckle, his sturdy fingers unclasp it and help me get him completely undressed. His pants fall to the ground and I just stare at the hard lines of his abdomen. My mouth waters, as well as my core.

"Enjoying the view, baby?" A dimple graces his beautiful face, as he smiles at me.

I gulp, nodding my head before getting on my knees for him. "You aren't the only one who can praise and worship." I place my hand at the base of his already hard length and then lick the bead of liquid at its head. I start moving my hand up and down him, spreading the liquid as I go. My mouth joins my hands in a steady pace. I don't know what I am doing but I do know he enjoys it, evidenced by his grunts and moans. His fingers find my hair and then fists it. His hips move with my mouth and hand, pushing him closer to finish.

Granger suddenly lifts me from the ground, grabbing my waist and placing me on the bed. "Hands and knees on the bed." I do as he says, facing the headboard. "*Eyes on me.*" He demands. I turn my head to look at him when he pushes inside of me, and a moan slips out of my mouth.

"Oh my Fates." I moan again before he starts his harsh pace of pushing in and out of me. "Faster." I listen to the sounds of us making love. Granger slaps my ass, and I keep eye contact over my shoulder as he lifts me to be flush against his chest. One of his hands goes to knead my breast, and I arch into him.

His kisses are searing and all-consuming. The connection between us is getting stronger the longer we are together, both in this embrace, and the more we emotionally get to know one another. The connection seems to be a physical tether tying us together. The more he presses into me, the more I feel his soul mixing with mine, as if we are one and the same.

Whenever the warmth of his seed spills into me, I follow him into bliss, waves of pleasure cascading over my body. Whenever they are done, I fall onto the bed, Granger right on top of me. Our heads lay on the softest pillows; we toss the decorative ones onto the floor.

"What are some of your dreams?" I ask as I lay my back against his bare chest. His arms keep me snug against his body.

"My dreams?" he asks, as if surprised I would care about his thoughts and dreams.

"Yes, your dreams. Your wants...other than me." I chuckle before adding on, "What did you crave before I came here?"

Granger shifts me so that I look directly into his eyes. "I wanted peace. I wanted my beings, my brothers, to get along. I wanted the death to stop. I wanted change." His jaw clenches tightly. "My father's death affected me more than I realized in those moments." He admits.

I run my fingers along his jaw. Slowly, softly caressing him in a way that makes me wonder if I don't already love him.

"I'm so sorry," I whisper. Our faces are so close, we could kiss. But now isn't the time for kisses.

"It's okay. It was so long ago now. When I ascended the throne, I was only twenty. That was about fifty years ago. I was young, that's why I think the chaos got so much worse. After a while, I couldn't control even my friends. My powers weren't where they are now; I hadn't mastered the shadows when I won out king. So, I retreated, along with my father's staff. Some of them were killed; beings I had known my entire life just...gone." My heart starts to crack just picturing a small Granger watching this hell. "But even still, I saved some of them." His voice seems distant, like he is reliving a memory that is painful for him in a way I may not understand. I haven't had any real losses in my lifetime.

"That must have been so hard for you." I continue running my fingers up and down his jaw, his face, his eyes. It seems to relieve some of the tension in him.

"It was. I think it was more so that he had been in the middle of training me. My powers were unpredictable, so when he was killed, I couldn't practice with any of the staff or else I might kill them. I was utterly alone in my misery, and my powers started rebelling against me due to lack of use. So, after a few years, I started training again. Once I could control the shadows, I gained respect from the North. I don't think the South will ever truly respect me, though." His jaw clenches, as if trying not to say more than he should.

"What of your mom?" I place my hand along his cheekbone; he leans completely into my palm. Granger scratches his face for a few moments before responding to my question.

"She died during a raid the South had planned. She had been nesting; she was expecting a few hatchlings. She never made it home." So, she lived in the North.

That must be why he seems closer to them. My heart aches for him, all the losses he has had.

"Oh, Granger I hate this war," I admit, feeling so raw from this conversation.

"I do too, Princess. Let's hope that the next few days we can come to some sort of an agreement." He licks his lips before biting the lower one.

My eyes drift shut with thoughts of finishing this war by whatever means necessary for these beings to move on in peace. For Granger to get a life full of happiness, he deserves.

His powers are truly unmatched. I think he could easily go against Father and the fight would be even. He must love his world to not just kill every being in the South; he is a better leader than most, his own father included in that. Father would have already killed anyone who didn't kneel before him. Granger cares deeply about this kingdom, and suddenly I feel as though bringing Father here isn't the best idea.

"*I love you, Capri,*" I swear I hear him whisper right into my very soul as I sleep.

Thirty-Seven

Capri

I have spent the last few days either in bed with Granger, training with Everett, or avoiding Killian's advances. Even after finding out I have accepted the mating bond, Killian tries to invite both Granger and I to his parties. I have been able to avoid him for the most part, but as I stand in front of my dresser waiting to go to the ball, I feel nervous that he may be able to corner me with the other lords taking up Granger's attention.

My dress for the night is a gold ballgown that is floor-length, the glitter in it matching Granger's eyes. My hair is all the way down, the wavy, honey-blonde locks reaching my lower back. I know I'll need to cut it eventually, but I don't want to just yet. If there is a battle, I definitely will. I like it long though. Atlas always claimed it could get in the way, saying that's why females could never rule because they care more about their looks than winning a fight. He doesn't know me very well though, because I can look damn good while winning the battle.

A knock sounds at my door, but when I go to open it, it's not Granger's eyes I look into. "What are you doing here?" I ask Eamon. His brows lift up almost to his hairline.

"The king is busy at the party; he sent me to escort you," Eamon explains.

"I see." I chew on my lip, unhappy with my current company. "I could just walk myself; you don't have to walk me down there. I am more than capable of making it on my own." I sidestep him completely, my heels making us almost the same height. If I just float up a little bit, I would be taller than him. I chuckle at the thought of showing him up in height.

"What's so funny?" His voice is gruff.

"Oh, nothing. Let's get going." I smile for myself. We slowly make our way down the stairs. There are hundreds of beings here, and I'm glad the space here is finally being used for something other than an orgy.

I grimace thinking of the many places that have probably not been cleaned well after Killian's parties.

"Something on your mind?" Eamon asks, not even bothering to lower his voice.

"Yes, I was just thinking about the many places Killian has thrown wild parties in here." Eamon makes a disgusted face before shaking his head. His hair is in a tight bun at the base of his skull; his black eyes seem scarier than before. "What have you been doing?" I ask while we wait to enter the ballroom. There are beings everywhere, some aren't even dragon shifters. Vampires, werewolves, sirens and humans alike walk around and mingle.

Some dragons are in their dragon forms outside; some circle the skies. They seem as if they might be nervous; they're probably from the North. They may be on patrol though, I don't know. I do know, this is the first time the South has welcomed the North for any type of conversation in years.

"I was at the nest. One of the lords will go check on our females and hatchlings every week. I decided to stay a while. I have a few hatchlings of my own about to crack their first egg." I look at this male again, suddenly seeing him differently. He must read my face though. "Just because I am about to be a father does not mean you should trust me, Capri. What I am, is a dragon lord who does not trust you." His voice holds no malice, though the words still hurt. "I want the end of this brutal war, and I will accept anything that will put a halt to it, but I still will not like you." He says honestly.

I look away, already knowing that no matter what, this kingdom will not like what I have to offer.

When we make it into the ballroom, everything looks so different. It all seems so much more elegant than before. Maybe because Killian recognized that most would not want to dine at a table he has had orgies on. Granger's eyes catch mine for half a second before a male pulls his attention away from me. I sigh before walking over to the table, leaving Eamon to chat with some of the seconds. I run my hand over it, realizing there are name tags. I don't find mine at the table I am standing in front of, which makes me wonder if I am sitting at the lords table. Granger will sit at the head of the royal table, alongside his lords and their seconds. I scan that table, still not finding my name tag and wondering if it might have been misplaced.

"Hi, I can't seem to find my name anywhere. Could you help me?" I ask someone on Killian's staff.

His eyes widen in panic for a moment before he schools his emotions. "Oh, um...yeah, sure." He walks quickly through the masses of beings before finally bringing me to a small table in the corner, all alone.

"Are you sure this is where I am to sit?" I ask, not thinking this is true. I glance around wondering if this might be a joke.

"Yes, Master Killian and Lord Airus insisted that you sit here." He gives me a curt nod before leaving quickly.

I nod my head, finally understanding what is happening here. I take my seat, and sit with my back board straight and fingers intertwining. This might be more difficult than I had thought the ball would be, but any battle worth fighting in, is going to be hard.

Thirty-Eight

King Granger

I clink on my glass, drawing the attention of every being who was invited into the meeting. This ball is unlike others; this is the first time since the beginning of the war that we have all been together. Tensions are high, and beings don't know how to interact with one another. So, I need to set an example.

"Hello and good evening. Thank you for gathering with me tonight to discuss some very important matters." I hold my glass high while I speak. "Such as ending this war and what it will take to bring forth such peace, so that we may all live together, happily enjoying the lives that the Fates have planned for us." I raise my wineglass, others following suit. "A toast, to an evening filled with compromise, understanding, and most importantly, an evening for peace." The crowd gathers and they all start for their seats. I scan the room, searching for my mate.

"Where is Capri?" I ask Caspian, but he just shrugs then pulls Eamon into our group.

"Where is Granger's girl?" Caspian asks in a hushed voice, since there are still some who don't know about us yet.

"I don't know. She walked away from me when we made it into the room." Eamon says nonchalantly.

I grab onto the front of his suit. "You lost her?" I growl louder than I intended. A few lone beings glare at me as if I might hurt them, and I would if I don't find my *mate*.

Caspian yanks Eamon from my grip. "Chill out, boss. I am sure we will find her." Caspian brushes nothing off of Eamon, pampering him more than he deserves. We all three are looking now, before Everett walks up and whispers in my ear.

My spine stiffens before I look to see if he is right, and sure enough, there she is...sitting alone in the corner of the ballroom. There is barely even enough light for her to see her meal.

Anger boils to another level as I realize what has been done to her. I don't think or say anything before making my way to Capri. Beings welcome me, praise me, females throw themselves at me, but my footsteps do not falter once as I stride to my mate.

"You look out of place; why don't I help show you where you belong?" I drawl. Fury builds up inside of me, not directed at her but at the situation I am sure Killian had a hand in. That bastard has been a pain in my ass since before I hatched. I place my hand out in front of her, and I see her bright silver eyes shine, as if she had been about to cry. That pisses me off even more. She grabs my hand while I grab her goblet of water and we make our way to her rightful place.

"What about my plate?" She starts to turn around, but I stop her.

"A queen will not carry her own plate, not to mention, that is not yours." She doesn't look back at the lone table that should have never housed her.

Capri tries to walk behind me, but I yank her forward. She will walk beside me, never behind me. She will not be thought of as less than anyone. Myself included in that. Whoever has made her feel that way should perish in the most brutal of ways.

Eyes glare; they follow their king. Probably wondering what I am doing with their mortal enemy. I almost throw mashed potatoes at a few males who seem to think it is okay to whisper about my mate. Killian looks up from his plate, seeming more than amused by the situation.

"Majesty, there is no room at the head table for a God," Airus says from his seat across from Eamon's.

I call to my shadows; they graze his throat. He stiffens as if knowing, I will kill him without thinking twice about it. "I could get rid of you then?" I ask, almost positive I could kill him and not one being here would question it. His second is more than ready to lead. His second would also be more than eager to agree to my terms.

"I think what Lord Airus is trying to say—but trying not to harm *her delicate feelings*—is that there is not a seat ready for her," Killian tries to explain. I walk over to Airus with slow and calculated steps. He stiffens when I approach.

"Is that so?" I ask tauntingly, waiting for his ignorant response. When it doesn't come, I yank his seat right out from under him.

Airus flies to the ground and laughter rings out, but I don't stay to watch his reaction. I simply stride to my seat at the head of the table, place the chair right next to mine, and call for somebody to bring the dish I made sure to have prepared for Capri. When I feel her approach, I tilt my head down to meet her gorgeous, glowing silver eyes. My hand goes to hers without permission, without a second thought. My body gravitates towards her without my mind telling it to.

Capri is everything I never thought I would have. I have lived alone in my father's castle for decades too long. I never thought the Fates would gift me a wife, let alone a mate. I grab a mint leaf and pop it into my mouth. I chew on the leaf, inhaling the minty scent while looking at the female who will either end my world or save us. I am scared to know that I would, in fact, stand next to her and watch it burn if she simply asked me to.

"Uh, Granger— Erm...King Granger. I can sit wherever, it doesn't matter. You know where I stand, you can speak on my behalf." Capri looks unsure of herself for the first time since I have met her. I still chew on my mint leaf, half a brow arched with a shit-eating grin on my face. I halt, still clutching her dainty hands in mine. I know there are more eyes on us than I would like, but that's because I enjoy my privacy...that is, until this female. Now that I have met her, all I wish is to be with her, show her off as mine. I want to memorize every part of her that I haven't already, I crave to learn every intricate detail about her life before coming here.

"I will never speak for you." My voice is so low it sounds as though my dragon form has taken root, and maybe he has. "You will speak for yourself, unless there is ever a time where you are unable to. Then and only then will I speak for you. Now is not the time for you to be alone in some corner. Not when there are conversations being held that involve you but you are not included in. Hell fucking no." I say as aggressively as I will fight for her on a battlefield if needed.

I am fully aware that I am less diplomatic than my father, or my grandfather. I just don't care. So long as I can end this war, my job as king will be done. I never wanted this; my father was supposed to live for thousands of years. He should have lived longer. I suck in a breath, hoping he will not be brought up tonight. I spit the leaf on Killian's plate before shaking the nasty thoughts from my head.

I look down at the two chairs, choosing to sit down in the plain wooden one and leaving the velvet tufted one for my mate. Capri stiffens right behind my chair. If all eyes weren't already on us, they are now.

"Majesty, I believe you are sitting in the wrong seat," Calix chokes out. His mate sits right next to him and her evil eyes stare daggers into Capri. I make note of every being staring at her.

"I am not," I say lightly before motioning Capri to take my former seat. Her plate is brought out at this exact moment. Perfect timing, a smirk graces Capsian's face. He enjoys pissing the South off more than he should.

"Majesty, here is the plate you asked for." The servant bows at the waist before depositing the plate on the table and leaving. Capri looks unsure for half a moment before sitting down, her chin held upwards as if she has embraced the role of my mate.

"Thank you, Hank," I call to the retreating child. I shove her plate in front of her and Airus chokes on his wine. I glare into each and every lord's eye, even my friends. Daring them to speak against her. Their eyes avert mine, clearly reading that I am in no mood to be tested tonight.

"Thank you." A small voice says into my mind, and my entire night is made by those two words. My shields are completely up, and my Capri still is able to speak to me, because the fates have finally given me something, no, somebody to live for, to fight for. They have finally decided I have lived through enough alone. Forcing myself to be alone for all those years was worse than any torture I have ever been through.

I whirl to her, my eyes boring into her glittering silver ones. My lips curve before I even register that I am fully smiling. It's a bigger smile than I have ever given anybody, but for her, it will never be enough. I know I must look insane. Maybe I am. I have fallen for the God sent to take my world away from me. The God whom I am keeping secrets from. The God who might be the ruin of me and my brothers, yet I would embrace any future so long as she is in it.

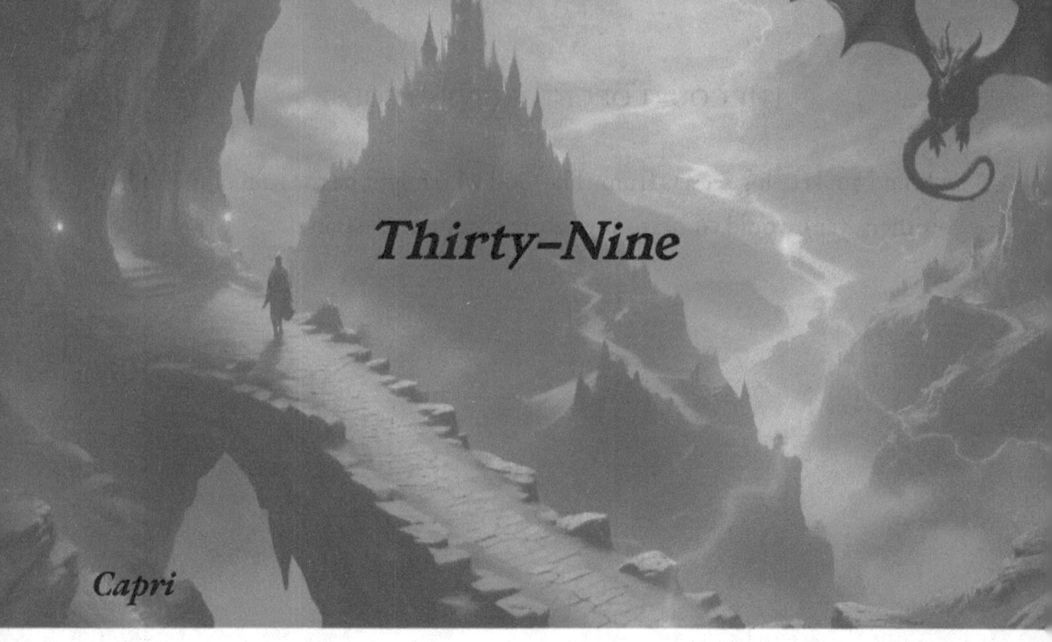

Thirty-Nine

I sit at the head of a table that I am completely unwanted at. I feel emotions clouding my mind, but I try to push them free from the grasp of my enemies. I don't want to focus on anything negative. I'm already too plagued with thoughts about what will fall if I fail to do what I came here to do. This Kingdom is at war. No matter how good these lords' masks look, they are not kind. They are not friends with one another; there have been losses so great that some of these males would gladly kill the other. There have been betrayals and there have been outright murders. I look around, knowing my side of things, but still looking at the South. I seek to understand them, but can't grasp it.

"Is the food to your liking?" Killian asks from beside me. I don't like sitting by him. He makes me feel uneasy now that I have seen his true side.

"It is perfect. I didn't expect him to do that. I feel extremely grateful," I say back to him sweetly, even though I know he wasn't trying to be kind. He is trying to draw attention to Granger treating me specially.

"I didn't expect it either. I wasn't aware we could request our own food at these events. I am a lord and have yet to get that type of treatment." His response is immediate.

"She will be queen after tonight," Granger growls, spitting a green leaf onto his plate. He clears his throat and takes a long swig of his wine before he stands up. "Listen. There is much that needs to be discussed tonight. If you are not a lord or their second, please exit the ballroom." Granger's voice booms in the large space and the sound of chairs scraping echoes throughout the entire room. Hushed voices and hurried conversations sound for several minutes before the large doors finally shut and the still room suddenly feels far too large for one table.

"What does that mean?" Calix asks, seemingly the only one who is brave enough to challenge Granger now. His mate stayed, but I have a feeling that if she misbehaves Granger will try to handle it for me.

"It means that once everybody clears out, I will explain. Not until then." He replies harshly. His eyes scan the last of the servants who make haste in gathering the plates and goblets from each and every table.

When every being clears out, the tables are also moved to the walls. "Shall we?" Granger nods his head towards a smaller circular table.

"Apparently, this is serious." Asher laughs softly into Callahan's ear. Calix glares at the two seconds, but it isn't he who responds.

"This is war," Amelie hisses, her face stone cold as she glares at him with pure unbridled hatred. Asher wipes his face clean of any amusement, and Cal clears his throat awkwardly.

We relocate to a round table, that way everyone faces each other. The North lords sit together, as the South do the same. I sit right next to the king.

"So, what is this, King?" Rafe asks, trying to start up our conversation. I notice the lords from the South don't call him "King" but "Granger," other than Killian. I believe Killian only does it when he wants to manipulate the situation.

"This is called negotiations. I know you are all unaware of what that means, but I would like to introduce you to what is hopefully the first of many meetings, in which we will discuss a way for us to all live happily ever after. Does that sound grand?" He says, sounding bored. Not one of the lords speaks up, so Granger continues. "I will start this by being honest with you. This is my leap of faith that I hope you will all follow." I gulp down my fear, swallowing it whole.

I know where this is going, and I don't know if I like it or not. I wish we could have had the mating ceremony before all of this.

"The Fates have gifted me a mate. I think it is pretty clear who they have picked to be mine." Granger says firmly, giving no room for questions.

Protests erupt from the lords even still, more than I would have thought, even from the North lords. I block it all out in hopes that they will all just stop talking.

"She is a God," Calix says in disgust, his lips turned down and his nose crinkled.

"For once in my freaking life, I agree. You cannot accept this bond," Eamon chimes in. Granger grabs my hand under the table and rubs small smoothing circles over the top of my hand. He doesn't look at me, but I know he is here right with me.

My heart sinks, ice-cold feelings trickling down my body as I listen to every insult thrown my way. I didn't expect them to sting so badly... Callahan looks somberly towards me. Granger squeezes his hand on top of mine when a tear builds up in my eyes.

"We are okay, this does not define us." I nod my head, knowing he is right. This doesn't define our relationship.

Airus tracks Granger's hand quicker than any of the others. "This cannot be!" He screams so loud it echoes throughout the room.

They don't stop, the sound of their voices getting louder and louder until I can't handle it any longer. I stand up and slam my hands on the table before me. "Listen, I think it is obvious that you all do not like me in general." I say in a voice that is not my own. A commanding tone that is harsh and cruel, and every being's nightmare.

I hear agreements, as well as Granger's growls. I ignore it all. "I am here to stay. I am here to end this war in whatever ways are needed. We can either come to an agreement tonight or we can meet on the battlefield." I shrug, knowing it might end that way, but I had hoped it wouldn't.

Granger's arms reach out around me and tug me towards him, almost as if preparing for one of the lords to strike at me. I lean into his seat as he gives me the floor.

"And you believe you can mate our king and that means we will bow to you?" Airus says with a sneer.

I scoff and shake my head slightly. "Of course, I don't want you to bow to me. I want you on your knees begging for forgiveness for what you have done to your kingdom." My voice is unlike my kind one. This voice is controlling and consuming. "I want you begging me to clean up your mess." His jaw clenches and his fists are white with rage. Calix's eyes are wide, as if just now realizing who and what I am.

Airus stands up, anger pulsing through him, his face bright red. Granger slides his legs out from under the table, preparing to stand up and fight if it comes to that. "You think you can speak to me like that?" His flesh then turns a grayish color, matching his dragon scale, before he gains control of himself and turns back red. Lightning strikes outside but I pay it no attention.

"I don't care how you think I should speak to you. Tonight, there will either be peace or death. It is up to you to decide," I say without hesitation. His face pales slightly, but Killian's does not. He is angrier than before. I don't care, so long as he understands there will be no more death after all of this is said and done.

"Let's all just calm down and talk." Granger's hands are out in front of him, looking every bit the king he is. The good thing is that I am not their queen, and I do not abide by their rules.

"I'll talk," Caspian says lightly.

Rafe nods his head before Airus chimes in, "I will listen to you, majesty." He says, directing his words to Granger.

We all sit down at the round table, eyes wandering to each other, not one of us speaking yet. Wine is brought out, possibly in hopes of making it a little easier to be around one another.

"When will your ceremony be?" Everett finally asks in a too-happy voice. I am grateful for his presence.

"Tonight," Granger answers, taking his wine and finishing it in one gulp. "More, please. This will be a long night," he grumbles out, seeming unhappy with having to be here.

"So, that's it? You are mating to a God?" Calix asks, not touching his drink.

"Yes, the Fates have gifted me with a mate who matches my strength in every way. In some ways, she even surpasses me. I will gladly take her if she will let me." My heart hammers with his words, my face blushes bright pink.

"Very well," Calix says, still seeming unsure.

"So, what is it that she will offer us that has not been offered before now?" Airus asks, his tone accusatory.

"She offers you nothing other than death if you so much as disrespect her again," Granger drawls, looking down his goblet at the lord.

I grab onto my goblet and take a sip, then another. "I will not kill you unless it comes down to that. I do not want that; I want to offer help. I want to rebuild this kingdom to its former state. Where every dragon clan can live however they wish to—"

Calix interrupts me, holding his hand up. "What if we do not wish to live like that anymore? We are not the North. We do not want to live in caves any longer." He scoffs as if the very mention of the North grosses him out.

"You do not have to. You can live however you want to, you just cannot destroy the way the North lives while you do it," I explain, which really shouldn't need explaining.

"Do you not know?" Airus asks, excitement suddenly coming from him.

"Know what?" Nerves start wafting from Granger.

"Do not act surprised. I will explain later. School your features or we will lose them." My back straightens with Granger's words in my head.

Airus smiles cruelly at me. "I guess you don't."

My brows lift. "Go on with it," I say as calmly as I can. Even though my body feels warm with anxiety.

Airus places his arms on the table. "Which secret are you begging to know?" Amusement paints his features.

I scoff and Granger's chair scrapes against the glossy floors. "I do not beg any male for anything, let alone a lowly lord. I am King Ragnar's only daughter, whom he will claim. I will destroy this realm in the blink of an eye if you continue to disrespect me." I say in a low tone.

The entire room goes deathly still; the air is almost sucked right from the room. Everett shifts uncomfortably, and Caspian's normal amused mood is now soured. I wonder if it's because of what I said. I will apologize later.

"We do not kill every God who comes to our planet," Calix says for Airus, who is seething but almost looks sickly happy. Like he is forcing it to come out, so he doesn't do anything rash. I wish he would come at me. My heart seizes in my chest. *Every God*, just now, realization strikes me in the head.

"So...what? You keep them and love them forever?" I taunt. "I guess that's lucky for me then." I wave my hands around as if to sarcastically make my point.

"Not really," Eamon mumbles so softly I wonder if he said it only to me. I lick my top teeth then grind them together. I feel as though Granger has a lot of explaining to do.

"*I will explain everything*," he hurries to assure me. I gulp before standing up.

"Your grandfather lives here. Well, not *here*, per se. Wait..." Killian holds his hand up, making a big show of this shocking news. "Is he your grandfather? Maybe he's your great-grandfather. I have no idea which one we kept and which was killed. The Fates, alas, gave us the upper hand. The problem is that the North wanted to keep the God King instead of killing them both."

I shake my head. "I see." I don't, but I don't want them to see me working through this in my head. I turn to Rafe, my chest heaving. "So, where is he then? I would like to see him." Rafe looks to his king, the male whom I no longer trust. The male who should have told me about my grandfather being held captive, and my great-grandfather being killed...

"He is alive and well," Granger speaks up. "I mentioned to you, darling, that the Fates gave us a gift. Our world is not just made up of powerful land. The very soil you stand on is the bones of Fates, the soil is magic in and of itself. Your grandfather and his father found this out. They wished to take our world from us. The magic that helps us use our power when we are not in dragon form, they wanted to take it away from us."

My eyes widen slightly before I place my mask fully on. I am not his *darling*, right now, I am angry. "Oh," I say, softly exhaling and running through every possibility.

"The dragons have only one common interest now—we all seek more power." Every lord and second nods their head. Granger gulps and continues. "The Gods wish to take it from us."

Is that why Father sent me here? Does he know about his father being alive or does he want to overtake this world instead of co-rule? The dragon shifters won't welcome Gods taking over their world. I don't understand what the goal here is...from either side. I intend to find out though. I feel sick to my belly after learning this news. Granger was going to mate with me, knowing full well he was keeping this secret from me.

"You may see him when this meeting is over; we will go," Granger says, looking directly in my eyes. I look away, flaring my nostrils. I know it is said that Gods have tempers and that that's why the Fates created dragons, in case we ever needed controlling, and we did. Dragons are supposed to be neutral; they aren't supposed to hold captives for decades. My eyes burn with the intense hate I feel right now. No, I may not know my grandfather. He *is* my family, though; he has my blood. Granger lied to me. That's what hurts, I realize.

"So, your land is created by the bone dust of the Fates? Let me come to this conclusion myself then... My grandfather and his father came here wanting what you have, which is power." I pace the table; each of the lords seems to be nervous. Their seconds aren't much better. "What does this have to do with your war?" I ask out loud, unsure where the dots connect here.

Killian chimes in, a nasty undertone to his words. "Well, you see, the North kept your dear grandfather from us for a long while. They use him, sweet, sweet Capri. If it weren't for him—"

Eamon stands up and slams his palms down on the table. "Enough." Granger growls loudly. Eamon doesn't stop, even though his king told another lord to. "We only used him because you killed our nests. You wanted us to live like fucking fae. We are *dragons*. We are the kings here. I don't wish to live like werewolves or vampires, I am better than they are." He yells.

I watch while the other lords' moods start to tumble as well. This is going nowhere. I may be upset, but this can't find the path back to war.

"Stop," I say firmly, but they do not. Rafe stands with Eamon, screaming about his clan losing half of their brothers and sisters. My mind is whirling with the fact that for years they have held a God... How? "Stop!" I say a little louder. They still do not listen to my harsh and firm tone.

"I said *STOP*!" My voice rumbles, the entire castle shakes with the intensity of it.

All eyes are on me now; they don't dare move. One or more of them whisper curses. It's then that I realize none of them *can* move. I have completely frozen their bodies. I gasp out a laugh. My father has this ability, but not for this many strong and powerful creatures. I clutch onto the power holding them all there while slowly walking around them. Eamon stands next to Rafe, his hand frozen on his shoulder. I run my hands over Everett's back. Their eyes follow me. It's eerily still. I kind of like the hum of power under my skin.

"I said to stop, you chose not to. Would anybody like a second chance?" I yank on the strand of power, just hoping it doesn't escape me. I want them to believe I am doing this with intent, and not by accident.

"Anyone?" The power I was holding Caspian under lets loose. His mouth opens and closes several times before he can come up with a coherent thought.

"How did...how did you do that?" His voice is raspy, as if he has ash in his throat.

"The power that I contain is none of your concern." I narrow my eyes on him. "Now, is that what I wanted to chat about whenever I released you? No, it is not Caspian. If you do not wish to tell me what you have done..." I shrug, barely holding onto the power holding them all frozen. "I could just go through each and every one of your minds until they turn to mush right here and now. I informed all of you...tonight will end in one of two ways." I take my time to look every one of them directly in the eyes. My silver eyes are glowing of my own volition. "Either we come to a peaceful agreement right here and now, or else I will kill every single being who dares go against me."

My voice doesn't sound like my own; I am almost scared of the Godly tone in which I am speaking. I release them now, waiting to see what they will all say. Also, unsure if I could turn their minds to mush. Even if I wanted to, I don't think I am strong enough to do that yet.

They are all gasping and choking for air. I furrow my brows. The only one of the dragons who seems more concerned for *me* over anything else is Granger. I may be upset with him, but he is still looking out for me.

"So?" I ask, making my way back to my seat. I motion for them to sit down. Calix doesn't seem to notice my gesture, so I force him to obey. His wild green eyes pierce into mine, and for a moment I feel true fear from him. His eyes scan to his mate, worry bleeding from him. I smirk at him, not showing that I feel anything other than happiness. Just as Father would do. Isn't this what a God is supposed to do? Make beings fear them? Shouldn't I feel good about this?

Everett rubs his throat softly. "You could have at least granted us oxygen," he says. His chest heaves up and down as he sucks in air. I swear my face pales. I didn't think about allowing them to breath, damn it. Horror hits my belly like a ton of bricks.

"School yourself." Granger's voice soothes me, even though I know I don't deserve his comfort.

"You could've listened to me. Instead, here we are, throwing threats around like they are sweets," I say right back to Everett, knowing in this moment I must be strong; I cannot be his friend right now. I clench my jaw shut, unsure if I can stop myself from the downhill journey I am on.

"Are you alright?" Even in his telepathic voice, he seems concerned for me.

"No. Why didn't you tell me?" Hurt floods into my system like frigid ice water. I see the moment he feels my emotions because his body goes still. I half wonder if I froze him again, but alas, I kept my power in check.

"I wanted to wait until the right time. There is so much more to this than you know. The Fates have played bigger roles with us. I want to explain all of this when I can actually speak to you."

I clear my throat, then look at the lords in question here. "Anybody care to answer me?"

To my surprise, Draven, Lord of Gosh stands. His white hair and white eyes scare me enough that I want to recoil when he walks right up to me and bends his knee. "You are my king's mate. I am tired of fighting for nothing to be changed. All my clan wants is to be able to accept those who live among us. We do not care for more land; we do not care for settling unpaid debts. We want peace as well." His voice is sturdy and low. "I will accept you as my queen, my king's mate, and my ruler." His hands are freezing, despite being a dragon. He kisses my palm, then stands up before grabbing his knife from his hip bone and cutting his hand. I don't dare reach out to stop him; I am sure he has a reason for wanting to bleed on my pretty gown.

"I, Draven, Lord of Gosh, promise my life to my king and queen. Now until the very day I pass into the next life." My mouth drops open, my eyes are wide, and concern rips through me.

After Draven, all the lords swear their loyalty—in blood—to me. I don't miss the fact that Killian and Airus are the very last to go. Their words are harsh and bitter; they hate me. I am okay with that, because they promise to stop their killing and to end this war.

"Over the next few days, we will all sit in on council meetings to decide what are the best plans of action here. Obviously, the South wants more land—"

I cut Granger off with my hand. "You want more land?" I ask the four lords. They all nod together. I raise my brow. "Well? Where? Which one of you?" My voice is bitter; I cannot fathom going to war over land.

"Not just any land. The North's land has more potent Fate soil," Draven answers my unspoken question.

"Whenever a Fate dies, their bones automatically come here?" His nod is all I need. He starts to open his mouth to explain but I cut him off. I don't need to know the details of the fate dust in the ground. "Alright, handled. Next concern?" Granger grins like he is proud of me. I am damn ready to get out of this dress and lay down in my soft bed...alone. I want the lords' blood off my skin, I want a rose petal bath, and I want my mom.

Over the next few hours, each lord goes over their wishes and demands. I tell them not everything can be fixed overnight. I will come and look at their lands to see where I can add some on. It's well into the night when the meeting is almost done. "My only request from you, lords, is that I will see my grandfather. I don't need to sit in on the council meetings. I wish to see him tomorrow." I yawn, my body feeling fatigued. Killian grins, while Everett looks like he is about to shit himself.

Caspian nods. "I will take you." His voice is low, almost as if he is unsure that I will accept him. "Callahan will sit in for me. I made my demands this evening. I wish for nothing more than the killing of our nests to halt, as well as dragonkind be the only to benefit from the Fates." Everything he asks for tonight is more than fair. Really, I tend to agree with the North. Their reasons are valid, their concerns for the nests break my heart.

I guess Killian doesn't like Caspian's request because the soil made from Fate bones...ew... helps stop the aging process for beings who are more like humans. He has been giving the soil potions to his partygoers. I didn't see a problem with it at first, but then it came to light that if other beings ingest the soil, for whatever reason, it always exacts a large price from them. If they take it for aging or illness, whenever they stop taking it, however many years later, they will age that number overnight. If they take it for an injury, they must continue to take it or else the injury will come back in full, but worse.

I almost threw up when Eamon told me about a human woman who went to the dragon shifter because she lost her arm to a siren. She stopped taking the potion after months of using it, thinking it would be alright. Her blood hadn't healed itself, the magic from the soil covered it up. The limb was rotted so badly that maggots fell from her swollen flesh. The black skin looked more like garbage than anything. The rotting had overtaken her body and killed her within a few hours. When he showed me what happened, it then brought up the question as to why Killian would continue allowing them to use it when it clearly reacted differently in humans' systems. He had been punishing those beings...giving them the soil, getting them addicted to it. Then he forced them to fuck him or do other outrageous things. If they didn't do it, then they'd die.

"I think that is more than reasonable, Caspian." I smile sweetly at him before walking away from the table. I get about ten feet before teleporting to my room.

I am done with this day. I am so tired that when my face hits the pillows, I don't even shift from my gown. I am out like a light.

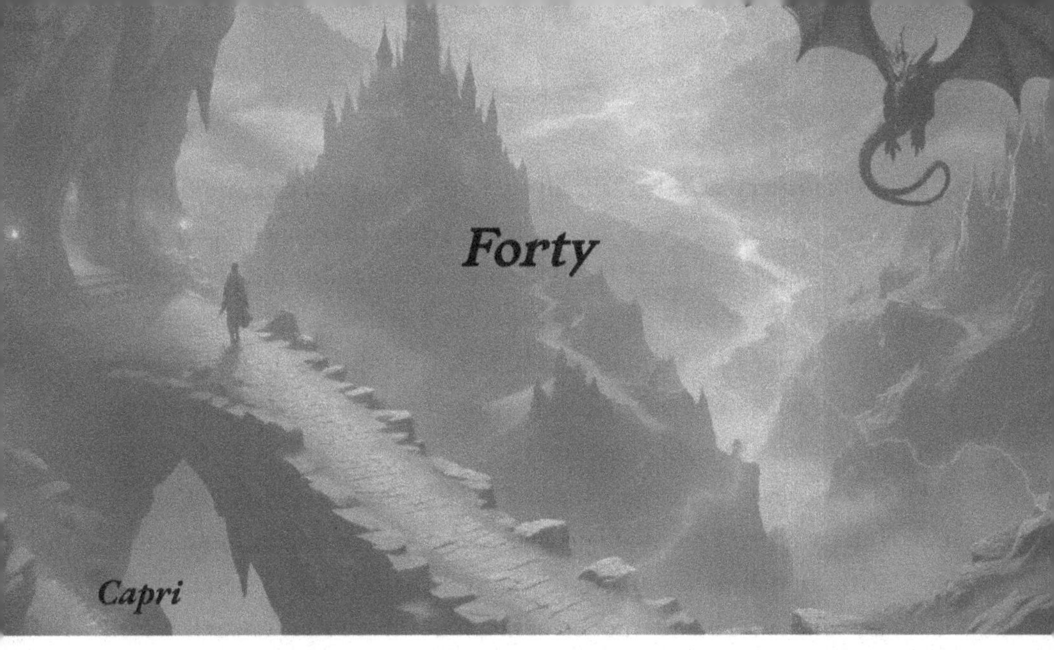

Forty

Capri

When my eyes drift open, I smell two things—breakfast and pine. I moan at the delicious scent in my nose. Then my still sluggish body shoots straight up, my feet hitting the soft plush rug. My fists are ready with fire and ice. A soft chuckle tickles my neck, before I blink at the male who has decided to invade my space.

"I am not invading, I was merely observing you sleeping," Granger mumbles.

"That is an invasion when you aren't invited to do so," I hiss out, looking for something to cover my body with.

"I have already seen it all, but I am also not looking. We leave soon and I wanted to give you some information beforehand." He runs his fingers through my hair, pushing a stray piece behind my ear. I lean into his touch, even though I am upset; the pull to go to him is so strong.

I reach for my blanket and wrap it around my body anyways. "Where is my gown?" I ask, now noticing I am naked under my blanket.

"I changed you; you had blood on your body." I bite my lip, unsure if I even wish to tackle that intrusion. Granger moves his hand slowly down my cheek; his thumb and forefinger grip my chin. "If you believe I would allow you to sleep with another male's blood on you, you are wrong." His eyes look down his nose at me, his lips slightly parted. I shake my head, not wanting his fingers on me right now, but also... needing them. I decide to ignore his possession of me for now. He finishes his chocolate muffin and plops a green leaf in his mouth.

It doesn't matter that he has "already seen" my body, I don't want him looking now. "Okay, why are *you* going? You need to be here for the council meetings. You know...for peace and all that?" I grab the plate already full of breakfast goodies. Granger leans against the wall, and watches me. His dark pants, tight shirt, and combat boots, alongside his morning stubble, make it hard to be upset with *my mate*. His knowing smirk is all the confirmation I need to know that he can hear every dirty and vile thought in my mind.

He slowly chews on his minty leaf, as I dig into the food in front of me. No meat is on my plate. "I can, and I do enjoy listening to your filthy dreams about me." His throat bobs as he swallows the minty flavor, and spits the rest of the leaf out of my window.. The very motion of his plump lips moving causes lava to hit my core. "But alas, we are busy. You and I have much to get done and we cannot start what I would like to and still make it to your grandfather." My legs clench together, the traitorous things forgetting we are mad at this male.

At the reminder of my grandfather and great-grandfather, I chomp down on my food and nod towards the chair across the room. "Why are you coming?" I ask again.

"Because I don't want my mate going alone. Your grandfather...he is powerful. The second most powerful God the Fates have created. He is upset and angry. But rest assured, there is a reason he is still here and a good reason he is alive." My brows raise. Who is the God who is more powerful?

"How do you know how powerful he is?" I tilt my head while asking.

"You heard us talk about when the Fates pass away their bodies turn to ash or dust, unless something is done to cause them to stay in form. They are then made into the soil of this world, that is if somebody or something hasn't already taken their bones." My mind whirls back to the cave where I found that Fate lying on the stone, all alone. "That is why it is so sought after by Gods. The Fates' souls still rest here; the world we live in is the most powerful one, other than the land of the Fates." His golden eyes are locked into mine in the intense way I'm used to. I don't miss the burning desire in his gaze. "There are places here where one could even speak to the souls of Fates. In exchange for things they may want, they will grant you things."

This gets my attention. "Such as?" I say.

"Beings could go and ask for longer lives, more power, for the Fates to kill their rivals. Anything really, so long as they offer something that particular Fate might want. Some of them want blood...some of them want sacrifice. It depends. Fates aren't all kind and pretty; they get bored in the afterlife. There is a reason they created Gods and dragons, vampires, and other such creatures that are monsters like us. They themselves are monsters."

Granger looks up, as if looking to see if a Fate will strike him down just for saying that. I chuckle. "Something funny?" he says, eyes darkening while looking at me.

"Yes, you are acting as if you are scared of them harming you. You are a dragon king, Granger." He makes it to me in two long strides. His warm hands grip my chin and force my eyes to his, even though they are naturally locked onto him anyways.

"I have plenty to be scared about, Capri. I killed my father because the power got into his head, he wasn't the male who had raised me. He had been the strongest king to have ever lived." Granger's eyes gloss over, as if reliving those moments. "He was killed as easily as we are standing here. I fear many things, and that is why I will live longer than him. I know I am not invincible, Capri. I know you also are not, which is why I would rather burn this fucking world down than even risk you." His chest is heaving now, as if he himself cannot believe the words he's spewing out. "That is why you will not be going to a grandfather who could kill you without even blinking. And he *will* try to. He will lie and tell you that you are family and should save him, but really, he wants out so that he can burn this world to a crisp for himself." My eyes widen slightly as I listen to the fear in his voice. Granger's chest is still heaving as hatred spews from his mouth rapidly, like he can't stop. "Your grandfather is tied up in a cave filled with Fates who are eating on his eternal soul. They wanted him, we gave him to them for something in return." Granger gulps. I can feel regret eating away at him. "Your great-grandfather died quickly, a dragon melted him whole. It was over before it began." Shame wafts from him in waves.

"That seems unlike you, Granger." Hurt flickers in his eyes at my comment.

"It wasn't me, but I will take the brunt of your anger if I need to." His eyes are downcast, and he runs his fingers through his stubble.

I grab hold of his warm and soft hands. I drop the blanket and call for combat clothes. Real ones this time, tight leather pants, a black t-shirt, and boots. "Let's just get this over with." I teleport us into the open garden where Caspian stands there waiting for us.

Caspian's brows lift slightly, but he clearly doesn't want to question his king, so he keeps his mouth shut. "Are you ready, Capri?"

I don't know if I am. I don't know what kind of state he will be in. I also have never met him. I doubt he will even know who I am. Why I am here to begin with? What will I tell him?

"He will know you. Your scent will force him to know you."

My eyes meet Granger's, his pleading for forgiveness. What he doesn't know is that he doesn't even have to plead or beg, I will gladly give it to him. Seeing him in pain causes my heart to clamp in ways I wish I didn't know.

Both males shift into their dragon forms, and I am momentarily stunned by how large Granger is. My breathing hitches and my mouth dries out. He has sharp scales on his large head, he is the color of nothing and everything. The beauty and terror of his dragon form cause me to gasp out. "Oh my—" My words stop when I look to see that the purple dragon isn't even up to the black's shoulder. "Wow," I say breathlessly. Granger's scales ripple as if he is shaking a bug off of him.

Everett comes behind me. "Are you good there?" He chuckles and my cheeks blush slightly. I recover quickly though.

"I am fine." I clear my throat and make my way to Granger. Everett stops me.

Everett's hand grabs onto my upper arm. "Caspian will still cart you around." His voice seems so small and muffled.

"Oh?" I question, but when I go to the purple dragon, Granger's dragon form roars. I stop right as my hand is about to grab onto the deep purple scales. "You want me on you?" I ask, startled because it seems as though I shouldn't ride the king. His huge head moves up and down, "I guess that's my answer." I shrug towards Everett.

"Majesty?" Everett has the biggest balls I have ever known.

"That is not fucking true, and you know it," Granger growls into my mind.

"He just questioned his king in dragon form. Yes, yes he does," I argue back, even though it is pointless. Some unspoken words go between them; Caspian seems

to be in on their conversation. I am reminded that in dragon form, the clans can speak to one another. Granger can talk to them all, but since strong mates speak telepathically, you don't have to be in the same clan. The Fates have made dragonkind complex for a reason. They have every power needed to kill a God.

Whatever is said causes Everett to back away and bow out. "Enjoy your family reunion, Capri." Everett gives me a soft smile before Caspian's purple dragon takes off into the sky.

"Thank you, Ev." I say, and Everett folds his arms over his chest as he watches me and his King. I look towards the enormous black dragon before he puffs dark smoke my way. It's the only signal that he is ready for me.

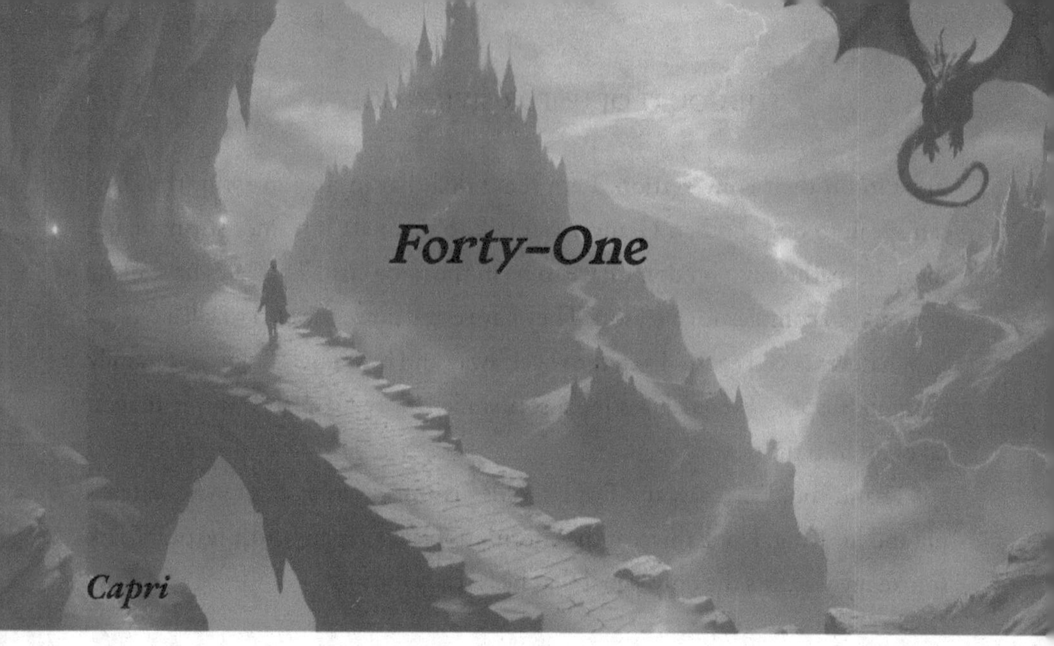

Forty-One

Capri

My legs are spread wide against Granger's neck, though not in the way they have been before. Though it's still a fun way, as we soar throughout the skies. The clouds are thick up here; the moisture hits my face and I can't help but open my arms wide and laugh. A full body laugh. I almost forget about the purple dragon trailing us closely. I look out over the green-blue sea. The beauty in it makes my lungs seize up. I haven't been out this way before; I hadn't realized there was land out this way.

"That is because no map will show it. Only dragon royalty will remember about this small speck of paradise."

For reasons unknown to me, Granger's voice comes in more clearly than normal, as if I feel more of a connection with his dragon form than his human form.

"I am never a human, mate. There is also more of a pull because you are falling for me. The love we have grows, and with that comes a stronger pull to be together. We will better communicate throughout our bonding until it is as if we are the same, body, mind and soul to one another."

The words are so clear, I would have thought I had spoken them myself.

I look out, and no longer do I only see water. Land comes into view, it doesn't seem unlike others I have been to, but the closer we get to the ground the stronger the pull is, and the more my power starts to thrum in my blood. It feels like a drug that I haven't taken yet. The feeling causes a moan to slip from my mouth.

"What is this?" I ask as we ready for landing.

"This is where most of the Fates' bones go. This isle is what every God has come looking for." There are thick clouds surrounding the land, and I realize that I don't know how we got here.

When my feet hit sand, an electric feeling courses through my body. Power comes so easily to my fingertips that I feel as though I could create worlds and break them within a second. Granger strides up next to me, his hand brushing against my own. "How do you feel?" he asks as his fingers slip into mine. I look over at him, his tanned skin glistening in the sun. He stretches his arms over his head, causing his muscles to flex in ways that do something to my insides.

"I feel like I am oozing power," I admit. "I know why my father wants this world, Granger. If this much power comes without even trying, I can't even imagine what he would be able to do." The feeling makes my stomach sour. I don't know if Father knows about this, but I sure hope he doesn't. I do not want him to be unstoppable. He doesn't need any more power than he already has.

Caspian shifts; his naked body has sand plastered to it. He starts to wipe it off with some of the water, splashing onto the powdery shoreline.

"Cover me, will ya?" Granger asks, and then yanks on my hand, pulling me into him. I don't have time to ask what he needs covering from before darts shoot out. His shadows explode the darts within a second. "Get down." His hand covers the top of my head before he is shoving me down. I duck down right as fire explodes into my vision.

"Granger!" I scream, but then remember he is fire-resistant. Caspian takes up the rear, a dagger in his hands, at the ready if we need him. He somehow had clothes here, because he is now in an almost sheer white top and tan pants. Not that it is a surprise to me. I have realized the dragonfolk of the North are simple. They do not wish for anything other than to live as they have always lived.

The heat of the fire burns my back. I realize Granger is covering my body with his. The fire scatters across his body, sweat pours from his large frame. The flames lick him in colors of purple, green, and blue. "It's almost over, just a few more feet," he says unbelievably calmly. He doesn't look at me, but I can feel how nervous he is.

"Alright." I nod my head even though I know he won't see it. After several more feet, the flames stop, the heat dissipates, and I almost feel cold without the blazing fire near my body.

"There are traps for any beings trying to get to the caves," he explains. Caspian follows right behind as Granger takes up the front, as if both males are scared I may be harmed. My heart flutters that they might just both care about what happens to me. I know Granger would, but Caspian doesn't have to just because his king is mated to me.

"*He does not wish his king to die,*" he says, even though his back is to me. I don't dare question why he thinks our bond is already strong enough that if something were to happen to me, it would hurt him too.

"*Because you fear what you will find if you question it?*" he asks again into my head.

I growl to his back, about ready to kick him the hell out of my head. His deep rumble tells me he finds me humorous.

"I do very much," he says, hushed.

"I don't find it funny. Stay out of my head," I say, even though I don't want him out completely.

Granger walks with purpose, his strides taking up what three of mine do. Caspian crouch-walks behind me. His gaze doesn't leave the tree line, as if he is waiting for an attack. "Do not leave my front." Caspian watches my gaze, like he thinks I might try to make a run for it. I wouldn't do that even if I thought I could survive this isle.

"I won't," I swear. The cave is right in front of us when a growl echoes through the trees.

"RUN!" Caspian bellows, and a huge black cat breaks out from the tree line. I don't have time to stop and help Caspian because Granger grabs my wrist and yanks me with him. He pulls me onto his back, and before I know it, the shadows have taken us right into the cave entrance. The kiss of the black smoke chills my warm skin.

My breathing is hitched and hurried. I look at Granger with betrayal in my gaze. "I can—" I start, right as Caspian is thrown into the cave. His limp body hits the gray stone walls and falls to the sandy ground. I rush over to him "Are you alright?" I try to heal him, but I feel drained.

"You cannot use power in this cave. He is also fine; the panther can only truly harm other beings." Granger explains. I don't have the energy to respond to him before Caspian sits up, sucking in air like it's his last few minutes on this planet.

A few minutes later, once Caspian's recovered, we walk in a line of three. The cave is lit only by candles that must have some magical essence to them because they don't even flicker. The cave is long and damp. The longer we go underground, the more I feel the power that had been leaking from my pores, leaving my body wanting. I don't know what it wants, but I feel as though I need to feed it something.

"Almost there, Princess," Granger grumbles softly beside me. Caspian stiffens when we come to an entrance that makes me want to turn around. I can't walk without the two of them pulling me forward. I don't like this cave, I decide; it must not like me either because I feel it trying to push me out. *Well, buddy, the feeling is mutual.*

"It's the cave's way of keeping your kind out of here," Caspian explains as he tries to drag me over the threshold.

After getting through the thick threshold, the push to expel me doesn't feel as heavy anymore. Instead of the cave wanting to push me out, I am face-to-face with the family member we all thought had been dead.

My grandfather's eyes bulge out for one second. That is all he gives himself to act surprised, then a mask of indifference is plastered on his still young-looking face. If I am being honest, he doesn't look more than thirty; he looks just as my father does. His handsome, chiseled face appears as mine does. We look alike, including his bright silver eyes.

"Hello, Capri." I shouldn't be shocked he knows my name, but I am.

"Hi." I don't ask how he knows my name, nor do I ask anything else. I do not want to.

My grandfather's silver eyes scan my body in a way that makes me uneasy, then he looks right at Granger. "So, you mated my granddaughter?" It is a question but seems like a statement, which Granger doesn't respond to because the God keeps on talking. "I am assuming my son does not know I am alive and that is why she is here, to take over this Kingdom for him to enact his revenge on this Godforsaken Realm." He all but spits the words out with venom.

"I guess you haven't had a good stay here then?" I tease, trying to lighten the mood. I can tell he loathes being here, his face looks pained. His eyes go straight to me. "Of course I loathe being here. Don't be daft. He may have been mated to you, but you are not his. He is the king of the dragons. Fate is cruel to us Gods, girl." His eyes rapidly go between me and Granger. "I wonder what price he paid to get you. That is why—" He hisses out in pain, and I realize that shadows have overtaken him. I look at Granger and he doesn't even seem fazed by the amount of power it must take for him to harm a God in this cave. "The King of Dragons does not love you," he grits out through his teeth, spit flying from between them.

"Do not insult my mate by calling her a girl. She is more of a ruler than your piece of shit son will ever be," Granger growls to my grandfather. The order doesn't make it's point though, because this God sitting in front of me only feels rage towards the dragon king.

"I want a moment alone with her," my grandfather states plainly,

"No," Granger says instantly. Shadows twine restlessly around his fingers, and the sight of it causes my body to want his. His protective dragon nature calls to some small part of me that has wanted to be a girl who needed help, and got it since I was a child. The problem? I have never been a damsel in distress, and I was never a child. I do not wish to be saved any more than I want Granger to be harmed in order to make me safe.

"I will speak with him; he is family after all." My eyes don't dare look into Granger's golden ones.

"Are you certain?" Caspian asks, and I realize it's because Granger has already walked out. I hadn't even heard his swift footsteps. I nod once, then make my way into the cavern that houses my grandfather.

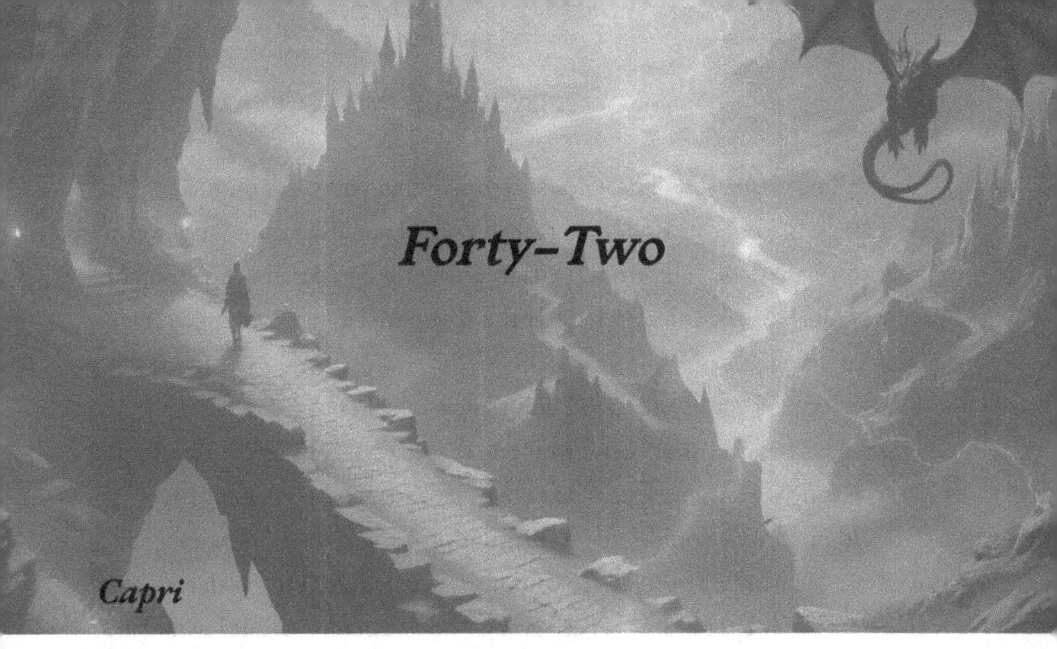

Forty-Two

Capri

"**M**y name is—"

I raise my hand to halt him. I sit crisscross about ten feet away from the God who looks like me but isn't remotely close to me. His curt nod tells me he knows what kind of meeting this will be.

"I don't need to know your name," I say. "I am not your family. I belong to no name, I have no family other than my mother." I state plainly.

His silver eyes scan me, and I notice that even though they are the same color, our eyes are nothing alike. His are ruthless, emotionless, and any thoughts about him being family are thrown from the door when he says, "So, your mother was a whore then? You are not a full God, but something else. I cannot put my finger on it. My powers have been sucked from my very being by these leeches, so..." He shrugs as if I understand him.

I scoff. "I understand you have been held captive since you came here. What do they want from you?" I ignore the fact that he asked me a question about my mom. If you call her a whore, you do not get answers from me.

"I have been here since that bastard betrayed me. He informed me that I would be welcomed, probably like you had been told then my father was skinned and melted alive. I was then brought here. The Fates took it from there. They create us to feed themselves in their afterlife."

My first thoughts are...well...*ew*. Then, "You're lying." I stand to leave but a sudden thickness in power makes me halt right in my tracks.

"You will not leave yet." His voice is commanding and thick with coercion. Sweat licks his brow; he must be extremely powerful because I cannot call to any of my power right now. "I have not used any power for decades, for this moment. I have saved it all up, or at least whatever the fates have let me build up. You will stay and listen to me."

"I won't leave," I agree, although I don't know why I do.

"I do not lie. I may mislead, but I won't do that to you." His lips purse, almost as if he is kissing something. I scoff because he truly thinks he's helping me?

"I would hope you wouldn't lie to me, I'm probably...what?" I pause giving extra effect. "The only person to see you in a few decades?" His harsh cold eyes give me all the answer I need. So, I keep going. "I don't need you, but I would like to speak to you, if you would like?" The silence is all I need to keep on. "Why are you here?" My voice echoes throughout the caves.

"I was sent here. I was told by the Fates that I needed to conquer this world. That us Gods were needed to take over, after the war between the dragons and the gods, I had thought the fates sided with us. It was a lie. They had seen me being captured before it had happened. They wanted to eat off me. My powers were far too great for them to allow me freedom." He shakes his head, and I can tell his words are true. "Why are *you* here?" His voice betrays none of his thoughts. I pace a few feet, then lock my eyes right onto his.

"I was sent here as well," I answer honestly. "Your son did it."

His eyes finally flash with some emotion. "He did, did he?" A moment of silence stretches between us. "Is he doing what he needs to in order to get me out of this mess?"

I swallow the hurt I feel, there is no reason I should feel it. "He sent me here, didn't he? I would figure he has some type of plan." My grandfather studies me for several long moments before he nods simply.

"So, what is your mission then? Kill the dragon shifters? I can feel your powers, I know you are strong. We can feed them to the Fates, and they will re—"

I make him stop talking with my power, hatred pours from him. And me...The strength it takes to make him stop feels like a pressure I have never felt. Like the cave is punishing me for trying to overpower it. I try to keep holding on but I feel it slipping.

"No, I will do no such thing."

His teeth grind together. "But you said—" he hisses out.

I smile, and I know he sees the moment of our miscommunication. "I did not say *I* was here to save you. You asked what my mission had been. I do not answer to my father. I will do what he thinks needs to be done, yes. But my mother and my mate are now my home. My father means nothing to me. I guess you could say the *whore,* as you called her, taught me well to detach myself from those who don't add value to my life." I hiss the last words out.

"I see it now." His voice is soft, almost as if he is accepting I am not here to save him. I don't know why he would insult somebody he thinks will help him.

"See what?" I ask, even though I am done with this conversation.

"What you *really* are." He says in a warning tone.

"And what is that?" A cruel smile kisses my face, as my icy tone betrays nothing.

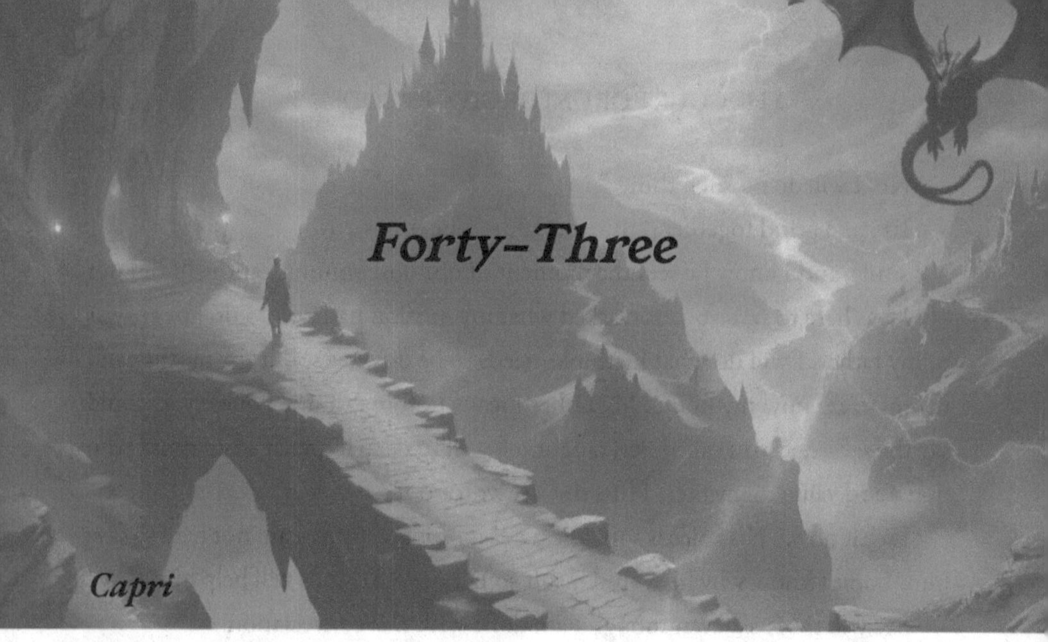

Forty-Three

Capri

Granger and Caspian wait for me outside the cave, my mind reeling, my heart in pieces, but I pick it up and continue this journey that needs to end with bloodshed. Just not my family's. Bloodlust coats my tongue, and I swallow it whole.

"What lies did the snake tell you?" Caspian asks. Granger is quiet.

"He wanted to know what the plan was to release him from this hell." We walk through the thick woods. There is no sign of the black panther.

"And what did you say?" Caspian chuckles, as if knowing I won't betray dragonkind. And I won't, which is exactly what I told *him*.

"I informed him where my allegiances lie." The questions stop when we get to the sand.

Caspian shifts into his purple form, Granger waits a moment longer. "I know that must have been hard for you." He rubs his thumb over my chin for a moment.

"Did you hear it all?" I don't mind if he did. He nods his head slightly. I lift on my tiptoes and press my lips onto his.

"Even if your voices weren't echoing throughout the cave system, I could hear it through our bond if I had tried to," he explains.

"I hadn't realized our bond could be so strong..." I think out loud.

"I don't think we know the first thing about our bond yet, Capri," he answers right away. I nod absentmindedly.

"I guess that means you also know what I am? What he said he could sense in me?" I don't dare say it out loud yet. The shock of it almost made me collapse, and if I hadn't been with him, I would have.

"I do. I thought I knew when I first met you, but he confirmed it for me." He gives me a quick but passionate kiss before shifting into his large, black dragon form.

The air feels warmer, as if we should hope for a future in which my father does what he said he would. He will give me this world and I will rule it with Granger, my mother along for the ride. Things feel hopeful on the journey through the thick clouds that thin out the further away we get from the isle. I feel as though I can accept the things that were discussed. The way the Gods were made into pawns to do the Fates' bidding... I can only guess that one too many Gods argued with a Fate and that's why dragons were created. Gods are not the kind to bow down, even to our creators. It seems to me like the Fates are the ones who need to be taken care of. But those thoughts will probably haunt me until my very last breath. I don't think anybody has truly killed a Fate.

"They are not killed in a way that we are, Princess. They want to die when they do. Either from being bored of old age or their partner chooses to move into their afterlife."

I absentmindedly rub a small circle on Granger's black scales. I want to comfort him even when he doesn't ask for it. Maybe I am the one who wants comfort *from* him. I don't know, I just know that touching him makes me feel better. I know that I am strong, and yet, I crave Granger to just pull me into his arms and hold me.

When we land, we don't go to Killian's. No, I realize we are at my palace. "Why didn't we go back to Drakon?" I notice Caspian isn't here, but before I can ask Granger about it, he answers my questions.

"We are here because I would like to spend time with you before our mating ceremony. It will be at my palace in five days. I think we should spend some time together, don't you?" The way he walks, even naked, is so sure and commanding, my breath hitches.

"I think that sounds wonderful, but do we have time for that? Shouldn't we be making decisions with them about the peace of your kingdom?"

Granger runs his fingers through my hair; I lean into his embrace. "We only have the time that we give ourselves, Capri. If we don't make time, we will never have it. You are my mate. I will not pick anything over you. Ever. My world starts and ends with you from now on. Nothing will come ahead of you...that includes my kingdom." He gets down on one knee, kissing my knuckles. The waves hit the rocky shoreline, a sweet smell blows into my face from my garden and suddenly it feels like everything is in place in my life.

"You haunt every part every part of my mind, my dreams, and my nightmares." His radiant eyes look right into mine, as I look down into his very soul. "I can't close my eyes without seeing you. I am finding I look forward to seeing every version of you that you allow me to see." My heart hammers so hard it might break through my ribcage.

"Please," he begs me. I don't know for what though. I fall down to my knees with him.

"Please, what?" My eyes look desperate to hear the next words.

"Be my wife, my mate, my everything, Capri. Give me your all, and I will give everything I have to you in return." He pulls out a necklace with a blood-red crystal. "Give your soul to me, and mine will be yours to do with whatever you please." My body feels possessed, my hands move of their own accord as they dive into his hair and draw him towards me. Our foreheads are pressed against one another, our knees tangled up in a web of us.

"Yes," I nod simply before he closes his eyes, his forehead still against mine. "Always," I whisper to him, as tears start streaming down his face.

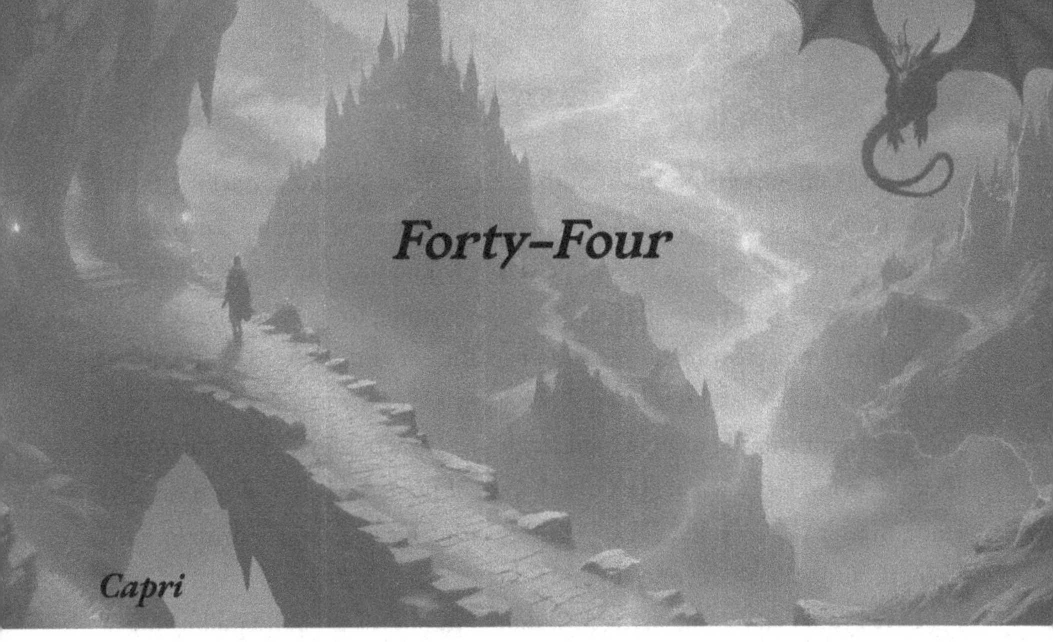

Forty-Four

Capri

After days of lounging and being completely and utterly useless, Granger and I decided to leave the bedroom. Against my wishes, of course, but he wanted to show me little bits of his world. I do want to explore, although I have no idea how we ended up here.

"Are you supposed to just like lying in the sand?" I ask for the fourth time.

"Yes. It is nice to just watch the water and see what swims by," Granger answers while lying behind me. He runs his hands through my hair. When his fingernails softly scratch a spot on my head, I lean further into him. Before I know it, I am straddling him, my hands on either side of his head.

"Are you not sated enough after the last few days?" He chuckles, his hard length bulging into me. I lean down and press quick, hot kisses to his neck.

"I don't feel like I will ever be completely sated when it comes to you." In all honestly, he consumes me. Every part of him eats away at my soul. These days together have caused an undeniable connection to form between us. Whatever the Fates wanted from us, I would gladly give it to them. I just need to remain as we are right now, in these moments.

"You are going to wreck me, aren't you, Little Goddess?" Granger grumbles out from under me, reminding me of another night entirely. He smirks down at me, as if remembering too.

"Only in the best ways possible, Dragon King." The waves come up to his toes but that doesn't stop him from reaching up and taking my top from my body. The waves take it with them.

He drags my nipple into his mouth, which causes a loud, animalistic moan to escape my throat. "So eager for me, huh?" He teases against my bare chest. I don't say anything, because I don't need to. He knows me already. He knows I need him more than I should. Our bond has nothing to do with that. I didn't have much family growing up and didn't get the amount of affection, attention, and care that a being who is loved should, outside of my mother. I didn't even know differently until I found Granger. He gives love to me freely and often. He is exactly what I was lacking but didn't know I needed. He has shown me that emotion isn't weakness like I had believed before. Having somebody to love is a strength, and valuable beyond anything else.

"I need you. I crave you, Granger." I don't know if it's the bond pulling me to need him more. I feel it, nonetheless.

My hands fumble for his pants; they are made of a soft fabric that slides from his hips easily enough as he lifts them for me. "I am yours, Capri. Just as you are mine." His eyes lay claim to me. They burn right into my very soul. I don't know if I can even remember a time before me and him. Which is crazy, because we have known each other for mere weeks, maybe a month.

"I haven't said this to you directly, Capri," Granger says, his chest moving so fast I think for a moment he may be nervous. "I think this is obvious, but I want to tell before we stand in front of all dragonkind. I love you." He declares. My heart seizes for a moment, so much so that I don't even notice him taking my pants off.

I gasp out as he pushes inside of me with ease. "I love you, Dragon King." I don't dare say *too*. I don't want my declaration to mean less than his. I need him to know that he is my world and everything inside of it.

"Is that so?" he whispers as his fingers graze my hip bones. It sends goose bumps to prickle on my skin.

"Yes," I moan out as he pushes inside of me more. My bead of pleasure scrapes against the firm skin below his navel. I press my palms against the hard planes of his chest, riding out every bit of pleasure he will give me.

"I will give you anything." His answer to my thoughts comes immediately. "I am in trouble, Princess." He leans up kissing the corner of my lips.

"What kind?" I ask against his lips, before drawing his lower lip into my mouth. He reaches his hand behind my head and pulls me flush against his body. His brutal pace gets quicker the closer we both get to bliss.

"The kind in which I would give up my kingdom if you only wished it so." He says rapidly, almost as if it is a promise. The loud sounds of our bodies almost drown out my words back to him.

"Then you may be in trouble, but I am right there with you." Right as the words leave my mouth, bliss hits me so hard I see spots. The sun beats down on us as my head lolls backwards from pure happiness. He sucks my neck into his mouth as his warm spurts of bliss hit him in waves as big as mine.

After several long moments of being together, still intertwined, we finally decide to take a dip. "Are you nervous, God?" Granger taunts me as my toes barely touch the warm, greenish-blue waters.

"No, I just don't know what's in there," I answer, although...I *am* nervous. Every other body of water on this planet has tried to kill me. My feet sink into the wet sand, almost up to my ankles.

"The water has not tried to kill you, the beings inside of it have." He tries to argue back.

I groan. "Same thing. There are still beings in here, aren't there?" I raise a brow right as he comes to offer me his hand. I don't take it.

Instead, I put my hands together around his neck and allow him to carry us waist-deep into the warm waters. "What all lives in your sea?" I ask while looking out, trying to see into the crystal-clear waters. I can see all the way to the white sand at the bottom. That doesn't help much though; perception isn't always correct. The water could be fifty feet, but looks as if it were only five.

"Merfolk live here, fish, mostly normal sea creatures. Maybe a siren going for a dip."

I wave my hands. "Exactly. They have tried to kill me." I lay my head down into the crook of his neck. My ankles crossed behind his lower back.

"They won't harm you when you are with their king," he declares.

"You don't sound too happy about that." I notice his body seems tense.

"I am not; you shouldn't be in any danger at all. Not just when you are with me, you should be safe everywhere. I also do not believe they belong here with us." Before he gives me any warning at all, he dunks us under the waters.

I dig my fingers into his tanned skin, so hard it must cut him. He stands up and grabs his neck, while still holding my body to his with the other hand. My ankles are crossed behind his back still, as if I were a baby moogroove. A monkey I have found that I enjoy more than any other creature I have come across. "Ouch," he says, rubbing his neck.

"You dunked me under with no warning!" I splash at him and he chuckles.

"You looked far too hot, Princess. I needed to cool you off," he says smoothly.

"Explain," I huff out; the sun seems to be baking us.

"Well, your looks are just—" I splash him again. "Again with the water?" He laughs, while wiping his face clean.

"Yes, tell me why you aren't happy about them being here." His body stiffens slightly before pressing a kiss to my cheek.

"They don't belong here, in Beithir with us. They are getting caught in the crossfire of a war they didn't start, nor do they want." His throat bobs. "Fae belong in their own lands, they don't thrive here. Sirens and Merefolk need more water than we have. Werewolves and Vampires need to be separated." Now that he has started, it doesn't seem as if he can stop talking. Like, he might have given this a lot more thought. "The Fae have been misused more than any other creatures here. They have a kingdom that is powerful for them. They could live a happy and healthy life." I listen to his words, not wanting to add anything to his emotions. "Vampires struggle to find food, and werewolves belong with packs. There are far too many beings here for our small land. The dragons were meant to live with dragons, the Fates said so." He declares rapidly. I decide it's time to speak.

"They said so?" I question.

"They did. The Fates have spoken to us many times with offerings we have given." My mind immediately goes to the beings they had to sacrifice in order to get answers. "The Fates aren't all bad, they are just as we are. Only, they have all power."

I nod in understanding at his assurance. "Okay," I say softly.

"The Fates created Gods first; they gave Gods different powers. Some water powers, maybe time control, mind altering. The list of God power is endless really. Some Gods even had Fate power where they could create things, but only in scale. Things they have had before, like you've done with your palace." My fingers move into his hair, running through the wet locks. It's cut closer to his head on the sides and longer on top.

"At one point, there was a God as powerful as the Fates. A certain Fate had poured too much power into him, he procreated, and then made even more powerful Gods. Originally, the Gods were supposed to be the enforcers for the Fates. To keep the other beings in their own realms in check." My fingers still.

"Then, one day, a God got out of hand and started taking beings for playthings. That's when dragonkind was created." The way he speaks about it is almost like he might have been there.

"I *wasn't* there, but the Fates showed me. No sacrifice needed for this information. Any dragon king will be given knowledge they need in order to rule their kingdom. I have access to all the memories of the past kings. There was a war between our kinds, a harsh and brutal war."

"That's why they hate us?" I ask.

"Somewhat. Dragons can kill Gods even though the Gods act as if they can do and say anything. It's petty really, but when Gods started showing up here because of the magical pull, dragons grew tired of the arrogance." I understand that more than anybody could know. I have lived with Gods almost my entire life, and they are not fun to be around.

"Anywho, I just think the beings who live here deserve their own realm, their own sort of freedom. Outside of dragon wars. They shouldn't be victim to our games we play with the Gods and the Fates."

I listen more about his take on the Fates and about the different ones he has spoken to. I love listening to him speak about his world and his life. One would never believe he is the king of this place. He seems so down-to-Beithir.

We spend the day swimming around, wandering the beach and the forest around it.

"It's about time to head back," he says from behind me.

"To where?" I ask, unsure where he wants to go with only days left until our mating ceremony.

"Home."

I grin at him. I know exactly where he wants to go.

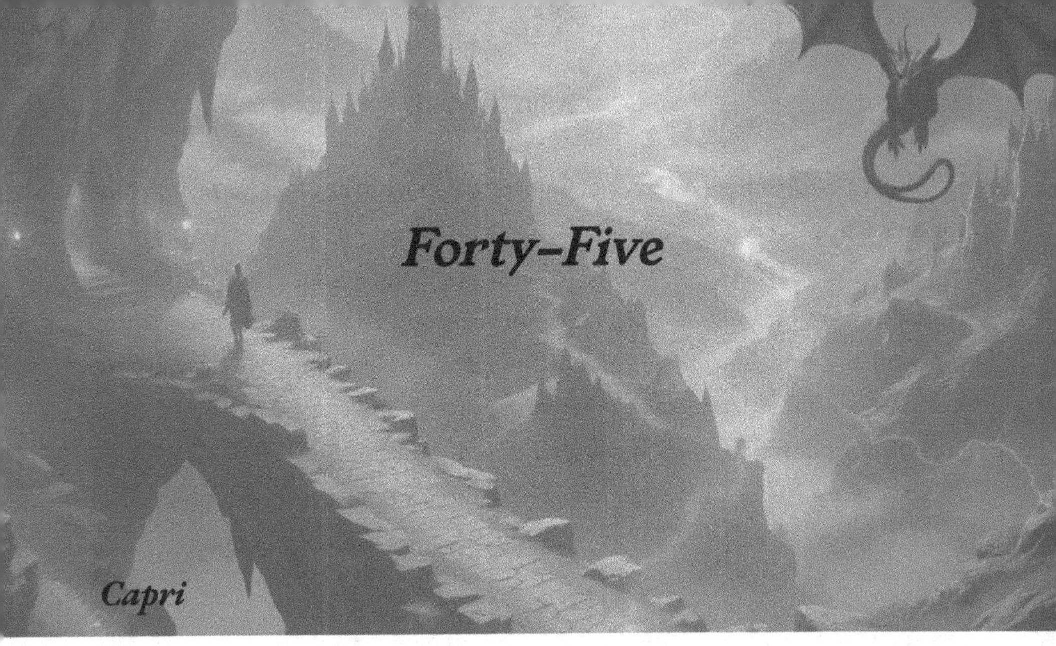

Forty-Five

Capri

My eyes open of their own accord, and not for the first time. Something doesn't feel right, but I don't know what it is. I know it can't be nerves for our ceremony; it isn't for another two days' time. Granger postponed the ceremony, giving us another few days to rest and just get to know one another. The lords weren't too happy about it, but Granger is their king. They will listen to what he says. Surprisingly enough, Draven was the most supportive of us staying. Caspian said the meetings were going as well as they could be.

Most of these dragon lords haven't been in the same room in decades, let alone participating in a discussion to create peace. So far, only a few fights have broken out, and they were quickly snuffed out. Everett has been a good source for gossip. According to him, Calix and Amelie have been fighting because of him vowing to protect me. I had a good ole laugh when Granger told me that little bit in the tub earlier.

A bang sounds from several steps down, and I am immediately up and on my feet. "Granger?" I notice his spot in our bed is empty. I run my hand over it and it's cold. "Granger?" I yell a little louder, knowing it must be him down there. "Where are you?" I hear clattering again, then muffled voices. I rush to the steps in only Granger's white T-shirt. "Hello?" I call out, panic bubbling in my belly, before I make it halfway down and am faced with two problems.

The first being that somebody, outside of my staff, has found their way onto my isle. The second is that they have Granger in their grasp and he is unconscious.

"What are you doing?!" I scream, my eyes widen with fear. Not for myself, but for my mate.

I am so baffled that I don't notice what's happening until it's too late. The air is sucked from my lungs so fast that I must pass out. Right before my eyes shut for good, the only thing in my vision is Granger, but I hear somebody whisper in my ear, "You should have known better than to try and change our world. You are nothing but filth, and trash will always be disposed of properly."

The darkest feeling I have ever felt sweeps into my body. Uncontrollable panic and fear ice over my body. Granger is in trouble, and I cannot help him.

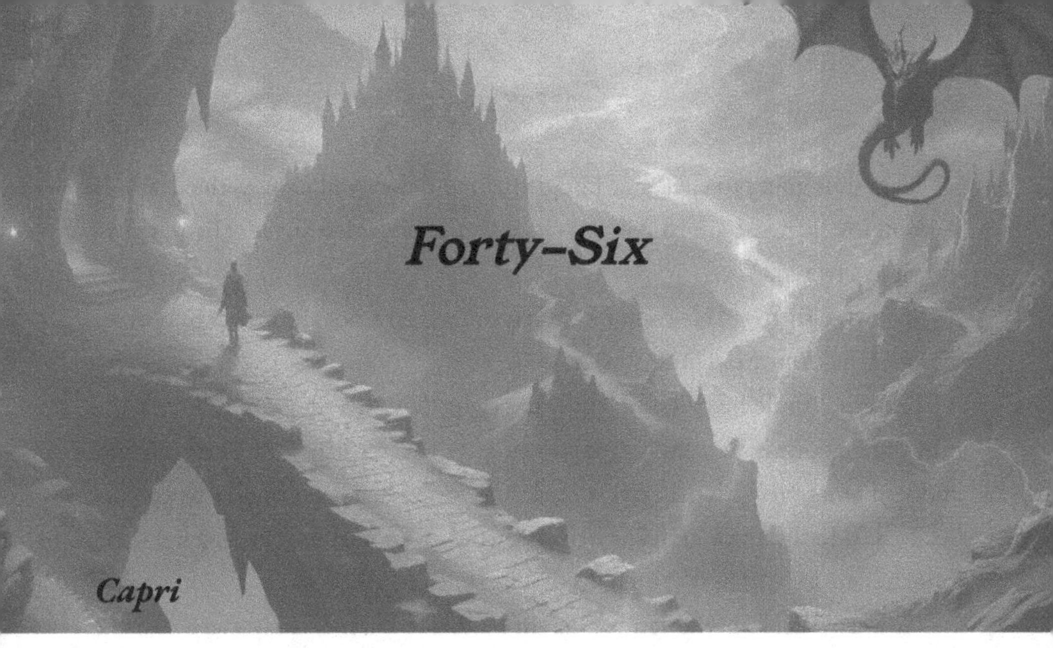

Forty-Six

When my eyes open, I'm greeted with a light so bright it can only be from a white dragon.

"Ah," I hiss out before trying to cover my eyes, but I am unable to. A harsh rope cuts into my flesh before the light subsides and I am faced with a huge problem. I am tied up and alone in a cave with whoever has taken me, and the last thing I remember seeing is Granger unconscious. I try to pull on my ropes and am unable to. A low chuckle sounds from deeper inside the cave.

When I look to see who it came from, I'm faced with who has brought me here.

"Asher... Is Eamon in on this then?" I ask the white dragon hoarsely.

"Who do you think sent me and my clan to get you?" He tilts his head in a serpentine way.

"So, where is he then?" I ask, unsure if I truly want to know.

"Where do you think he is?" I try to call to any of my magic and can't. My body is drained, my power is non-existent. I need to focus to try and build something up so I can save myself and Granger.

"Enough with the questions, just answer me," I snap, feeling uneasy. My heart feels panicked, what could be happening?

"I don't have to do anything, little God. After this night, you will be dead and Beithir will have a king who isn't afraid to kill those who need to be killed." He punches my stomach hard, and I gasp out. Not because it hurt—really, his punch was weak—but because that means they plan to kill Granger.

"Who?" I breath out.

"Eamon is going to challenge him tonight and they will fight to the death. If Eamon loses, then I am to kill you since you're powerless here." His lips turn down in a frown.

My brows furrow. "He couldn't even beat me...how does he expect to beat his king?" I shake my head in confusion.

The cruel smile he gives me chills me right down to the bone. "That's the fun thing about mates. Even though you guys haven't had your ceremony yet, it doesn't matter. With the extra special time you've had, your bond is as good as secured." He cracks his knuckles before hitting my eyes with a blinding light. He punches me so hard in the forehead that he splits my eyebrow.

"You can't kill him, though you might be able to kill me," I say sharper than I should, given my circumstances. "You cannot kill him, Asher. He is far too strong. Don't do this." I warn with panic in my tone. Then, as if my words mean nothing to him, the light intensifies only to give him enough cover to punch me in the nose, again and again. Bright-red blood sprays everywhere right as he kicks my side. I grunt but can do nothing as he hammers into my body with everything he has to give.

"The good thing is, he will wake up as dazed and confused as you were. Then..." He grabs my face, yanking my attention back to him. I growl at him, but he just laughs. He drops his hand, my blood all over his fist.

"You are signing your death stone," I declare right as his boot connects with my ribs, over and over, as if I hadn't just threatened his life.

"Then, *Capri*, he will realize you are in danger and be so distraught he won't know that many lords are trying to kill him." His smirk causes fire to boil in my bloodstream, but when I call to it, nothing comes.

"Just answer me this—why can't I use my magic?"

He stops his assault for just a moment. "Because this cave stops your kind from using magic." His eyes narrow on me. I don't dare show him how much pain I am in. "This cave is different from the one your grandfather is in. This one is stronger." He smirks. My blood is speckled across his face, and he slowly licks the blood from his lips. I cringe at the way he seems to enjoy my blood on his tongue.

"That shouldn't be possible," I snap. It's an abomination to take away a beings power, these caves shouldn't exist.

"It is possible though. Granger may have shown you your grandfather, but he didn't tell you everything. Why would he? He is the King of Beithir, you are God filth." My face blanches of all color. Dread drains me completely. "We have learned enough about your kind, Fates, maybe we keep you alive after Granger's death and test on you." I clench my jaw so hard, I swear my teeth shatter under the pressure.

"You will not kill him," I swear again, a vein bulging in my throat.

"Maybe not, but one of you will not make it to morning."

Fury bubbles over in me. "Oh, yeah?" I challenge.

"Yeah."

My face turns to one of anger. "The problem for you, Ash, is I wasn't raised as anything other than a fae. And I learned how to fight...*as a fae*," I drawl out right as my rope snaps and I get to my knees. His eyes widen slightly.

"You still don't have powers," he grounds out, backing away from me.

"I didn't grow up with the power of a God, I grew up with nothing. I had so much fear that I would be found out, I never used my powers. I grew these powers later into what they are now, they didn't make me powerful." I pound my fist on my heart.

"This is what made me strong... I fought then to protect my mother, now I will fight for my *mate*," I swear, right before I throw sand into his eyes, keeping him from being able to attack me with his light magic.

"Ah!" He bellows loudly.

I elbow him in the side of his temple, knocking him out before I rush out of this hell of a cave. My powers don't come back, but I have been here before. I have had missions just like this. I can survive; for Granger, I will. "I'm coming." I say, hoping he can hear me and will fight until I get to him.

My feet hit solid ground, my fists pumping so hard and fast I swear I have the speed of a vampire. I wish I really did right about now. I hear Asher roar, and I just hope I can make it to the beach and get my power back so I can teleport right where I need to be.

I just hope I can make it there without looking at a map. I am only in a shirt, and I don't have the pants with the map in the pocket. I don't dare slow down when I hear branches break and feet pound behind me. I run harder and faster than I ever have; faster even than the times when I stole bread from the market vendors so Mother and I would have another meal. It's in my blood. I can do this.

Forty-Seven

Whe my eyes open, I can't figure out how I got here. The only thing I know for sure is that she isn't here with me. I don't know where Capri is, but I cannot feel her within our bond. The feeling of her absence causes fury to build up so strong it might break me.

Before I can even think, flames scorch my skin. It's dawn; the sun is coming up and I vaguely hear shouts of fury. When I look up, finally clearing the fog from my head, I see what is happening. All seven lords have gathered around, and Eamon stands right in the middle of a dirt circle. The seconds are all here, except one in particular.

"*I will kill you, you know,*" I growl into Eamon's small mind.

"We will see about that, Rhodes," he calls from the twenty or so feet he is away from me. "I have told the Fates about my plans. They didn't answer, so I decided to take fate into my own hands." He stalks towards me. I grab at my side, feeling sore. "I called the lords together to challenge you. You are a weak excuse for a king, and I believe I can do better."

I scoff, standing up to my full height. I am bigger, stronger, and more powerful than he is. "You could try. I doubt any of them would follow you." My feet start to shuffle, the dirt is soft. I look at Caspian, my brother from another life.

"*Please,*" I beg him, hoping he will understand what I need. The only thing in this moment.

"*Already done.*" His throat bobs. "*I don't like it though. You need us.*" I give him a curt nod before Everett leaves.

The green dragon takes to the sky. Eamon's eyes follow him for half a second before focusing on me. "You won't find her," he claims.

"Maybe not, but he will," I say before we begin circling one another.

"She isn't worth it," he hisses in disgust.

"Even if she weren't my mate, she would be worth it. She has changed me in ways I can't even begin to describe. She will change our world, our kingdom, and all others. I have seen it."

His face blanches of color. "Not if she is dead she won't."

I growl, a low rumbling sound from the depths of my chest. "She will not die today. She will not die tomorrow," I declare, because I know. Deep inside of me, I know she will make it. She must.

Right as I have those feelings, something burns deep inside of my skull. Only it's not *my* skull hurting, it's *hers*. The piercing pain almost shatters me, but I circle the prey in front of me.

"You feel it, huh?" He taunts me as his clumsy feet move slowly. Unlike him, I prowl. I watch his movements carefully, the years of being alone in my palace taught me patience. Something most, if not all other dragons struggle to find.

"I do," I confirm. There is not a reason to deny our bond.

"Well, it looks as if you and her will not be able to finish your bond. How sad, truly." He tries to blind me with his light magic.

"I suggest you go by dragon law, or else he will suffocate you with his shadows within a minute," Draven says as calmly as is appropriate for the situation. Eamon grinds his jaw.

"He knows that with magic our king defeats him every time," Killian adds in for good measure.

Calix didn't bring his mate, which shocks me but also gets me wondering if they might have planned this.

"So, one thing you all agree on is that you want my spot?" I taunt. Rafe stiffens, Airus clears his throat.

"I don't want your spot," Caspian says firmly.

"Me either. I swore my loyalty, and I meant that shit," Airus says swiftly. Rafe nods his head, I look into the group.

"So...what? After Eamon dies, you're next?" I ask Killian.

"I will challenge you, yes," He confirms.

"Good to know your blood is on the menu." I respond. Killian shows no signs of being scared. "What about you?" I ask the only other lord who hasn't said if he is going to follow me or not.

"Enough!" Eamon charges at me; his balance is shit but right as he comes at me pain laces my side. I grunt before taking a solid hit to the face.

"One thing about mates is that even without officially bonding you to her—" He pauses as he throws another punch, but I evade it. He strikes out again and I block it with my forearms. I shove him back.

"What about mates?" I ask through my teeth. His feet drag in the dirt as I shove and shove.

"Anything done to you, she feels...and vice versa," he grits out. He ducks down and tries to charge at my midsection, but I am too strong for him to take down.

"Luckily, nothing will happen to me," I say, while trying to unlatch him from my torso.

"I never said we'd focus our efforts on you..." He threatens. At that same moment, pain laces through my entire body as if I am being electrocuted, though I stand unharmed. I grunt yet again, unsure what is happening to her. Eamon strikes again and again, blow after blow, and I dodge every single one. Pain ricochets throughout my body in waves, all coming from Capri.

Finally, I have had enough of this. My hands grab his head from my midsection and twist his neck so hard the crack echoes throughout the empty field. The sun is fully risen now, and when I stand up, stepping away from his limp body, I look into the eyes of the next lord to challenge me.

"I hope you said goodbye to your boy, Killian. You will not live to see tomorrow," I threaten, hoping he will bow out.

"I didn't need to. Unlike Eamon, I have been training for this moment since your father died." He says plainly.

I growl, showing all my teeth. "Step up then." I raise my voice. "Show your king what you have been planning!"

When Killian steps into the circle, the air changes. It intensifies to another level. He looks back to his second-in-command, a dragon I don't often see. He keeps to himself and his small family mostly. "Solomon, you know what to do." The second nods sharply before stepping forward.

"I will challenge you on behalf of my lord." The large male steps forward. I am big, but Solomon is bigger. His muscles are bigger, and he is taller than me. The scars on his body show the hours of countless training he has done. Little does he know, I may not have scars, but I have trained nonstop for decades.

"I accept his challenge." I step forward, meeting him.

Even during battle, my mind whirls to Capri. I need to know she is safe from whatever Asher is doing to her. I am fully aware she is strong. I know she is brave enough to make it, even if I don't.

"Solomon." I nod my head in respect, he does the same.

"I am sorry, Majesty. Things were too bad for far too long." He truly looks saddened. I am unsure if it is because of me, or the fear he might lose and leave his family without him.

I swallow, knowing he isn't wrong. "I agree." I move to kill yet another male I do not want to.

My eyes meet Killian's. "Where is my mate?" I ask in such a threatening tone that Solomon pales. My voice cracks slightly, sharp pain hitting right in my nose. A small trickle of blood starts pouring from my face.

"Apparently, exactly where we intended for her to be." He smirks right as his second charges at me.

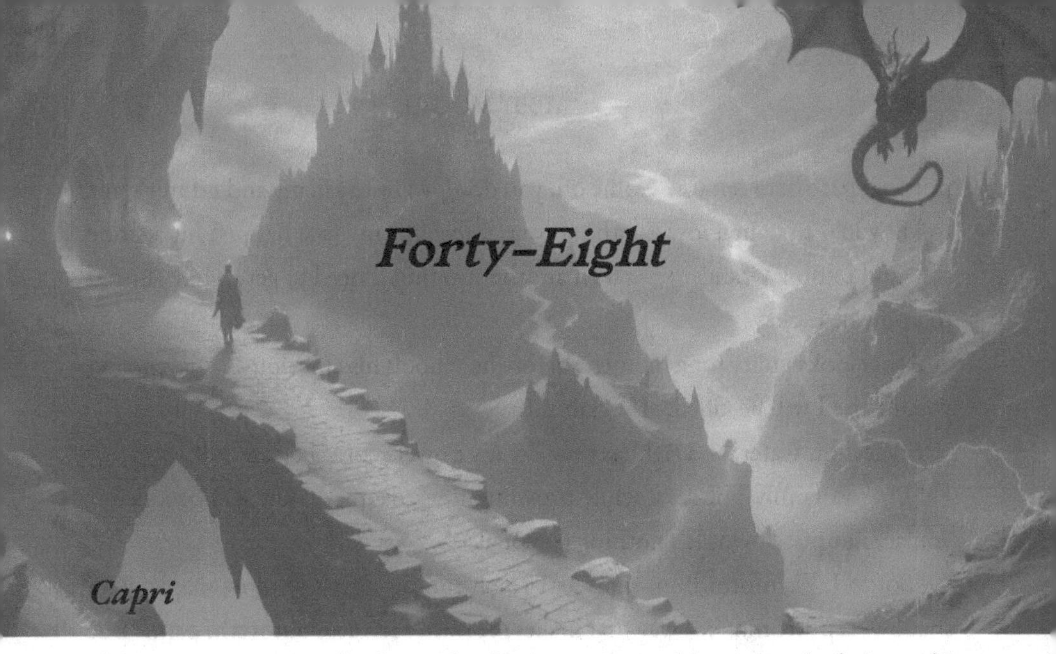

Forty-Eight

"Asher, let's talk about this." My voice trembles. My side feels as if I have been getting hammered with blows. The very air in my lungs was sucked out when I felt as if my ribs shattered. Granger must be in a fight; one in which I feel each and every blow.

"There is nothing to talk about. If one of you dies, the other will be weaker. We need Granger brought down; his laws are outdated We need a new king." Asher swears as I punch him right where it hurts. His balls. I try to grab for anything, feeling uncomfortable that I'm in only a T-shirt.

"That was very naughty." His voice is low, as he cups his tiny balls.

"I know." I cringe; I hate hurting him. The closer I make it to the beach the more I feel my magic coming back. Not enough to use, but the strength of it coming back at least. I strike out again, but he grabs my wrist and head butts me. My nose starts to spray hot, thick blood again. "Ugh." I growl out. He yanks me around, my back to his front. "This isn't a position I enjoy." My voice is sugary-sweet, and it causes him to pause long enough not to tighten his strong grip. I stomp on his foot hard, then, when he leans forward, I rear my head backwards, hitting his own nose. He screams right as I whirl around. I throw more sand into his eyes. He screams while trying to rub at them.

"You are a bitch," he hisses while trying to get the mounds of sand grains out of his eyes.

"Possibly, but I wasn't born this way," I swear. No, I was thrust into this cruel reality. "I know you weren't born like this either." I say as I slowly backpedal, putting space between us. "Come on, you don't want to kill me and I don't want to kill you." I say in a low, soothing tone. I feel like my face has just hit a stone wall and I know Granger has taken another beating. I need to get to him, I need to know he is okay.

Asher looks guilty for a moment before he schools his emotions. "I have to kill you, or else I will be killed." He claims.

My feet hit water, and right as they do, my powers come back in full.

"I have a family," he says, while prowling towards me. "They will be killed if you are not put down. It's nothing personal."

"So do I," I inform him, right as I reach for Granger's shadow magic. The shadows capture him in a way that makes me hurt. His face contorts in pain. "But I can't allow you to live if you are going to harm my mate." His eyes widen slightly before I tighten the shadow's hold on him. Then, as if he is inhaling the smoke of them, they flow right into his nostrils, into his mouth, in his eyes. Everywhere. The shadows go anywhere I command.

"I'm sorry!" he screams around the shadows, the black mist engulfing him.

"Too late," I say softly while I watch the shadows devour him whole. A roar sounds in the distance, but I don't dare look. I owe Asher the respect he deserves to at least watch his final moments. Another roar sounds. I don't know if it's friendly, I don't know how many there are, but I will wait to see.

Suddenly, I pull the shadows to constrict around his heart and every major organ, to finish the torturous job of killing him. Then, as if listening to my very thoughts, his body explodes. Tiny bits of him spray all over me. Blood runs down my face, the warmth causing me to vomit. I hunch over and spew my guts up, then, whenever everything is out of my belly, I dry heave.

"It's okay." Everett's calm voice hits my ears like a feather falling swiftly into the water. Then, as if a wave rolls over the top and pushes the feather under, *I realize*.

I whirl on him, fists up and ready with Granger's shadows. "What are you doing here?" I ask in suspicion. His hands go up in surrender.

"Hey, Capri, it's me." His voice is soothing, like a lullaby a mother would sing. Mine just never did.

"Yeah, I know it's you. Where is Granger?" I ask, looking around. "If you think you can take him down, you can't. I will kill you." Shadows and fire come to my hands without me even asking for them.

"I don't want to take him down, but the other lords do. They and their seconds are challenging him. He needs you." His eyes are filled with worry.

"Show me a map." Understanding dawns on him a moment before I reach into his pants pockets and find what I need.

"Hold on tight; I wouldn't want you to fall. I have no idea where you would end up, and I don't have time to waste looking for you in the stars." I say and his body tenses for a moment before we teleport away. Right to where my Granger is.

Forty-Nine

Capri

When we land, I see males standing around the edge of a big dirt circle. There are torches lit all around it. Each torch is a different fire color—one black, one white, one purple, one gray, another green; there's a red, a blue, and a pink. One for each dragon breed. I gulp when I see Granger on the ground, my own body filling with pain and hurt at the sight of him.

"No," I breathe out right as Everett, Caspian, and Callahan hold me back. "Let me go!" I hiss.

"I cannot. If you step into that ring, you will be accepting the fight as your own." Caspian says harshly. His gaze filled with worry as he takes in my condition.

Granger is down, limp. His body looks half-beaten and bloody. His forehead is pressed into the dirt, while a large beast of a male circles him. This male looks as if he were created to fight. His body is all muscle. I have never seen a stronger male before in my life.

Even still, the male has bruises and is bloody too. Granger has gotten hits in. Killian stands on the edge of the circle, bouncing on his toes. He's eager, I realize, for blood. I yank on the males' hold on me. "It doesn't matter, don't you see? If he dies, I die. There is no *me* without *him*." I cry out in pain. Because the very thought of losing him causes my chest to constrict. I look Caspian in the eyes while telling him exactly what my heart feels. Their sweaty hands slip on my skin. I rush forward before Caspian grabs hold of me again. His eyes lock with mine in understanding.

"I see now, I was wrong." His voice is calm and reassuring. "I don't know why the Fates did what they did by mating you two together. I doubt we will ever know, but I can see it." He tilts his head towards the middle of the circle where Granger lays.

"Thank you." I say, a hot tear falls from my lashes. His grip on me tightens slightly, and my eyes narrow on him.

"What?" I ask, needing to move to where Granger is hurt.

"Be careful. This male is the toughest of all of us. He has trained every day for this moment. Killian made certain he would be ready to challenge Granger." Caspian's eyes scan my body. If he feels any type of way about the blood coating my skin, he doesn't say anything about it.

"I will be ready." I make my way around the lords.

Each of them part for me. Some of their nostrils flare, more than likely smelling whose blood is on me. I make it to the front of the circle, right next to the lords and their seconds. Or I guess, what is left of them.

"Weren't male enough to challenge him yourself?" I ask Killian, studying Granger. Killian doesn't even look towards me.

"Not mate enough to die along with him?" He taunts back. It doesn't hit the mark he thought it would.

"Asher is dead," I declare with no emotion, and get no reaction.

"I figured," He replies calmly.

Granger is on the ground, his face is beaten so badly I hardly recognize him. I just know my heart is pulling me towards him.

"He will die tonight," Killian says.

"Let me get this straight, Kill," I say, taking one small step into the fighting ring. His eyes track the movement.

"When I beat whoever this is, and challenge you by name, you cannot say no?" I ask, even though I know he can't. Granger's arm is bent in a way that looks broken. My own arm is feeling the pain from his bone being shattered.

"I don't think you'll make it out of the ring with Solomon, so I have nothing to worry about, now do I?" He sounds so sure of himself.

Little does he know, I am pretty damn sure of myself, too.

I look right back at him from several feet into the ring. "Get ready." I whisper, before cracking my knuckles and readying for the fight.

He nods his head deeply, slightly bending at the waist. The only show of respect he will ever show anybody. When I come up on the male beating Granger down, I place my hand on his shoulder. "As Killian was able to have you fight for him, I will be taking your king's place." The male stops, then looks towards Killian. Whatever he sees causes him to stop. Granger's blood trickles from this male's face.

"Fine by me. You'll die quicker, God trash." He spits his vile words at me.

He takes several steps backwards, then places his hands behind his back. "You have one minute," he warns.

"Thank you so kindly." I roll my eyes.

Right as I touch Granger, every nasty and vile thought I had in my mind disappears from my body. Everything slows down when his head finally lifts and his once radiant eyes meet mine.

"Princess." Blood drips from the corner of his mouth. "Why are you covered in another male's blood? I thought we talked about this," he teases softly. He then coughs up more bright-red blood. Tears swell in the corners of my eyes.

"I know, we did talk about it. I thought you were being possessive." I reach for him, trying to heal him.

"Don't bother wasting your magic, I'm just resting. I'll get up and win this fight." He says so quietly that I almost can't hear him.

A low chuckle escapes me. "Yes, I believe you." My warm golden healing magic starts running into his bloodstained flesh.

"Seriously, Capri. Don't waste your magic, in case you need it. If I die, you flee. Promise me." His eyes are locked onto mine. Right as I am about to tell him he isn't going to die, he lifts up and presses a hot, firm kiss onto my lips.

I meet his kiss tenfold. "I love you," I say against his lips as he continues to give me quick kisses.

"I know," he assures me before he keeps going. "*Look at me.*"

My eyes open to look directly into the face that I couldn't ever forget, even if I wanted to. "Okay." I nod my head, then press my forehead firmly against his. His hands go right to my hair, digging into it, grabbing onto my head as if he can't not hold on to me tightly.

"Thirty seconds, you two," Killian calls. We both ignore him. I can't tell Caspian he needs to drag Granger off right away. I just hope he knows. I don't dare break contact with Granger to try and plead my case.

"Capri, I cannot afford to love you." I inhale sharply. His fingers grab my chin pulling my attention up to his. "But I will spend the rest of my life earning you. Bowing to you only, worshipping you on my hands and knees." Tears start falling down my face. I bite my lip to keep from crying out.

"You see, he isn't the king we need!" somebody calls out. Granger's shadows whip out and hit him.

"Eyes up here, they don't matter." His dark lashes flutter. This is the moment, the time. I know it is.

"Granger, I'm sorry." His eyes flicker with panic for a moment before I meet Caspian's gaze and nod once.

"Capri?" His tone is filled with concern.

"I need you to survive this war, Granger. They don't deserve you; I don't deserve you." My voice cracks and tears stream down my face. Then, I let his shadows go to work. Betrayal wipes across his face before the shadows cause him to pass out. The lack of oxygen helped, of course, but I know he may never forgive me.

"You better win," Caspian and Everett say at the same time.

"I will try to. Get him far away from here." I stand up to face my own fate, looking into the eyes of a male who is nothing to me. He is nothing but a male who needs ending. And I will be that end. Everett looks over his shoulder one more time before focusing wholly on his king.

They drag Granger away; his limp body causes my blood to start pumping. "Say it," I say, even though I am facing nobody.

"Say what?" the male they call Solomon says.

"Say you have betrayed your king. You will rot in whatever hell the Fates toss you into." I turn to meet the large male's gaze. Solomon takes a step forward. The seconds all chant things about *God trash* at me. I don't listen. Callahan is the only one cheering *for* me. Draven stands there stone-faced, as if he doesn't know what to make of me. I don't know what to make of him either. I just hope I have some time to figure it all out.

Fifty

"I don't know what will happen with our king, but I hope for his sake he dies when you do," Solomon taunts, blood dripping from his nose and mouth. I know I don't look any better than he does.

"I hope for your sake you die in this ring. Would you like to use power then since your side of the world chooses to live unlike your dragon kin?" If my threat of power usage scares him, he doesn't show it. This male is a brick house, and I realize it is because he doesn't care if he lives or dies. He lives for his lord and his lord only. His family must mean nothing to him for him to sacrifice his life like this.

I don't have that advantage; I care if I survive. I have Granger and my mother to worry about. I can't let my emotions get in the way. Too many lives rest on my shoulders. I came here for my mother, I will not leave here without knowing she has a safe place to live where my father cannot get to her.

"Let's get this over with then. I have things to do and beings to see." I don't dare look away when males continue chanting things at me. Callahan starts nervously pacing behind the other beings.

"You know, it is a shame. A God like you is too pretty to just die," Solomon says with a sneer. Several males start chuckling as I try to focus on the threat in front of me.

"It is a shame," I agree.

"So, you agree you'll die?" He tilts his head.

"I agree it's a shame a pretty God like me has to look at your face for a moment longer." I take off sprinting towards him; he chuckles before bending down to stop me. His hands are out in front of him, but I slide on the ground under him. I slide right between his legs and kick the backs of his knees to cause him to falter. I don't dare stop. I keep going, wrapping my arms around his neck and choking him as strongly as I can. He claws at my arms before I finally let go. He is strong, but I was raised Fae. I am quick and clever.

"Is that all you've got?" He gets to his feet as fast as his body will allow him to. I rush at him right as he gets his balance, throwing myself into him. He yanks on my hair as I slam my full force into him. "I'm shocked you are even playing fair, God," he taunts in my ear as he rips at my hair.

"I must, or else it won't count as a win for Granger. He will not be shamed by my lack of knowledge." I say as I kick out, hitting him right where it matters. I roll away from him quickly.

Irritation rushes across his face before he shows his teeth. "You know nothing about our kind!" He screams as he runs towards me. I move aside right as he throws a punch my way.

"I may not know everything, but I know as much as I need to in order to win this fight." I swallow before I do something I never thought I would. I try to make a dragon mad.

"I guess you are just a weak little boy who never got enough love from his mommy," I say bittersweetly. "Was that it?" I fake being surprised when he rushes again, swinging uncontrollably. "Was your mommy killed in this war you created?" I keep on, noticing what seems to set him off and what doesn't. "Maybe it wasn't your momma. Maybe your daddy just didn't love you and that's why you fight females?" That seems to get him going, and his eyes turn to dragon slits. This is my chance.

I zigzag in his blind spots before I get right up to him and jump onto his back.

"Solomon! You fucking idiot!" Killian screams. I press my elbow into his spine so hard I hear bones crack. But I don't stop there. I press my hand against his back with every bit of God strength I have until I pierce flesh. His body goes limp under me before I yank his heart from his body.

I hear Granger screaming and thrashing against whoever is trying to hold him, but that doesn't stop me from prowling my way to Killian. The other lords take several steps backwards right as Caspian loses his grip on Granger. "Capri." He rushes towards me but stops when he sees what I hold in my hand.

Black blood seeps down my arm, and muscles and tissue hang loosely between my fingers, spilling over my small, dainty hand. "I thought you might like this, since you attempted to take my heart from me tonight." I drop the heart right at the lord's feet before looking for my mate.

When my eyes finally meet his, my own heart starts beating again. My steps are hurried as I make my way to him. I shove past several males before falling to my knees in front of him. "It isn't over, is it?" I ask softly, not caring that we are surrounded by traitors.

"Not even close," he swears, shaking his head. We both look as if we have been to war. Granger takes a deep breath before grabbing my face between his large silky-smooth hands. "I am afraid we have bigger things coming our way." He licks his lips before looking to the sky. I blink several times before responding,

"What is happening?" My brows furrow.

"Your grandfather has escaped the cave. He is gone."

I fall onto my butt as if I have been struck. "How?" I breath out, unsure if I can even process this.

"I don't know, but the Fates aren't happy with us. They wanted him, now he is gone." I shake my head while Granger places his hands in mine.

Caspian walks up, interrupting us. "We need to make a choice here," Caspian whisper-hisses.

"I don't need to, it's already done," Granger swears. I look between the two of them, unsure what to even think about right now.

"Where did he go?" I try to backpedal but they are already somewhere else. Granger stands, yanking me right up with him. He pulls my beaten and bruised body into his.

Granger tucks me into his side, his arm dangling around my shoulders. "Everybody listen." Granger speaks with the authority of a king. Because, well, he is still their king. Over the ones who are loyal to him, and even the ones who are not. "The God we had is gone." Voices erupt around the circle.

"What happened?" a female asks.

"We have another God right here," a male says, then several voices agree.

"Send her!" Beings start pointing towards me.

"She is not going anywhere," Granger says sharply, putting his body in front of mine. "Capri will be your queen tonight," Granger declares right before more protests roar out.

"You can't tie us to a God," somebody says.

"Yeah, she deserves to die for coming here." Beings of all kinds start screaming, *everybody* is screaming, and I just want it all to stop.

"Stop!" I scream out right as my mind feels as if it explodes. Bright blue light hits every being who isn't a dragon. They scream out, and then, one by one, each and every one of them disappears. They gasp out as they all go *poof*.

"Where are they going?" Airus asks, brows furrowed and he looks around as if worried he might be next.

"I don't know. Bring them back!" Killian yells loudly.

"I won't," I say calmly, even though I am not calm right now.

Everybody stops right there. They stop panicking, they stop breathing. I dip out of Granger's hold and pace in front of him. "The Fates aren't happy. Those beings weren't safe here. This is a war between Gods and dragons. Vampires and werewolves, even the fae and humans, none of them deserve what is coming for them," I say with as even a voice as possible.

"Where did you send them?" somebody asks, and more voices join in.

"Yeah, where are they all?" a female dragon asks.

"I sent them home. The fae and humans live in similar realms. There is a kingdom where humans thrive. And the fae are better off living in their own magical lands. They will live happier lives. Maybe confused—"

Killian steps forward, rushing at me. Everett stops him, shoving his hand into Killian's chest. "My boy!" He screams. I don't even stop when he starts thrashing. Pink scales start to shift into view before Granger steps forward.

"I wouldn't, Lord Killian," Granger threatens in a low voice.

"Really? You're fucking mate just took my family," He roars with the most emotion I have ever heard from him.

"Your family were fae and other beings?" Granger questions.

"You know they were," Killian seethes.

"Then you know exactly how we all feel," Caspian says, before others join in with, "Yeah, you took our families from us. This is payback."

I run my hand over my face. "Everybody stop!" I yell over them all. They look to me as if I have all the answers. "The vampires and werewolves are fine, sirens are fine, the humans and fae are all good. They will thrive in their new lands. There are already beings of the same species there living full and happy lives." I look to Granger before he nods, giving me the go-ahead. "My grandfather has escaped, which means one thing and one thing only." Killian shoves Caspian, pink flames dancing around his hands. "The Gods are going to come. We need to be prepared for anything." I don't know what I expect but I do know my grandfather will not sing my praises to Father.

"Why would you help us?" Somebody in the crowd of dragons asks. The crowd has grown full of naked dragon shifters. I look to where the dead second, Solomon, lays limp. His equally still heart lays in the dirt.

"Because of two reasons—I am mated to your king." I lick my lips.

"Not yet!" Killian hollers, I roll my eyes, ignoring him.

"Tonight, that will be changed," Granger responds calmly. I smirk at Granger. He doesn't even notice because his eyes are glued to Killian.

"The second reason being I am not Fae and God, as I had been told. I am a God...and a Fate."

If I had thought all hell had already broken loose, I wasn't even close.

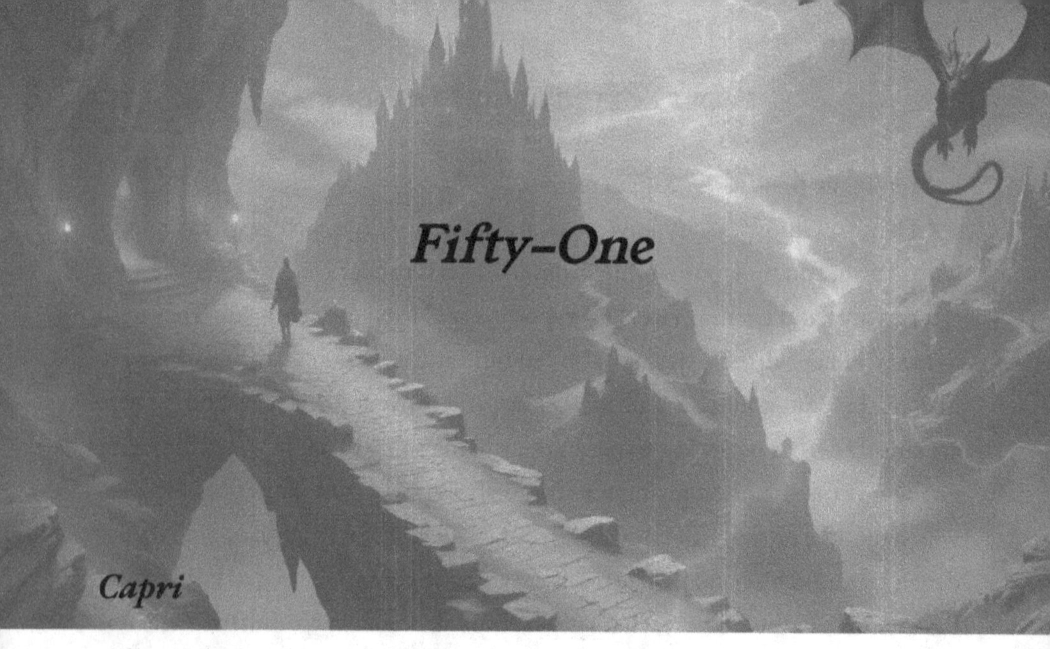

Fifty-One

Capri

"Who told you this?" Draven asks immediately.

"I had a theory, and I tested it out." I shrug my shoulders.

"How could this happen?" Airus asks Granger.

"We don't have the answers yet, but the only thing we need to know now is that tonight will be mine and Capri's mating ceremony." Everybody hushes, I notice Amelie push through the crowd and into her mate's arms.

"And?" Rafe asks.

"And we need to deal with the traitors." Granger eyes Killian and Calix. "So?" Granger asks them.

"So what, Majesty?" Calix asks. His mate is glued to him as if they were connected.

"Are you a traitor, Lord of Dracol?" Granger tilts his head in a reptilian way.

"I am not," Calix declares. Amelie looks terrified for her mate.

Granger looks to me for an answer. "I don't feel as if he is being dishonest." I chew on my lower lip, not wanting to get to Killian.

"And you? Would you like to plead your case?" Granger asks the traitor.

"I don't believe I should. I challenged you, and my male lost." Killian shrugs his shoulders.

"True, so you accept the punishment then?" Granger asks.

Killian walks up to another male. He bows his head. "Do you accept Lord of Drakon?" The stillness in the field is so tense it feels as if nobody can move.

"I will." The male's muffled voice is calm and collected.

"Step forward," Granger demands. "Declare yourself loyal to your king and queen."

The male doesn't hesitate before striding to us and kneeling. "I declare my heart, soul, and mind yours. I will follow you, protect you, and obey any laws you deem fit." The male's voice doesn't even fluctuate when he speaks. "Do you accept me as a Lord of Beithir?" The male bows his head as low as it will go without being on the ground. Granger looks at me for an answer.

"We will," I answer as Granger takes my hand in his. "Killian will no longer be your lord. He belongs to no clan other than if his new lord will accept him. That is between you and Killian." Granger says, before he turns, my hand in his, forcing me to follow him.

He leans into my ear. "Did you really mean to send them away?"

I look up into his eyes. "Yes. You told me you thought they deserved a better life, and I agree with you." He leans down and kisses my cheek.

"You don't have to be so agreeable," he whispers to me as we make our way to the coast. Our two palaces seem as if they are right next to each other, even though they are hundreds of feet apart.

"It's easy to be when you are right."

His eyes widen slightly, his brows furrow, and he covers his heart with our interlocked hands. "I do not deserve you. Truly, the Fates may be cruel, but them giving me you, even if it's for a small time, is the kindest thing they could have done."

I lift a brow. "Where to?" I ask, even though I already know in my heart where we both belong.

"Home." His answer is immediate.

"On it, King."

As I lay upon Granger's front, I run my fingers lazily through his hair. "Tell me one more time," I say against his neck, pressing kisses to his warm skin.

"We're going to be mates by tomorrow," Granger says for the ninth time.

"We already are mates." I correct him for the ninth time.

"Our ceremony will change nothing, Capri, I know that. But it will strengthen our bond, which we already have."

I nod into his neck. "I know."

The wind blows in my long, honey-blonde hair, and I lie completely flat on him. "Is this bad luck?" I smile while biting my lower lip.

"What?" He leans up, and the sun shines into his golden eyes. His muscular arms strain as he holds his head up, while he watches me watching him.

"You know...being together before our ceremony."

He half smirks at me. "Isn't that a human thing?" He sits up, knocking me off.

"I don't know. I guess it is, but they got it from somewhere, didn't they?" He laughs at me. "I like this," I say before he can even respond to me.

"Like what?" He runs his hand over my stray hairs, pushing them from my face.

"Us. Not being king and queen but being Granger and Capri."

His face turns serious. "Capri, if I could give you that, I would."

I lean into his embrace. "I know, and I don't want that. I am thankful your beings have you as their king." I shake my head before continuing. "I am just grateful for these moments."

Right as we lean into each other, Amelie interrupts us. "It's time to get ready," she announces. I look into her soulless eyes and wonder how the Fates could give somebody like her a mate. That gets my mind going as to how I am a Fate...or at least partly. Since I am one, I wonder if I could speak with them without sacrifice.

"I'll see you soon." Granger stands, putting his hand out for me to grab onto. I pull myself up, and as I'm about to dust myself off, he beats me to it.

I smile softly at the male I am tying my soul to. "Thank you."

He leans in to kiss my cheek. "I look forward to eternity with you."

Granger straightens before turning to Amelie. "If you even think about harming her, your life will be void. I will kill you before the thought can even process." He threatens her with ease; it isn't hard when she doesn't ever smile at anybody other than Calix. She doesn't even bat an eye at Granger.

I look between the two of them. "I can ready myself," I declare. Because I can. I don't want her messing me up or getting in the way.

"I will treat her as a queen." Amelie says too sweetly to Granger. The sound of her trying to be kind doesn't feel right coming from her.

Granger shifts into his large, black dragon form, his scales shimmering in the light.

Granger takes one more moment to look at me before huffing hot steam into Amelie's space, then he takes off into the sky. His castle isn't a far flight, but I have a feeling he is going to fly until our ceremony.

Dainty fingers grab onto my arm, but my attention is pulled elsewhere. As I watch Granger tilt and soar throughout the skies.

"Are you coming or do you plan to stay in that?" Amelie crosses her arms, her eyes filled with disgust.

"You are not the ray of sunshine I would like to spend the rest of this day with," I admit as I follow her up the sandy shores of my isle. "How did you even get here?" I mumble.

She stops and looks back at me. "You do realize I am a dragon?"

I roll my eyes. "Of course I know that. But you are *dressed*," I point out.

"And you don't think I could carry clothes in any four of my claws?" She volleys right back. She has a point.

"I guess. I just hadn't thought of it." We start the long climb up the rocky side to my palace.

"Just because you enjoy staring at the naked males around here doesn't mean we all are like that. If you had taken the time to stay during our meetings, you would know that," she snaps at me. I huff a breath. This is going to be a long day.

"You are right," I agree with her, thinking it will just be easier to do so.

"Not to mention the fact that you sent all of our closest friends away. Did you know—" She pauses, and I run into her back. She stumbles a few feet. "Wait. Did you just say I am right?" She asks in shock.

"I did." I nod, looking into her eyes.

"Calix is my mate, and I still don't think he has ever told me I was right." She narrows her eyes at me in suspicion. I shrug my shoulders.

"You are right. It was selfish of me to leave during those meetings, but I wanted to meet my grandfather." I motion for her to keep walking.

She starts walking—more like climbing—until we make it to the side door that opens into the scullery. Her fists clench several times. "I am surprised you would admit that." She chews on the side of her cheek before looking around at what I have built. "So, you really are a Fate then?" She asks in wonder. I start walking towards the large staircase that leads to my room.

"I guess so, but I don't think that's how I made this." She follows right on my toes, even though I notice her wandering eyes.

"How would you explain this?" She asks as she looks everywhere she can see.

I stop in my tracks and turn to face her. "My father, King Ragnar, has a similar ability," I start to explain before continuing my long trek up the stairs. "He can make things from objects he has had in his possession. Maybe this was a Fate's ability. I have no idea, and nobody to talk to about it." She hums before we make it to the third floor and walk into the narrow stone staircase. "I am kind of new at all of this. I hope you'll give me time to figure it out. I didn't mean to kill that dragon when we first met." I gulp down the guilt I feel as I continue rambling on to her.

"I know you didn't," she says, almost in a whisper.

When we walk into my room, I go straight to the tub. "I am going to wash the sand from my body. I don't have many gowns; there isn't much to pick from." Granger has brought me several gowns that belonged to his mother, but I used all the ones within my reach already. Not to mention, most of them were far too revealing for this type of ceremony.

"I'll check it out," Amelie says, nicer than I would have thought she could.

"I do not expect you to help me if you don't want to," I say as emotions threaten to clog my throat. "I know we are enemies, we don't have to pretend right now. I can ready myself." I say again.

"I told my King I would take care of you as a queen; I do not lie to my King." She says before making her way to look through my clothes.

Fifty-Two

Capri

After several long hours, the sun is starting to go down. The sky is light-pink and orange on the horizon; it seems as if nothing else matters but these next few hours. Amelie finishes up my hair, but I couldn't care any less about how I look. I want to see Granger; I want to be in his arms.

A whistle sounds from behind me, and both Amelie and I turn to see who it is, even though I already know. "Ev." I smile at my friend.

"You look..." He shakes his head. I give him a big hug, wrapping my arms completely around his waist. "We have to do this now before Granger sees you; he might kill me for laying my eyes on you." He pushes me back gently to get a good look in. He whistles again. Amelie snorts. "Would you like to run away with me?" I playfully slap his upper arm.

"Of course. Where would we go?" I joke with him, and a large smile paints my face with happiness.

"I am afraid there is nowhere in existence Granger Rhodes wouldn't find you, Capri." Tears swell in my eyes from his words.

"I think that there is nowhere I wouldn't feel him either." I declare softly.

Amelie excuses herself, claiming that our strange friendship creeps her out. When she leaves, we sit down on the bed.

"Are you ready?" Everett turns serious.

"I am."

He grabs my hands, his are rough and hot. "I know this world is hostile to outsiders, but after tonight, you won't be an outsider. You'll be as good as a dragon."

I squeeze his hands. "Thank you for being such a good friend to me, Everett. You didn't have to be, but you did." He smiles widely. "I can't thank you enough for showing me kindness when you didn't have to." My eyes sting from the tears I am holding back. Everett clears his throat. "For welcoming me to your home, when nobody else wanted to." I bite my bottom lip.

"Let's get you mated then, huh?" He stands straight, holding out his arm for me to grab hold of.

"Let's do it." I nod once before standing solidly. I walk barefoot down a few stairs before backpedaling. "You know what, Ev. Let's go in style." I smile at him before he gives me a knowing grin.

"It's your night." He shrugs.

The wind whips my curly, long hair. I hadn't thought about messing it up, but I also don't care. I could go to this thing in nothing but a T-shirt, and Granger would be glad I made it. Listening to Amelie talk about her relationship with Calix earlier made me realize that mine and Granger's bond is different than theirs. Mating bonds aren't ever going to all be the same, but I can tell ours is different than any other. Granger respects me in a way that feels special. And I intend to tell him all the ways I respect and love him.

When we circle the palace, which now houses hundreds of dragons, nervousness starts to bubble in my chest. "What if they hate me?" I whisper. Everett roars his response, which I can't understand. I see so many dragons down there; most don't fit inside.

"They don't need to fit inside." Granger's voice comes in my head so softly that I want to lean into him. My heart aches knowing my mother won't be here to see this.

"Why won't they need to fit?" I ask down our bond. The more I use it, the easier it becomes.

"Because we will be outside. Come down and I'll show you."

I pat Everett, signaling to him that I am ready to descend. He heads down, towards my future, my mate.

When Everett lands, he stays in his dragon form while I hurry inside to find Granger. My eyes scan his palace, which I haven't even been inside of until now. "Excuse me." I hold my gown up as I quickly walk around others. They whisper about me. Some move out of the way for me, others don't. Some deliberately block my path. I simply push past them, my eyes only looking for one male.

The pull to Granger gets so strong, I start up some steps before I find myself walking down a hallway. I don't know where I am going, but my heart does. There is nobody else in these halls, and my pace quickens when my heart feels like it might explode from being apart from Granger. When I round a corner, I run right into him. My sharp inhale causes his eyes to widen.

Granger grips my shoulders, concern lacing his eyes. "Are you alright?" His face scrunches adorably.

"Yes, I just…" I shake my head, giving him a soft smile. "You literally just took my breath away. I had been searching for you, then my feet just started moving until I ran right into your chest," I explain, taking my time to check him out.

The tight white shirt he wears under his navy jacket fits his strong, muscular form in a way that makes me clench my thighs together. His nostrils flare, and his eyes track my movements. "Princess, don't do this to me right before we are needed elsewhere."

I bite my lip. "Do *what* to you?" I blink slowly, playing with him.

"Beg for me to take you right here when we are needed outside right about now." This calms every other thought in my body.

"Right now?" I question in a whisper, before he grabs my hand and guides me into a room.

This room has bookshelves stacked against the wall; it smells musty and dry. The books all look worn and old. There is a desk that has paperwork spread everywhere on top of it, ink smeared all over the pages. "What room is this?" I run my fingers over a small patch of the desk with no papers. There is a thick layer of dust on it.

I hug him from behind, holding onto his body, as if I might lose him. "My study," Granger answers before throwing open the windows. He gestures outside. I look around from where I'd been hugging his back to see exactly what he is trying to show me.

Twinkling lights are spread everywhere outside. Small white chairs are scattered across the lawn. The grass is bright green and there are flowers everywhere. Some of them are even constructed into different shapes. Right then, my eyes snag on a particular place. My jaw drops and my brow lift to my hairline.

"Did you have them make that?" I ask in awe. Granger spins towards me, his arms caging me against his firm body.

"I gave them very strict instructions."

I bounce on my toes. "I'm ready." I say cheerfully. He chuckles deeply at me.

"Then I guess I will meet you down there," He says right before backing away from me and jumping right out the window. We aren't that far up, and he is a dragon, but *still*. He lands with grace and agile skill. I gasp, but then he looks up at me, straightening his jacket and winking at me before turning away and walking towards where I can only assume I need to be.

I spin on my toes to go meet my forever. When I turn around, I am met with Everett and Caspian, Callahan right behind them. My eyes widen a fraction before I stride to them. I gather all three in my arms, even though they don't fit. "What are you guys doing here?" I ask in wonder.

"Mating ceremonies are kind of like human weddings; typically, somebody will walk you down," Everett says, his eyes scanning me once more. I scratch behind my ear, trying but failing to bring my mind away from the fact that I have nobody.

"*You have me*," Granger says immediately. I sigh.

"*Yes, I have you, and that is all that matters,*" I softly confirm.

His swift response explains why the males are here. "*You also have family in them. They care for you, too, Capri.*"

I gulp down any emotions that might clog my throat before speaking, "So, why are you here then?" I ask them, even though Granger just told me. I want to hear it from them. Callahan sneaks a peek from behind the males.

"We would like to walk you down, please." His manners catch me off guard. Everett steps in, adding to the pile of emotions I am already feeling.

"You might feel alone here, Capri, but you aren't. You are family to us, and we love you." I smile before Caspian picks me up and hugs me tightly. My feet dangle in the air as this large male hugs me tighter than I have ever been held. I giggle before informing him that even though Granger is allowing them to walk me, he wouldn't be fond of all the touching.

Granger's low grumble confirms my suspicion. "We need to get going before the other dragons eat all the food inside the hall," Everett says, grabbing onto my hand and pulling me forward.

"You're concerned about the food?" I ask, arching a brow. Even though I, too, am hungry.

"Well, yeah. It isn't often we get a nice, cooked meal." Everett says right away. I shake my head at him. Caspian looks at his friend as if thinking the same thing I am.

"You have eaten well the last month and a half. And you chose to live here with us. You can leave." Caspian says with a curt shake of his head. I laugh, covering my mouth before Everett looks towards me.

"You are a traitor," he hisses out at me. I hold my arms up in surrender.

I point my finger right at his face. "Hey, no, I'm not. But you did decide to live here." He pushes my finger gently away, and we all laugh.

We walk down the steps arm in arm. Callahan is following right behind me.

"Just because I wanted to live in the North doesn't mean I didn't want a home-cooked meal sometimes," Everett whisper-shouts into my ear. I swat at him before we come to an arched open door. Caspian looks down at me, then narrows his eyes at my feet.

"You aren't wearing shoes," He comments.

"No, I am not," I confirm. He side-hugs me once more before we step outside. "I knew I liked you. I am just sad you have to be mated to *him*..." He tilts his head to where Granger stands. "It could have been us." He says in a joking way.

"If only," I tease him right back. He kisses my cheek before stepping back to allow me to walk. My bare feet press into the silk on the ground, my toes crinkle before I begin my short walk into my future.

I never would have thought something like this would happen for me. I had always believed that I would be lucky enough to even have one being love me, my mother. Maybe if I had prayed to the fates for a while they might grant me Val. Even though I knew deep down I couldn't have passion for Valor like I do for Granger. I never knew that true and pure happiness could be this easy. That somebody could love me entirely without needing anything in return.

Looking at Granger right here and now though, I know that fate planned all of this for me. For this moment, they knew my love had been waiting for me, as I had been for him.

I know that the moment either one of us stops breathing, it will end both of us

Fifty-Three

Capri

As soon as my eyes see Granger, I am ready for this to be over with and to be in bed with him.

"Be patient, Princess." He says simply down the bond.

My bare feet hit the lush green grass, after the silk runs out. There are pink flower petals scattered all over the ground. Chairs split the walkway; dragon lords and their seconds sit in the front row. Other dragons who I have never met sit scattered around in different rows. Each chair is occupied, some are even at the tables placed all around. Still more dragons circle overhead, fire pluming from their throats.

I realize the twinkly lights I had seen from above are actually fire. There are candles and flames lit all over. The flower arch where Granger stands is my favorite thing I have ever seen. The flowers are in full bloom, whites and pinks, the prettiest combination of colors. I think I may have Everett to thank for that. I walk as quickly as I can to Granger and the male I don't know, who's standing beside him. Granger laughs at me. "You aren't supposed to run." He gives me his hand, and I swear tears are gathered in his eyes.

"I couldn't wait any longer." I shake my head, placing my hands in his waiting ones. I face him fully, ignoring the male and every other dragon here. Granger is the only male my eyes will ever go to again.

The male clears his throat before speaking. He is a pale male with plain features. "Thank you for coming," He says to everybody, but looks at me when he speaks. A dark hood is placed over his head, although it conceals nothing of his features.

"I didn't know it was optional." My response gets several laughs. Granger tightens his grip on my hands. He smirks at me, before his eyes start their slow descent down my body. The gown I am wearing is pure white. It hugs my every curve before fluttering out around my ankles. Amelie informed me that every queen deserves to look like one.

"You look better than any queen I have ever seen." Granger whispers before the male draws our attention.

"It is not every day the Fates grant such a gift as being mates, but especially with a Fate herself." The male looks to Granger. Granger gives him a tight smile. "It is a special moment for dragonkind to accept this female as our queen." The male grabs our already joined hands. He places a white cloth over them before chanting something in an old language. I look at Granger for an answer.

"This is the old tongue. He is bonding us." Granger explains.

The chanting gets louder before I feel it. Granger drops one of my hands. He squeezes my other hand tightly, rubbing his thumb over my knuckles.

I feel Granger inside of me, inside of my very soul. The male then pulls out a huge knife and places it in Granger's open hand.

Granger takes the knife before slicing his own hand. Bright blood pours down, staining the white cloth. Our hands are still underneath it.

"I, Granger Rhodes, King of Beithir, accept my mate the Fates have given me. I vow to protect her always. I will put her above all else. My soul will forever be locked with hers." Granger hands me the knife, his blood still coating it. I wait a moment before Granger nods softly. I slice into my hand, hissing in pain. I bring my bleeding hand over our joined ones as I just watched him do, and repeat the exact words he has just spoken to me.

When my words end, I add on for good measure, "I will always be faithful and loyal to you, Granger. I will love you, protect you, and put you first." I swear to him.

Right as the words leave my mouth, my body feels as if it is floating, even though both my feet are still planted firmly on the ground. My soul feels as if I am not only me; I feel Granger inside my body and my mind more than I have ever. I realize now how important this ceremony is. How close I had thought we were previously is nothing compared to now. I can't even feel the difference in his emotions versus my own. Maybe there isn't a difference anymore.

Granger seems to feel the same because when his eyes meet mine, both of us seem to feel the shift.

"The Fates have given you both an incredible gift that not many get to experience. Your blood is now one and the same. I can probably feel as much as any of our brethren that you two have one of the strongest bonds I have ever felt. This will do well for our kingdom," The male says, confirming what I had already thought. I look down at the cloth, our hands are no longer injured, but the blood mixed together.

When Granger's eyes meet mine after also looking at our hands, his eyes are hot and ready. Love shines within them. "I love you, My Queen." He kneels in front of me, kissing the top of my hand. "Capri, you are my family. You are the beginning and end of every day for the rest of my life. Anywhere you go, in time or space, I will gladly follow you to the ends of any world we travel to. You are mine, now and forever," he vows, bowing his head in respect and love. Then, as if setting off some type of response, the other dragons in attendance do the exact same thing. They all bow down, their chests all the way to the ground.

All together they chant in unison. "All hail our queen." It sounds a little creepy, really. Granger stands, drawing all my attention back to him. As it will always be. "What would you like to do, My Queen?" His plump lips pucker. I lean into his ear while the male who performed the ceremony takes his leave.

"I would like to get you out of this suit right away, Majesty," I whisper before grabbing hold of him and teleporting us away.

I chuckle as Granger finds his bearings; he almost looks a little sickly. "You would think after weeks of doing that it would be easier on me." He holds his belly as if he feels sick. Which I realize also makes me feel ill.

"This is going to take some getting used to," I admit, while frowning. Granger is on me in a moment. His hands fumble with the gown's buttons until he gets so annoyed he just rips the gown right down the front. "Granger," I gasp out as my breasts fall free.

"You weren't wearing anything under this?" He asks in surprise while taking several steps back to look his fill. His eyes are wild with need as he licks his plump lips. I bite down on my lip as I, too, drink him up .

"No." I shake my head before prowling to him slowly.

"You allowed us to keep on with those silly words while you were naked under here?" He asks, lust filling his voice. I press my palms against his chest, pushing him backwards until the back of his knees hit my bed frame.

"I did. Although, isn't everybody naked underneath something?" His gaze heats as my breasts bounce with every step.

"*Capri*." He grabs my hips before spinning us fully around.

I fall down on the soft bed, giggling while he kneels in front of me. My legs are spread wide open before him. "I don't think those words were silly," I say, lifting my chin as his hand plays with my belly. He moves it so slowly up my body that goose bumps spread across my hot skin. Before he dips his head to my core, his gaze meets mine, his brows lifted all the way up.

"You know as well as I do how much I love you. What I would do for you is endless. I will remind you anytime you need, but I hope that my actions show my feelings more than any words ever could." He says with such passion, my eyes sting.

A single tear drops from my eyes. I bat it away. "I never had a family," I say before he licks at my core, his eyes still on mine.

"You had your mother," He says against my most sensitive bits.

"I did, but I mean *more* than that." My head falls back as he starts with his fingers. They play with me while his tongue goes to work.

His forefinger presses on the bundle of nerves at the very center of me, his tongue lapping up every ounce of pleasure it can. "You'll remind me when I need it?" I ask. My eyes are closed. I am already dangerously close to the edge as he sucks my bead of pleasure into his mouth. Dots cloud my vision.

"I will spend every waking moment showing and telling you every bit of how I didn't live until you came into my life. How I was a vessel until my heart started pumping again." Bliss hits me right as his words leave his mouth. I scream out in pleasure as I ride his face until the waves stop.

"I feel the same," I whisper as he climbs up my body to meet my mouth.

I taste myself on his tongue, the moment almost too emotional. My eyes sting again as I blink away any unwanted emotions. Granger unclasps his pants, letting them hit the ground before pumping himself several times.

"You know, you never told me if there was some type of birth control potion I need to be taking." I had taken one before I came, but haven't since I got here. Atlas made me take it one night, but gave no further instructions. Granger stops right at my entrance. I regret saying anything at all now. I push my hips, hoping he might just slide in. He moves his hips slightly away from me.

"Do you want to take one?" He asks, fisting himself. He holds himself just out of reach of my still throbbing core. I move my hips up so that he will move against me. I toy with him, moving my hips around so that he plays right at the center of me. He allows it this time, his eyes closing slightly.

"I wouldn't want to bring a child into a war," I say as he glides his thickness against my slippery center.

"I wouldn't either. Which is why, since I am a dragon, I can control when I am fertile." He presses into me in one full thrust. I gasp out as his thickness stretches me completely. He stops when he hits as far as he can go. "Dragons lay eggs still, so males can decide when they are and are not fertile. I have not been fertile with you; we will discuss babies at a later time." He grunts.

I grind my hips in a circular motion against him. "Later time?" I ask as he starts to move his own hips slowly. His hips move in a small circle, rubbing right on my clit.

"You don't want mini-mes?" His eyes dance with amusement.

I go up on my elbows, our chests brushing against one another's. "I want more mini-*yous* than you're willing to give me, more than likely," I tease.

This is a strange feeling really, because all the bliss he is feeling from my body, I can feel. And I know he can feel how amazing my body feels from the pleasure he is giving me.

"I'll give you anything you want, Capri. If you want a hundred babies, I will give them to you. If only to see you smile."

I push on him. "I want you harder," I breathe out. "And I want baby talk later, not while we are in the throes of passion," I say in a husky tone.

"Get on your hands and knees," Granger demands. I obey so quickly that he falls out of me. Right as I am facing the headboard, he shoves himself back inside. The wet sounds are deafening. He fists my hair in one hand as his other hand plays with me. He drags his fingers softly down my back. It causes me to arch further into him. I press my ass as far into him as it can get. He slams into it, and I shake it for good measure.

"Stop it, or else I am going to blow right here," He warns. He pulls all the way out of me, running his thick head down my center before pushing into me again. He repeats this motion several times before staying inside of me. My arousal is so apparent that I am not surprised when I start dripping down my leg.

"Even your pussy loves me," He teases against my back. I push harder into him, meeting him for every stroke.

"I love you," I say in response. Granger's hands reach down to my front and pull me upwards. He continues his brutal pace of pounding inside of me, as his hands keep me upright. My back is to his front as he takes me fully. He sucks on my neck, causing me to start the blissful fall to pleasure. "I'm coming," I say breathlessly. He tweaks my nipple between his fingers as his mouth presses long, hot kisses to my throat.

"I am, too." Right as he says it, I feel his cock twitch inside of me, spilling every bit of himself into me.

After several long moments of staying just like that, Granger picks me up, wedding style, and places me inside an empty tub. I stand in the bath, evidence of our mutual pleasure dripping out of me and onto my thighs.

"Well?" I ask, a smirk already on my face.

He motions towards the dry tub. "I don't have water power. Can you fill that for us?"

I chuckle for a moment before bringing water to my hands. "Are you going to contribute to this moment?" I lift a brow as I stand in cold water. "I figured I just gave you the orgasm of a lifetime, you could also warm it up, maybe?" Granger says on a chuckle.

He steps into the tub and the water starts heating right away. I hug around his neck.

"Very kind of you, Majesty," I say against his lips. He smiles against mine.

"I thought so." He teases me back. He leans his forehead against mine and nuzzles my nose for several moments. "I love you, Capri." He turns serious as he kisses gently.

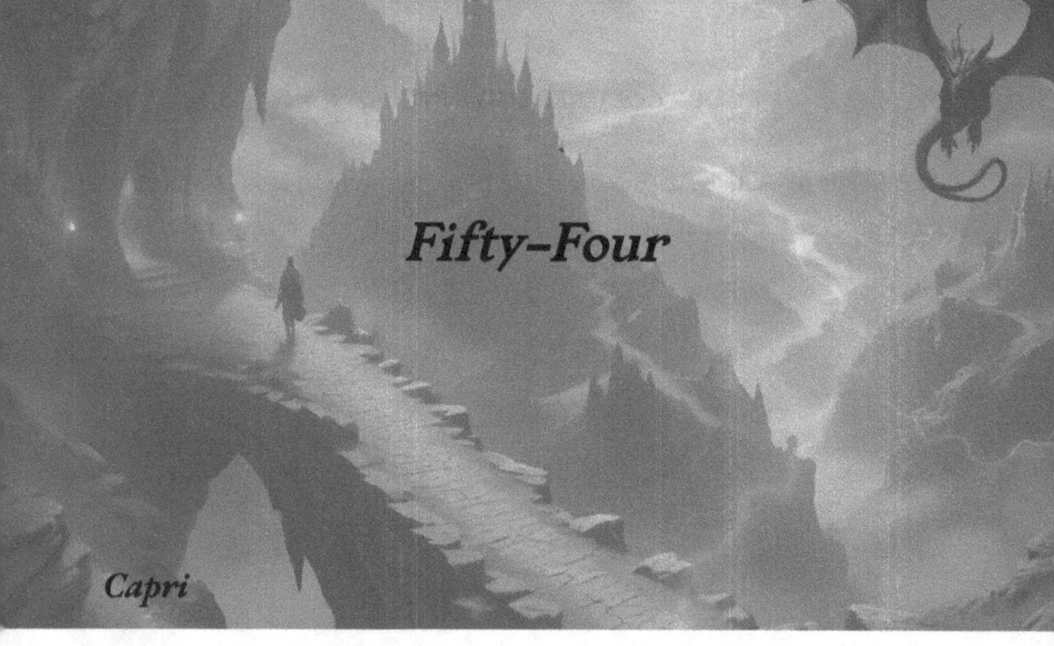

Fifty-Four

Capri

My legs are sprawled out over Granger, my arm across his chest. After our bath, we made love for several long hours until we both passed out. His body is a beacon, signaling me home. Anytime I stray too far from him, he pulls me back in. His arms wrap me up as if I am a delicate butterfly hibernating in a cocoon.

The only thing that wakes me from my deep slumber is the shaking that causes me to plummet to the hard floor. "Oh my Fates," I curse. Granger is up and out of bed, grabbing onto my arm before I even realize I am not fully awake. "What just happened?" I ask in confusion. I rub my already sore head.

"I have only one guess." Granger picks me up before walking to my open archway that looks out to the sea. "Your family is here, Capri," Granger says, but my ears must not hear his words.

"What?" I rub my head before walking right up next to him.

"Your family, or maybe just some of them, just got here," He says again, and this time I understand his words.

"How do you know?" I ask, looking up at him before scanning the still-dark skies. Is it even morning yet?

"The ground just shook," He says, feeling nervous. Or maybe I am the one feeling nervous. I can't tell. "It is both of us." He confirms what I had already thought.

"Did it shake like that when I arrived?" I ask as we both dress quickly. I watch as Everett and Caspian fly towards us, a few dragons in tow behind them. They appear as though they are flying sideways.

"No, but you are only one God/Fate. I can only assume it is probably your father, brothers, and grandfather...if he is stupid enough to come back."

I suck in a breath. I knew they might come, I knew Father *would*, but I didn't think I would have to face him this soon.

"Don't be scared, darling." He grabs my face while footsteps pound up the steps. I scratch my head, right where I hit it.

"I am not scared for me," I admit.

"Don't be scared for me." He says softly before adding on. "Get dressed, we have company." He tucks a stray hair behind my ear right as Caspian, Everett, and Draven come bounding up and into my room. Right in time for me to call for some of Granger's clothes I had found earlier.

"Something is here," Draven says, seemingly out of breath.

"Where are the others?" Granger moves before they even have time to step completely into the room. They start down the steps, and I follow behind.

They take the steps two at a time, so I do as well. When I get tired, I just float down them. I realize too late that I am barefoot. When we make it to the bottom of the many steps, I see that there are dragons everywhere. Some of them seem drunk, a lot seem tired. Some of them make themselves comfy in my home, and I smile. This was the dream, for both sides of their war to come together. I didn't think it would be because of my family though.

"Because they are drunk," Granger confirms out loud. "Sober up, lads. We have a long night ahead of us." The dragon shifters stiffen at their king's words or tone, maybe both.

"Sir?" One of them asks in a shaky voice.

"I don't know what we are facing, but the North and South need to prepare for war just in case." Granger warns everybody, some of the females clutch onto a nearby male. I can feel their fear, taste it even.

I stop dead in my tracks when one of the females starts to cry. "He wouldn't come here for war," I say softly. In reality, I don't know what he would do. I don't know my father very well at all. Granger's eyes soften slightly before he looks towards his clans.

"I don't know what is going on but we will figure it out. Take the hatchlings and females who cannot fight to Morologo," Granger tells Caspian. Caspian grabs onto Granger's shoulder, worry written across his face. "If I need you Cas, I will call for you. Right now, I need you to take care of the females and hatchlings. Please, brother." Granger begs.

Caspian nods slightly before heading out. "I will care for them. Be safe, brother." Caspian says over his shoulder and another female wails out as she walks away from what I can only assume to be her husband.

I rush to Granger's side, not knowing what to say because I don't know what I will tell my father when he demands things of me. I listen and watch as everybody goes to their designated places. Hurrying everywhere, as if their lives depended on it. And they might.

"Granger, let me speak to them. I need to see what is going on. Maybe he just wants to use some of the soil, and then he will leave." I grab his face, and the small stubble of his beard presses into my hand.

Granger takes a moment, his eyes darting from my mouth to my eyes. "You will not go alone," He says, before grabbing a goblet and chugging it down in one swig. "I guess it's time to meet my father-in-law." He slams the goblet down on the table.

I follow right on Granger's heels, feeling as if I am a duckling following its mother for food. "This isn't how I wanted you to meet my father," I say from behind Granger. I watch as this lethal male straps knives to his body. Then he bends down and straps some to mine as well.

"If all else fails, you defend yourself, no matter what." He looks me in the eyes.

"They are family, Granger. He didn't come here to harm anybody," I say again, but I am still not so sure.

As we make our way outside, I can sense them here. I feel the tense air all around us. "There is a hidden system under my castle. Take any remaining clans there and hide. There is enough food stored there for all my staff and everybody that can fit." I look to Everett. My eyes are filled with worry, him returning the same worry as mine. "You need to go, now," I whisper as I see them. Everett's brows furrow before he looks to his king.

"You heard your queen. Get them and hide until I tell you otherwise." Granger doesn't take his eyes off my family. "Yes majesties," Everett says, his voice cracking but I don't dare look back as he guides the others to safety.

My chest fills with panic as I see all of my brothers, my father, grandfather, and mother all standing with...*Killian.*

"Are you ready?" Granger asks right before he shifts. *"If anything happens, Capri, you run. If anybody catches up to you, you fight until you are dead. Do you understand me?"*

I climb up his back leg, digging my feet in until I reach his neck. "I understand," I say sadly.

I don't understand, but I need Granger to focus. The sky is still pitch-black, and the clouds are foggy, lighting and thunder boom and crack in the distance. The air is hot and thick with moisture. I tie my hair back with a blue ribbon right as we land on Granger's isle. I jump from his back before calling out to my father.

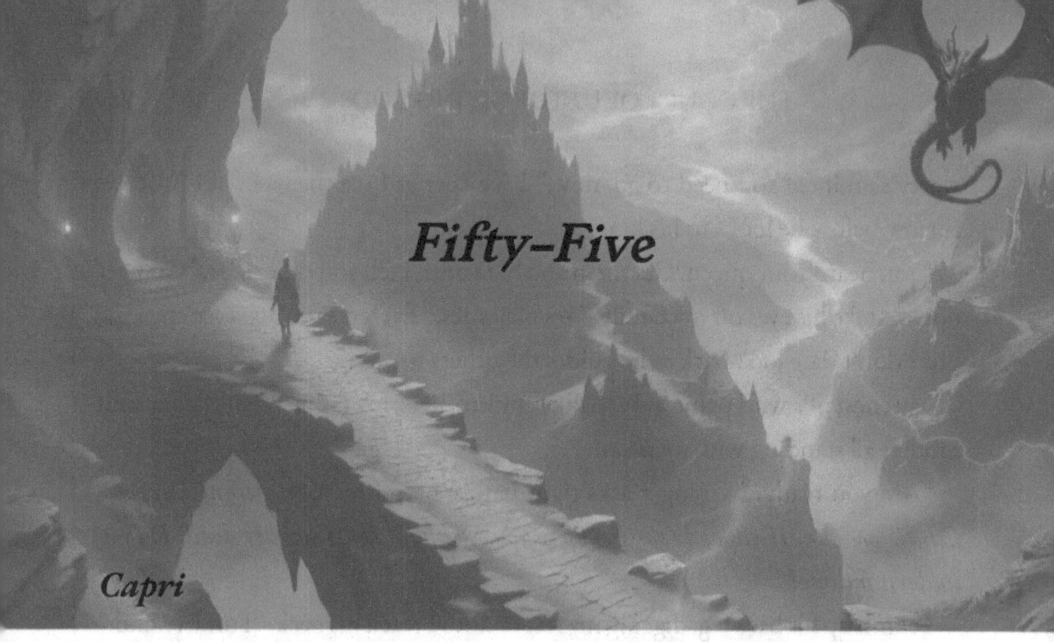

Fifty-Five

"Father," I say as he floats down to meet me. Granger prowls in his dragon form. Grangers claws clinking as he stalks towards us.

"Hello, Capri. I see you have done more than your job." My father says cruelly. Lachlan laughs an evil laugh. It causes me to raise my defenses just a little. "Mother, are you all right?" I give her a once-over. She seems okay, intact at least. Father snaps his fingers at me. His eyes go to the large black beast that stands guard behind me. I stand between the front legs of Granger.

"My father has informed me of your situation." Father's nostrils flare slightly in disgust.

"Which one?" I ask, playing dumb.

"Don't be coy with me. Flirting might work for other males, but I don't fuck my kin. So let's start this over." My face turns down in disgust at my father's remark. Granger blows steam from his mouth, baring his extremely large teeth as a threat. Father has the good sense to take a step back. My brothers stay with my mother and grandfather. I notice Lachlan holding something, swinging it as if it is a toy. It looks like a burlap sack.

My mother hasn't answered me yet, so I try again. "Mother," I say, just slightly louder. My father draws my attention back to him with his power. He can't control minds, per se, but he can persuade them to think a certain way.

"Capri, did you do what we agreed on?" His voice is chipper, unlike how he typically talks.

"Why are you here?" I ask, instead of answering him. Granger begins pacing behind me. His tail almost hitting my father. My father takes several steps backwards.

"I heard you were mated to the dragon king. Was I not to see it?" He tilts his head, his eyes cruel.

"I'm sorry you missed it." I inform him.

Then my father's eyes go to my neck. "I guess it was a good time then?" My hand tries to cover up the marks Granger left on me.

"It was." I nod my head, feeling so uneasy with everything.

"We brought you a gift," My father says. His words don't seem kind though. "We can call it a wedding gift, yeah?" He asks even though it doesn't seem like a question. It sounds like a threat.

"I don't need anything, you have already given me so much," I say, trying to appease him.

"I have, haven't I?" My father begins walking around all the tables.

"You have. More than I probably deserved." I say, still trying to calm whatever it is inside of him. Granger growls loudly in protest.

My father walks over flowers, stepping on them, crunching the gorgeous little things under his boots. He shoves things off the tables, and I wince when he throws a chair out of his way. "I am so sad your mother had to miss out on watching her darling daughter be mated. But alas, I brought them all here for you." He gives me a half-smile. I gulp the spit I have gathered in my mouth.

"Again, why are *you* here?" My suspicion has risen to another level.

"As you know, *my* father disappeared quite some time ago." My father walks to another table, picking up a drink and smelling it. "Alongside his father. Well, and several other Gods. If you could call them that."

"I didn't know. I guess there is a lot I do not know about our family," I say, mirroring his movements on the other side of the round table.

My father lifts his brows, slowly morphing into the ruthless God King I know him to be. "I guess so. Like how the Fates somehow gave you their power. I tested your mother, you see." He motions to her and she shakes; she is so scared. I don't know if it is for me or herself.

"*She will be okay,*" Granger says, down our bond. I nod my head slightly. My father tracks the movement.

Father narrows his eyes. "Strange, isn't it?" He looks to Atlas, and it's then that I look into my brother's eyes.

"It really is." Atlas confirms whatever my father is trying to figure out. "Fate would be so cruel as to give a bastard daughter the power I have craved for a millennium," Atlas says harshly. I don't show any emotion to their cruel words. My grandfather grunts his agreement. I don't know who to look at.

"*If things turn south, you leave, Capri. Tell me you will,*" Granger's voice chimes in again.

"*I can't leave my mother, Granger.*" A low growl sounds from deep inside his chest.

"Anyways, you will give this world over to me, as well as your power. You will live, eat, and breathe for me." Father lifts his brows before dumping out a drink onto the table.

"I will." I agree.

Granger's dragon slits look right at me. "*No, you will not be his slave,*" Granger says harshly into my head.

"*No, I won't. I just need him to let my mother go before I can act, Granger. I need her safe. I don't care about them, I just have to play the part for a moment longer until she is away from here.*"

My father *tsks*. "Enough with this talk between you two. I need to hear from the dragon king." My father then looks right into the eyes of his biggest enemy. "Will you speak to me yourself, or will you stay hiding behind your shield?" Father taunts him. Granger doesn't answer with anything but blowing smoke towards him.

"*He deserves nothing from me.*"

I blink several times, feeling unsure if I will be able to de-escalate this.

"*You cannot. One side will die tonight.*" Granger declares harshly.

I roll my eyes at Granger; my father watches. He studies us and then laughs deeply.

"You know, Mara told me I should have killed you. I am glad I didn't listen to her now." Max steps forward, narrowing his eyes on Granger. I feel Max's power immediately. I start towards Granger to defend him, but Atlas grabs my mother by the neck. "Who are you going to save?" Father asks as I feel mind control pulling me in ways I don't want to go.

"What?" I grab my temples, my head feeling full. Granger's large dragon head starts to swivel. He can feel exactly what I can. Max is attempting to control his mind. Granger blows small flames from his mouth. "My mom!" I scream as he blows fire towards my brothers. It would kill them instantly, but it would also kill my mom. Granger looks to me, desperate for anything I could give him to get us out of here.

"I will give you anything, Father. You want power, you can have it." I throw my arms out in surrender. There is nothing I can do right now. I didn't plan for this to happen.

My grandfather chuckles. "Girl, you know nothing. But like I said, you will learn at some point."

Granger roars, more agitated. "You can't have him!" I scream, starting towards Granger.

"Who do you pick, Capri? Her or him?" My father asks again.

"Both." My mind is whirling as I try to solve how all of us can make it out of here.

"I will give you a deal then, yes?" My father starts towards me, along with my grandfather. I don't know what his power is, but I can feel it emanating from him. Granger is still mind wrestling Max up ahead. I send a windstorm whirling towards my brother, pushing him back enough to stop his mental assault on Granger. Max glares at me with a newfound hatred in his eyes. His carefree personality is long gone and replaced with a vile creature.

"There is still a way for us all to get what we want, Father," I say as I watch them walk towards me. Granger is right at my back, trying to fight off Max still.

"Yes, there is a way for us to get what we are owed by the Fates, Capri. That is the game, isn't it?" Father says harshly, he kicks another chair.

"*Capri, you need to leave now,*" Granger warns, right as harsh waves of power rush into both our minds. I scream out, clutching my head.

"It is crazy how bonded you can be after such little time. I wonder what will happen when you two are apart?" My father asks cruelly. Panic bubbles in my chest right as my grandfather makes his way to me.

No, he isn't at me. My brother is right in front of me. My father and grandfather have split their paths. I try to track them but my mind feels as if it might explode. I blink several times, not knowing what is happening. Max's assault on my mind is so powerful that it forces Granger to shift back. His naked body lays on the ground as he writhes in pain. "Run, Capri!" He screams...but I can't. I can't move.

I look into Atlas's eyes, pleading for my brother to just help me once. "I thought we agreed," I cry quietly before Atlas licks his lips.

"You agreed to give me this world. And I kept your mother alive. Our deal is fulfilled little sister." Tears streak down my face as I realize what is happening.

Then my grandfather grabs onto Granger's body before I can stop him, and disappears. I scream, incoherently, I scream my lungs out. My voice is breaking from how hard I use it. Spit flies from my mouth as I wail louder than I have ever before. "No, Father, bring him back! I will give you anything!" I yell, but he doesn't listen. My body gives out on me and I fall to the ground. I hit the ground with my fist, and my body feels icy cold without Granger. "Where did he take him!" I push to get up but I can't fully so I crawl.

I rush over to where Granger had just been on my hands and knees, running my hands over the grass, thinking I can call him back to me. My mind is still hurting from the mental attack on it.

I whirl on all of them. Standing up tall, sniffing in any snot dripping from my nose. "You want to play games Father?" Spit comes out of my mouth. My father smacks his lips.

"Ah, so if you had to pick, it would be him then?" He playfully asks me. I look up towards my mother, panic swirling in my belly.

"Do not harm her." I warn, my entire body shaking with either fear, hatred or every awful emotion I can muster.

My father *tsks* again. "Don't worry, I need you to listen to me, not disobey me. You will do exactly what I ask, and if you do, then you will get your mother and your mate, intact."

I swallow, looking up to where my brothers and mother had been. Where are they? They must be walking down to meet us. "What do you want?" I narrow my eyes on my father.

"Everything. I want this planet, this kingdom, and the Fates to listen to me. I want the power they gave *you*. Because they gave it to the wrong GOD!!" He roars so loud my ears start to bleed, and the ground under me shakes.

"I can't control who they give power to," I say, while holding my ears.

"No, but you can make them give your abilities to me. Because you are no Fate. You are barely a God. A disgrace is what you are. You will make them listen, and if you can't, I will use any means necessary to extract the Fate power from your body." He walks to me, and grabs onto my neck as if I were merely a toy, and not his daughter. His fingers press hard into my throat.

I vaguely hear Lachlan laughing manically. "I like this kingdom; it has un-touched waters." Lachlan says cheerfully.

Max rolls his eyes. "Who cares about the fucking water, Lachlan. Can't you feel the power bleeding from the soil?" Max bends down and runs his fingers along the ground. He moans out as power seeps into his body. I have so many things running through my head that I didn't notice the burlap bag Lachlan holds is leaking. When Lachlan tracks my eyes, he elbows Max in the side. "Should we give it to her now?" Max nods and smiles playfully. He has my mother in his tight grip.

"I don't want a gift from you," I tell them, then look to my father. "Give me my mother and Granger, and I will do whatever it is that you need from me," I plead with him. *Please just listen to me.* My father drops my throat and grabs my face, pulling my full attention to him. He yanks his grip on me because to him, I am replaceable. If he kills me, it will inconvenience him. He will not mourn me, nor would he shed one tear.

"You will do what I want, or else I will kill everybody you have ever even spoken to and then force what I want either way." He threatens, and I know he will do exactly what he says he will.

My eyes flit to the bag again, curiosity and dread winning out. "What is in the bag?" I ask, tilting my head up as much as my father will allow. The scent hits my nostrils at the same moment the boys make it behind our father. My father lets go of my throat, and my knees give out on me. The loss of Granger is too much to handle already.

"Boys, give your sister her mating gift." I am not prepared for the screams that leave my throat. If I weren't already on the ground, I would have fallen to my knees. Valor's head rolls right in front of me.

"No, no, no, no, NO!" I scream. My voice is betraying me. It breaks right as my heart does.

"Capri, I will give you one last chance. You can listen to me and help me keep your mother and boyfriend alive, or they can both die, and I will torture you. Which is it?"

Hot tears stream down my face. "I'll help," I croak out, because my voice doesn't work any longer. *I* don't work anymore. I grab onto what's left of Valor, clutching my best friend to my body. As if that will do any good now.

My mate is gone, my world tilted upside down, and there are dragons under my castle with food reserves for only two weeks. My mother hasn't spoken a word since getting here.

My father slaps the side of my face several times, almost playing with me. "Good girl. We will have some fun, father-daughter bonding. You'll have to tell me all the gory details about your time with the dragon king," He taunts, and my brothers all laugh. My mother stiffens, the only sign she is even alive in there.

Granger is truly gone. I can't feel him. *Where is he?* I try to say the words out loud, but my voice still won't work. Hot tears stream down my cheeks as they all walk inside of the palace, my mother being dragged behind them. I can't seem to make my legs work correctly either, I can't move. Panic beats down on my body so hard that I don't know if I can go on without knowing if Granger is safe.

As soon as I am fully alone, I finally find what little voice I have. "Where is my mate?" I gasp out, as pain overcomes my body. I have never felt this level of sorrow and devastation before now; this cuts deeper than any sword could have. *I lost him.*

I curl in on myself, Valor's head now curled in my body. I hold onto him as I wail. My body feels numb, I feel as if I can no longer move or go on, I feel nothing.

WHERE ARE YOU? I scream down any fragment of the bond I might feel, over and over again.

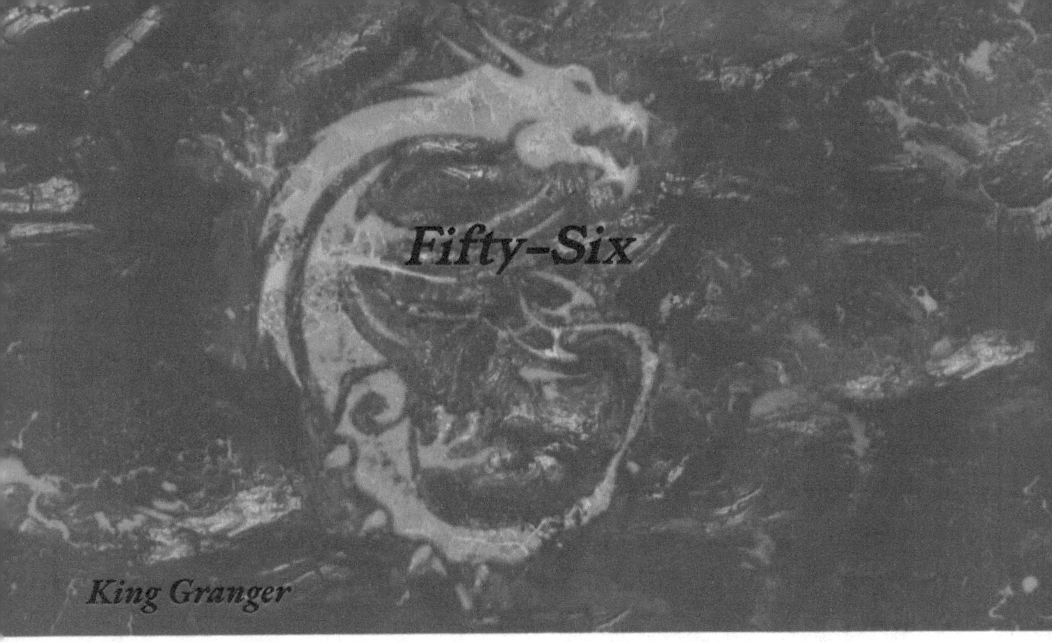

Fifty-Six

When my eyes open, it takes several minutes for them to adjust to the bright light of the daytime. How long has it been? I can't feel her any longer. What has happened? She can't be dead, right? I would be dead too, so she must be alive. I just can't feel her.

"Capri?" My throat feels scratchy. It feels raw. A voice finally echoes in my ears. A voice I know all too well.

"So...like father, like son," Capri's grandfather says.

"I guess," I confirm, looking at the second most powerful God there has ever been.

"You tortured me for...what?" He scratches his chin in a show. "Your entire life?" He keeps going, but I don't respond to his taunts.

"Where are we?" I ask, looking around, even though I know.

"We are where it all began, Granger. I watched you over the years. You grew so fast, of course. Watching your father torture Gods would do that to a boy, wouldn't it?" He walks up to where I am chained.

"The Fates don't want me," I say, hoping I am correct.

"I don't care. I, unlike my son, do not need more power. I am the strongest God there has ever been."

I correct him immediately. "Second." He hits me hard enough that blood sprays everywhere.

His eyes glow with rage. "What?" He grabs my face so hard my teeth dig into my flesh.

"You heard me," I say between my clenched teeth. "You are the *second* strongest God, and my father still defeated you. She can too." He punches me again, so hard that without my dragon form, I see spots cloud my vision.

"She is not stronger than I, especially after my son takes the Fate garbage from her," He swears before shaking his head. "They ate from me for far too long for me to allow it to happen. Although I get the feeling we will be seeing them soon." My eyes widen as he cuts into his flesh. "Let's see if we can't get the Fates to listen to this measly God and dragon king, shall we?"

I grind my teeth, knowing I am in no position to make demands. I just need Capri to survive. She should be safe with her family; they won't actually hurt her. Gods are evil, but they won't kill her. Will they?

I spit blood out of my mouth before looking into the eyes of the God who killed my father. The God who forced my hand when he controlled my father's mind, and wouldn't let him stop killing dragons until his own death. I was forced to kill my own flesh and blood because of mind control that was far more powerful than any being should possess. That story is one I will never speak about though. I killed my father, nothing else matters.

"It looks like you might make your wish come true...killing two dragon kings," I say right as he shocks my body so hard I pass out. He whispers into my ear right before oblivion takes me.

"I will not kill you until you get to watch what my son has in store for your clans, the humans and fae that his bitch of a daughter sent away, and your fucking mate. She will never know another moment of peace." It's those words that haunt me well into my sleep.

www.ingramcontent.com/pod-product-compliance
Lightning Source LLC
Chambersburg PA
CBHW010654100726
47901CB00012B/2547